BRANDON WICKS

AMERICAN FALLOUT

sfwp.com

The characters and events portrayed in this book are fictitious. Any similarity to real persons, living or dead, is coincidental and not intended by the author.

Library of Congress Cataloging-in-Publication Data
Wicks, Brandon, 1979-
American fallout / Brandon Wicks.
pages cm

Summary: "For Avery Cullins—library archivist, one- time teenage runaway, and gay man from a small Southern town—"family" means a live-in boyfriend and a surly turtle. But when his father, a renowned nuclear physicist, commits suicide, Avery's decade-long estrangement with his mother, who now suffers from dementia, comes to an end. With his boyfriend's help, Avery takes custody of his mother and, in a rented U-Haul, the trio heads cross country, back to an apartment in Cleveland and an uncertain future. The journey soon becomes a pilgrimage into the past as Avery sifts through his mother's mementos and a story of love, family, and loss emerges as his parents make a home, lose a child, and test the boundaries of marital love in the 1970s. Meanwhile, Avery must confront his own struggle with a mother who doesn't recognize him and a lover who, despite his cries to the contrary, is growing older, closer, and more domestic"—Provided by publisher.
ISBN 978-1-939650-42-9 (pbk.)
1. Gay men—Fiction. 2. Gay men—Family relationships—Fiction. 3. Cleveland (Ohio)—Fiction.
I. Title.
PS3623.I29A36 2015
813'.6—dc23

2015016698

Published by SFWP
369 Montezuma Ave. #350
Santa Fe, NM 87501
(505) 428-9045
www.sfwp.com

Find the author at www.bpwicks.com

Contents

For Katie,
for my parents,
and especially,
for "Gary"

"Journeys to relive your past?" was the Khan's question at this point, a question which could also have been formulated: "Journeys to recover your future?"

And Marco's answer was: "...The traveler recognizes the little that is his, discovering the much he has not had and will never have."

—*Italo Calvino,* Invisible Cities *(Trans. William Weaver)*

"To pause there would be to confirm the hopeless finality of a belief that two atomic colossi are doomed...to eye each other indefinitely across a trembling world."

—*President Eisenhower's address to the United Nations, 1953*

I

Fear of the Atom

1

I need to explain.

All of my growing, I did in the womb. As a macrosomatic baby, I spent forty-four weeks in gestation rather than the traditional thirty-eight and, once born, measured in at two feet and seventeen pounds. Hell on my mother, as you can imagine, but not so easy on me either. Consider me there, *in utero*: a distended, pink homunculus, feeding far too long on everything she fed on—a steady diet of saltines and canned tuna, gall and anxiety—who, in enough time, would be nurtured more by the stress hormones that pumped through her blood than by any sugars or proteins. So now, thirty-seven years later, I am a shrunken animal, denatured, hardly 5'4". I rarely tip the scales over a hundred and twenty, and my face is more spotty mange than beard when left unshaven. My skin, if you pinch it, gives enough slack to suggest I've lost thirty pounds or more, which isn't the case. Rather, it was anticipating a bigger man, growing in that womb for so long. Since its conception, my body has carried with it the expectation of something bigger than myself—big enough to hold the histories, the stories and lives, of my parents.

For years now, I have been estranged from them both. The exact number is fluid, most conveniently dated to my mother's stroke, though our separation precedes that in ways which are difficult to mark on any calendar. It's been ample time, however you count it, for the maps to change and for all the old words to lose their fixity. Home for me now is Cleveland, a little apartment off Lorain Avenue from which, if you hang your head out the southfacing windows, you can almost smell if not see the weekend bustle of the West Side Market. It's the smack of Lake Erie at five in the morning, cold and fishy. It's the hush of the university archival stacks where I work. And family…perhaps the most unstable word in the English language, the loudest artillery in the political arsenal of reactionaries and radicals alike…*family! family!*…a word whose ever-shifting boundaries have drawn battle-lines and alliances in the human species since the earliest kinship patterns practiced by hominids on the Serengeti…for me, that's been complicated. I make of it what I will: family, in this season of my life, has come to mean a long history of friends and lovers, a surly box turtle named Dorothy (Allison, not Gale, for the record), and my partner, the happy profligate, Freddie Luc. But as with so many of us, I was birthed from a popular American myth: that the family is a nucleus, and splitting that nucleus risks obliterating life as we know it. The responsibility is enormous. And my job—as I first saw it through the red vellum light of my mother's navel, gestating too long for this world—meant holding together all the unstable elements of our little suburban household, tucked among the horses and sandhills of South Carolina.

Last week, I had just returned from biking when my father's lawyer rang with the news of his suicide. On weekday mornings I often pedal along the streets that skirt Lake Erie, trying to increase my stamina. More than the exercise, it's the peace I'm after. The balance of stillness and motion. Before dawn the city holds its breath, quiet enough to hear my spokes whir through the alleys. It's the hour of solitary figures: a middle-aged man coughs from a fire escape, another hoses rotten produce off the sidewalk, a delivery truck idles by a fire hydrant in the damp chill. In this, I can find my center. By 7:00 a.m., the halo of early morning light and fog burns off the high-rises. The rumble of traffic cranks up and the streets shake themselves fully awake.

I had just gotten my handlebars into the apartment, breathless from the perspiration and smog and two flights of stairs, when I heard Freddie in a dull murmur at the kitchen counter. All the lights were off. He had the phone pressed to his ear, massaging his eyelids over and over. "Yeah, wait. Hold on. Avery," he called to me. He hadn't been home long enough to crawl into bed, the funk of stale smoke still clinging to his shirt and boxers. "Florida. Some guy. Your dad," was all he said, shuffling off to the sofa. I wiped the earpiece off on my shorts and said hello.

I had never spoken with this man, Vernon Rossi, before. He introduced himself, taking only a moment to loosen the phlegm in his voice before stating that he was the executor of my father's will. From there, it didn't take more than ten minutes for him to lay down the particulars and offer his condolences. After hanging up, I made travel arrangements, and we flew down to Florida the next day.

Vernon Rossi's account was elliptical, but certain images stuck with me at the time. Since then, I have gleaned enough details from Rossi and others after the funeral that the fragments can be pieced together in something close to a narrative whole.

Earlier that week my father, James Cullins, at the age of seventy-three, had been spotted leaving his ground-level condominium one sunny morning in Tallahassee on an errand to end his life. Before leaving the condo, I imagine he had followed a familiar routine. That he had adjusted the thermostat after waking, that he showered and prepared breakfast—black coffee and toast—and stacked their plates by the sink when finished. That he parked Carlie's wheelchair in the mid-morning glow of the television set and called to confirm her nurse for early the next day. Then, he set out from the condo, charting a course from which he would never return. Shortly after hitting the sidewalk, however, he bumped into a former colleague on a power walk. Dr. Neil Langer. This would be the last eyewitness to see him alive, a man with whom James sat on the board of trustees at Florida State University, a casual acquaintance. Inquisitive, beet-faced, he pressed two fingers into his neck to time his heart rate. James! I usually don't catch you out! Keeping busy? Getting exercise? The man patted his own rounded belly. Hah-hah. James straightened his hair with trembling fingers and laughed, answered yep, yep, yep to all the questions. His right hand began to tremor more violently, so he swept it through his hair again, which was wet and parted. His beard was not quite kempt, crawling with untrimmed curls at the throat. A pallid complexion, a foggy mental air about him, sickly almost.

James had always been a little awkward. A man who apologized when he bumped into inanimate objects—never quite sure of what might be a human being, and what might not. But here, James didn't even stop to talk. He nodded, waved, fumbled those few words but kept marching down the sidewalk, slightly stooped, in quick mincing steps, as if he were a doddering old man. This, in a time and place where men his age thrived, where they were robust and confident in their health, and planned to take their grandchildren on RV trips to see America's living history, or scuba dive with their spouses off the Keys as in commercials for joint life annuity plans. This old colleague of his, a man who had known James for years, noticed the snub. He studied James as he went, forgetting his heart rate, and decided to call out: Getting over the flu? James waved from a distance, said nothing. Unknown to everyone at the time, least of all me, James had been diagnosed with Parkinson's Disease. He had been living with it, in fact, for at least a year. Twenty minutes later, he bought a handgun.

This hadn't been his first trip, of course. He had previously applied for the purchase so that on this day, James, a one-time customer, could squeeze through the doors of Big Tiamo's Pawnshop and More with a .22LR semiautomatic pistol, a Plinker, as gun enthusiasts call them, and a pasteboard box of ammunition, all cinched in a black plastic bag. To the late morning commuters, maybe he looked exactly like what he was:

a retired professor, a nuclear physicist with a dyspeptic gut, shuffling through the thick Floridian air. He cradled the parcel in the crook of his arm. His gait became lighter and smoother, his forehead cooler then. Maybe as the traffic picked up, as the sun baked the streets, an anonymous relief crept in. Perhaps, for the first time in months, his muscles loosened and regained some of their autonomy. When he finally arrived home, James carefully sat the package by the microwave, defrosted a container of tomato sauce, and set pasta to boil on the stove. Capellini. Angel hair spaghetti. A bottle of red wine came down from the cupboard. That afternoon, he wheeled my mother up to a rare candlelit dinner while a 24-hour news program relayed dire pronouncements on national security in the adjacent room.

The following morning, he awoke before dawn. A habit ingrained since his twenties. In the bathroom, he paced while dressing and softly narrated the day to himself, the same way he had rehearsed decades of auditorium lectures. He knotted his tie, cinched the hasp on his slacks—let out another inch this year, but no longer by Carlie, no, not for a long time, but rather by a Trinidadian tailor across town. For this morning, this solemn occasion, he kept the television off. The house was quiet.

My mother slept. Fully dressed, he studied her while she lay on the bed, softly snoring, with the black bag hanging from his hand. What did he see there? A wife of fifty years. Mother of his two children. The rust and heft of a fifty-year leg iron around his white ankle. An albatross. A noose. And then: a twenty-three year old girl riding shotgun in his battered '64 MGB, laughing as the black bell of her hair shakes free of its kerchief and flies up in the wind. And finally: a seventy-two year old woman, fine down on her lip, who, if she was allowed to wake on this day, would wake into a world suddenly devoid of her husband, of the caregiver who oversaw every facet of her life.

Eventually, he boiled coffee, called the front office and left a message, a reminder that the nurse should arrive early that day, 8:00 a.m. sharp. Bringing the hot mug to his lips, he paused. A switch flipped in his brain. A small flicker: a gentle thought. James was never a wasteful man but this morning, without a sip, he decided against the coffee and poured it down the sink. Instead, he decanted the last full glass of the previous night's wine, grabbed one, two powdery doughnuts from a box of Entenmann's pastries, and settled out on the back patio. He left both gun and ammunition by the microwave.

After all his preparation, at 5:46 a.m., my father watched the sunrise from a wicker chair, carefully set his empty wine glass on the patio brick, and then voided his life insurance policies by, of all things, asphyxiating himself. A plastic dry-cleaning bag and a "Wine Saver," a cheap TV gadget shaped like a can of WD40. He belted his head with the bag and shot a hefty supply of argon gas cartridges upside his neck before gently passing on into daybreak. Later at his funeral, while most people avoided broaching his suicide, one retired chemist placed his knobby hand on my shoulder and whispered, I suppose, as a form of condolence: "The noble gases are painless."

How much pain James felt, physical or otherwise, in his final moment is hard for me to gauge. He had left an unaddressed note on Carlie's nightstand, which couldn't have been for her, since by this point my mother could not read. All it said was: COULDN'T DO IT. No addressee, no subject, the *I* removed. An abbreviated message initialed *JaC*, the way he used to sign any household reminder. It was his only gesture toward an explanation. Police later found the Plinker still in its bag beside the microwave.

So we flew to Florida. Freddie and I have spent five days in the condo, sorting through decades of my father's belongings, subsisting on cheap lo mein and vitamin water, while my mother languishes in state custody at a nursing home. Outside, a purple meniscus cuts against the condos' skyline; crickets begin to trill in the tiny patch of grass despite the cars whooshing along Blairstone and Mahan. Freddie paces the condominium's patio, where my father spent his last hour, as another balmy evening draws down on what will be our last full day in Tallahassee.

In the kitchenette, our return travel arrangements are changing. While I wait on the house-line, I watch Freddie from the window, sweet-talking into his cell phone and sneaking cigarettes. He takes long, nervous drags with one eye on the door. Once again, he's trying to placate Henri Sellier, co-owner and namesake of their joint business venture, a cocktail lounge called Henri's Closet, so named for the double entendre, of course, but also for the fact that its maximum seating capacity will be ten people. If it ever gets off the ground. The project has stalled in construction for a third time, leaving Freddie and Henri in need of $10,000 and with no remaining capital. The entire trip, Freddie's been on the phone at all hours trying to scare up the money. It's what a Freddie does, after all: finds money, loses money, looks for more. Still, he's tried to be helpful with me. I've put him to task on manual labor all week, cleaning and packing, but ten minutes after he starts, I always find the boxes hardly touched, the mop leaning against the wall, and Freddie out on the patio, plying another potential investor for an eleventh-hour recovery. After the calls end, he's still only half here, staring vacantly at the unpacked boxes with his hands jammed into his pockets and a queasy grimace on his lips.

Even without the stress, Freddie has always been claustrophobic, itchy, in domestic spaces. An historic aversion that bordered on disgust. Before we started dating, he liked to say that monogamy itself meant putting our collective LGBT card-carrying heads on the chopping block of assimilationist culture. *It's repressive—* he'd proclaim, brushing cigarette ash lightly from his pant leg—*This slavishness to domesticity. It goes against everything we should be celebrating. And marriage rights, don't get me started. Marriage rights have corrupted the shit out of the best people I've known. Brainwashed. They'd have us all drinking the Kool-Aid of Heterosexual America and keeling over.* Of course, he said this right after I declined a private invitation up to his apartment. I had been dating someone else at the time. The truth is, Freddie was a fling, an adventure for me. He had a history of traveling light, docking from one guy to the next. Our relationship was never supposed to last. But here we are, four years later in Tallahassee, deciding what to do with my late father's wicker patio furniture.

I finalize details with the moving company, jot a few notes, and hang up the phone. I don't call Freddie in immediately. Instead, I busy myself with a cheap Rand McNally atlas, highlighting the route we'll take in the morning. I wait for him. I practice my mother's sense of timing.

It's been nearly a decade since my mother had her stroke and James cut me out of the loop. An act to purge everything he thought that had gone wrong in his life. A mistake, no doubt, that complicated his last years. Because who better than me to take care of her? Who better than me, who knew the many lives of James and Carlie Cullins better than they knew themselves? Who had been yoked since childhood with their failed marriage? A Libra, I balanced the whole mess. I knew how their scales measured.

By the time I arrived, my parents, James and Carlie Cullins, had passed through a gauntlet of deceptions and jealousies, of violent tragedies and replacement babies; they had died and were reborn and died again, only to emerge, once and for all, as mutual antagonists in a domestic drama that would endure beyond death. So by the morning of October 1, 1978, as my malformed bulk came crowning into this world, my parents—if not transformed—had become fully *translated.* They had arrived at a new and altered meaning of themselves, and so much was lost in the process. No equivalents, no transliterations.

In these new lives, there were no longer two hundred and fifty words for *passion*, no longer thirty-two ways for saying *us*, and an utter semiotic mess of meaning for *love*. So restricted, they stopped using these words. Worse yet, the few they had remaining became a confusion of language. Even uttering the simplest terms of daily communication—say, for instance, "newspaper" or "dirty socks" or "dishwasher"—could set each other off into a sputtering rage. Groping for a right word and finding none, unable to be heard, my parents would finally storm off to their divided ends of the house.

Lost in such a marriage, my mother began to seek meaning in the long departed. She researched the genealogy of every possible branch of the Robicheauxs, her family tree. Traveling the country, she visited parish churches and town halls, leafed through the necropoli of early census records to sort out our mud-scuffled ancestry in the new world. She drafted letters to France, Germany, and Nova Scotia. She left the house often. From such trips, our cavernous living room turned into a repository. The built-in bookshelves were wedged with family albums, histories, facsimiles of death records and marriage certificates. Plastic crates of photographs and newspaper clippings buried the sofa and the sideboard in a chaotic filing system. Her collection even pushed into the adjoining greenhouse, where bundles of mildewed accordion folders suffered from jungle rot under the leafy shelter of bromeliads and frangipani.

The mustiness of these things alone could have kept my father away, with his uncontrollable allergies. But more than dust and mold, these were the rooms where my mother set up camp, where she ate her meals, drank her coffee, and frequently lost her reading glasses under the Xeroxed news clippings. She talked on the portable phone to unknown people in unknown places—making hopeful connections with others we might be related to—hunting, gathering, while on the turntable Herb Alpert and the Tijuana Brass crooned in the background. And the collection didn't end with print materials. Over the years, all my parents' original furniture became displaced by antiques salvaged from this or that relative—wall clocks, foot stools, rocking chairs, coffee tables, an oak fireplace mantle, and even a wagon wheel which she turned into an orchid trellis. And with each piece, cross-referenced in my mother's brain, was a formidable catalog of anecdotes. The great-uncles, dead cousins twice removed, and great-to-the-fourth-power grandmothers who had owned these things—carried them, marred them, loved them—and left them with a piece of their souls. That was the way she organized the family: by objects and stories. While re-gluing a table leg, she once told me, "There are two kinds of death, baby. As soon as something's forgotten," she blew a raspberry, "that's it. It's truly dead and gone." Later, when my maternal grandfather developed Alzheimer's, Carlie became zealous in hording these end tables and clocks, turning over their naked wooden bellies to record their provenance in permanent marker—the dates and initials of their owners—against the failure of her own memory.

My father, feeling outnumbered by my mother's kin in the next room, began heralding his own ancestral banners, focusing on one figure alone: his mother. He had already missed the genetic lottery on the strong Irish features running through the Cullins name. So instead, he looked to Antoinette Passantino Cullins for guidance. From her Sicilian blood he became a born-again Italian-American well into his forties, redefining himself, his history, through recipes—bolognese, primavera, ricotta gnocci, and his catch-all standby, *pasta and sauce*. Cheeses in particular gained Old World inflection in his speech. "Do you want some *pah-mee-jahno*?" he'd say, holding up a green can of pre-grated parmesan as we sat over plates of capellini. Or, over lasagna, "What do you think? Too much *ree-COT-ta*?" Strange powers were charged through these words. While doling out hefty spoonfuls of rigatoni, each meal he made became an occasion to remind me, "You know, Termite, your Nona was Italian. That means you're Italian, too."

"We're all Italian," I'd say, a child of five, learning this new world of family politics.

"No, your mother is definitely not Italian."

"Thank God for small favors," she'd reply and ask for the *cheese*.

These are the pieces, the old meanings of family, long since relegated to the archive. Now with one phone call an emphysemic lawyer in Florida has reprised all that. He did for me what my father had lost the chance to do: he invited me back. But more than a reunion, I now realize, he has given us all the opportunity to rebuild anew.

And so we are doing just that. We're going back to Cleveland, yes, but by a detour through Copeland, South Carolina. With my mother we have the chance to make a fresh start and reconcile my family's entire story. Tomorrow morning, we spring her from Florida state custody and hit the road. After all the cleaning and purging, after hours of sitting at Rossi's tiny desk, while he hacked up phlegm and mopped his face and laid down the legal details of my father's life; after the wake, the damp handshakes, the condolences mumbled by retired FSU faculty; after the week-long mental hemorrhage to keep the universe together despite so many years of separation, massive brain trauma, disavowal, and childhood—I am bringing my mother home. I am bringing her back to me. But if I'm to have any hope of this, any help, I have to bring her back to herself, first.

"Well, that took forever." Freddie pops his head in through the patio door and sees that I'm off the phone. He coughs once, adding another stick of spearmint gum to the one already in his mouth. He sizes up the boxes around the room as if they might have multiplied. "When do we get the trailer?"

"We don't," I say. "We're trading the car in for a truck."

He stands—jacket through his arm, hands in pockets—like a businessman on the world's longest layover. He forgets to chew. "I thought we were getting a trailer hitch for the rental car?"

"They don't have any more hitches. All they have is trucks."

"I thought we made a reservation."

"We did. But now all they have is trucks."

Freddie stares blankly at me. "Where am I supposed to sit?"

"In the cab, I imagine. Unless you prefer the cargo bay."

"All three of us? With your mother? We can't ride like that. We'll be armpit to asshole."

On the atlas, I squeak the highlighter over another inch of secondary highway, halfway through Georgia. "The fourteen-foot truck is supposed to seat three adults comfortably."

"For chrissake..." Freddie goes to sit on a box, and I leap over to stop him. Breakables are inside. He opts for the floor, hitching his legs up to his chest with a groan of discomfort. "Fourteen feet." He laughs at himself, looks around at the room. "Well, I guess all of this is definitely going, then."

We are returning to Copeland because I alone am responsible for our history. Those many weeks I spent in gestation, preparing too long for this world, I was fed the lives of my parents. I heard their conversations between the palpating beat of my heart and that of my mother's. I absorbed their voices through that murkwater, listened to their stories, and saw into their lives further back. The song in their synapses became my song. The neural switchboard of their memories became the impulse of my nervous system. That life, that self, split from me at the moment of my birth—the part of myself that lives within my parents' story, not as the father and mother I knew, but as the James and Carlie Cullins I had never known. Now I am being asked to reverse the process. I am asked to find the vestigial umbilicus, rank now from the old amniotics, and tether myself up again at thirty-seven. I am asked once again to keep the record.

And so I will. But let us at last set that record, if not straight, then truthfully queered, the way it belongs.

These then are the people we once were.

2

Here's the trouble: this begins twice. Three times. It begins over and over, *ad infinitum* as any story does, and though we might already know how this one ends, the particulars of each beginning change the story and so change its meaning. How can I say this? I could begin, for convenience, by saying this is when James and Carlie first arrive in Copeland, South Carolina, and where everything gets its start—but that would be a lie. I suspect that's why the Greeks scrapped the whole messy concept of beginnings. That's the real trick hidden in the narrative: If it all springs *in medias res* from the muse's head, then the storyteller has no accountability for getting it right. But I've got no goddess to intervene on my behalf and kickstart the show. (Well, maybe one, but I need to save her for later.) At any rate, it should be enough to say that this is when James and Carlie come back to Copeland for good.

When they arrive in town early that summer of 1971, they are young but not that young. They have paid their younger dues. They have followed James' academic path from Florida State to Harvard to MIT, working together to support his addiction to higher education through two Master's Degrees and a PhD. No leaders, no followers here; they have allied together in support of each other, in support of this joint destiny with all of its quirks, twists, and hardships. They have lived through New England winters in a mobile home no warmer than a Quonset hut; they have subsisted on cold vienna sausages and english muffins; they have broken through the fiscal year with only two dollars and twenty-eight cents in the bank; and, in the course of multiple relocations, they have sold all their worldly belongings, twice.

To put it another way, in the common punchline of that era: they were married.

By the time they pull up to the construction site of their new home, nestled in the hinterlands of a small South Carolinian town, my parents are now thirty years old. From this new vantage point, James and Carlie see all their trappings stretch out before them into the future: the house, the family, the spacious two-acre yard where children and dogs gambol as in elementary school primers, and where neighbors, once they get some, wave distantly from newspaper bundles across the street. It's a prelapsarian scene: a return to the garden, a return to the place where you belong, which offers respite from your toils, where you cannot be ashamed and from which you can never be banished. Homeownership, in the American mythos, is nothing less than Eden, an undoing of the Fall. So, with 20% down on a $40,000 price tag, James and Carlie have achieved the sacrosanct social contract of their day. LIFE, in capital letters. They have arrived.

Love is what happens when someone shows you the world freshly. When they throw open the shutters and the view from your little window suddenly brightens with strange and exhilarating colors. The air tastes crisp and more peculiar. The whole world tingles with a sense of possibility that is almost, but not quite, placeable: it hints at the life you might yet lead. It's in the knowing glance while people-watching on busy streets, or in the hidden pattern of sunlight as it plays on the sidewalk, or in the intelligent synchronicity of a flock of starlings as they swoop into a field and form an enormous black teardrop. *Look out there, do you see that?* they point, the beloved. And your lips part in awe of all the beautiful, unspoken promise in the world.

It also helps if you've had sex.

When Carlie Robicheaux Cullins steps out of the car and into the sunlight, five months pregnant, she loves what she sees. The house stands wide on a two-acre lot, amid the sand and pine scrub, with a team of men laboring on its structure like ants on a limb. They scale the roof, they nail the flashing, they haul materials in and out of the open door frames—their hammers echo in the neighborhood.

"What do you think?" James calls out, slamming the car door.

She flashes him a big smile. Carlie isn't petite. She even stands an inch taller than James when he's standing slump-shouldered. Dark and lovely, she is a little apologetic for her stature and tries to hide it at times; other times she doesn't, the way she doesn't try to hide her boisterous laughter, which seems to draw attention to her physique. Today she wears a smart maternity smock that she has sewn herself, the fabric a black and white geometric pattern. Her joy makes her gargantuan.

Carlie rubs her belly and watches and listens. The skin of her arms puckers like gooseflesh. Maybe it's the sound of the hammers. Their noise echoes through the absence of the neighborhood which, at the moment, is more streets and trees, horses and stables, than houses. Out of two hundred wooded lots, theirs is only the third house. And what a house! She loves its name. A Mid-Century Modern. A Mid-Century Modern with that asymmetrical, low-leaning roofline which, if viewed from above (as she often studied the blueprints and imagined), resembles a square spiral. It's not very large, but it is open and has dramatic angles and lines, and plenty of wide windows from which to view the world. No boxes. No Boxes for Living, thank you very much—side by side, shoulder to shoulder, piled high atop each other like a termite colony. This house expands from the landscape like a Frank Lloyd Wright starter kit. It breathes with its surroundings. And maybe that's exactly it: the landscape. Sure, the yard is a construction site, a mess of clay and sand churned up by a hundred heavy-treaded work boots and truck tires; and piles of scrap brick and lumber lay everywhere; and straw is laid down to keep the soil from washing away.

But see this: plenty of strong pines still stretch from the rutted turf to the sky, and the sun is warm and tickles her nose, and even from the woods native azaleas bloom an impermanent pink satin. Having spent the last two years living under three feet of snow, of winters that had almost erased the bright memory of her native Louisiana, she feels she has finally stepped out of the cramped, fourteen-hour car ride of her soul. Her body unknots itself. How to possibly put such relief into words?

"Well?" James prompts, shielding his eyes. "What do you think?"

Carlie's breath hitches, catching on the little spud suddenly shifting inside her belly, and she declares with tears in her eyes: "I think I have to pee."

Before my father proposed, they planned. After two years of dating at Florida State, among those balmy, shaded avenues in Tallahassee, they laid out the schematics of their life together. As with every preparation, my father pulled out a pad of quadrille lined paper and a stubby No.2 pencil. Years later, those pads would chart the weekly chore lists for my brother, then for me, graphing us into fine upstanding young men one clean bedroom and tooth-brushing at a time. They would also chart our vacation schedules *(Washington, D.C. Fantastic Facts Fun Zone: 2:30 p.m.-3:45 p.m.)*.

"Okay," he said, drawing two columns and writing *CARLIE* at the head of one, and *JAMES* at the head of the other. "If this is going to work, I mean, if we're really serious about this, then we have to know what each other's expectations are. That's why so many marriages don't work. Isn't that incredible? I find that incredible. Nobody ever thinks to take the time to talk about these things."

"That's a really good idea."

"So," James said, underscoring Carlie's name. "Tell me your expectations."

Carlie sat in the dinette chair with her hands in her lap, palms up, while James stared.

"Okay, well, here, I'll go first," he said. "One. I think together-time is important. Down time. We go out a lot with the kids here, I know, but I like to keep it low-key." By kids, James meant his roommate, Carlie's roommate, and the forty-two year old Japanese mathematician they had all become acquaintances with. "I think that's important to building a good stable environment, you know? No carousing, no bar-hopping; things get seedy. Unseemly."

"Well, we really don't do that much now, James."

"I know, we're not swingers. Two. I think education is very important."

"Oh, absolutely."

"So is financial stability. That should be Three. They kind of go together. So I wouldn't want to have kids at least until my dissertation. I believe you should be able to support your family."

"Me, too."

"Four. I think we need to support each other. Solidarity is important, as man and wife, you know?"

"I'm so glad you said that."

"Things just get too lopsided if one person has to shoulder all the weight."

Here, Carlie thought of her hard-drinking father—a good man, but absent in the way of any 1950s father—and her mother, a woman of wry wit, though buttoned-down by propriety in the way of any

1950s mother. And never the two met or mentioned the other, it seemed, except over the breakfast table. And even then. Her father had his political organizations, her mother had the kids. When James had jotted down the words *mutual support*, Carlie's heart thrummed, it positively vibrated.

"Twelve." James quickly scrawled notes as he spoke. "We should work on a savings account. That's the only way to be independent."

"Okay," she said.

"Now," James said, and underscored her name for a third time. "What do you want out of a marriage?"

Carlie locked her elbows, thought, and let out a puff of air. "A big family," she said. "Really, that's the only thing I can think of. That's the one other thing I think is really important."

James bopped the pencil eraser against his lip. "Okay, big family. How big? Can you tell me why big is important?"

"Well, I'm the third youngest of six. And, I don't know, you always have someone to go to. It's balanced. It's a family. Three would be good, too. And I suppose I could be okay with two, minimum. But no, I take that back. Two's not really big. Three kids would be ideal. To begin with."

"All right," James said, scratching at his ear.

Under Carlie's column he wrote *big. fam. kids*.

In two years' time, the wind will howl outside their little trailer in Nashua, New Hampshire, and they will have planned again, this time with actual blueprints. A house plan that James' father had drawn up years before he died, something his parents had considered for retirement, but one that he and Carlie have modified. Three bedroom, two bath. A small greenhouse and a sunken living room, with a lofted study and a stone fireplace that climbs all the way to cathedral height ceilings. Outside, the frozen wind chimes my mother had hung in a spirit of indefatigable optimism will swing, clinking icicles against the siding. In the morning they will drive the hour to Cambridge, Massachusetts, in sleet and black ice, both to the Massachusetts Institute of Technology—

my father to his classroom laboratory and my mother to her desk job as secretary to the dean. No leaders, no followers. And together they will squirrel away every red cent she earns toward that blue vision of home on the paper.

Stretching from the car ride, James relaxes into the slouching posture that he had perfected in college, the one that placed him (he thought) just beyond bookish and into hip. Because despite the hawkish nose, despite the thick prescription lenses, despite those skinny, glaring white legs with the knobby tennis knees that protrude from his Bermuda shorts, he knows he looks good. And he is right, if for one magical reason: sheer confidence.

A drafting table stands in the sparse shade of a loblolly, roughly banged together from scrap two-by-fours and a piece of plywood. The blueprints are weighted down by a small plastic radio. A young man approaches them from this table—the framer, still in his early twenties, meekly smiling.

"Mr. Cullins?"

James waves, then shakes his hand in a tight-knuckled grip.

"Dick warned me y'all might drop by in a day or so to look at the place." The young man is sweaty and baby-faced up close. "Ain't y'all coming down from Boston or something?"

Unlike Carlie, James is from Bay Shore, New York. But he had been in the South long enough to soak up the colloquial. To be at ease with the referents and sounds that slip from his wife's mouth, to swim in that culture, but also to possess enough cagey cunning to argue head-to-head with anyone—be it Akira Toshiyama in the engineering department at FSU, or some Bocephus down at the local watering hole—about the dark and dangerous history lurking just below the surface. Here, he has cultural authority and moral authority. And enough modesty not to dangle it over anyone's head.

James grimaces in the sunshine. "More or less. I just finished up my doctorate. MIT."

"Shoo. That's a big school for science, isn't it?"

"Yeah," James says. "It's all right."

"I bet you work at The Bomb Plant then?"

"The bomb plant?" He pauses momentarily. "You mean the nuclear facility?"

"That's the one."

James rights the glasses on his face, grinning out of the corner of his mouth. "They don't make bombs anymore. We just remediate them. Waste is my specialty. But yes, I start work next week. Are those sloped box cornices you're doing there?" He points up to the roof's overhang. He points to show that he is not just a brain, but also a man, and a hand, and capable of identifying manly and handy things.

"Well, yessir, they are."

"Good, good," James says. "That's a good detail. I know a little something about it. My old man was a carpenter." James claps the younger man—and he can say that, younger man—on the shoulder. "It looks like excellent work you're doing here. Excellent work."

Carlie has joined them. Holding her small belly, she wonders if she could discretely disappear into the woods and squat when the blueprints catch her eye. She lingers over them for a while, distractedly, as the two men chat. Confusion knits over her face. Finally she asks, "Where are the windows?"

"Don't worry about the schematics, Carlie," James says in high spirits. "Just look up." The two men grin at each other in that knowing way: *Women!* Out here in the sweat and the sawdust with the men, it's cute, you got to love them.

"No, I mean the windows," she says, this time shielding her eyes from the sun and pointing toward a high blank wall on the house. "The windows that are supposed to be all up there."

The framer suddenly looks abstracted. "What are you talking about?"

She taps her finger against the blueprint. "The windows that are right there."

At a service station across the bypass, James drops a coin into the slot and waits for Dick Durgess, the contractor, to pick up. He counts the trucks that go by while Carlie visits the women's restroom—there have only been two that he's noticed. They live, technically, outside the city limits of Copeland. Counting objects (trucks, telephone poles) keeps his thinking together.

They have seen Dick Durgess in the flesh only once. A busy guy. But accommodating, very friendly. Endorsed with slight reservations by Map and Minerva Price, an older couple, friends from another beginning. Well, perhaps not *endorsed* by Map and Minnie. Maybe even slightly discouraged. But Durgess was willing to do the job for eight thousand less than the other contractors, which was really the only endorsement the man needed.

James gets his secretary on the line, a polite teenage daughter.

Carlie appears from the rear of the building, carefully stepping around the broken glass and pop tops, and looking in need of a strong disinfectant. Or at least a bar of soap.

"That's him, James, I think that's him," she points at a blue pickup turning into their development from the bypass. They pile in the car and follow after.

They pull up to the property just in time to catch Durgess before he climbs back into the cab. He waves, seemingly caught out, slightly embarrassed.

"Mr. and Mrs. Cullins!" he calls as James approaches, redoubling his volume. It isn't Dick Durgess, they realize, but the foreman, a man who introduces himself as Leo or Leonard or LeRoy, James doesn't catch it.

"Teddy just informed me about the window situation," he says, hands up, guilty as charged, sweat stains under his arms. "Now we got the wood siding already up, but don't worry, we can cut some holes in that stuff, no problem, punch in a couple of frame supports, and have those windows in for you, a week, tops."

"I wasn't worried."

"Well that's good, cause there's no reason to."

"Absolutely. My wife was worried, not me.

"I understand."

"You encounter an obstacle," James says, "you find a solution. It's only a matter of working the problems out."

"You got that right. I can tell you're a logical man, Mr. Cullins. You got a way with words."

"It's my line of work. My specialty. I seek solutions."

"Walls instead of windows doesn't seem that minor to me," Carlie says doubtfully. "I'm a little concerned with the fact that your framer couldn't read the blueprints."

"See? My wife is the concerned one."

"Oh, he can read blueprints, ma'am. Ted is just a little wet behind the ears, is all. A little eager to make good. He just married in, after all."

"Married in?"

"Yessir, to Dick's eldest. The one that answers his telephones."

"So you're saying he's Durgess' son-in-law."

"Yep. Now," the foreman pulls a small spiral pad and pen from his breast pocket. "We can give y'all a buzz later in the week when we get those windows knocked in. You can come take a look, check up on the progress."

"I certainly appreciate that. It'll put my wife at ease."

"So where're you folks staying?" He levels the pad on one knee.

James glances back at their car, a fifteen-year-old Nash Rambler. Most of their matchstick furniture is lashed to the roof and trunk, like a wagon lost from the caravan. The backseat is crammed with suitcases, bedrolls, boxes of scientific texts. "What do you mean?" he says. "We're planning on staying at our house."

"In your house…" Leo runs his tongue over a chapped lip, his pad at the ready. "In that house?" He nods toward it.

"Well, yes. The deal with Durgess is that we contracted him to build the shell, and we would do our own finishing. We'd do most of the interior finishing ourselves."

"No, no, I know."

"Collaborative habitation," James says. "We live in it as we work on it."

"Uh huh. Well, we don't exactly have the electrical in yet. We can get to it first thing tomorrow. Have it done in about a week, no sweat."

"A week," James repeats. "I start work at the nuclear facility this Monday."

"The what?"

"The Bomb Plant."

Leo nods again, slowly. "Mr. Cullins, that house is dried in, but it ain't exactly a home yet. Did Durgess know that's what you were planning?"

"Well, I—" James raises his hands, swats at the empty words around his brow. "The house is supposed to be near completion by now, isn't it?"

"We're a little behind schedule."

"How behind?"

"Two months."

On a return trip to the service station, James jams more change into the pay phone and waits for an answer. The one he gets, of course, is from Dick Durgess' daughter. Her mouth sounds full of hard candy. He leaves a long message with her and climbs back behind the wheel.

Both are silent.

"Well, I guess we could always get a motel," Carlie says.

"Carlie, we haven't budgeted for that," James says. "We have a lot of work and money yet to invest on finishing the house. And I mean, I have everything itemized down to the cent. A week even in some flea-bag motel would kill us."

"What are we supposed to do then?" They have spent the past three days in this car, driving, eating, living. "Sleep in this thing? We can't even put the seats back."

James faces her. "What about Map and Minnie's?"

Carlie gives him a cautionary stare. "James, they are old, pleasant people. They don't need us showing up on their doorstep unannounced like a pair of stray cats."

"We were planning to visit them anyway, right?"

"Visit, not impose." Carlie rubs both hands over her belly. For the moment, it is a crystal ball in which she can divine portentous clouds rolling over the landscape. The thought of trying to sleep jacked upright in the car all night, with all that weight pressing against her bladder, occurs to her. That and a rusty gas station toilet for her bathroom. A bed sounded nice.

"Well, let's at least call first."

James considers this and fixes the glasses on his face. "I don't have another dime."

3

I am asked to keep the record. And keep the record, I do.

Unlike my mother, I am an archivist by profession. Specifically, I am an assistant archivist who specializes in the acquisition of Americanist cultural ephemera. That can mean anything from association copies of James Fenimore Cooper's *The Deerslayer*, to the tax returns of a Gullah root doctor, to a vitrified bottle of snake-oil circa 1900. The field is wide open. We keep our ear to the groundrails of faculty rumblings. On the top floor of the Special Collections Archive, I sit at a burled walnut counter and act as the primary liaison between visitors and the materials collection. To the few undergrads who are forced to use our arcane services for a class project, I am just the library troll, the small red face of bureaucratic control who nags them to keep their personal items in the assigned cubbies. To the grad students, I'm an indispensable tool and occasional savior. To most of the professors, I am part of the furniture. But I can appreciate what they do. They hunker over the research tables, muttering to themselves in a funk of coffee-breath, and quietly puzzle the world together from its many pieces. The ritual goes like this: I bring them the requested folder or box, then on go the cotton gloves, out come the foam support blocks for the older texts.

They immerse themselves in the materials, turning manuscript pages one at a time with both hands. Fingers to corners, palm to center. Holy and reverent. It's the orthodox religion of academia. In the quiet atmosphere, they sniff, they snuffle while scribbling notes. The occasional cough from a church pew. Some don't even know my name, though I've seen them nearly every week for six years now. I observe the observant.

My work life is a second skin that follows me home. Each morning, I change in front of a full-length mirror before work, suiting up for my 6:00 a.m. ride, with Freddie twisted among the disheveled bed behind me. I peel back that skin and stand naked, studying the material facts: the faded white scars of old body and facial piercings that no longer hold a single stud, the blurred indigo of what used to be a heart-shaped warhead tattooed on my shoulder, the growing discoloration of my teeth. I inspect for that red, receding hairline hidden against my scalp, which I ritually shave for cycling. Trace the deepening acne scars that bracket my mouth. Prod the sagging muscle tone on my chest and legs. Every year, it seems, I become less myself. So in this way, I try to remember: I catalog my body as it fights against middle age. At work, every year brings more new freshmen, wandering the library and populating the campus grounds. Another fall. Another spring. They stay permanently nineteen whereas the faculty and I grow another year older.

So it goes. I watch the scholars come in and scratch their heads over these pieces for hours at a time—I watch them rub their eye sockets dry—sequestering themselves in the quiet rooms, among the walnut and worn leather, analyzing these fragments to create a coherent narrative. There is a beauty in making meaning, making order, from where it doesn't exist. An art form to configuring the oddments of another life, another history. These are the people who keep you alive long after your loved ones have failed. Even if it's for a study of gendered leisure practices of the 1930s, you're there, part of the world again.

Which brings me to Minerva Price. A personal Mnemosyne to the Cullins. I knew her only after she exited the scene: whenever Carlie told stories about our immediate family, she always began with Minerva Price. Her husband, after all, was my namesake. However, I don't have to defer to some cheap Proustian trick to conjure her. I have the words from her own hand, her own pen.

During the time of my great gestation, Minnie wrote some fifty-three letters to my mother. A one-sided correspondence that, once discovered, was kept secret in my household. As an eight-year-old boy, I unearthed the bundle crammed in the back of my mother's night stand and began stealing them one by one. Many were discolored by that point, their flaps peeling dried glue—bent, spindled, *par avion*—specked and mouse eaten at the corners. Each envelope bore stamps, but no postmark, as they were never actually mailed. And almost every one contained a simple store-bought greeting card which Minnie then defaced with found images, expressing—or hiding—herself through a bricolage of cut-up photos, old magazine ads, and ink drawings. The lost-and-found quality mesmerized me as a kid, and still does to this day. The face of one such card is decorated with three-cent stamps from WWII. When opened, one sees that Minnie whited-out letters in the preprinted message, like a cryptogram, to spell a single word (AGAPE). By this point in her life, holding a pen became difficult, so she rolled the card itself through a typewriter to fill every inch of marginal space with text. Flip it over and on the reverse side is "A Chronology of Picture-Thoughts," followed by a grid of eight tiny human faces, snipped out and pasted from personal photographs, yellowed through the years. Some are of Carlie and James, some Minnie and Map, others I don't know.

They are love letters to Carlie, that much is clear. Though as a child, I felt they were addressed to me, too. A compilation of anecdotes, stories about my parents, reflections on the world they once inhabited together. The prescience of Minnie Price—that she knew my family and seemingly wrote to my future self—distracted me from what the letters truly were. Freddie calls them works of art and says that I should frame them.

I consider them a historical record of sublimated desire. Each began with the same oblique greeting: *Dear Pony Paradise*, the name she had christened our home. Each ends with another signifier of place: *Agape, Hoss Creek*, for the stream that ran through her back yard.

Sentimental? Maudlin? *Treacly?*—as one faculty member calls his students' writing. Certainly. Her letters smack of a peculiar naiveté, if not mania or depression. But even the most critical among us, in our unguarded moments, believe in the power of our words to enter the collective consciousness. The First Amendment, confessional poetry, and letters to Santa—they all are born of the same belief. So, too, are the armchair oaths uttered during a UNC basketball game, directed at a television screen, to say nothing of the language that we *record*: think of the innumerable diaries locked in drawers and stowed under mattresses; the travel journals from a summer of backpacking across Europe; the goofy voice recordings and skits filmed with friends in middle school; the anonymous postcards sent to websites that specialize in broadcasting secrets; the online comment forums teeming with flamewars, trolls, and hotheads; the endless private thoughts publicized on blogs, or the unblinking *I* of the latest social networking system, stored for eternity in the massive glowing server farms of Butte, Montana; and the earlier analogs still keep pace, too: the dry erase boards in college dorms, the messages chalked in kaolin against concrete stanchions, the overpasses sprayed with graffiti, the initials carved into park benches, all the charms, spells, and incantations of everyday life—Jesus Christ, we are all screaming, at one point or another, that *someone* somewhere out there must be listening amid the crush of human life. They hear us and do something with our voice, with our stories, something we assume that we cannot.

Where does this need come from? From that navel-gazer in the full length mirror after a long day of work. From the need to watch ourselves, see ourselves, in relation to the world around us. These cards, these letters—addressed to Carlie, to the house in which we lived—are a reflection of desire. A way for Minnie to see and be seen; to hear and be heard. And that's the simple power of the archive. By its existence we are allowed to believe that every little object we touch gets imbued with a life, a voice. They whisper of another reality between the living and the dead. Even something as simple as *Couldn't do it. JaC.*

4

But let's not forget about Carlie, who speaks to us, even by limited means, across that hazy divide of past and present. Part of Carlie's anxiety about surprising Map and Minnie Price came from knowing they were childless. Forty years of marriage had borne no fruit: no grown children, no grandkids, and so they lacked the security that a family—as she understood the word then—is supposed to provide. The older couple knew that she and James were expecting (she had sent letters), but Carlie didn't want to go parading her second trimester up in their private space. And private space, it seemed, was the defining feature of their life.

Map and Minnie had set themselves up in a little cottage fifteen miles outside of town, off a secluded byway known as Auscauga Lake Road. It was an axle-rattling road that people flew along without ever stopping, only slowing enough to toss an unwanted cat or puppy out the window. Auscauga Lake itself was a nowhere—a myth, a confabulation, a faux-Indian name used to mysticize white-owned land—at most, a manmade fishing pond hidden somewhere on a private acreage. Several creeks rambled through those woodlands, creating a stream-fed marsh that attracted deer and foxes and, with these, the echoing rifle-shot of hunters. Map and Minnie had tamed their own parcel of wildwood to commune with nature. Or at least that was the assumption. They lived in social refuge—two little leaves of grass—with the birds and the raccoons and the towering pines, and the occasional sportsman who had blown off his own foot.

"You're going to miss it, slow down, slow down," Carlie taps her window.

When James and Carlie arrive, cutting the engine under a carport rusted and heavy with pine straw, it is evening already, a dusky blue.

Stepping from the Rambler, the air smells of loam. Of natural deadfalls and beaver dams and running water. The world is a dampness, a lushness, a falling, an echoing. Everything set into the earth is dewed with water: the cottage foundation, the broken concrete, and the brickwork. Even the little stepping stones under their feet are slick and fresh.

They mount the porch steps, knock against the screen door, and call hello to the empty bamboo chairs. They wait. From the woods, insects teem in a hypnotic twilight reverie. The trees are older here, more fragrant; a last light hangs from their branches.

Carlie inhales deeply and slowly releases, lamaze-like in the last breath, through her lips. She watches the woods, relishes what she sees. "I could die out here," she says. "Just plant me in the yard."

"Maybe they can't hear us," James mumbles. The screen door snaps as they invite themselves onto the porch and try knocking at the kitchen door.

Everything sweet smells of decay, Carlie thinks, putting her hand on the mildewed wood of the porch mullions. She imagines cozy afghans with that whiff of cedar. Musty and pleasant. James knocks against the glass.

"Maybe they're not in?" Carlie offers. "I don't see Map's Caddy."

A dark look sets in James' face. He nods toward the unfamiliar hatchback under the carport. "Then whose is that?" He raps again, louder.

"Careful, you're going to break it."

"Something's not right," he says. He calls out, his hand cupped to the glass: "Map? Minnie?"

"James, I don't think they're home. They're probably out to dinner or something."

James sucks on his upper lip. He has recently grown a mustache. "Maybe we should break in."

"What?"

"Think about it, Carlie. They're in their sixties. I think something might have happened to them."

"What do you mean?"

"Way out here? Any number of things. Like a burglar or something. Or maybe they had a heart attack, or fell down in the shower. "

"The both of them," she asks dubiously.

"It's entirely feasible, Carlie. Bad things happen." He cups his hands around his glasses once more and tries to peer inside. "It's best not to be naive about this," he says. "I think I should maybe break the window."

"James!"

If anyone, at that moment, could bust the glass and winnow into the inner ear of James' memory, perhaps they could hear the little voice of his paranoia. Maybe they would follow it to his Junior year of college, when he returned home from class one evening to find his roommate, Ronnie Shorr, hiccupping on the toilet. After calling his name for five minutes, James gently parted the bathroom door to discover Ronnie sitting in his boxers, red-eyed from fright and crying. Then he saw the assortment of empty pill bottles scattered on the bare tile. "James?" Ronnie faced him, pale as a pat of butter. "I've done something really asinine." And then began James' mad scrabble, trying to induce Ronnie to vomit, shoving his own fingers down the boy's throat, knocking over bottles of caster oil and mouthwash, wrestling each other in a flurry of arms and legs until he dragged Ronnie by the ankles into his beat-up MG and sped to the hospital.

But these epistemological whisperings rarely go noticed. As James searches the porch for a blunt instrument—against Carlie's protest—a different voice calls out to him, this one musical and cheery through the pines:

"Yoo hoo! Down here!" Blurry through the porch screen, the speck of Minerva Price is trudging up the backyard slope, bowlegged as a bulldog.

James and Carlie absently trail off from their bickering, trying to get a good look…Is she? They pause. Yes, she is. As her shape comes into focus, she definitely is: soaking wet and stark naked. Naked as only being nude in the woods can be stark; as only skinny dipping by twilight, in the creek behind your own home, can be stark.

It takes effort, real effort, for James to uncork his lungs and blurt, "Minnie! Sorry! Geez!" He backs into a set of wind chimes; they gong and clatter. "We didn't know, I mean, you shouldn't have let us..." Every attempt to quiet the bells keeps them ringing. Fumbling, James stammers out apologies as loudly as he can, to make himself heard, or perhaps to make her stop, to make her turn back or do something discrete with her body to save them all more embarrassment. But she keeps on coming. Her arms dripping and folded against the chill, Minnie mounts the porch steps flatfooted—*thump thump thump*—wringing out her hair as she walks, drumming the porch with heavy spatters of water. Slightly breathless, she sings out, "My apologies for the peepshow, dear hearts, but—Suwannee! Look at the size of you!" Minnie pauses, staring at Carlie, who blushes. "James, you lucky duck. There's something positively magical about a young woman in the plump of life." She grabs another limp fistful of hair, which is gray and thinning on the scalp, and gives it one last twist. The brown aureoles loll beneath her arms as she does so, exposing the veins that lace her sagging belly and breast, drawing the eye to every inch of territory on her shrunken white body. By now, James is so red, it's as though all the oxygen has been cut off at his neck. "Apologies for greeting you in my birthday suit, but it's difficult for me to get around sometimes. I thought about sneaking round to the front door, but it's locked. And then I would have been one more old lady with her bare keister facing the world. Anyhoo," Minnie huffs, refreshed and wrung out, "this door is always open. We lost the key years ago. It does require a good fat push, though." After an expectant pause, she glances up at James: "Could you, dear heart?"

When James approaches the door he sees their three distorted reflections in the decorative windowpane: the large blur of himself, and the two distant woman-shapes on either side behind him. With the cool brass in the palm of his hand, he has the disturbing shock of looking backwards into the future, and a horrific notion suddenly occurs to him: that this is what his wife will look like. Before and after. His young, beautiful wife. In that moment, he spans decades, falls through a wormhole of time. He imagines waking up one morning, still young and virile himself, next to this suddenly aged and desiccated body. Brittle white hair and papery skin. Shrunken bones. And the smell. The lingering odor of slow decline. Of incontinent bodies. Of unbreatheable talcum and mothy nightgowns and dentifrice and just pure unsettling grandmotherly age. A tiny pin hole, a small perforation, appears in the fabric between James and Carlie at that moment; insignificant and nearly invisible, but he can just begin to feel the whistling air on the other side.

He uses his shoulder. The door breaks open.

"Thank you, dear heart," Minnie says, squeezing his arm as she moves him aside. "What would the world be without good strong men."

Minnie speaks to them from the bedroom where she has gone to towel off. Her voice makes an uneven melody, like a music box with a warped spindle, the tines missing every third or fourth key as she talks about the pleasant nonsense of everyday life in the boonies: electric outages, pregnant cats she has found and lost, the number of times Horse Creek has swelled and wreaked havoc on the beaver dams.

The kitchenette and dining table are tiny, too warm and too cramped to entertain, so they migrate to the living area. There, a large picture window dominates the view. Forty square feet of plate glass with one dramatic curtain drawn to the side like a stage. It faces the northern exposure and an open vista of the woods. Carlie stands full-length at its glass and watches small birds flit through the gloaming, disappearing into a forest of fir branches. Little has changed about the cottage over the years. It's still decorated with exotic Asian bric-a-brac: figurines depicting lumpy Taoist monks, alabaster vases, dried flowers, a dusty wall scroll, and lacquered boxes on the marble coffee table. Each is a reminder of Minnie's pen pals or Map's tour of duty during WWII. In the dinette, the old fashioned brass oil lamp still hangs above the table, a bit gunky from use or lack of use, Carlie doesn't know which. The Silverstone electric organ sits by the front door, sheet music propped open. Carlie eases herself into the sofa while James paces the room, hands in his pockets, distractedly inspecting small objects and photos. He clicks on the Silverstone and immediately the fan starts humming like a small aircraft preparing for liftoff. He clicks it off and it wheezes, exhaling into silence.

The last time they had seen the place was for a New Year's party two days before they left for New Hampshire. (James enrolled in the spring semester, so there they were, moving in the dead of winter like fools.) The New Year was always a gala event that overran the Prices' entire property, glowing like a pagan bacchanalia amid all those dark woods. Luminaries dotted the hillside. A bonfire crackled down by the creek where revelers, swollen with laughter and drink, stood around its heat. People spilled onto the porch, etched by the colored lights and votive candles, while inside, the howl of the electric organ played to a packed room. And all around, the light frost, the chill at Carlie's face. More than friends and neighbors, it seemed that people from all over the state came to Map and Minnie's parties—my sister's husband's second cousin, Map said of them all when making introductions. They crowded the porch bar where he concocted round after round of Harvey Wallbangers, littering the picnic table with discarded Donald Duck orange juice cartons. Map moved through that scene like a natural-born movie star, one who never made it to Hollywood. While talking with him, nagged by the impending move—just two days!—Carlie remembered one misstep in the trip ahead: they forgot to renew their driver's licenses. James in a turtleneck, glowing from the alcohol, waved her off. Carlie, we don't have time. We'll just have to get by without them—we just don't have the time. But they were already driving around with expired licenses, what would happen when they got to New Hampshire? Map handed her a fresh cocktail, smoothing his mustache and grinning like a fox. Give them to me, he said. I'll take care of it. You kids just drive safe—and then an uproar drowned them out as the countdown began on the old Admiral television inside.

On the morning of their departure, they received an expedited letter at their door. Inside was a pair of new licenses and a note: *I simply explained to the attractive young woman at the department that, no, these did not belong to me, but were the property of two dear friends of mine, and would ease the burden to us all if she could simply process them. What more would she need to hear?* This was Map's only explanation.

"James," Carlie whispers, patting the sofa cushion beside her. "Come sit by me before you wear a groove in their carpet."

He doesn't seem to hear her, lost in some algebra of thought, a trace of sweat on his face. Then he pauses, looks up. "No," he says. "That's all right."

"What's wrong? You look like you're about to run out the door."

Abruptly, James turns. By now, he's jingling the keys in his shorts' pocket, clicking them together like an agitated insect. "This was a bad idea. We shouldn't have come."

Carlie tries to straighten up in the sofa, lowering her voice again. "Well it's a little late for that now."

"We haven't asked to stay the night yet. We can beg out right now."

"James, we just got here. At least let's wait until Map gets home so we can say hi."

He stares at her now, as if he hasn't heard her—as if maybe he isn't considering the conversation at all, but rather considering her, in a way that makes Carlie feel removed from him and a little uncomfortable. Pregnant and beached on the sofa. James breaks his thought and goes back to pacing. "Yeah, you're right. We'll wait on Map. Then we'll call it an evening."

"Okay, but where else are we going to go?"

"I don't know yet. I'll come up with something."

Carlie pushes herself forward, just to be clear: "I am not sleeping in that car."

Minnie emerges from the bedroom affixing a pair of earrings. Her hair is done up in a wobbly mass of chestnut curls which, Carlie realizes for the first time in her life, is a wig. "Ready to be in the world again!" Her movements are brisk, concise for a small body. She struggles with one earlobe. "I hope I didn't startle either of you. It's an old habit, really. You live way out in the hokey, and things tend to get a little freer. You start shedding inhibitions like winter coats. Pappy couldn't stay in his long johns longer than five minutes. Been back in town long?"

"No, actually..." Carlie begins but James throws her a glance. A tea kettle begins to whistle and Minnie jumps up, excusing herself to the kitchen.

"Don't go to so much trouble," James calls out. He clears his throat. "So where is Map, anyway? When's he due home?"

A few clinks and rattles, and Minnie reappears bearing a tarnished salver with three porcelain cups and a steaming pot. She pauses, momentarily stunned. "Pappy?" Her eyeglasses slip down her cheeks, intense magnifiers that look owlish. "Why, dear heart, how could you not have known? Map, why—he's dead."

She sets the tea service down on a hassock between them.

Smiling, Minnie settles on the edge of the sofa and clasps her hands over one knee. "So," she says, a widow living alone on four remote acres of backwoods pine forest, "tell me all about the new house. How is life among all those marvelous horses and ponies?"

5

We begin. We began. We begin in Copeland as Carlie steps from the car into that bright afternoon, a film of sweat glistening on her forehead. But that is firmly in the past now, as Freddie and I have entered her story, hauling box after box of her history up the gangplank into the moving truck, until well past midnight, with drops of perspiration clinging to our noses and chins.

So, instead, she stepped. And we continue.

She stepped. And in an airless room with light dawning through the curtains, I whisper.

6

I whisper, "Ma," even though she sits in the wheelchair, awake. I kneel down to get a good look at her, to examine her face, her eyes. It seems like the first look I've gotten since we arrived—the first hard look in over a decade. I've kissed her cheek, and hugged her neck, and warmed her knuckles. I've clutched her padded armrest at the funeral as though she might be wheeled away, kidnapped if I was inattentive. But not this, not just the two of us. What I see in her is a startled clarity: her pupils dilate, tick over my face, focus on me. The irises expand, contract; twin lenses of tawny brown apprehension, flecked oddly with blue imperfections that I hadn't ever noticed before, not even from my earliest memories. She doesn't dare say it, but her expression does: *Yes?* A question for all the unknowns in her life, as if she has misplaced everything—purse, keys, reading glasses, along with names, faces, the current year, and sense of place. And so she fakes along as best she can. I place a palm against her cheek. It feels cool.

"Ma, it's me. You ready to go?"

A hesitant, troubled smile passes her lips. *Whatever you just said, sure.*

Carlie's stroke was a bilateral hemorrhage that left her partially immobilized, aphasiatic, and lost in her own memory. One of those lightning strikes that burns a dead streak down the center of a person and hollows her out. From a distance, the illusion of my mother is that she still appears to be a very capable woman. A healthy seventy years, full-faced, robust if also a little settled in her weight from spending most of her time in a wheelchair. Her hair, a brushed nickel-gray, is styled to the short no-fuss wave of many women her age. But when spoken to…the kind of aphasia she has leaves her with a limited range of simple words and constructions: *yes, no, maybe* are the clearest, with only *or, and, but* to connect her ideas. Gone is so much of her vocabulary, but the intelligence is still there.

I stand so I don't have to confront the confusion in her face. "Looks like the good news is they didn't move you in here for the long haul." I grab her suitcase, a tartan-patterned cloth thing, and shoulder a book bag that looks brand new and is stuffed full of her incidentals. Her room is shared, divided by a curtain down the middle. Her "suitemate" snoozes on the other side with audible respiratory problems, inhaling like an iron lung. Vivian. Freddie and I said hi to her only once, intruding on her afternoon Court TV, but her name stuck. All the names in this place, men and women, sound like they should be extinct species of flowers. Vivian. Inez. Cecil. An early morning light seeps in from the window blinds, doing little to lighten the dark beige walls everywhere. "Andiamo, Mamma," I whisper and grip the handles of her chair.

We hurry through the hall, the carpet purring beneath the wheels as we pass room after room, each door shut. No windows in the halls. Only bleary watercolor prints of sailboats and hibiscus in bloom. Here and there a reading nook, a cul-de-sac with a settee, or a pair of low-setting Victorian knockoffs with a table lamp in between. Dreary things that are supposed to add color. A gray pre-dawn light fills the front entrance, makes the glass and metal of the automated doors luminesce weakly.

"Mr. Cullins," a voice calls, heavy and close in the carpeted silence. In the wake of my father's wake, of all the eulogizing and remembrances and invocations, this name punctures but does not pop me, like a magic needle through a balloon. By this, I mean it takes a second for me to realize that I am Mr. Cullins, and not my father, though he would have been Dr. Cullins, anyway. We halt—chair, luggage, son, and all—and I glance back to the receptionist's desk, eager to be on our way.

"Yes?"

The receptionist is a large woman, dark, her cheeks riddled with angry acne; she wears a tropical fish print RN smock. "It's 5:45 the morning," she says.

"Yes? And?"

"I told you: you cannot take her out of here," she says, hitting the beat of each word, and though her voice is grim, she's whispering, pantomiming almost. Everyone whispers at this hour.

I'm at the counter in two strides, glancing back at Carlie as if to say *just a moment.* "This is my mother," I say. "Her name is Charlotte Marie Robicheaux Cullins. I am her son. Her legal guardian. All this week I have filled out and notarized every document pushed at me so that the state of Florida will recognize this relationship to my own mother. I have signed my weight in ink and paper so I can take her out of here."

Still seated, the woman slowly shakes her head no as she speaks. "Mrs. Gutierrez handles all discharges; she has to sign off for the release."

"And when does Mrs. Gutierrez get in?"

"She won't be back in until Monday."

"Monday?"

Her face sets harder, more rigid. "Mr. Cullins, lower your voice."

"Monday. I'm sorry, what are we supposed to do, camp out in the lobby? Or maybe I should call my lawyer? Look, we've already made arrangements. All her things are packed and ready to go. The whole nine yards." I begin fumbling through my jacket pockets. I don't know what I'm looking for exactly, something to assert my authority. "There is no way we can wait that late. We have jobs to get back to. Lives." And then I come up with a card, one of Freddie's stray business cards, this one from the nightclub-to-be. I scratch out the name in heavy ink, circle his cell phone number, and add my own name to the back. "Here," I slide it across the counter with the pen. "You already have our address on file and our lawyer's number. Tell Mrs. Gutierrez to give me a call when she strolls in on Monday morning with her cup of coffee. We'll have us a nice long talk." I grab Carlie's wheelchair handles. "We're going now. Thank you so much."

The receptionist shouts my name in a hushed way.

"Have a good morning."

She rises behind the counter but does not desert her post. I elbow the button for the automated doors and we roll out.

Freddie waits by the moving truck, a big yellow box on wheels that idles under the carriage porch with only a few inches of clearance. He stands with his shoulders hunched, the collar of his blazer askew, checking his cell phone for signs of Henri, no doubt. From a distance, it's clear that Freddie's beauty is reaching middle age. He fills his suit differently, tighter at the waist, a softening to the once hard lines. A new welt of flesh now appears under his dimpled chin whenever he smiles. Dark circles raccoon his eyes. I've never been pretty, but over these past four years, all my cycling has kept me in shape, whereas Freddie's late nights have been turning his boyishness to fat. It's hard not to notice sometimes, a reminder of his inattention. His short-sightedness.

Freddie runs one hand down his face, yawning, as he stands in the white vapor that stutters from the tailpipe. Behind him is the dull glow of the interstate in the distance, its lights discharging their sodium haze. He perks up when he sees us, ditching the phone in his pocket. The entire scene suddenly strikes me as ridiculous: the truck ready and idling like a getaway car. Freddie, the bleary-eyed point man. "What took you so long?" he says, hurrying around to unbolt the cargo door.

"I didn't know we were being timed. Here, grab her things." He hefts Carlie's baggage into the loading bay as I wheel her up to the cab. The passenger door suddenly looks more precipitous from here. "Freddie? Give me a hand. All right, Ma, here we go. Arms." I hold mine out like a brace.

We've had limited practice with this, and absolutely none with a door as high as this truck. My size turns out to be an advantage here; I can get under her, provide leverage. I can't help but think of our friends Stacy and Yvette, and their son Emile. Whenever they go anywhere, getting Emile in and out of his kangaroo seat is a stage production. Complete with introduction, climax, and denouement. I've seen their biggest fights erupt over struggling with that childseat. And the wasteland of Cheetos bags and broken Happy Meal toys that Emile leaves in his wake.

Up she goes—grab, wobble, but we steady her. One leg, then two. It proves more difficult for her to scoot into the middle of the bench seat than to climb up the cab. I give Carlie's lapbelt a test-tug and rub her knee. "Sit tight for just a sec, all right Ma? I'll be right back." She nods in a distracted way, breathing heavily.

Behind the truck, Freddie wrestles with the wheelchair, then gives up in a fit of swearing and laughter. I help him collapse the frame as quick as I can. Glancing over my shoulder, I check for the dark shape of our receptionist through the doors—Dorothy, I think her tag read—but there is no sign of her.

Once folded, I hoist the wheelchair up into the loading bed and pause. It took us three hours to load the truck last night, but it seems so empty now, a long cavernous hall leading to the far end, where all her belongings huddle together. I get to work, strapping the wheelchair to the side with elastic cords.

Freddie wipes his nose. "Remind me: why aren't we flying?" I can hardly hear him over the engine rumbling.

He juts his chin toward the truck and repeats himself.

"Because road trips are fun," I say. "They're an American tradition, a gateway to self-discovery."

"Ah." Freddie pockets his hands and kicks the back tire. "Self-discovery might be easier if we had this stuff shipped."

I slam the shutter down, and we climb up into the cab. "Got everything, Ma? Comfy?" Carlie sits between us, stock-still, without saying a word. No *yes, no, maybe*. The purse in her lap contains all her necessary identification, medical alert information, and various pharmaceuticals. The book bag has other necessaries, adult diapers and such things, stowed at Freddie's feet. He mashes it further beneath the dash and scrunches himself closer to the door. He tries for his seatbelt, then gives up. "Does she have enough room?" I ask. I double check her belt, make sure she's not constricted. While leaning over Mom, I notice the molecules inside the cab have changed, something acrid under the scent of cracked vinyl and vanilla air freshener. "Just out of curiosity," I say, glancing up to Freddie, "were you smoking?"

Freddie's huddled against the door, legs crossed, gazing out the window. "I haven't had a cigarette in eight months. You know that." He rubs his stubble and smiles at his reflection. "The exhaust. Maybe you didn't notice, but I was slowly asphyxiating in a cloud of carbon monoxide for twenty minutes. Remember?" He blows me a kiss.

Then, beyond his window, I see her: the shadowy but unmistakable shape of the receptionist. Next to her, the broad-shouldered figure of what has to be security personnel. They stand behind the glass doors, watching us. What I assume to be Carlie's dossier hangs from her left hand; a long folder, stuffed with forms and documentation. Official release, official acknowledgment, names, numbers, verification of her place in this world. I don't know how long she has been watching us. And I can't guess, for all those files and that large guard, why she hasn't come outside to stop us.

I pop the truck into gear and we crawl from under the carriage porch, the tires slowly catching asphalt as everything in the cargo hold lurches and rattles in our wake.

"Here we go," I say, checking the passenger mirror for those silhouettes again, who are still lingering, still watching and conferring behind the glass, as we proceed from Florida into the world.

In real life, there are no quick getaways.

7

For Carlie and James, there was no escape plan, no Plan B, no clearly marked exit sign. So when confronted by the shocking news of Map's death—or any shocking news, for that matter—my parents responded with the typical politesse of respectable people the world over: they tried to ignore it entirely. With bewildered little smiles stapled to their faces, they kept mum. They didn't ask when it happened. They didn't ask how it happened. They didn't know if they should. What, after all, could they say? *Map? Oh, he's dead, is he? How interesting! What's that, our house? Why yes, it is behind schedule. Yes, I know, how terribly inconvenient.* They spoke stiltedly with Minnie, their smiles fluttering, dumbfounded, against her breezy demeanor. They checked their watches. They silently wondered where else they could go this late in the evening. Most unnerving, Map was now laid to rest out in the middle of the woods—she nodded toward the large picture window—where the deer could visit him. From that and the few platitudes Minnie offered, a general idea took shape: the prognosis was inevitable, so Minnie had pulled him from the hospital, and Map spent his last, dying months on the back porch. Day and night, through delirium and growing incapacity. So weak and bone-thin that he soiled the mattress every day.

Minnie had been a trained nurse at one point in her life, after all; it was the automatic thing to do. ("But listen to me prattling away! You poor dears don't have a home to go to!"— Carlie had let that bit slip.) When Minnie extended an invitation to stay, they tried to decline, but she insisted ("Nonsense. Pappy wouldn't hear of it!"), offering up Map's own bedroom, which had the queen-sized bed, after all ("I've been sleeping in the spare for some years now. He was always such a terrible snorer!"), and so considered the matter settled. While she whisked off to gather sheets and towels, James and Carlie realized the cold truth: there was nowhere else they could possibly go.

After dragging in the suitcases, Carlie and James shut themselves up in the bedroom, afraid to touch anything. They prepared for sleep, trying to acclimate to this new atmospheric pressure—the strangeness of invading a dead man's bedroom. They poked around; they whispered. The entire room looked undisturbed, if not exactly preserved. Map's flannel shirts still hung in the closet; a bathrobe lay folded on the bureau; the scent of tobacco still lingered in the half-bath. Carlie sat on the bed cross-legged and worked cold cream onto her elbows, which had begun to get rough and patchy lately.

James returned to the room, having just vomited, and gently shut the door. He was a little less pale, a little less green, but still gingerly rubbed his chest.

"Are you okay?"

"Just my stomach," he said, stifling a belch. Five pairs of his slacks and dress shirts hung neatly from the curtain rod, avoiding the closet. "This is highly unusual. Highly unusual." He began laying out neckties across the open lid of the suitcase. "What are we doing, staying in a sarcophagus?"

"*James.*" Carlie leaned across the bedspread. "Keep your voice down."

"I mean, don't get me wrong, I appreciate Minnie's hospitality and all, but can you believe this? Map is dead and we don't even know? And Christ, look at the way she's acting. Flitting about, making tea. It's like he's on a business trip or something. All nonchalant and casual about the whole thing."

"Maybe she was expecting it?"

"Expecting it? If we weren't expecting it, why would she?"

"That's a silly thing to say. He was her husband."

"That's what I'm saying! People expect babies, Carlie. Not this. I don't care how close someone is to the end, death is always a shocker. A *surprise*. And Map, he might have been on in his years, but come on, he was still spry."

"Everyone grieves in a different way," Carlie offered. Then she grinned mischievously, edging closer on the mattress. "After you die, I promise to wear all black for a year. I promise to gnash my teeth and rip all my hair out."

"Laugh. You do realize that you're sitting in a deathbed, don't you? That we're climbing into a dead man's bed—and it could still be warm for all we know."

"Hush! Don't say that." Carlie readjusted her legs. "Minnie used to sleep here too, you know."

"Yeah, yeah. I was right, though. Out on the porch? I knew something was wrong. Ugh," James rubbed his stomach again. "I'm in knots. I can't believe I'm starting work on Monday. First day of work and I don't even have the comfort of my own damn bed."

"It'll only be a week, sweetie. The foreman said they'd be ready for us to move in then."

"They'd better or there'll be hell to pay. It kills me that I'm going to be living out of a suitcase for my first week like some traveling salesman." James poked around the room in his tee-shirt and boxer shorts. "And what kind of commute is it from here? I'll have to time it tomorrow morning. I bet it'll take me an hour and half to get to the plant. And who knows about traffic?"

Carlie pulled the bed's afghan up to her cheek and inhaled. "I've never seen you this anxious before," she said, which was untrue. The preparation for his dissertation defense had swelled into three long months of dyspepsia. She spoke with the cover pressed to her face, watching him, "You're making yourself sick."

James began picking up and setting down framed photographs from the dresser, examining them. "Yeah, well, it's the whole set-up that's doing it," he said, lifting a small portrait. "Hey," James whispered. "Carlie, look at this." She slid out of bed, heavy-footed, and came to his side.

On the dresser was a yellowed photograph of Map. In the photo, he stood atop the rocky outcrop of a mountain, buck naked except for a pair of cowboy boots and a pistol holster slung around his bare waist. His back, or rather buttocks, faced the camera as he shot a grin over his shoulder. Beaming with a healthy physique, fists firmly planted against his hips. The Frontiersman's New Clothes.

"That's nuts," James said. "What were they, nudists?"

"No," Carlie said, smiling, working her knuckles where the rings had been a few moments before. "I think they were just in love."

James shook his head, studying the picture. "Who would keep this in his own bedroom?" As Carlie slipped back into bed, James returned the frame to the dresser, facedown.

* * *

Early the next day, they escaped Minnie's house and returned to the construction site. Alone together, and in view of the house, the future once again seemed more certain. The Rambler was still chock full of their belongings, carrying the reminder that, soon, the construction would be done. "Home," James said after cutting the engine. He huffed at the sight of it, feeling an exasperated relief. They had come to give the foreman Minnie's phone number.

The crew was smaller this day, about five men. The ruckus of hammers and hauling chimney stone was noticeably diminished. They couldn't find the foreman. They spoke instead with the towheaded framer who explained they would be getting to those windows soon, the schedules being ironed out as they were. While James scrawled down their information, Carlie looked over the house again, envisioning the windows. She squinted against the daylight. It was difficult to imagine them; the scene still didn't look right. It couldn't be a failure of imagination on her part—Carlie had been seeing this house in her dreams for the past two years. Then, her mouth fell slightly agape as the problem revealed itself. She had expected it to be there, that's why she hadn't seen before…because the windows were supposed to be there, too, and they weren't, which had thrown her off.

"Where's the balcony?" She said this carefully, as if smelling smoke in a crowded room.

The two men stopped, looked up. Teddy, the framer, chewed his bottom lip. He looked down to the blueprints on the table.

"The small balcony," she clarified, "that is supposed to be below where the windows are supposed to be."

Teddy's face pinched in pained concentration. He straightened up, smiling nervously, and asked James, "Could you please not bring your wife around here anymore?"

8

Ah, but Carlie, you can never go back. You can never return home. Or you can never leave home, depending who you get your clichés from. Or try this: there are only two plots in the world—a man rides out of town or a man rides into town. Town being the stand-in for home, of course, a sense of belonging and place in the world. Such notions are too simple, too precious to be of much use. The truth is far more complicated. You can both never leave and never stop leaving home in the same breath. The return is unthinking, habitual, coded in our smallest daily practices. Rice gets washed three times before cooking, then once more for good measure. Dark roast coffee only, brewed strong enough to burn a hole through your colon. Butter and eggs go to the back of the shelf, not near the refrigerator door where they will spoil quicker. And then there are the active countermeasures: opting for whole grain bread, a certain aversion to the hard sciences, life without a television set. Cycling at six in the morning, sweating all the impurities out. With these habits, you can never stop tearing down that place you have known, knocking holes in its walls and drawing up a new blueprint to live by, only to rebuild your understanding of the world with what you have already demolished, those same raw materials. These are the only bricks and mortar you have: those faces and names and gestures cast within the first two decades of life. Though the house you build takes a different shape, your every action and reaction points to home.

We make a pit stop every two hours. I know from Carlie's nurse that she hasn't had a bowel movement in three days. The RN supplied me with a stool softener, but it's not constipation, I'm pretty certain. She's just uncomfortable on the toilet. I think all the change, all the disruption in her life has made her nervous, retentive. Sun-up glares off the metal gas pumps and interstate signs at every brief detour. Pitted sidewalks strewn with butts, steel doors flaking rust. Keys attached to large wooden paddles. Loose deadbolts that you have to jiggle to open. A reminder of a lifetime of traveling, no doubt. I try to avoid these gas stations, opting for newer ones, or ones that appear newer, with the chance of indoor restrooms.

In Dublin, GA, around nine in the morning, I manage to get her into one. We pull the truck alongside a combination gas station and fast food restaurant.

"Bathroom, Ma?" I say. "Do you need to use the bathroom?"

She starts awake with a snort, and I repeat the question. A sticky heat radiates from her body, and it occurs to me that she might not have had a proper bath since my father died. It takes her some time to get her bearings. She looks concerned and says, "Yes and no. But yes." Nodding vaguely.

"You have to go?"

Her voice is hoarse, cracking. "You know, yes. But."

Freddie moans next to her, wedged into the door. Incredibly, he's been sleeping—sleeping like he's under narcosis, fraught with deep dreams. His blazer is wadded between his cheek and the window; he sweats, stirs once, and doesn't wake for anything. "Freddie. Get up." Mom tugs on her seatbelt so I pop out and make preparations as quickly as I can. From the truck, I opt for the walker over the wheelchair. She might need to stretch her legs. I bang on Freddie's door twice before he cracks it open, shambles out, nearly tripping. We help ease Mom down—a bigger challenge than going up, which involves a lot of physical and moral support, enthusiastic instructions about where to put her feet. Afterward Freddie climbs back onto the bench seat, eyes still pinched shut.

A blast of air conditioning and the smell of bacon grease greet us inside. The place is busy with senior citizens having their discounted coffee and biscuits. Mom drags past the counters and I follow slowly at her side, like an usher. Eventually, I push the women's room door open for her. It's a multiple occupancy bathroom, but luckily, at the moment, there are no other women inside. "Mom, do you need me to…?" But she trudges past me without a glance. I lean against the wall and wait.

A few women come and go, a mother and small daughter, a tiny woman my mother's age but able-bodied, clutching her purse like I might yank it from her. Five, ten minutes pass. Freddie shuffles up, stretching and rubbing his face. His collar and hair are sticky from dried sweat. "I'm amazed you're up," I say.

He stifles a long yawn and looks about, a sour grimace on his face. Still pre-verbal, he leans on me like a puppy. He scratches his throat.

"Here." I pull cash from my wallet. "Go get yourself some breakfast and meet us back at the truck." Freddie studies the money for a moment, unsure of the denominations, then shuffles off.

By now she's been in there too long, I'm sure of it. I approach a cashier, a teenager girl, and tell her that I need to get inside the women's restroom. She stares at me, lip curled. "My mom," I explain. "She's disabled."

She mentions her manager and disappears. He arrives after a moment, a man with a thick neck who smells strongly of antiperspirant.

"She hasn't come out," I explain, but he's already flipping through a ring of keys, whistling, and pulls a slippery-when-wet cone from the janitorial closet. After a quick knock knock and cautionary hello, he kicks the bathroom door open with one wingtip and props the cone in front of it.

"There you go." He folds his arms.

The handicapped stall is partially open. I step in, gently wrap on it, and peek through. Inside the stall, Carlie starts awake from where she had fallen asleep, slumped between the toilet and the wall. She looks at me, bewildered, a seam of confusion—and a red mark from the concrete bricks—creasing her forehead. A pair of lilac underwear is stretched across her knees. Inside the crotch is an adult underpad. We have an opened stack of them in her day bag that the nurse gave us. Some absurd name like Prevail or Dignity written in a flowing script across the package. I forgot these in the cab. Too late now. I turn to the manager, "Could you?" He snatches the cone, whistling to himself, and the pneumatic door wheezes shut to allow us some privacy.

"Mom, do you need help? Tell me what you'd like me to do." She stares dead-center at me, embarrassed or overheated, as if trying to figure something out. I notice then that the toilet seat is up, and she's sitting on the bare rim, her pants draped to the floor. "Are you done? If you are, let's get you up off that." I pull myself into the stall, roll an excessive amount of toilet paper around one hand, and hold it out. At this time of the morning, the bathroom still smells strongly of bleach and that pink liquid soap that has a citronella tang to it. The tiles underfoot still glisten, if not exactly clean, from a fresh mopping. She absently plucks at the wad of paper and tries to speak, but the words won't turn over, *Gnh-gnh-hnh, hn-hn-hng*, like a flooded engine that won't start. Finally she clears her throat and gets it out: "Home."

"Yeah, home," I say. "We're going home. Do I… do I need to help you here?" I tentatively point with the wad of paper, gesture at her legs. "You know, with cleaning?" Suddenly, she attempts to stand and plops back down. On the second attempt, she grabs the toilet rim to steady herself. "Don't, Mom, that's got to be filthy…" Then she grapples with the handrail and walker to get to her feet. "Here, I really think we need to get you cleaned up. Just say the word if you need me to..." I stand there, toilet paper in hand, watching as she struggles to tug her underwear back up. "No? Okay, well. If you're fine with that, I guess...I guess we're good." I peek into the toilet bowl. Urine. "Shall we go?"

Once we finally settle back into the cab, Freddie's more chipper, if also groggy. He has a twenty-four ounce can of energy drink and a carry-out bag in his lap. "Everything go all right?"

"Yep. Perfect." I buckle Mom up, tear into a few moist towelettes, and begin rubbing them over her hands. "Easy."

"Doable?"

"Completely doable. Amazingly doable."

"Good." He nods. "I bought everyone breakfast." He then produces a variety of prepackaged goods, laying them out across the dashboard. Snack cakes, potato chips, cookies, powdered doughnuts. I see there is a protein bar there for me, the kind I usually eat after cycling. Freddie explains, "I didn't know if Carlie had nut allergies or something. All that healthy stuff has nuts."

"Nope, no allergies. Resilient as a battle tank." She passively holds her hands out as I finish the job, then I reach over to cram the used wet naps into Freddie's bag. The cab stinks of alcohol. As we take off, I crack the window an inch, convinced that I can smell urine.

It's mostly back roads and minor highways between here and Copeland, South Carolina. A rural scenic route. We bump along the riddled asphalt of Georgia Highway 26, a gray, eroded ribbon that flashes sunlight like a mirror. The road curves and cleaves through a vast horse pasture, then farmland with rolling irrigation pipes, where another small town has petered out.

The wind whistles through the gap in the window. I feel the warm, clear air on my scalp and focus on the steady rush of highway. Without the air, cars make me a little ill. I glance over and see Freddie asleep again, despite the sugar and caffeine. Sprawled sallow-faced against the door, the drink can wedged in his crotch. Carlie has nodded off as well, her mouth canted open and bucking gently against the headrest.

Late at night, I used to tell these family stories to Freddie, whenever I stayed up long enough to hear the deadbolt slip open. He would come home already wired from some elevated state of consciousness—the necessities, he says, of doing business—and I'd be wandering through my own Nod after a few bourbons, the old stories rattling around in my head. In truth, I'd be waiting up for him. Just to see him, to remind myself of something. Of what, I can't remember now.

But on these nights, we usually dragged chairs to the windows facing West 25th, as if they were a porch, listening to the 2:00 a.m. traffic—laughter, car alarms—and catching a faint breeze between the buildings. Lights off, feet up, the orange glow from the street lamps on our toes. Tinkle of ice. At that hour, Dot stirred in her terrarium like a cranky neighbor. Scratch, scratch: Keep it down. Digging a hole in the glass that would never appear. Those were the nights in which I could feel a wind whistling through my chest, an empty space where my other life used to be, and so I filled Freddie with stories of that place, chapter after chapter in the fragmented chronicle of Copeland. Pointless anecdotes that seemed important at the time.

Freddie never had much to say, only nodded until I spun my stories out. Occasionally, he groped at his chest pocket for a cigarette or, if finding them gone, settled for another glass of bourbon. He was a rootless army brat, after all, born in Paris, and had lived in so many places that none of them stuck. Childhood, a place called home—those are experiences in orbit somewhere, completely detached from him. *Tabula rasa.*

Those nights always ended with me shuffling off to bed, while Freddie stayed up long enough to greet the sun.

9

Peacetime Products for a Safer Tomorrow, the unofficial slogan went. But peace is not a very profitable industry, a niche market at best. Consider the economic returns of World War II, that fantastic windfall of domestic consumerism—the two-car garage, suburban housing and homeowners' subsidies, a Tomorrowland furnished with new vacuum cleaners, television sets, and microwave ovens. Good spoils for any economy, but underlying this shift was the ghost of Hiroshima, the shadow of Nagasaki. Our creation of The Bomb—and the subsequent arms race toward mutually assured destruction—had birthed an advertising campaign of ecstatic terror that ran through the Red Menace and tied all markets to a national identity: the massive upsizing of consumer goods, tank-like American automobiles, crates of canned ham, oil drums of peaches in heavy syrup, Sears and Roebuck bomb shelters, and the ramped-up mass-production of a national defense industry which danced through the green fallout of Joe Public's expendable income like a Busby Berkeley grand finale, singing at the top of its lungs, *We must be prepared for tomorrow!*

To this day, nothing has captured the American ethos of destructive optimism quite like nuclear fission.

In the 1950s James' employer, the Savannah River Site, was the largest producer of fissile material for nuclear warheads in the United States of America. Situated on three hundred square miles of government secured land, SRS drew its workforce from five counties and in doing so, accounted for a quarter of the South Carolina economy. An army of laborers, engineers, research scientists, military personnel, and administrators worked in a nuclear complex three times bigger than the city of Charleston. A sovereign no-fly zone, a Vatican of new era ingenuity that drew the best minds from around the country, heavily patrolled not by a flamboyant Swiss Guard, but by the earthy olive-drab, machine gun-toting U.S. Army. Locals both revered and reviled it as The Bomb Plant, but bombs were never made there. What this massive facility produced was the essential plutonium 239, californium 252, and a classified amount of tritium, for those bombs—all those manmade elements that could only be manufactured in the atomic blast furnace of a nuclear reactor. In short order, an entrepreneurial enthusiasm for all things radioactive bled into the surrounding towns. Local bars cropped up with names like Ground Zero or The Fallout Shelter; brand new aluminum signs for Atomic Auto Repair and Chain-Reaction Motors hung along the byways, squeaking out the praises of industrialized progress with each passing car. National security, after all, meant business. Big Business. Private industry kept its hand in the pocket of that one wealthy uncle everyone seems to have: Uncle Sam.

But in 1971, the nuclear business was beginning to flag. Chemical agents and synthetic rubbers were all the rage for the Vietnamese lineup—which meant DOW Chemical, Monsanto, and DuPont won all the profitable contracts. So with the uneasy Cold War détente (and the impossibility of nuking Vietnam), federal powers scaled back the production of weapons grade materials. Two reactors were shut down, and the small bedroom communities broke into economic fever chills. So what was the product now? The advisory board at SRS scrabbled for a new market: Radioactive waste remediation? Vitrification? Isotopes for the medical industry?

A little of everything. SRS spent millions on brilliant young physicists toward a twenty-year plan that had a finger in every pie. For James, his slice of that pie was in waste. In 1971, K-Reactor became the first production reactor in the country to be automatically regulated by a computer. Aside from eliminating lower-level jobs, its activation meant more heavy water—the coolant that keeps a reactor from a meltdown which, in the process, produces an extra four million gallons of irradiated byproduct per year. There's a Zen koan locked up somewhere inside that water, flowing to, then flowing from, the fuel rods: cooling, calming, polluting, poisoning. Once an earthly element, now imbued with a celestial terror. However, figuring out how to remediate all that contaminated waste was less about prosody and more about drawing in government bucks.

For James, this meant a staggering dollar investment in his brain—and the knowledge of it kept him awake. Monday morning came with the singular speed of an accelerated neutron. At 4:00 a.m., his young wife, the old widow, and all the fat little birds huddled in the wet branches were still peacefully asleep. James, however, sat at Minerva's cramped kitchen table with a cup of weak tea, his stomach churning like a volcano. Starchy suit, pressed shirt and paisley tie, shined shoes, and new briefcase—he could hardly breathe. It felt like the waiting room to his life, like waiting for his number to be called. He didn't want to arrive too early, but to be on time, punctual to the dot, so he measured his movements, counted the seconds, sipped his tea. At a quarter to five, he moved to the carport. The Rambler had been completely unloaded the day before, all the cheap furniture and boxes stowed in neat stacks under the carport. Of course life hadn't begun, that was the evidence: seeing their possessions dumped together on the damp concrete, waiting in the gray, unfamiliar quiet of the world. Marriage was only one part of the equation; the child, another. Both things seemed far removed from him in this limbo, at this place and hour. Today, he was finding himself at the other end of the equation. Today, he had the calculus of breadwinners: briefcase, clearance cards, and a full tank of gas. He stowed his briefcase and gently depressed the Rambler's trunk until it latched. Everything clicked into place. Before leaving, James upchucked a thin gruel of tea and stomach acid into the hydrangeas by the carport and felt a little relief.

He drove for an hour in the twilit murk, along misty roads that made the windshield perspire. On the outskirts of Copeland, he joined a line of traffic that crawled through the hamlet of New Ellenton. This was the daily morning influx. They could have been campers, a stream of vacationers heading to the lake, trying to get an earlier start but getting stuck in rush hour traffic nonetheless. Sunrise glared through the windshield, casting a steamy light on the few cinderblock buildings that bordered the road—anonymous barbeque restaurants, bait shops, a tiny post office—which, after another forty-five minutes, bottlenecked directly into a controlled toll gate and the only means of accessing Savannah River Site.

The gatehouse guards wore military fatigues and carried M16s.

James cranked down the window and fumbled for his pass clearances. Several identification cards hung from a lanyard around his neck, coded for different levels of clearance, and he shoved them all through the window. Wordlessly, one of the military personnel moved his hand from the stock of his assault rifle and thumbed through the cards until he found the right one. He signaled the barrier and waved him on.

From there, the main artery split into a hydra of narrow roads that wound through 78,000 hectares of native forest, each turn posted with small delphic signs. Many of those winding roads were in poor repair; most of them, in fact, belonged to Ellenton before the entire town was evicted to make way for SRS in the 50s. Homes, schools, and churches were hauled away on flatbed trucks, and what couldn't be moved was half-heartedly demolished. What remained was a vision of the apocalypse caused not by nuclear devastation but by its progress. Old highways were left to grow over with kudzu while furnaces, chimney foundations, and aluminum houses rotted in the woods. Family cemeteries were dug up and bodies transported. The few abandoned homes left standing may have foreshadowed Chernobyl, but no one fled in the midst of Sunday dinner. The populace had been given an eighteen month eviction notice. Enough time to prepare but not to fight. Enough time for one young displaced resident to draft a response, something of a handwritten letter to the editor, tacked to a post marking the town limits of Old Ellenton during that exodus back in 1950:

> IT IS HARD TO UNDERSTAND WHY OUR TOWN MUST BE DESTROYED TO MAKE A BOMB THAT WILL DESTROY SOMEONE ELSE'S TOWN THAT THEY LOVE AS MUCH AS WE LOVE OURS. BUT WE FEEL THAT THEY PICKED NOT JUST THE BEST SPOT IN THE U.S., BUT IN THE WORLD. WE LOVE THESE DEAR HEARTS AND GENTLE PEOPLE WHO LIVE IN OUR HOME TOWN.

Prosaic? Natch. But more than that, one can see the disturbing symbiosis of love and destruction that permeated the local mindset. The frustration, pride, and complacent acceptance that such an industry engenders. After all, they picked the best little town to nuke the world from. As far as I know, that sign still stands today.

But for James that morning, all these details passed him by. Pulling into the main perimeter, his vision opened up to the secret city within the secret wood, drawing back the boughs that hid a new world capitol: there were the great industrial and administrative buildings, gleaming glass and steel, harboring the architectonics of the future; there were the walking paths and electric cart paths that ran through the woods, following the shade of beech trees like a golf course; the labyrinthine parking lots divided by tight security gates, sparkling with a thousand cars, the orderly ranks of the elect each with a designated space; and again, more security booths at each of the sector buildings, where personnel flashed their numbered badges; and above it all, the top of the newly automated K-Reactor that crested the treeline like a mountain summit, home to an atomic guru.

James stepped from his car. Like a wandering acetic himself, a seeker of answers, he had come from spiritual rigors into a vision of nirvana. From the New York public school system, clawing into higher education by scoring a tennis scholarship, pushing ahead of the large, anonymous pack at FSU by doubling up his course load, cleaning the laboratory equipment in his off-hours, then part-time admittance into Harvard, transferring into MIT, late hours in the student labs, 1:00 a.m., 2:00 a.m., exacerbated by the long commute home to New Hampshire, contending with every affluent son of a judge, or an aluminum die-casting tycoon, or any number of the well-heeled family names of the northeast whose patrimony meant something to the admissions board and school endowment, and then every maladjusted crank of a professor with whom he had to strain to gain their notice because he wasn't there on international scholarship. His own father had been an ice and coal salesman, then a carpenter, who always spoke big of education, as if it was the promised land, as if it was the milk and honey long due to their tribe. And even when James' studies in high school drew him further away from his father—they no longer spoke the same sentences, no longer understood the universe through the same mathematics—the old man still sold half his business to send him safely on to the other side. Now his father was three years gone, now the turbulent and demeaning moratorium of school was behind him, now he had a wife and a child on the way. James had walked barefoot through the searing desert and finally found his place in the world. A retinue of technicians whirred by in an electric cart, looking like soft G-Men: buzz cuts, white shirts, black ties. Their chests were pinned with pocket protectors and ID tags, their eyes framed in thick black glasses. Beyond them was another small group of lab personnel, white coats, talking around a picnic table while having a smoke. They might as well have been taking Socratic walks and plucking asphodel blossoms for their lapels. Isolated here in nature, James saw a utopian community. An Amana colony for physicists.

What he saw in these men (and at that time, only men) was this: a fraternity of boundless intellectual freedom.

* * *

"One: don't send any off-site correspondence without the expressed authorization of at least two Level II managers.

"Two: don't contact any affiliated research teams without your intermediary liaison.

"Three: don't access restricted-use data from an off-site location; that means any of the three other quadrant buildings.

"Four: don't let restricted-use data leave the licensed site.

"Five: don't allow any subsets of correspondence data at the end of your project to remain unmitigated."

"Unmitigated?"

Phil Doyle paused long enough for James to catch up in two strides. James had just come from a five-hour orientation in an airless room with ten other men. He relished stretching his legs again, but the pace made the air tingle in his head.

"Administrativese: Undestroyed," Phil said with a smirk and continued on. Phil Doyle led him on a tour of the G-Wing corridor, one hand in his suit pocket, the other gesturing freely while he spoke. His hair was sprayed in a shiny auburn sweep that seemed untouchable. "But don't let all those 'don'ts' throw you. I like to get them all out of the way early, so we can focus on more productive things," he said, ridding some lint from his serge blazer. "We really do try to engender creativity here." Thirty feet underground, the corridor they walked through had exposed pipes overhead, constantly roaring, and a few twitchy fluorescent panels that lit the passage.

"Manual C lists any form you'll need. Supply and personnel procurement, materials contracts, consent of council. Use form 1021-B to petition for budget requests—and whatever you get, don't spend it all at the candy shop. There are random compliance audits to make sure you're following operational procedures. Here's your office!" Doyle braced a door open, like a quick motel room inspection. Windowless, the office was little more than a bunker. A metal desk and adjustable shelves were bolted into the wall. A dusty model of a water molecule had been left behind on the topmost shelf. Doyle furrowed his brow, though still smiled. "You'll probably want to start by requisitioning some office supplies."

Farther down, the hall dead-ended into the research facility and an emergency exit. Doyle approached the door and keyed the punch-button pass code. A mechanical bolt unlatched. "And this," he said, "is your team." Inside, a single man occupied the table at the far end of the room, making notations beside an electron microscope. "Whit Shirley, meet the new project researcher for waste remediation, Dr. James Cullins."

At the sight of the lab, James' soul breathed again. The hybrid computers with their tiny green blips, the clipboards and punch cards, the chemical sinks and micro pipettes, the brilliant white wattage of ample overhead lighting. And there, a gamma ray spectrometer; over here a neutron detector, two large nitrogen canisters for the separator, and a few small deuterium supply bottles that stood like a row bicycle pumps on the shelf. Here were all the instruments designed for measuring and understanding the unseen energies of the cosmos, arranged in haphazard, practical beauty. The lab itself was just one of three shared workstations attached to a larger research facility. Through its observation windows, James could glimpse the cavernous chamber where an isochronous cyclotron was housed, a particle accelerator with color-coded pipes, and a network of cables and vacuum components. Set into the far wall of the main facility were the hot cells, small isolation chambers shielded by a foot of leaded glass and sets of mechanical arms—master-slave manipulators, in the brutal parlance of the time—for dealing with hazardous materials. The sweat, the anxiety, the burning claustrophobic fever of managerial protocol flushed from James' pores and slid right off his skin. This room alone was the one true religion, his calling, the irreducible building blocks of the universe: waves and particles.

And then he noticed his "team" staring at him. A lone technician, a biologist, James knew. But this man did not look like a scientist. He looked like a paunchy, retired golf pro, a once famous has-been who'd seen too much sun. Dirty yellowed hair and the blistered, creased skin of a plucked turkey. The man reclined in his chair, metal squawking on concrete, and drew his smile out like a knife. A leering and almost predatory look. Later that day, James would catch sight of Whit Shirley speeding from the parking lot in a dusty El Camino—and notice the bare gun rack in the rear window. Phil shut the door on Whit Shirley before anyone could say hello.

"You two can get acquainted tomorrow," he said. "Let's see, what else. There are upper, middle, and lower level managers that deal with the technicians—Level I, II, and III, respectively. Your team and any research assistants are overseen by Level II. Since you're the principle researcher, Bob, Al, and I will be your go-to guys. Bob Pendergast, unfortunately—PenderGasbag. As for the upper management, well…we all know how *that* is." Phil widened his eyes and shivered theatrically. "All right. I think that about does it. After you fill this up, Bob'll be leading the end-session orientation at 4:00, so take your time."

Phil's secretary had followed several paces behind the entire time so that James had forgotten about her, but now she stepped forward with what looked like a first aid kit. Unsnapping the box, she held out a little plastic cup with a securely fastened lid.

James took it in hand. "A urine sample? I already did one of these this morning."

"I know, it's a hassle. But all part of the protocol, especially on Day One."

James noticed that they had stopped in front of the men's room. It had no door, but rather a U-shaped passage like the pass-through to a horse paddock.

"Oh." Doyle snapped his fingers and paused for a beat, as if finding his words. "One last thing. Don't send any new research proposals directly to the Level I managers. It tends to clog things up." He shrugged. "You know, when people jump the chain of command. Besides, those geezers will shoot anything down without a Level II to champion it." He grinned and pointed at the cup in James' hand. "There are instructions posted in the stalls. Hand that to Leanne when you're done. She'll wait." And then Phil Doyle disappeared down the hall.

James lingered inside the corridor for a moment with Leanne, who remained silent and refrained from making eye contact. He excused himself.

The men's room smelled of concrete and mildew. As promised, inside the stall was a laminate poster with explicit instructions on how to pee into a cup. Step-by-step illustrations explained how to fill the sample, including when to unzip his fly and how to angle the container like a beer glass. James imagined himself before the toilet, holding the plastic cup in one hand and a PhD in Physics from MIT in the other.

All right. Okay. Fine.

He dutifully filled the cup, secured the lid, and washed his hands. While snatching paper towels, he noticed a green little box mounted next to the dispenser. James studied it for a moment. Someone had crudely painted SUGGESTIONS on the side. Below that, another person had scrawled RETIREMENT FUND in ballpoint pen. He had seen no actual suggestion boxes anywhere on the grounds; this one had to be a joke, and an old one at that, as the box was coated in a thick layer of dust. There wasn't even a lock, or a hinge. No way of opening it that he could see.

James smirked. Shaking his hands dry, he carefully took a slip of paper from his pocket pad. On the tiny page, he wrote:

Re: Urine Sample Protocol addendum

**Nowhere on instructions does it say to remove lid from cup.*

—JaC

Folding the paper neatly into the box, James exited the men's room with a spring in his step and a warm bottle of urine in his grip—making the first move in a game that, less than a decade later, would end his career.

* * *

That same morning, Carlie had laid in bed for hours. Though she had been vaguely aware of James rising and shuffling about, the simple, perfunctory slam of the car door outside woke her in a panic. She was late! She wasn't ready, she wasn't even dressed yet—she had to grab the essentials and run outside before he took off. Where were all her things, her coat, her purse, her keys? But then a cold despondency shocked her back into reality as the Rambler trawled away, blooming gritty exhaust against the windowpane, and Carlie realized that, no, she wasn't going anywhere, at least not with him, not now, not anymore. James was off on the first morning of his new career.

This, after a thousand mornings of boiling coffee, of driving to work through twelve inches of icy slush, of helping James through school, of phoning surveyors, estimates, and work orders for their house. They had come this far together…but now what? Stroking her belly, Carlie wondered if this would be the nature of motherhood, too: to have your child, who has been part of your body, part of your every waking minute, shake free from your grip on his first morning to school. (She had a sneaking suspicion it would be a boy.) No, Ma, I gotta go. Thanks for everything and all, but I don't need you anymore.

So she laid there, afraid to move, afraid to get up, afraid to disturb her foreign surroundings. Don't touch anything, don't call attention to yourself. If this day could just pass her by, then she might not feel so lost in the universe. This was the bed, the comfort she had wanted while they sat outside that gas station, after all. She considered bundling herself into a cocoon and hiding until James returned that evening. The sheets wrapped her in an unfamiliar smell, a scent like dried violets and aniseed. A hazy spring sun eventually passed through the window sheers—they were nibbled with tiny moth holes, she could see—and crawled across the bed until reaching the covered mountain of her belly. She drew the afghan up to her eyes, pressing her face in its rough wool. All around, the house awoke without her: the water pipes running, the back door opening, the brass ticking of a clock somewhere, the creak of the floorboards in the den.

A dusty sunlight filtered through the windowpane, beyond which she heard the muted chirping of birds. It was the end of spring, and she felt like a convalescent. She wanted to make herself invisible, undetectable in the house. A ghost. She refrained from coughing, from making the hard bedsprings groan. Luckily, morning sickness didn't occur in the morning for Carlie. But she did have to pee. She held off as long as she could, curling up, repositioning herself in bed until 9:00 a.m., when she tiptoed in her nightgown to the en suite bathroom. The rush of urine was so sudden and loud, she cringed. Instead of flushing, she lowered the toilet lid and crawled back into bed.

At a quarter to noon, Carlie emerged from the bedroom, fully dressed, her face scrubbed and her hair back. She crept to the kitchen like a mouse, clasping her hands together, and poked her head in.

"Oh, good morning!" Minnie whispered, as though someone might still be sleeping in the house. She was lifting a hot kettle from the stove. The red wig, the dangling earrings, the fortuneteller's glasses all looked loosely affixed to her head.

Carlie waved to her, or waved her off, energetically. It was the first morning—the first time, really—they had ever been alone in the same room together. She felt like a guest who had stayed too long. Someone who had made a fool of herself the night before and passed out in the coat closet.

"I don't want to be an obstacle," Carlie said. "Just go on about your day."

"Oh, okay." Minnie came around with a steaming teacup and saucer. They seated themselves as Carlie spoke.

"If you have any errands to run, just go ahead and do them."

"Oh, will do. Certainly."

"I'm so sorry that we're upsetting your schedule like this. Taking up your space. We'll try not to be in your hair too long."

"Oh, it's no bother."

"So don't let me stand in your way."

"Okey dokey."

Both women stared at each other across the cramped breakfast table, waiting for the other to speak. Minnie smiled, absently stirring her hot tea. The *tink-tink* sounded like a distant railroad crossing, or a clock treading over the same second again and again.

"So, do you have anything...?" Carlie prodded. "To do? That you need to do? Something...out?"

"Oh?" Minnie leaned in, her spoon poised. And then, understanding that was the extent of her question: "Oh! Oh, no, dear. Nothing." She shook her head, still smiling, and settled back. *Tink, tink.*

Carlie nodded slowly, folding her hands in her lap. She wanted to run back into the bedroom and bury herself under the covers.

Then Minnie's face brightened. She pointed one knobbed finger toward the stove. "Tea?"

"Yes!"

She hurried to pour a cup. Carlie accepted, even though she knew the caffeine would play havoc with her stomach.

Before taking a sip, Carlie hesitated. "Minnie, I just want you to know, I'm sorry..."

Confused, the older woman stared at her from across the fruit bowl. "Oh, dear heart, I already told you. It's no trouble at all."

I mean for Map, Carlie wanted to say. But then, in a moment of honesty, she realized that she didn't want to say it. She didn't want to get anywhere near the subject of Map. He was now ambiguous territory: a path leading down somewhere she didn't want to go, without knowing why.

Minnie kept staring with a faint rosy blush, as though enchanted, grasping for something to say. "The two of us could take a little stroll..." she suggested. "The fuchsia is bursting this time of year."

Carlie said, "You know, I should get a hold of Dick Durgess. Do you mind if I use your phone, Minnie? I should really give him a call to see how things are going. Just to make sure."

"I Suwannee," Minnie declared, thwacking the tabletop. "First-rate! Be my guest, dear heart."

Carlie stood to dial, working her knuckles through the telephone cord. After several rings, she made contact with Durgess' daughter. No, her father wasn't in. No, she didn't know when he'd be back. No, she really couldn't say anything about the progress of their house, she was just the receptionist and nobody told her anything, she was really sorry. Carlie rested the receiver on its hook as if it was made of glass.

"Any news?"

"No." Carlie glanced at the kitchen clock. Only five minutes had passed since she emerged from the bedroom. "So, Minnie," she said, inhaling deeply to buoy up a smile. "What do you do today?"

And Minnie, scrunching her shoulders up to an apologetic smile, only shook her head behind those owlish glasses as if to suggest: *this was it.*

* * *

James came home in the evening disheveled but excited. Mashing up forkfuls of pork chops and spinach casserole, he talked in a disbelieving frenzy about his day—the project plans, the budgets, the people, the *paperwork*. "My God, you wouldn't believe the amount of paper they push at you, you'd swear they were deforesting the entire country. I have to fill out a form just to take a leak." He laughed, somehow enjoying the idea. Carlie had never heard him talk so much. Or eat so much, for that matter. He bared his teeth against the bones and gnawed them clean; he drank glasses of milk like a growing teenager; he had seconds and thirds of anything that remained on the table. Carlie sat at the edge of her chair and listened with the fork in her hand, and didn't eat at all.

After dinner they relocated to the den, where James helped himself to the bar. He made drinks for everyone, a round of Harvey Wallbangers and a Shirley Temple for Carlie, his tie unknotted to one side. How easily he stepped into that role, man of the house, king kahuna, doling out the juice, splash, splash—no Donald Duck?—floating the Galliano with Map's silver muddler so that it shimmered on the ice. As they clinked glasses over the coffee table, he said, "'I wonder what the poor folk are doing'—eh?" and Carlie cringed. The expression had been Map's quip at every toast, every meal—Map, who said his entire family had been cut down during the Depression, never to recover, and so was sent from home at an early age. Again, she felt the call of an ominous path whispering behind her. Someplace she didn't want to look. Instead, Carlie watched for Minnie's response, but the older woman simply smiled and raised her glass. James sucked the vodka from his lips and eased back, stretching his socked feet onto the coffee table. Carlie had to nudge him twice before he removed them. "You know, Minnie," James said, adjusting himself. "You should really see about getting that door fixed."

"Pardon?"

"The back door." He nodded to the kitchen. "The one you can't lock. It worries me. You being by yourself out here now and, well, everything. Not too safe. I can get around to taking a look at it if you want me to."

"Oh, no, I don't think so."

"You sure? It'd be no trouble."

"Oh, yes. Quite." While glancing at Carlie, Minnie caught a dribble from her lip. She blotted it with a cocktail napkin and excused herself to the bathroom. James and Carlie were left alone on the couch with the radio playing in the kitchen, a barely audible country twang crooning from behind the sink. "I really don't think Map would be too happy with that," he said, mostly to himself.

Carlie slid in closer to her husband, curling her legs underneath herself.

"I was thinking," she said.

His brow rose. "Uh oh, a dangerous sign."

She nipped him with her fingers. "No," she said. "I was thinking I might drive you into work tomorrow, so I could take the car. I couldn't get a hold of Durgess on the phone today. If we could speak to him face to face, I think things would go a lot faster."

James set his drink aside, rubbed his face, and yawned out a small amused sigh. "I really don't think that's possible—you should see the security regulations at work. It wouldn't even be worth the effort." He stretched his arm around her shoulders and gave a brotherly hug. "I'll get it all taken care of this week, just wait on me. I need to focus on getting settled in at work first."

She only nodded, resting her cheek against his shoulder. Worried about the next morning with Minnie. Worried about the next fifty years.

10

Last night, I dreamed that Freddie and I were on this road trip alone. Miles of thin, flickering road spooled out before us between vast stretches of cow pastures and peach fields, and the truck was empty and light, so light in fact that it was only on the periphery of my awareness. But then I realized it was not this trip. That we were younger, quite young, and I recognized the long dark highway and oncoming headlights from a precise moment in my youth. I was running away. I was eighteen again and running away from home, running away from my father, running for the first time toward an uncertain vision of myself. And Freddie was beside me in the dark of I-20, wearing a hand-me-down army surplus jacket, and we were laughing under the stars with our thumbs out, trudging between interstate exits to the distant sodium glare of the next Georgia town, the next truck stop, anticipating a hot cup of coffee and the next ride. I watched the moisture bloom from his laughing, from his lips, and thought: if only we had met at this age. If we met now, how different everything would be.

And in that moment, I woke up, unable to breathe. That had not been the first time, either. Ever since Vernon Rossi called, I've been waking before daybreak, choking. My lungs hitch and won't unlock during sleep, my respiration freezes. So at four or five in the morning, I bolt upright gasping for air. After the first few lungfuls of oxygen, my heart rate settles, and in the silence of my own breathing I inevitably begin to imagine the view from my father's dry cleaning bag: the blurry vernal sun bent by odd creases of the plastic, each breath shifting the aerosols and plastic film, distorting the warm and womblike universe around my head. Even there, I have to note that James chose not the penetration of a bullet, but the vaginal suffocation of a plastic bag. Eventually, the gray reality of the bedroom reasserts itself; the grainy, vaporous light of a streetlamp leaks through the blinds. Then I melt back into bed and lay awake until dawn takes on full force, listening to the traffic. Freddie hardly stirs at these jolts. I watch him, an insentient mound with the covers bunched to his cheek.

I think: those mornings that Carlie awoke at Minnie's, dreading the day ahead—what did they talk about to fill the hours? For three days, it was the same dreary routine. The clock on Minnie's china hutch chopped at the time until James arrived home. Did they ever talk about Map's illness? Did Carlie ever guess what felt so dangerous about the subject? Minnie might have hinted around the spiraling misdiagnoses: first as a rare form of pneumonia, then cryptococcal meningitis, then encephalitis, finally to be labeled as an unclassifiable, terminal disease. He suffered through countless lesions and ulcers, hallucinated from severe weight loss and diarrhea. His deterioration was so rapid, so feverish, it soon became clear that Map would spend his last days in a sterile observation room. So Minnie stormed the hospital. She fought with doctors and nurses so that Map could die in peace, at home, from his mysterious illness—an immune-deficiency syndrome which wouldn't be properly identified until the mid-1980s. For the few weeks that followed, his hospice was a rented cot and argyle blanket on the back porch of their Auscauga Lake home, facing the stream. This flamboyant pair. Did Minnie ever suggest the surrender and freedom she felt when putting him in the ground? Did she take advantage of this opportunity with my mother and confess her motives for hiding his grave in the woods—that headstone bearing my namesake, Milton Avery Price—to be quietly buried by years of falling pine straw? Or hint at the felicities of their double-lives? Did she reveal how at last with Map's passing, Death, that great chiseler, had tapped her on the knee with his mallet and demanded, "Now speak!"

No. They talked of nothing. Only in her letters do these details emerge. However close I imagined Carlie to be to that woman, they were never close enough. Not while she was alive.

11

Number Four. Was it Number Four? Yes, it was. Solidarity. As man and wife, they would be a team. They were in this world together. Carlie laid on her back—increasingly the only position she could find mild comfort in—and reminded herself of this. I imagine Carlie and James in those early years as two travelers walking a country lane that suddenly diverges. Those first steps at the fork, they pause to look at each other, young, slightly confused. What are you doing? Aren't we going…? This way leads home, doesn't it? Silence falls as they point in opposite directions. A weak wind, noticeable now, runs its fingers up the scalp and through the hair, and will stay with them waving those first farewells even should they decide to continue walking together.

Why now, why here? Because Carlie feared she would spend her whole life in this bed. That the inertia would settle into her sheets like a heavy silica. That her legs would atrophy and shrivel, that her fingers would become stiff and numb, that her brain would wither like a piece of spotted fruit. She would forget the little things first. How to brew strong coffee. Songs that she knew by heart, first their notes and then the lyrics, flecking away word by word. How to trickle charge a car battery; how to jumpstart her daddy's '57 Chevy Biscayne with a church key; how to change a flat tire; how to drive a stick. How to replace the ribbon on a typewriter or type without pecking; how to negotiate the intricate social hierarchy of a workplace. Then the larger forgettings would come, tearing through the moth-eaten holes of her memory that the smaller absences made. How to drive; how to lift; how to carry; how to run; how to walk; how to interact with people at all; how to voice her own thoughts amid the babble of the world around her. Because by the third morning, with the bed sheets twisted and knotted around her body, damply lying in that raw dawn light, Carlie had finally given a name to her fear: uselessness. And once a thing is named, the map of its certain future is laid bare. All road signs pointed toward one direction. She was becoming useless, irrelevant. They, she and James, were supposed to be a different generation of men and women, different from their parents. And they had been. So why didn't she feel like that now?

By 7:00 a.m. Carlie forced herself out of bed, showered, and threw a crocheted smock over her dungarees. In the kitchen, she was absolutely ravenous. Wordlessly, Carlie chewed through two bowls of cold cereal, a half pack of soda crackers, a limp and sticky box of old raisins, and the last black-spotted banana in Minnie's fruit bowl. She then punctured and drained three 4oz cans of cocktail juice filched from the bar.

Having finished with breakfast, Carlie found herself again trapped at that tiny table. This morning, the back door was open for the breeze. Wind gusted through the pines at irregular intervals, like cars passing on the highway, leaving the steady, sedate burbling of the creek in its silence. How many mornings of this? A week? A lifetime?

From the living room, Minnie suggested they practice a song together and patted the bench. She sat at the old asthmatic organ, dolled up as if for church for some reason.

"Minnie," Carlie said, watching the pines sway. "I need to give Durgess another try."

She steeled her nerves, stood, and dialed. Minnie watched from the organ bench, a chord book in her hands. After several rings, Durgess' daughter answered again. Carlie had the sudden urge to reach through the telephone and strangle her. Why? What exactly had this girl done? Nothing. And maybe that was it: the absolute nothingness of her. She wanted to tell her *stop answering the phone. Stop having nothing to say. Tell me who else I can talk to*. They battled through the same useless questions and answers. The girl was simply a myna bird—echoing only those things she heard, those things fed to her. Carlie could do nothing to make her change her tune. She cut the conversation short by saying, "You tell him to call us, you hear me?" her throat clenching like a fist.

She hung up.

Minnie eyed her from the organ, depressing a few keys to produce a deep churchy rumble. Carlie kept her back to the older woman, one hand pressed to her forehead, holding herself together.

Minnie released the notes, quiet hung in the air, and she said, "He won't call."

Carlie jerked around. "Oh, for Christ's sake, don't you think I'm smart enough to know that? But what else am I supposed to do, just sit here and—" An angry sob pushed up her throat. She couldn't catch it in time. Carlie clamped a hand to her mouth as though she was going to vomit, shocked that she had fallen into such an outburst.

Years later, many years later, Minnie would write of this moment in one of those fantastic letters of hers. The feeling, she said, was like those mornings at dawn, during her deathbed vigil over Map, when she would spy deer creeping from the woods to the muddy creek. Quietly, they appeared from nothing: emerging from the grainy light and fog. A mystical experience, as she described it. Knowing she couldn't touch them, but wanting to stop time in that moment. Wanting to hold them in her gaze for as long as she could in order to understand their beauty and, in some small way, become a part of it. Minnie switched off the organ and quietly left the room. Carlie, alone by the phone nook, stunned by her own mouth, called out, "Minnie, I'm sorry—I'm so sorry! Please!"

By the time Carlie uprooted her feet to follow, Minnie had reappeared and they nearly collided. She stood, squat as a bulldog, with a heavy black purse pulling at the crook of her arm. "Time's winged chariot, dear heart," she produced her car keys and jingled them, "is quite useless when it's just in park. I believe your new home has been long overdue for a proper inspection." She took Carlie by the elbow, adding, "You and me, Cisco. Let's went."

* * *

Shortly after his death, Minnie had traded in Map's Cadillac for the glossy green AMC Gremlin. Even in this half-sized automobile, at 4'10, she could hardly see over the steering wheel, which perhaps was for the best—that no one could actually identify the maniac who piloted the vehicle. Perhaps that's how she had evaded the law for so long, Carlie was thinking: as a ghost car briefly appearing along the highway, sans driver, clocking in on the radar at ninety MPH. They roared along the back roads, Carlie passenger to a blind, blustery red wig with knuckles. Minnie released her foot from the accelerator only to take the curves that bent through sleepy residential boroughs. Signs flashed by in black and white streaks, reading twenty-five MPH. They traveled with the windows cranked down, their hair whipping in a whirlwind. Carlie kept one hand to her hairband, the other on her belly, and used both her elbows and knees to wedge herself in place. The bangles along her arm rattled with every bump.

"I apologize again for the other evening, dear heart," Minnie began, getting conversational at this speed. Carlie tried to smile but didn't respond. She pressed her tongue to her teeth to keep from biting it, fearing that any break in the woman's concentration would send them careening into the woods. "It's usually just in the mornings when I strip down to my skivvies for a dip in Hoss Creek. Nearly every morning for thirty years, you know. Like clockwork. It gives my little ticker a good jolt of reality. I lay back, wet my hair like a polar bear, and wait until my toes melt. I skipped this morning, not knowing if you'd be up." Big earrings jangled with each stiff bob of her head. "But I dare say this is loads more invigorating. I should keep you around." She reached over and gave Carlie's knee a good pat.

Once free of the mill valley, they hit Copeland. Minnie inhaled deeply. "Smell that air—I do believe we're near." Carlie couldn't help but smell it too: the hot, earthy odor stirred up by the horses. The Gremlin decelerated and the blurry landscape came into relief. With the car slowed, the pastures here were like an ocean floor, raw and undulant in their beauty. Bare patches in the sedge revealed a fine, sparkling sand. On the roadside embankments, wheat-colored manes of sawgrass stirred from their passing. And farther back into the trees, Carlie could see the horses. "I Suwannee," Minnie crooned under her breath, the car now crawling at a snail's pace. "There they are. Just look at those pretty ponies. What par-fum! Eau de Equine."

In 1971 there were probably no more horses in Copeland than there are now. But at the time, that's all there was to see in town. No glut of banks and credit unions, no tanning salons or coffee shops on every corner, no mega-retailers with their economically landscaped concrete medians; only the horses, and the sparse pines, and large prisms of granular sunlight breaking through the boughs.

They coasted into the neighborhood. Few of the acreages at that time were developed, the land cut by rambling plank fences, tarry with creosote. Along those fences, spotted palominos and jet black foals stomped up dust, pausing in their gallops to watch the novelty of a car passing by. They leaned over the rails, drawn by the glinting green metal.

When Carlie and Minnie arrived at the house, they confronted a dismal sight: absolutely nothing had changed. Nothing. The construction crew had thinned out considerably, loitering around the house like vagrants at a bus station. Some played cards, others chatted under the shade, fewer still even deigned to eye the Gremlin as it parked alongside the property. Only the framer, Ted, was out in the sun, sweating on the blueprints and squinting at the house as though deliberating over some particularly difficult algebra. Carlie pushed her head from the car.

No trace of the new windows or balcony. In fact, the entire site looked at a standstill. She forgot all about Minnie then. She forgot about James. She forgot about the anxiety and dread which earlier that morning had sapped her body and will.

Before Minnie could crank up the hand brake, Carlie had opened the door and was well on her way to hoisting herself out.

"Excuse me?" She had approached the framer from behind, giving him a start. "Excuse me, what's going on here?"

"Ma'am?"

"Where's the foreman?"

"Oh. Well, he had to head off. He left me in charge in the meantime."

"I can see that. Where'd he go off to?"

He hemmed for a moment before scratching the answer out from behind his ear, "I'm not sure exactly."

"Well when was the last time you saw him?"

Deliberating on what to say, he stared at Carlie's belly. He scratched at his cheek with a perturbed determination. "Same as you, probably."

"You mean to say last *week*?" A needle of panic stuck in Carlie's throat.

"More or less." He added, "He comes by every now and then to check up. I think he might be out conferring with Mr. Durgess. But he did leave me strict orders." And here he ventured out on a more authoritative limb, straightening his posture and pointing toward the house. "Right now, the way it looks, I'm afraid we're just going to have to proceed as planned and forgo the whole window and balcony issue. There's just no way around it."

Carlie's mouth clenched. "Uh huh," she said. "I see. And how come no one let us know this?"

"Ma'am?"

"How come we were never notified."

The framer hesitated a moment. "Well, shoot, we must've tried five or six times, but no one answered."

"Is that right? When?"

"What?"

"When did you call? And what number? Do you even still have the number we gave you?" Frustrated, Carlie held up a hand, erasing the question. "You know what, forget it, buster. I want to talk to your father-in-law. Forget the foreman, just tell me where I can find Durgess."

The framer glanced uncomfortably toward the road, toward the little green car, licking his lips as if he had the DTs. "Your husband with you?"

With that, a dark disappointment clouded Carlie's eyes. In the passing shadow, she became aware of all the men idling in the yard, watching her conversation with a snickering amusement. "No, he's at work… can you please tell me where Durgess is?"

At once Carlie understood this was a mistake. This momentary plea, the politesse of her gendered upbringing with all those sirs and ma'ams, had revealed a crack in her demeanor, a gap through which all of her bargaining power escaped. The framer put his eyes on Carlie anew, on her face, and saw that she was a woman. Understanding this, he looked relieved, friendlier. He wiped his brow with the back of his sleeve. "Honestly, ma'am, he spreads himself across a whole bunch of projects. He could be at any number of places." And that was it. A sudden weight plunged down through her chest, and Carlie knew she had lost the only opportunity she would get.

"Pardon?" Minnie spoke up from behind Carlie's elbow, surprising them both. She leaned in, cocking her head to the side: *the better to hear you with, my dear.*

"He could be anywhere."

Puzzled, she shook her head and pointed to her right ear. The framer repeated himself, stammering a little.

"I'm sorry, dear heart. One more time."

Teddy shouted, full staccato volume: "I said, there are half a dozen places he could be!"

"Wonderful!" Unsnapping her purse, Minnie pulled out a pad and a red felt pen. "Here, write them down for us." She pressed the pad into his limp hand and patted it like a grandmother. "Starting with his home address."

* * *

Dick Durgess had a deep affinity for his town. For the Savannah River Site with its influx of relocating families, for the budding retiree community it produced, and all the other migratory flocks, too, especially those Northerners who wintered in Copeland for the polo. He considered them all his special émigrés and had an abiding faith in the depth of their pockets. As Carlie and Minnie drove the map of Copeland, circa 1970, Durgess was building no less than twenty houses at once, many on spec, and doubling the kitty by stretching the same thin team of sub-contractors across all of them. For Durgess, gambling on construction in this way was not unlike a roulette wheel: as long as you kept it moving, you had hope.

That afternoon, he hunkered over the warm hood of his station wagon, scribbling down a whole sheaf of receipts for three tons of misplaced chimney stone. For a life of high anxiety, Durgess still had an ample belly and ruddy cheeks, and his only sign of stress was concealed under his hat: a balding scalp spotted with angry, peeling scabs. An engine idled up behind him and then cut off. Two car doors slammed with the brisk authority of bank creditors.

He cautiously thumbed up the brim of his hat to find two women approaching. One was tall and pregnant, pressing her lips together in a terse, closed smile; the other was a little old lady whose black purse sank and swung like a sack of doorknobs. If his muscles relaxed any, they shouldn't have.

"Mrs. Cullins!" He beamed, placing her quickly. "I was just on my way out to see your house. What brings you all the way out here on such a gorgeous afternoon?"

"I'm surprised to catch you at your home like this, Mr. Durgess," she said.

"Am I home? I hadn't even noticed. Work tends to follow me around."

"Your son-in-law gave me your address."

"Ah, yeah, Teddy. He's a good boy, isn't he?"

"I figured I would leave a message with your wife, but I'm glad to see you here."

"My wife?"

"Yes, since I've had some difficulty getting a hold of you."

"Yeah, business is slamming. It's got me up against the wall."

"I have some concerns."

"Concerns? Naturally and understood. Well, fire away, I'm all ears." Durgess braced his hands against his meaty hips, still clutching a fistful of damp receipts. His overalls were rank with perspiration and pale orange brick dust.

"Yes, about the framing errors with our house."

"Yeah, I heard about that, and I'm deeply sorry. It's a hell of a business—if you'll pardon my language—keeping these rowdies on track. But I also know the boys are right on it. Why, is that you, Mrs. Price? You're looking good—I hardly recognized you. How's Map doing? Haven't seen him in ages."

"Splendidly."

Carlie spoke louder: "The foreman told me the exact same thing last week. Unfortunately, he hasn't been on the job site since then. I was told he might be with you."

Durgess adjusted the brim of his hat once more, grimacing and sweating and not entirely because of the sun. "No, no he isn't. We've been looking for him though."

"What do you mean you've been looking for him?"

Durgess picked at his scalp. With the canvass hat pushed back, Carlie could see rosy scabs of alopecia through his thinning hair. "Well, Mrs. Cullins," he said. "In the parlance of your husband's profession, you might say he's on sabbatical."

"What you're saying is he's disappeared."

Durgess laughed once and shook his face, reddening from both embarrassment and apology. A skittishness overtook him, as with the framer, and he would not lay his eyes on her. Durgess palmed his mouth like a sobered up drunk, baring nicotine-stained teeth and—why not?—chuckled once more at his miserable luck. "I'm saying I have no ever-loving idea where he is."

Carlie said, "I am thrilled that you find this so funny."

"Oh no, trust me, I'm mad about this, too. Downright furious—that sucker's going to be on the switch once I find him. You know how much this screws up my day-to-day operations? Let me tell you, Mrs. Cullins, you have no idea."

Carlie nodded, repeating almost absently, "I have no idea." She weighed each of those words carefully, tossing them up and down in her palm as she moved closer, turning the full biological heat of her pregnancy, her height, her livid motherhood upon him. "Let me give you a little insight on the idea I do have." Suddenly a phrase her daddy often said popped into her mind, one he used when drinking on the porch with his buddies late at night—*got me by the proverbial balls*—and it left her a little giddy and power-drunk, because she now realized that was exactly where she could have Durgess. And why? Because these men with their swagging testicles could not, she discovered, *look her in the eye*. They scratched their groins and pulled at their flies in a manner that suggested they could just pick up their manhood, sling it over one shoulder like a gunnysack, and haul it from town to town. *Mo-bility*. Like sailors on shore leave. Boasting and bragging about what they had in their sack. But pregnant and unconfined to a house, she made these men uncomfortable. Because here was the evidence of their fluid, their little ineffable squirt of selfhood—and that's what they all came down to, little squirts, tiny ejaculations—made flesh. Housed in woman-flesh, no less, and dependent on it, inseparable from it, *bonded* to it. And it—*she*—could chase into the world after them.

Carlie put a single finger to Durgess' mouth before he could open it, and the shock of this intimate gesture electrified the straggly tips of his hair. The words that followed were beyond anything she had rehearsed in the car. "Here's my idea. My idea is that I expect to have a home ready before my child is born," she said. "My next idea is, if I do not have that house ready, then I am prepared to drop this baby right in your front yard. I will howl through the night and spill my birth and cut the cord with my own teeth. Right on your front porch. And there we will camp, everyday, every morning, and I'll nurse my baby from that cute rocking chair you've got, morning, noon, and night, and we will wave to your neighbors passing by. I promise you this…" Here, her eyes glittered and a sweet, sweet vitriol curled from her sugared voice. "In time, I will turn your wife against you; I will turn your daughter against you; I will drag you into my life. And then, I swear to God, I will find me the highest tree I can and I will string you up by the balls. By your actual balls." She felt Minnie's cold knuckles lace themselves through her own free hand. Either to comfort, to calm, or to say that she would help pick out the tree. Carlie squeezed back.

She took a deep cleansing breath. "So now tell me your ideas, Mr. Durgess. Just what do you plan to do about my house?"

12

Horses. Copeland is full of horses—and the geriatric. They are made for each other. Paddocks and nursing homes, stables and assisted living communities, they all amount to the same thing: free-range pens. (Which also cost the same: exorbitant.) That was the sense I had as a sixteen year old. But I know the past twenty years have turned the post-nuclear dream into Dick Durgess' vision of heaven. At least for a brief time. Sixty years old, seventy years old—during the housing bubble, these were the second childhoods, the time to spend those 401(k)s and live a little, the new halcyon days of a free market economy. The nineties and aughts saw retirement as the new youth. And since then, those with money in their pocket still relocate to the Sunbelt—or above the Floridian Hurricane Belt—to gentler climes. Toward a Copeland with gabled and gated communities, mixed-use condos and retail space, to dine where you shop and play. To summer concerts on the green in Copeland Gardens. To buy, for the able-bodied and independently living, vast plots of real estate and develop second homes, away from or toward the children and grandchildren. But toward, first and foremost, the horses. Their proud iconic heads adorn the street signs; they stand in plaster casts downtown, painted by local artists; they leap from garlands and banners: *Historic Copeland is Horse Country!*

We arrive around noon.

The south side of town is the usual anonymous center of commerce found in any small burg in America. A grid of powerlines, stoplights, and retail stores that expand to all available spaces. The intersections smell of unleaded fumes, of sizzling asphalt, of greasy chicken and pulp-meat from the fastfood drive-thrus. Mostly treeless, sunlight glares off the traffic poles.

As we merge onto Whiskey Road, traffic becomes heavier but tree-shaded. Our truck scrapes a few low-hanging branches, rattling toward downtown Copeland, toward the picturesque boulevards and fountains that appear on billboard advertisements, the golf courses and quaint gardens featured at the South Carolina welcome center. Live oaks and magnolias dapple the street, hugged by ornamental brick walls. Freddie perks up, wipes his chin. Carlie is still out; her breathing is deep and ragged, disturbed only by a gurgling indigestion. I lightly rub her knee. "Look, Ma. Look where we are."

She stirs, groggy, and focuses her attention out the window. "Yes," is all she says, trying to clear the fog. My mother, once so voluble with me over the phone. In a perverse way she reminds me of Dot, our turtle, in her terrarium. Frequently, I worry that she's not stimulated enough in her little glass enclosure, that through boredom, her mind and body are only shriveling. That she's trapped and knows it. Copeland crawls by outside Freddie's window. She silently soaks it in.

When we pass the Triple Crown Country Club, I crank down the window and relax a bit. Beneath the midday exhaust comes an odor sharp and sweet, the fresh scalded water smell of spring. Pine needles, dogwood, wisteria thick with a sexual perfume. Freddie loosens his collar to get some air, rolls the passenger window down, too. He hangs one elbow out and whistles, marveling at the private estates. Behind a screen of poplars, their long cinder drives lead to white porticoes and horse-head knockers. "Do they do ghost tours here?" he says, folding a stick of gum into his mouth. "It looks like they'd do ghost tours. You know, haunted mystery tours."

"This isn't Charleston," I inform him. "It's a real town. Not a tourist trap." Once we pass the courthouse steps, however, it becomes clear that a re-marketed sense of yesteryear has been good to downtown Copeland: boutique grocers, sidewalk bistros, wine sellers, and gift shops abound. Everywhere we turn, the blocks of parked cars read like summer vacation at Myrtle Beach: Michigan, New Jersey, Pennsylvania, West Virginia, Maryland, New York. "Good God, Ma. Look at all these license plates. No one is actually from here anymore."

Freddie threads his arm behind Mom so he can poke me. "Look," he says, pointing to a massive orange Hummer with Ohio plates. "That one's you." He pops his gum, leaving a pungent whiff of spearmint.

"I'm not from Ohio."

"Oh yeah? What's your license say?"

"U-Haul."

"Not the plate. The one in your wallet."

"Freddie," I say, scouting for our turn, "these people own second or third homes here. They claim residency for tax purposes. I was born here. I was shaped here. I am the legitimate product of perhaps the worst public education system in the nation because of the state's low income and property taxes. Therefore, I am not these people, dear Freddie. I—" and then I see it, our hotel, sandwiched between a pizza parlor and a dog bakery—"am a proud native."

"I bet they all are." He sails a wet kiss at me from across Mom.

I pull under the carriage porch of the Heart of Copeland Inn, which is a renovated Holiday Inn from the 70s, pillared and painted a pale pink. The requisite rocking chairs and potted topiary sit out front. Freddie deems it "fabulous." It takes us about half an hour to reach the check-in counter—first unpacking the wheelchair and decamping Carlie, then circling the blocks for a parking space that could fit the truck. When I show up with our bags jammed under my arms, Freddie and Mom are still waiting outside by the entrance, looking very much like a hospital release. "Inside. With the air conditioning. Don't make her sit out here."

"We were people-watching."

The lobby is clean but shabby, falling just inside of kitsch with its beaded lampshades and mismatched antiques. A baroque, gilded mirror sits behind the counter, catching our reflections as we glance around the room. I can imagine the proprietor here: a man in his late sixties, a "lifelong bachelor" in the parlance of small southern towns, who has a penchant for tasseled loafers and dotes on a pair of twin Yorkies. He makes a mean squash casserole for Sunday brunches, *the old fashioned way, just like Mama did: with ranch dressing.*

The receptionist confirms everything on her computer. Two double beds, non-smoking. Down the east wing, on the second floor, which shouldn't be a problem for Mom with the elevator. As the receptionist checks us in, Freddie whispers: "Just one room?" He leans into the counter, shoulder to shoulder with me, to block Mom from the conversation. "You squeeze us together on a single bench seat for a fifteen hour car ride. And now we're going to share a bed, too?"

"There are two beds, Freddie."

The receptionist pauses, thoughtfully offers, "Is there a problem?"

"No, no problem. We can live. My mother has mobility issues. I need to be close at hand."

"I can check to see if the adjoining suite is available if you like."

Freddie raises his brow as if to say *See?*

I rub a hand over my scalp, feel that my hair is getting long again. Before I can respond, the receptionist hits a few key strokes and lights up, her lips shining, "You're in luck! The adjacent suite is still open."

"No, I really don't think that's necessary."

Freddie snaps his gum. "You never even asked me."

"Asked you what?"

"Never asked me about the rooms. I thought we'd have our own room."

The young woman smiles nervously, unsure of what to do with herself.

"In a situation like this, Freddie, what we want doesn't matter. We need to consider what's best for my mother."

He shifts his elbows, as if settling in, as if refusing to budge from the counter. "You never even thought to ask me, did you?"

"Now is not the time to be jealous of a seventy-year-old stroke survivor."

"It's not that. It's not jealousy."

"If I may," the receptionist interrupts, speaking softly. "The conjoined suite is a bit larger. The layout might be easier for," she nods to Mom, "for navigating a wheelchair."

Freddie studies me with a buoyant light in his eye. I know this look: it's the question of leveraging something practical to his advantage.

"Fine," I say. "It's extraneous, but fine." And the receptionist merrily inputs the additional room.

"You're a peach," Freddie says, and hugs onto me. He rests his chin on my head, the way that I dislike in public. "You're a doll."

I grab the key cards from the desk, shrugging him off. "Just help me with the bags."

* * *

"Our goal here is to stir the senses. To invigorate ourselves, to excite both the heart and mind," I say as I unpack Carlie's clothes, letting the wrinkles out. She's parked in her wheelchair by the window, while Freddie paces in the adjoining suite, talking to a stricken Henri in heated tones. Swish-swish, he moves back and forth behind the open door. "What will quicken our numbness? Small things." I snap a lilac blouse and fold it neatly. "Small, touchable, tasteable, smellable things. For instance, we can go to Copeland Gardens, see the azaleas. Get a good whiff of their tart perfume, listen to the fat bumblebees wheeling around."

Swish, Freddie passes, one hand pinching his waist.

Swish.

I'm trying, he says, speaking into the phone.

Don't worry, he says.

"We can tour the town, too, see what's changed. Most of all, we can visit the old house. Get the old sensory juices flowing. We will stuff our cheeks with a million soggy madeleines." I slide the dresser drawer shut, neatly arrayed with her folded skirts and blouses.

About this time, Freddie walks into the room, throwing his cell phone onto the bed. He grips both hands at the small of his back, like it might need the support. "I don't know what I'm doing wrong here," he says. "It didn't used to be this hard. No one is giving me the time of day." He rubs his face and then yanks both hands through his hair, as if he might rip it out by the fistful. "I got to freshen up. I have to be fresh."

"Don't take too long. We're leaving for lunch in just a few."

"Where?" His voice disappears into Mom's bathroom.

"Cafe Soleil, right down the street. It used to serve a crab bisque that Mom loved. Does that sound good, Ma?" She is still slumped in her wheelchair by the window, looking dejected. "Mom?" No response. So I try, "Carlie?" and her head lifts, swivels my way. "You remember the Soleil? Cafe Soleil?" Again, nothing. Instead, she looks away, leaning her cheek into her good hand. "We'll see the house after lunch. Does that sound good to you?"

The air conditioner kicks on, rattles and chokes, blowing tepid air against the glass. I see that she is wearing tennis sneakers. New, generic running shoes. Pink and gray. I don't know if I ever remember seeing my mother wear tennis shoes. What did she used to wear? Sandals all the time? Flats? If so, what did she wear in the winter?

"How about this, huh?" I take the aluminum walker from the closet, unfold the sides, and prop it next to her chair. "Let me know when you want to use it." I give a quick inspection. Tap the tennis balls with my foot—tennis balls for the tennis shoes. "Do you want these things on? I bet this was James' doing. Practical and stylish."

Exhausted, I sit at the edge of the mattress. As I do, she eyes me, as if we've sat too close together on a bus. Her eyes still have a fluid, rabbit-like nervousness. Left-brain strokes often leave people quiet and anxious. So I talk about everything we have planned for the day, in careful detail, to help her feel included. No surprises. Gradually I lean closer, searching for eye contact. I take hold of her hand, hoping she'll look at me. Her palm is tough and clammy. Quietly, I ask, "What is it you want, Mom? Can you tell me?" She removes her fingers from my hand, rubs her own knuckles. From this angle, we both have a clear, unobstructed view from the window. For a moment, we watch The Alleyway below. It's an old street from the winter colony days, cobblestoned and open only to pedestrian traffic. Couples amble along while young families dawdle with small children or push strollers. Others lounge with drinks on the sidewalks, their dogs tied to café tables.

Thinking of nothing else, I clap my hands together and say, "I'm thirsty. Are you thirsty? How about I go get us some ice. A couple of cool glasses of ice water. All that sugary sweet stuff Freddie got us for breakfast, you must be feeling dehydrated, too. I'll be back in just a minute. All right? And when I get back, I'll get changed and we'll all go out for some lunch."

She looks at me, searchingly. She clears her throat as if to speak, but then settles for a slight nod.

Ice. When at a loss, keep active. I watch her from the door for a minute before silently stealing out. I have to convince myself that she won't fall from her chair and break her neck when I turn my back; she won't choke to death on her own saliva. Adult Protective Services won't find her crawling with roaches and remand her from my custody. Still, I hurry.

The ice machine is down at the far end of the hall. Down the fire retardant carpeting, with its red and gold geometric patterns, that dampens my footfalls. Past the dull, forty-watt wall sconces. I press the button and wait for the asthmatic thing to cough up its first cubes.

When I return with a full bucket of ice, Carlie is mostly as I left her, turned to the bright window. I grab a fresh change of clothes—jeans and an old soccer shirt—and a pair of water glasses. The bathroom door is cracked open, so I slip inside.

That's where I catch Freddie doing key bumps in front of the vanity. Catch isn't really the right word. He was taking his time. After a moment of deliberation, I drop my roll of clothes onto the toilet lid and pull the door shut behind me. "My mother is ten feet away from this door," I say. "And you're in here doing blow."

Freddie tucks the bag into his coat pocket, checks his gums in the mirror, and licks them clean. "I'm just following orders." He doesn't look at me, but grins slyly to himself in the mirror. "How did you put it? I'm invigorating my senses."

The words hang heavy between us. Finally, I push my arms through the soccer shirt and shrug it over my head. He gives me ample space when I move to the sink to fill the glasses.

He starts again: "Avery, look, we've been at it for a week now. A week. Of packing and funerals and, God, shitty rental cars and now trucks. And it'll take us, what, at least three more days to get to Cleveland. Meanwhile," he gestures to the suite, groping for words, "meanwhile, Henri is flipping his *shit* and there might not even *be* a lounge by the time I get back. I'm trying here. But if you want me to be my usual charismatic self, if I have any chance of pulling this off, then you need to leave me room to operate. I'm practically suffocating."

"What I need," I say, "is for you to put others first. Try practicing some restraint."

"What do you think this is?" He nearly laughs. "I should be in here with an 8-ball, for chrissake." Freddie runs his hands under the tap, rubs cold water against his face and neck. "Besides, I seriously doubt your mother will care."

I stop at the door. "She's not a vegetable," I say.

"I didn't say that." He wets his hair.

"Sure you did."

"No, I said that I doubt she would care. She's a seventy-year-old woman. Not some ten-year-old ward of the state."

"She was, in fact, a ward of the state—past tense—and I'd like to keep it that way."

"What do you think I'm going to do? Land you in jail? Get her deported?" He cuts the tap, shakes his hands dry, and sees me staring at him in the mirror. His blue eyes, weary, are laced with sticky lashes; they blink twice. "Look, just tell me what to do, and I'll do it."

"How did you even—did you fly with that mess?"

"No, of course not."

I feel my jaw tense, spasm. I say nothing.

"You want me to stop?" A bead of water clings to his nose. "I'll stop. Consider me stopped."

I grab the door handle to leave, but pause. I consider telling him that everything must change, that it has already changed, that Cleveland most certainly will not be like we left it. Instead, I flash an unhappy smile and I say, "At least close the door next time."

"Thanks. Thanks for the credit." His voice echoes softly inside the bathroom.

By now, I'm ready to beat the door down for some fresh air. "Ma, you ready for a walk? Want to grab some lunch?" I find the television on and Carlie's chair parked two feet away from the screen. "Did you turn this on?" I ask Freddie, knowing it's a foolish question. I watch her for a moment, in something not quite like disbelief. She stares at the screen intently, then waddles her wheelchair a foot closer, pops the channel. A 24-hour news program lights up against her face, vivid tickers and captions. She doesn't budge, doesn't make any sign of hearing me. "Mom," I say. "Carlie. Ready to go?" I linger by her shoulder. She stares at a commentator with immaculate hair and waxy make-up. "We can watch TV anytime. Come on, let's go see downtown."

When I reach to turn the set off, she barks *No!* and grabs my wrist. A moment ticks by. I can feel her callused fingers dig into my veins. Even after she eases into watching the program, she doesn't let go. I glance across the room to Freddie, who looks as if he has stepped into a domestic dispute. So I kneel beside the wheelchair, my wrist still in her grip.

We wait like that, watching the endless news cycle for nearly half an hour. We watch Carlie watching the talking heads and headlines that swim across the screen, two feet from her face.

* * *

The streets are buzzing, the sidewalks busy with townspeople and spring vacationers and dappled shadows, shades of green and blue stirring from the dogwoods. We push along toward lunch while Freddie chatters non-stop. It's hard to say what finally got us out of the hotel room. At a certain point, Mom reached up and punched the TV off mid-prattle. Who knows why. But five minutes into the standoff—amused maybe—Freddie had flopped down on the bed and, propped by a nest of pillows, got into watching the media pundits. Freddie doesn't watch programs so much as participate in them. He began a running commentary with Mom and the television, really enjoying himself. The breezy conversation hasn't stopped since. So mesmerizing, in fact, that she has been replying. Every time he ends a sentence with *You know?*, she says *Yes*. Now he strolls by her side, talking endlessly about Cleveland, the cocktail lounge, the whole continuing drama of refurbishing it. All the setbacks with financing, the lucky breaks and bureaucratic twists in licensing the place. While he prattles, I try to get my bearings, connect the dots, whatever are left to connect. Many of the old buildings downtown have been contracted, sold, and subdivided into luxury condominiums; half the storefronts hawk souvenirs. Horses on everything. Shot glasses, coffee mugs, bumper stickers, and tee-shirts. Galloping, leaping, trotting.

Window displays are emblazoned with green steeplechase jumps and white magnolia blossoms. I point out a dilapidated piano bar that I got booted from in my youth. Nobody, it seems, wants to hear the story. My legs still throb from squatting for thirty minutes straight.

As the cafe comes in sight, Freddie stops short. He stamps his foot, cackling. "Ghost Tours!" He points across the avenue. In front of the Visitor's Bureau, a fat man sits atop a horse-drawn coach, wearing civil war britches and a tattered waistcoat, fanning himself with a gray cap. By the wheels, a placard advertises THE GHOSTS OF CAROLINA HAUNTED PLANTATION RIDE.

"No," I say. "Never." Shaking my head, I lean into the wheelchair to get Carlie rolling again. She takes notice of a cardinal pip-pip-pipping from the dogwoods.

"Square," Freddie says. "Killjoy. Remember Boston? That guy with the hand? That was a gas. Didn't you say your mom used to travel a lot?"

The bird lights out, swoops low across the street. "Our time here is in short supply. I guarantee you that's nothing but a solid hour of antebellum stereotypes and Lost Cause nostalgia."

"Well, no shit, Professor, that's what makes it *hilarious*. Come on. I bet your mom loves horses. Like any vestal American virgin. Let's go for a ride. Let's travel back to a time of petticoats and bloody slave uprisings."

"Lunch, Freddie. I'm starving. I bet we're all hungry."

"Yeah, yeah. I get it." He spits his gum into a trashcan as we continue. "You don't like the competition."

At the café, we choose an outdoor table under the awning. Gladiolas decorate the salt and pepper shakers where we wheel Mom up. Freddie sits back, empties his pockets on the table—phone, wallet, keys. He fits right in with the affluent snowbirds. Loafers, no socks. Collar open at the throat. Bouncing his foot, he examines the people passing by. The waitress greets us while busing the next table, her arms full of used water glasses and sloppy plates. She moves with the hurried confidence of a college student, her body decorated in shoulder tattoos under a sleeveless tee. We look over the menus, flimsy sheets ringed with water stains. "Hey, look what I see," I slide over to Mom. "Look what they have on the menu. Crab bisque. Do you think you would like that?"

She considers the possibility. "Maybe, you know," she says, giving the menu some scrutiny. "But yes."

"Yes to the bisque?"

She stammers the word *bisque* with difficulty, confirming it again and saying, "Yes," with a nod.

"Did you hear that? Bisque! All right. Excellent. Bisque it is." After the long drive this morning, after the nursing home and gas stations and hotel rooms, the act of ordering this one thing feels like an enormous relief. It feels like we've settled in. I order a tuna salad and Freddie gets the beef au jus and a glass of beer.

When the waitress returns with our order, Freddie takes a long thirsty drag off the top of his beer. As we tuck in, I notice Mom lift the spoon to her nose. The action is shaky and slow, using her offhand. She sniffs the soup, then after a moment of consideration, drops the spoon back into the mug.

I hesitate. "Do you need help?"

"No," she says, quite simply, and pushes it away with her knuckles.

"What's wrong?" I peek into the mug, stir the creamy lumps. It looks fine, doesn't seem too hot. I offer it to her.

"No," she says blocking the spoon. She shoves the mug further away from her, abruptly.

"Mom, you wanted this. I asked you and you said yes. Are you not hungry?"

"She doesn't like it," Freddie says, his mouth full of roast beef.

"She used to love this stuff. She'd come here every week when I was in high school."

He reaches for the spoon and stirs the bisque around a few times before taking a taste. After smacking his lips, he gives his verdict: "Imitation crabmeat. I wouldn't eat this either."

"It's not—" I take the spoon from him, sample it. I wipe my lip. "It's not imitation crab. This tastes just fine. Here, one taste, Ma. Just try it." We go back and forth like this two or three times until she shoves the mug at me, knocking it over. Hot crab bisque spills through the grates in the patio table and all over my lap before I can pull away. There is no napkin dispenser. I flag the waitress. "Okay, this was not necessary." I push the chair out; my fingers and legs are coated. I flick chunks of crabmeat. "What else can I get you? You need to eat something."

"We could get her some of those adult milkshakes," Freddie offers. "You know, the kind in the cans. She drank them at the nursing home."

"I'm not pumping her full of a chemical slurry. She deserves real food."

While I look for a place to wipe my hands, Freddie's phone rings—he had set it to "The Girl from Ipanema" while in Tallahassee, tall and tan and young and lovely. He checks the display. "Who do we know from this area code?"

"That's Florida," I say, wiping my hands. "That must be Vernon."

He passes the phone to me.

"Avery?" There is the sluggish beat of a dropped signal, then the unmistakable cough, as Vernon Rossi shifts his girth and shuffles papers at a tiny desk two states away. I press the phone to my ear, waiting on more napkins, hands sticky and thighs sopping with warm bisque. "I got a call this morning at about 9:00 a.m. from a Mrs. Gutierrez at Perkins Hall. She claims that you hauled your mother out of there this morning like a longshoreman."

"I don't even know what that means."

"Good, so you weren't there."

"No, of course I was."

"Don't tell me this. At five in the morning, you take her out of there?"

"More like six."

"But without being released from the home. Great." A world-weary sigh, tired of dealing with unaccountable shmucks like me. Vernon clears his lungs again. "Plus, she also claims that the nurse or whatever on duty says you were hostile."

"Vernon, I wasn't hostile. I had already signed everything they wanted me to. This is my mother—I'm her legal guardian. Honestly, what can they do?"

"File kidnapping charges."

I look over to Mom, to Freddie. She has a menu gripped in her hand, her cheeks taut with concentration. Freddie has his elbows on the table, tearing off bits of crust that he pops into his mouth while following our conversation.

"Honestly?"

"No, not honestly. I'm joking. Your father couldn't take a joke, either. But they are filing a breach-of-contract complaint with the state—nitpicking for money which will either come from Florida Medicaid or your wallet. Either way, you made more work for me."

"Look, can we discuss this later? We're at lunch now."

"Good for you. I have to work through mine. What are you eating?"

"Currently, I'm not eating anything. Mom just dumped her crab bisque all over me."

Vernon grunts. "Crab? I thought your mother was allergic to crab."

I pause. "What are you talking about?"

"Crab, on her dietary restrictions."

"She used to eat crab all the time," I say.

"You sure?"

I look to Mom, uncertainly. "Yes." She's meticulously trying to make sense of the menu, her hand reaching out for the straw in her water glass. The waitress arrives with a dish rag for me to clean myself. I hold the damp rag in my hand, unsure of what to do, of what to say. I look to Mom. Again, I say, "Yes."

13

Ten years, twenty. Over thirty years ago: the evening after Carlie's successful manhunt across Copeland, James loosened his tie before the mirror, scrutinizing his wife's reflection, and said, "*Mr.* Clarence?"

Mr. Clarence, it turned out, had been Dick Durgess' impromptu nomination for a new foreman.

"That's how Durgess referred to him, and he said he could start work tomorrow."

"If we're paying the man, we shouldn't have to call him Mister!" In the claustrophobic space of the bedroom, James banged his elbow against the dresser, which wasn't even theirs, and began cursing.

"Oh, it's not worth making such a big fuss over. He's probably just an older gentleman."

"Older gentleman. So is Durgess, technically speaking, and I'm not about to start calling him *Mr.* Richard! Mr. Clarence...doesn't anybody have a last name in this line of work? Where the hell did Durgess even get this guy?" James dropped his slacks to the floor, then hastily stepped into a pair of shorts. He jerked up the zipper, and fastened the hasp.

"James, Sweetheart, Darling," Carlie leaned into his chest, gingerly unbuttoning the collar. "If this man will put the last nails into our house, then I am willing to call him Roy Rogers if he wants me to."

James pushed away her fingers and unbuttoned the shirt himself. "The problem is, I can't believe you ran off and did this without me. Who knows what kind of foreman we'll be getting now. You have to think, you have to be careful—you have to know what you're getting yourself into. He could've just pulled a fast-one over on us for all we know."

Carlie's hands went numb. "I was in the man's kitchen. I saw him make the call myself," she said.

"That's not the point. The point is, people like Durgess can see people like you coming from a mile away."

"I thought you said he did good work."

"Just because he does good work doesn't mean you should trust him. Jesus, it would be naive to trust any of these people. First and foremost, they're out to make a buck. You watch, this new guy, this Mr. Clarence, is going to turn out to be Durgess' brother, or brother-in-law, and in the final reckoning will cost *twice* what we were initially quoted. All because we felt like we were over a barrel. It's a classic bait-and-switch, Carlie."

"I don't..." All she could see was his back: the narrow spine in a fresh white T-shirt, the dark shag of his hair unruly after changing clothes.

"You know, I thought we were going to support each other," he continued. "I told you to give me time, to this weekend at least, and now I'm going to have to stop by there after work tomorrow and check in on this character, straighten all this shit out. Jesus, you're going to rush me for the rest of my life, aren't you?"

"I don't—" she hiccupped. "I thought you said you'd be more comfortable being in our own home..."

"I also said I didn't want to deal with any major ordeals in the middle of my first week! And this is our *house* we're talking about here. The house we'll be living in for the rest of our lives! It needs to be perfect—"

They were interrupted by a polite knock. James thumped over and cracked the door to find Minnie's cherubic face in the three-inch gap.

"I'm sorry..." she whispered. "Is this a bad time?"

James turned to Carlie, who was facing the window. "No, Minnie. What can I do for you?"

She held a beat-up manila folder in her arms. Documents curled from the sides, crinkling as she shifted her grip. "I hate to trouble you, but I recently discovered this squirreled away in the closet. They're Map's mostly—finances, I believe. And I didn't know what to do. I thought about hiring a lawyer—"

"No, no, you don't want to do that. Here, let me take a look at them for you." James groped at his breast pocket for a pen and discovered he was in a T-shirt. In the interval in which he turned to his briefcase, Carlie pushed through the gap and out the door. He let her go.

Carlie thought about leaving, about grabbing the keys and marching barefoot to the car, but she had no idea where to go. Also, she would have to storm back into the bedroom for the car keys. She decided on a long twilight march along Auscauga Lake Road to vent her steam, but on the porch, she reeled. Carlie grabbed for the door and missed, catching her body against the frame. Without actually falling, she had the sudden sensation of hitting the ground, hard—the sickly lurch and impact. She needed to sit, be still, or else her guts would split and everything would gush out. She eased into one of the wicker chairs, tucked her legs underneath, and closed her eyes. There was a need to make herself very still, and very small. Unnoticeable. Carlie rubbed her belly, apologized to it profusely through her teeth. The rungs were damp against her thighs and the night air was thick; a brief rain had happened and she hadn't even noticed.

After some time, the door braced open and shut again with a fat push. Minnie stood on the porch with her, the heavy black purse clenched in her grip. Carlie smiled to herself, eyes still closed, and said, "I'm not going anywhere."

Minnie hovered by the other chair, not yet taking the seat. "Oh, I assumed not, dear heart. I thought I should let you be, you looked so dejected, but…but there's something I've been mulling over all afternoon." She took the seat then, primly and properly, and hoisted the bag onto her knees. "Anyway, here. I decided you should have this." Dipping into her purse, Minnie produced an oily cloth bundle and gently set it in Carlie's lap. It had a heavy, cold weight, as if the rags contained a spare engine part.

Carlie peeled back one soiled ear. "There's a pistol in my lap," she said.

"Now, it only has room for six rounds, but that should be plenty," Minnie continued.

"Plenty?"

"You might want to replace them, however. It's been quite a while since it was fired."

"It's loaded?" She watched the pistol like a rattlesnake. "Minnie…I really don't have any need for a gun."

"Oh, dear heart, life is full of such necessities." Minnie gave her knee a pat. "I just watched you today and was so impressed. I thought to myself, now what can I do for a woman like that? Well, here you are. The perfect thing."

"But what am I supposed to do with it?"

"Use it for peace of mind. Tuck it deep into the closet. Drive around with it in the glove compartment. Mostly, just know that it's there."

Then Carlie remembered the bedroom photo, the nakedness, the holster. "This was Map's gun, wasn't it?"

"Yes, it belonged to him. He'd be delighted to know you have it."

"James would croak if he found out we had a gun."

"Oh, I know dear. James is a wonderful sport, but sometimes he's not too bright. Besides, it's not for him. It's for you."

The moon crested the pines and miles of tree frogs chirped in the dark.

"Well," Minnie suggested, "Why don't we say that I hang onto it for you, until you need it."

"Yes," Carlie said, still a little dazed. "Why don't we say just that."

The pistol disappeared from her lap. The purse was taken inside. Carlie understood then that Minnie had been carrying that gun around all day long.

* * *

When James and Carlie arrived at the construction site two days later, they were greeted by a short, sun-darked man sporting a trim Errol Flynn mustache and one crossed eye. "Polio," he said as a way of introduction, pointing to the in-turned eye, and grasped James' hand. With each pump, his grip tightened like a rope. He wore an old khaki jumpsuit, unzipped down his sweaty chest. Over his heart, James caught a glimpse of the faded indigo tattoo: WE BUILD, WE FIGHT.

"Mr…?"

"Clarence."

Both James and Carlie gazed over the man's head to their house, expecting to see it listing to one side like the disaster of Pisa, the angles following the plumb line of Mr. Clarence's crossed-eye. But instead they saw the molding of four new windows, blocked in a graceful row. They saw the armature of a small balcony, braced up by four-by-fours. Later they would learn Mr. Clarence had spent his life repairing roofs, painting houses, and building airstrips in the Pacific Islands under heavy flak. Sawdust and brown paint flecked the hair on his forearms. He was maybe fifty-five.

"It's a disgrace and a travesty and it sickens me to death," he said. "The workmanship that's been going on here. That balcony," Mr. Clarence pointed to where his left eye couldn't see, "Was supposed to connect with a main support beam running through your living room. We'll see what we can do without it, but I wouldn't recommend doing any major calisthenics out there when we're done. If you catch my drift."

Carlie scanned the work site and ventured, "Are we missing some people, still?"

"Missing? No. I fired them."

James nearly choked, thinking of all the delays they've had so far. Delicately, he ventured, "Is that your job?"

"Hell yes it's my job," Mr. Clarence boomed, angry, it seemed, with no one in particular. "It's my job to get this behemoth done and done right. If Durgess doesn't like it, he can deal with me. He shouldn't have hired such halfwits in the first place." Mr. Clarence cut his good eye to Teddy, whose ears burned red while hauling slate, pretending to ignore them.

He squared his knuckles against his hips, standing with an air of SeaBee efficiency. "It'll be a good house," he said.

"It's my father's house," James said. "Almost. He designed most of it."

Mr. Clarence only nodded. Behind that silence and cockeyed gaze, perhaps he knew that as much as any slab foundation, houses are built on people. On personal histories and beliefs. And that to truly understand a person, you take his house's flaws—impractical balconies, excessive window placement, cheap water heaters—and appreciate them for what they are.

Standing in front of their home together, Carlie remained silent and laced her fingers into James'. The next week they moved in.

* * *

On a broiling afternoon when the exterior was nearly complete, Mr. Clarence dragged a Styrofoam ice chest from under the framer's table where it was being shaded from the sun. My parents weren't there, but they got this story third-hand, which was the same way they later learned how the new foreman had physically removed the other workers prior to their arrival (by picking a fistfight with two of them). From the ice chest, Mr. Clarence pulled out a plastic bowl, a plastic spoon, and a sweating block of strawberry ice cream. He carefully peeled back the paper folds, licking off his thumbs, and cut into the soft block with a putty knife.

"Knock them out," he said with Teddy, the framer, standing at his side.

"Sir?"

Mr. Clarence ladled a frosty pink spoonful into his mouth and nodded toward the completed balcony. Two rough-hewn timbers kept it supported from the earth. Teddy studied the man's expression for the punchline, unsure of where it might be. Mr. Clarence cleared his palate and cut into the ice cream again.

"Knock them out."

Teddy scratched at his throat. "Well, it seems to be doing okay the way it is."

"Those supports aren't supposed to be there." He sucked the plastic spoon and then pulled it through his teeth, getting all the good, sugary cream.

"It's also supposed to be anchored to a main beam running the length of the house," Teddy said.

"And whose fault is that?" Mr. Clarence called to a pair of builders, "You two. Grab some sledges. We're going to see if our work can stand." The two obliged despite Teddy's silent plea. Mr. Clarence leaned against the table and watched as the men squared themselves at either corner under the balcony. Teddy slowly backpedaled, one heel after another, out of Mr. Clarence's sight. They swung. The first strike connected; the supports shivered and shook the entire overhang. One man paused, looked up, and readjusted his position a little farther out as he got a better grip on the handle. Gradually, everyone stopped working—the brick masons, the electricians, the carpenters. One roofer shimmied to the eaves to peek over.

The second crack connected like a baseball bat, echoing across the yard. One strut splintered free while the other flew and whumped into the dirt. There was a loud pop like the sound of timber falling through the forest, shaking the west façade of the house. The entire structure eased and groaned. The balcony held aloft.

“Lookee there,” Mr. Clarence said, licking his spoon clean. He put the empty bowl aside. “Now you can be the one to tell them never to use it.”

But Teddy had already passed out, spread-eagle, on the ground.

“Mail him back to Durgess, would you?” Mr. Clarence told the onlookers. “His work here is done.”

14

In the sweatbox of August, they kept the patio doors open to ventilate the house. The sharp pleasant stink of wet paint clung to the walls. Fresh carpet crackled as they unrolled the bolts of shag. By this time, James' initial idea of collaborative living had been fully realized. He and Carlie awoke each morning to the whine of a circular saw in the yard, then struggled up from the floor of their new bedroom where they camped on a double mattress. A fine grit of wood dust, glass, and masonry debris covered the subflooring wherever they walked, crunching beneath their slippers for that first pot of coffee. They worked on finishing the kitchen and den, prepping the floors for carpet or linoleum. To ingratiate themselves with the workers, James had bought a small efficiency refrigerator and filled it with iced beers, deviled eggs, cold cuts, and jars of sweet pickles as a community chest. Carlie tacked up blue bed sheets to act as privacy screens over the empty doorways and a heavy curtain of upholstery fabric for the bathrooms. After these developments, some of the crew took to using the house toilets instead of the port-a-johns in the yard, which she wasn't too keen on—greeted as she was each morning by a slurry of muddy bootprints and urine on her new laminate and cigarette ash all over the toilet bowl. She discretely removed the front curtain and designated the back bathroom as Women's Only.

Scaffolding still occupied the sunken living room and foyer. Up went the massive chimney and hearth, stone by stone; up went the masonite; the men called in unison as they heaved the fieldstones or panels into place. An open loft overlooked the progress—James' upstairs office—its banister lathed by Mr. Clarence himself, as if in reparation for the sister balcony outside. The ceiling stretched up twenty-two feet, a gospel-singing height crowned in windows that glowed with the hot western sun each evening. The eastern side of the house, both the den and dining room where my parents worked, faced the woods through large sliding glass doors. In the lulls of stagnant heat, they would sometimes glimpse horseback riders trotting by on the bridle path, preceded by the soft ambling thunder of their hooves.

Few of the crew remained once the finishing got underway, but for those that stayed, Carlie had become something of a darling on the work site. The sight of her kerchief tying back all that black hair, with finishing nails lined up between her lips and carrying what looked like prize-winning watermelon under her smock, inspired both respect and irreverence. Among themselves, they laughed. They predicted that the boy—convinced it was a bouncing boy inside that massive womb—would pop out truing a piece of lumber with a thumb-sized hand plane. She was going to give birth to a square set. She must've made love to a tapered reamer. She'd nurse him with a caulking gun. Lord knows, she must've had sandpaper down there—fine 220 grit. Smooth a man's bedpost right down to the nub. Best of all, they loved seeing James follow after her like a mother hen. Clucking and squawking and fetching. The jokes about his lack of rooster-hood went on and on. But mostly, the workman observed Carlie from a distance. Chewing egg salad sandwiches or sipping from cola bottles, they would stare at her and move on. So it happened that one afternoon, a lanky mason passed into the kitchen to grab what he could from the small fridge when he spotted

Carlie, eight months pregnant, balanced at the top of a ten foot ladder, tapping in picture rails in the den. He wiped his face with one dirty forearm and squinted up problematically at her. Normally, he wouldn't have said word one. This time, however, he was moved to ask, "You need some help with that?"

She paused, belly bumped out from the wall, and smiled, "I'm fine." The nails made it difficult to speak.

Within seconds, James appeared at the base of the ladder as if responding to the call of danger. His hands were blistered raw from nailing, ripping up, and re-nailing deck planks. "Here," he patted a ladder rung. "Better let me take care of that."

"James, I'm perfectly capable."

"But the baby…"

And, rolling her eyes, Carlie climbed down the ladder. She spat the nails out into his hand.

Five minutes later Carlie knelt on the floor in the hall, cutting carpet padding, her long dark hair spilling free from its bonnet. A DIY Madonna prostrating herself with a large razor in her grip: rip, cut, rip. Suddenly James' hot breath was at her ear, heavy with fatigue, bent as if reading over her shoulder. He whispered, "Isn't that a strain? Hunched over like that? I mean, doesn't that put an awful lot of pressure on your stomach?"

She paused, stabbed the box cutter into the corking, and then struggled up to her feet. James took her place, sweat running down his chest like a marathon runner, his knees popping.

"So what about the picture railing?"

As James settled down with the carpenter's knife, he pointed toward a postal truck pulling up to their yard. "Hey, look there. We have mail." He began cutting rough squares. "Why don't you go see what it is?"

Carlie marched up the acre of front yard without saying a word. On August 14, 1971, our house was christened with a simple card, a small red envelope addressed only to Pony Paradise. The first of Minnie's many letters. Its cover showed a large live oak onto which Minnie had cut and pasted several small pictures of horses, dangling from the branches like wind chimes.

The Japanese magnolias and tulip trees are now in their second bloom, a little piqued but glorious in this weather. The hydrangeas are frothing mad and foolishly beautiful once more. You are loved. Welcome home.
Agape,
"Hoss Creek" S.C.

After reading the card, Carlie held it to her breast and looked around. The yard had been sodded with centipede grass, a scraggly growth from which barren patches of earth still sparkled like beach sand. From those spots stinging nettle sprang up in clumps. Prickly pear cacti. Most of all, pine scrub in dull greens and browns. While she sucked on a tooth—her mouth had tasted of old pennies since her third month of pregnancy—a flatbed truck bounded down their drive, carrying what had to be a delayed shipment. She followed after.

When Carlie caught up, the men were unloading what looked like large canvasses wrapped in butcher's paper.

"Are those the interior doors?"

One of the men paused. "Yes, ma'am."

"How many are there?"

"Five."

Carlie bit her thumb and thought for a moment, holding up the crew. "You know what," she said, "take them around back if you don't mind. Just put them in the spare bedroom for now. James and I will take care of them ourselves later." The lead man only shrugged, and then the wagon-train of interior doors rerouted itself to the backyard.

Back in the kitchen, Carlie propped the housewarming card on top of the mini-fridge for display. She grabbed the discarded tack hammer, fingering its handle. What she needed was a screwdriver for those doors. Maybe a mallet. James entered in a sweat and chugged down several glasses of tap water. All day, cicadas had razzed from the trees, which swelled and swelled over his psyche like heatstroke.

"Here," he sputtered, wiping his mouth and looking at the hammer. "Let me do that."

"Do what?" She folded her arms. "No, tell me. What was I going to do with this?"

"If you're not careful," he pointed to her belly, still breathless. "The baby."

"And what about me?"

"We're parents now, we have to think about more than ourselves."

"Listen to me, James. My back hurts, my feet are throbbing, and all my insides feel like they're being squeezed through a jelly press. If I just sit, I'm going to be doubly miserable."

"Look, all you have to do is take it easy. That's your job. Personally, I'd love to do that myself."

"I don't want to take it easy. There's nothing easy about taking it easy. I need something to do."

"Okay." James threw his hands up, frustrated. "All right. Why don't you stain the cabinets? This way, you have something to do, and I don't have to worry about you."

She studied him—the T-shirt stretched out of shape, the tiny holes dotting its yellowed collar—and handed over the hammer. "Fine."

"I'll be out back working on the deck," he said. "Just stain the cabinets."

Their new appliances—the stove top, the oven, and soon the full-sized refrigerator—were outfitted in Golden Rod, Harvest Gold, Buttercup Yellow, all the warm colors of 1970s kitchens. Carlie spread a tarp of newspaper across the floor. She carefully arranged the cabinet doors against the newsprint and set to work. Twenty-one cabinets, shorn of their hardware. After one hour, half were carefully rubbed with a chestnut stain. Carlie took her kerchief off, dampened it, and tied it back. Traces of the stain crisscrossed her forehead like dried blood. With nine cabinet doors left, she was running out of room. She sniffed, pressing the back of her wrist to her nose, her temples pounding. Stain, paint, and glue fermented into heady, winelike fumes in the rank heat. The windows were open, but in the den, she noticed the glass door was shut. Now who would close that damn door? Dizzied, Carlie wobbled into the den, where she snapped off her glove, unlatched the handle, and slid the door open. More air breezed in. The smell of sunshine on concrete, the sharp folic tincture of pine needles. She breathed two, three good clear breaths while a wren piped from the nearby nandina bushes.

"There," she said, and left the door wide open.

In the kitchen, her head began to tingle—blacking and blurring in time with the pulse in her body. When Carlie stooped to catch herself, a warm bubble released. Heavy heavy water—the nuclear Zen koan returns, cooling and containing different fuel rods. It ran like mercury down her thighs, taking form, taking shape against a cabinet door, distorting its glossy finish like a gazing pool.

"Oh, shit," Carlie staggered down, pitching into that mercurial future, smearing one great palm-print in the stain, breech water, amniotic memory, mercy, and terror.

"JAMES."

Within seconds, James bolted through the door in his paint spattered T-shirt and cut-off shorts. "I knew it," he exclaimed. "I knew it!" Floundering much like that hen now, shrilling with panic and joy.

As they sped out of the driveway, the yard crew bust out laughing and hooting, crowing proudly after: *cock-a-doodle-doo! cock-a-doodle-doo!*

* * *

Carlie would later say that she missed out on the child-birthing experience. Her penultimate word upon entering St. Joseph's Hospital was a guttural *help*. Her last word, new to her lexicon, was *epidural*. Like other women of this era, the continuous infusion of lidocaine and fentanyl that she subsequently received not only obliterated all sensation below the waist, but seemingly detached Carlie from her own body.

James, however, had front-row seats thrust upon him.

As a flight of orderlies wheeled Carlie away into the delivery room, a pair of eager candy stripers accosted him from either side. "Here, you'll need to suit up to enter." One kept him by the elbow while the other unfurled the sleeves of a paper smock, holding it out like a straightjacket.

"What? No." James zeroed in on the gown, flapping his arms free. "No, no."

They struggled for a few seconds, throwing words and helpful hands back and forth, their volley of *baby! wife! miracle!* hitting him in the face. The volunteers, high school girls, couldn't have been more than seventeen and were doing their best to manhandle him into the delivery room—a new husband-won privilege that was gaining ground in 1971. Eventually, a staff nurse stepped in to halt the commotion and put the girls on new rounds.

Alone, James stood in the hallway and watched from the tiny port window in the door. He stood, shivering on his feet, for what seemed like an eternity. Whoever said this was a beautiful experience? It was horrible, it was disgusting—he had never seen so much hemorrhaging and loss of fluid from one human being. Gradually, a dark dread began to settle into his bones until, at last, the horrific truth occurred to him: his wife was going to die. His wife was going to die in labor and leave him with this creature. He could already hear it mewling in the dead of night, echoing through the half-carpeted hallway of their dispirited house. Up the staircase, tucked away in a distant corner of his study, the cradle: a detached homunculus inside, howling for James' hairy teat.

Boarding school. Yes, there was boarding school, that could be one possibility. But what until then? *Years* until then—a child had to be what, eleven, twelve to be enrolled? Could he bring it to work until then? Hide it in his briefcase? A purplish-red bundle of fat and wrinkles, grasping at his pens and slide rule, documents sticking to its damp skin.

James staggered backwards and bumped into another passing nurse. Seeing him glassy with nausea, she took pity and escorted him into the waiting room. James plopped into a chair and put his head between his knees to keep from passing out. He glanced up. On the TV, a Braves game played with the volume turned low. He wiped his grimy face with the tail of his T-shirt, picked at the paint flecks on his arms, rubbed his palms together, and nearly blacked out.

"Christ Almighty, James, you look like you just dug out your own grave."

"Whit?" James lifted his head too quickly and felt the blood drain out. Whit Shirley sat on the small vinyl bench with a dark spray of gore staining his field shirt. He smelled of musk. Deer urine, if James could have placed it. A fishing magazine balanced open on one knee. "What are you doing in the waiting room?"

Whit nodded at the receptionist window. "Waiting," he said. "Rich and me were out hunting and he ran into a little accident. Leapt right into an old fence post; got him, oh," Whit pinched two inches of his soft side, "right about in the appendix, they think. Anyway." He idly flipped the page. "He's got a splinter the size of a switchblade in him right now. That's him squealing like a stuck pig in the back." He peeked above his tinted glasses. "Dr. Cullins, I got to say. You look like you're in serious need of some medicinal nourishment. I'm talking d-r-i-n-k."

At that moment, a nurse pushed her head through the door and called James' name. In his uncoordinated state, James glanced from the nurse up to the television. He saw the flashing blue light of the ending credits to *Hawaii Five-O*. How had that happened? Wasn't Phil Niekro just on the mound? She had said: "Your son is here to see you."

He followed the nurse down the corridor, his eyes glued to her white heels, until he came to a large Plexiglas window.

"Would you like to put this on now?" She held up the paper gown.

He nodded.

"Wait right here."

James looked over the line of anonymous baby faces, tight and discontent in their institutional bassinets. Old, egregious men, every one of them. Power brokers with wrinkled jowls, who should be chewing on wet cigars. What genetic grievance did they inherit, what hateful biology, to make them look that way?

"Here you are." The nurse eased what looked to be a bundle of rags into his limp arms. Inside was the tiny, corked up face of his son. A large port-wine bruise covered half his cheek and swollen eyes.

Holding that warm cocoon, my father became displaced in time (for the second and perhaps last time in his life). He felt every atom of his being disassociate and slip away, like pollen molecules through an endless spring wind. He felt diminished, he felt bare, he felt—not the sense of immortality that progeny are suppose to bring—but the fleeting vanity of his own life. He could feel the breath leaving his body even now, and more than ever, James understood that he will pass; he will molder; he will rot into humus beneath the trees. And this, his son, will outlive him. This son will see him to his grave, will place fresh-cut flowers in a brass urn, and offer a few candid words. And bring children, and those children's children, to that engraved spot on the cemetery lawn. His son will visit him and place flowers every year on his birthday, on Christmas Day, on Father's Day, and will remember him in this world. It was a pleasant feeling, strangely, as if he himself were wrapped warm and snug in the folds of this cotton swaddling. The child shifted, soft and infinitely vulnerable. It was a comfort.

James released a long, nervous breath, one that had been pent up in some compartment of his hypertensive, adenoidal body since the day he was born.

"Mr. Cullins," the nurse whispered, placing a gentle hand on his shoulder. "When you're ready, we have some paperwork for you."

* * *

Later, James would say: "Labor? Hah! More like a coffee break. It took no time at all!" To which Carlie, unamused, would remind him, "Eight hours. It would take a hell of a lot of coffee to fill eight hours."

And that was the way the story began, the way they told it before I was born, before my brother died, before everything they had once shared in love fell apart piece by piece by piece.

II

The Nuclear Dream Deferred

1

My father's funeral was perfunctory, but well-attended. Circumstances being what they were, one of his colleagues—the same man, Dr. Neil Langer, who bumped into him that morning he purchased the handgun—volunteered to arrange the service and I accepted. As a result, the wake was geared toward the university faculty and therefore became the academic memoriam of Dr. James Cullins, the chairman and scientist, within those hallowed walls. The remembrances came from people, from stories and moments, that were all foreign to me. They spoke about a man I didn't quite know. In all, six people approached the podium to eulogize my father, some impromptu. I myself abstained. Freddie, Mom, and I sat in our funerary best, isolated in the front row, darkly and distinctively out of place.

Afterward we shook a hundred hands at the receiving line, while my ill-fitting collar dug deeper into my neck. The service took place in a nondenominational university chapel, the way James would have liked it—an atmosphere of dignity, of virtue, without any actual religious affiliation. In the annex coffee was served in paper cups, a foldout buffet laid with paper table cloths and finger food sponsored by the Engineering Science Department, all of which had the air of a Christmas party held by a department that had experienced recent budget cuts. A few of his former grad students lingered in the wings by the refreshments and potted fronds, observing everyone, whispering and smiling among their milieu. The tenured faculty shuffled in single file to give their turn at condolences. Polite, deferential, academic—all the mannerisms one would expect, including the older gentleman who attempted to ease my burden by informing me that the noble gases would've painlessly displaced the oxygen in James' brain, making for no last minute gasps or regrets. Shaking hands and nodding, I stood there rehashing all the old grievances, the unsettled arguments, the unbridgeable rifts between us…the Real James, as I thought at the time. A desire to casually drop damaging remarks about him crept into me as people took my hand. The man that I knew and that these people had never known. Monomaniacal. Insecure. An abusive husband and an unwilling father, twisted by a need for normalcy. But then I noticed the way his old colleagues laid their hands on Carlie, even as they echoed the same stale sympathies down the line. It was strange, how much they touched her, how earnestly. They placed their hands on her face, her shoulders, her arms, eagerly, maybe unknowingly, as though they might heal her or themselves from what had happened, from what must inevitably happen. The reassurance of the touch itself struck me—complete strangers clasping her cold knuckles in what has to be the oldest and most sincere protection against death.

Later, during the ride to inter my father's ashes, I had asked Freddie, "What do you want done after you die?" We bounced in the backseat of the limo, where he grinned to himself, staring out the window. He had been in the thick of it all day with me, charming, smiling. He can pull out a quiet charisma when called into service. Introducing him as my partner met with the requisite number of awkward exchanges. His eyes looked beaten, as though bruised or smudged with mascara.

"One," he had said, clearing his throat softly after a moment of thought. "Set me on fire. And I don't mean like cremation. I'm talking like those Norse gods played it, on a pyre. Like the Vikings and Hindus and whatever. Light the match on some remote beach where everyone gets pelted by cold wind. Let the whole thing burn to cinders and walk away.

"Two: Put me in the ground, no box. No steel vaults or vacuum-sealed freezer bag. I mean the open dirt, so all the sexy worms can dig me.

"Or better yet, Three: Just float me away."

"That sounds more Viking-appropriate."

"Anoint my body in oil, float it in the water, and let me drift down river out of sight. That's the best way to do it, I think: an actual goodbye. Really leaving, going somewhere. Not the wax dummies you get in open casket wakes dolled up for eternity. No offense to anyone's last wishes."

"I see you've put a lot of thought into this."

"I just thought of that last one."

I remember thinking then of Minerva Price, floating naked in her cold-water creek. Bobbing between two worlds. We turned onto the highway strip of Tallahassee, passing bright fast-food chains, car dealerships, pawnshops, and title loans. My father's urn, in a box, rattled in my lap. "I really figured you for something more ostentatious. A sphinx maybe—something bejeweled. With neon."

Freddie had smiled broadly, rocking in the turbulence of the backseat. Mom was being kept by an orderly from the nursing home. "It's grandeur would only be a pale imitation of the man it housed," he said. "And subsequently pillaged."

It occurs to me now that what I had meant to ask—with my father between my knees to be interred in Bellwood Memorial Gardens, a transaction not unlike a safety deposit drop—was really: What are we *supposed* to do with the dead? Crystals are an option now, I read somewhere. We can compact their carbon into gemstones and carry our loved ones around in platinum settings, gold chains, filigreed broaches; pass them down to grandchildren like wedding rings. Ashes to carbon, dust to diamonds. And so they can re-enter the chain of physical being, beyond interment, in an everlasting mineral form where death does not exist. Forget for a moment the moral crisis of pawning your dead relatives to pay off credit card bills. The point of this new funerary rite is that our most cherished keepsakes can, in fact, be our most cherished loves. Love that is compressed into a noun, a direct object, and not a verb. A Thingness. Maybe because verbs are too terrifying. We must actively *do* them for them *to be*, for them to arise wet and glistening from the creek bed. And like all verbs, once we do them, that's it. They become past tense. There comes a point when they are over and done.

It's the same problem with the living. How do we keep them while they are alive? For a year following my mother's stroke, I did what most any child of my generation would do: I armed myself with a surfeit of useless knowledge. Knowledge as self-defense. Imagining the Dickensian cruelty of my father—locking her away, feeding her gruel, doing everything wrong or self-servingly—I overdosed on statistics, facts, and testimonials to figure out what I would do in his place. It was a useless exercise because I was nine hundred miles away, living my own life. It's still useless now because, for all the case studies I read, nothing could tell me how to both grieve and accept the terms of her stroke. The texts I found were too medical, too technical to be of much emotional preparation. And the few professionals I spoke with in passing were cagey, if apologetic. "Stroke, huh?" They would flip through lesson plans or sip coffee from the student union café. "That could mean a number of outcomes." Other avenues proved equally unhelpful. Success stories dominate the Internet, heralding full recoveries. Stories that are couched in the language of miracles or the Horatio Alger School of rehabilitation therapy—unwilling to give up! as if failure to convalesce properly is a matter of personal choice. Whether they celebrate divine intervention or personal industry, all the stories are about family members who have "come back," people who are "themselves again," who have "returned home." Always, that much mythologized return home. Their language makes the stroke sound like a sabbatical, a journey, a temporary leave of absence. (To say nothing of the caregivers who can no longer "be themselves" because of this new role thrust on them.) Poisonous rhetoric. This attitude seeps into the groundwater to set impossible expectations. I have yet to find the story of the mother who still "isn't there," whose mind is trapped behind the inability to speak and see as she once could. Whose mind is a failing vessel, her old self somewhere in there, rattling around like a dropped screw. What happens to those people, to these cases? Where do they go? They are conspicuously absent from the pages of AARP. They have no heartwarming entries in the campfire of Internet forums. They are quietly dropped from the world, I suspect, because they contradict our most fundamental beliefs about self-improvement, redemption, and progress. Because they are incurable, they occupy no space in our social conscience. There is no Race for the Status Quo. No pink blenders or buckets of fried chicken to buy in support of an unchanging condition. Instead, these mothers and fathers are put away into the grandkids' old converted bedroom, or enrolled in nursing homes where the curtains are drawn, where they can be fed and bathed and out of the way. Nothing I have found has prepared me to live with a parent who is no longer herself. I sit across from my mother and watch her lick the spoon after her bisque is taken away. She licks the spoon clean to stare at her concave reflection. Nothing I have ever read told me how to reconcile the stranger she is with the person she used to be.

Where do we begin, in order to accept such change?

It bears saying that Carlie was accepting, graceful even, when I came out to my parents, even if she was seven hundred miles away from me during that particular milestone. She had been out trolling public archives in Shreveport and Baton Rouge for much of that school year, my senior year, in the height of her genealogical obsession. James and I kept house like a pair of old bachelors, shuffling around in our bathrobes and boxers. Those mornings I lived on instant breakfast drink mixes, chocolate powders, mostly. When I graduated to coffee, my father stared at me like he was peering into a broken mirror. "What do you think you're doing?" he asked. "Having breakfast. What do you think *you're* doing?" I would nod toward the individually packaged, industrialized snack cake in his hand. "Is that your power breakfast? Little Debbie help you start your day?" "All right kid, don't be a wiseass."

Walking around on broken male eggshells, the way that fathers and sons do, trying our best to avoid the usual arguments. Alone together, we were affable all that fall quarter of my last year in high school. It stayed that way until one late-night errand to the grocery store, a last minute run to buy coffee for the following morning. We were idling at a stoplight, staring at its red glare through the windshield where the entire intersection was deserted. Patiently law-abiding nonetheless. The radio was on. It was tuned to an AM frequency, a talk radio host that James always listened to, one of those bombasts who sits in an isolated sound booth and levels his safely-guarded vitriol against the world in the middle of the night. Tinny and slightly distant, it sounded to me like an alien transmission from Pluto, a single voice directed solely at us, evangelical in its cadence, surreal. Two hundred miles away, a gay pride march was taking place in Atlanta, and the spectacle was shameful. Talk of AIDS, Clinton, and moral diseases. At that time, I had no defense against such public mouthpieces. But I also didn't feel it mattered in my own home, not in my own adolescent bubble. Plenty I hadn't admitted to myself at that point, let alone dare admit to others. One eye toward the excitement, one eye to the door. Both eyes shut to myself, as first experiences always seem to happen in the dark—mine being those quick and sweaty trysts on school field trips. The intimate overnight bus rides, with all eyes asleep, bound for band performances or science camp. And then James broke our awkward silence, looking perhaps for some father-son connection, or maybe foreseeing the future of my coming-out, forestalling the inevitable. With his eyes on the empty intersection, he said, "What I don't get is why these people insist on putting themselves on display." He hit each word carefully, shaking his head at the idea. "Why do they think that everyone wants to know that stuff? I don't want to know what you do with your life. That's your business. Not mine."

The light turned green. And that's when I left the car. Zipped out of the seatbelt and bolted from the door before James had a chance to call after me. I dashed into the woods. The station wagon followed me along the highway, crawling at a snail's pace with my father calling out the window, its headlights blazing between the trees. I didn't stick around to be found out. In retrospect, it was all very melodramatic, slightly embarrassing. My entire flight was surreal in the way of an impoverished imagination, in the way of having seen this very scene before, even as I was running—a nostalgia, a *déjà vu* from so many made-for-TV movies and subplots in film. And the rightness, the correctness, I felt with that recognition stayed with me while huffing through the woods. Yes, I thought, this is what's supposed to happen. I have seen it before, as on TV, and now my life accords with it. Maybe this is what remains of rites of passage in our culture: when we can recognize reality falling into accord with the formulaic representations. When we can recognize our life fulfilling the weakly scripted requirements of bad television drama. I didn't return that night. I hitchhiked to Atlanta, the same as a friend I knew. In fact, this was something I had been considering for some months, below the level of my own consciousness. It was a two and a half-hour trip by car, and I told prospective rides that I was in the military; that I was traveling to surprise my girlfriend, that I was going to pop the question and we would get married. I was amazed at how easily this story opened car doors for me. And that was how, by using this officially sanctioned fairytale of heterosexual love, I more or less began my adult life as a queer.

Carlie, of course, flew into a rampage when she returned home to find me disappeared. Dutiful son, three days later I called to let them both know I was safe. She and I spoke for hours, racking up the collect call I had made from a payphone. She was livid that I had done such a stupid thing and relieved that I called; she reconciled, she doted on me, encouraged me to come home, she said that I was always different, since day one. Since before day one. Since pregnancy, since conception, even. Way before she felt the first kinetic rumblings of the womb, she knew I would be different. And when she said it, it didn't sound so bad. In fact, it sounded like relief.

When James picked up the phone, he echoed an apology, but his voice was flat. It was startling to hear, because I had almost forgotten about him. He felt it, too, I think. How suddenly irrelevant he seemed. A stranger fumbling to keep pace with the moment that Carlie and I had shared. So, while groping for words, he chose an opposite path instead. He found his stride in an age-old paternalism, which became clearer and clearer as he picked up steam: We must shepherd the young through their phases and confusion. We must save the young from themselves. His lecture was broken by Carlie screaming at him in the background. New battle-lines had been drawn in the sand between them, and it had been with my toe.

The point of all this rambling—the funeral, the blow-up of my sexual epiphany—is to say that a decade down the line, when Carlie had her stroke, I think he remembered. I believe a part of him remembered it as a personal failure, the moment—to his eyes—that his vision of family irreconcilably fell apart. So after my mother had been stabilized, he called me from her hospital room. By then, in his early sixties, James had an appointment at FSU, an endowed chair, and lived between Tallahassee and Copeland at different times of the year. He told me briefly what had happened, and what the prognosis was. Scrambling around my apartment with the phone to my ear, snatching clothes and keys, I told him I'd leave straight away.

"Son, I don't think that's a good idea," he said and stopped me cold. I could hear nine hundred miles of that same AM frequency static, silence, and bad blood between us. "It would only confuse her."

If he couldn't reclaim me, a twenty-seven year old man traveling a path so threatening from what he knew, then he could reclaim his wife. It was one of the last conversations we would ever have, following the example of his own mother, Antoinette Cullins, whose ability to cut family ties my mother had witnessed with a sublime fear. Cutting an artery to staunch the heart. After that, he packed her up, sold the house, and moved everything to Florida.

2

Long before I became their biggest bone of contention, James and Carlie were preparing for a different family crisis.

Within seventy-two hours of Bradey's birth, the mothers would descend. From Bay Shore, New York, and LaBauve, Louisiana, they would come thundering to the call of grandchildren. Separately, Antoinette Cullins and Mary Alice Robicheaux would square their personal belongings into fastidious hard-shell suitcases, and they would set out for steamy rails, they would set out for sooty Greyhound stations. They would leave their husbands—one already buried in the ground, the other in the quarrelsome, undetected stages of Alzheimer's. These women came from hard Catholic backgrounds; they came from neighborhood apartment buildings where the pipes clanged overhead and from cinderblock houses shaded by ancient pecan trees; from four stories up and from one hundred feet below sea level; they came from games of pinochle and card tables of bourre; they came from unfiltered cigarettes and Prohibition Era bottles of homemade Cherry Bounce, thick with dust. They came bearing the torch of good advice—the right way to feed a child, to burp, to change, to dress, to protect, nurture, and cherish—two of the Lord's own personally appointed Horsewomen of the Motherhood, and He only needed two, not four, they were that efficient. Carlie could read the signs that preceded them, could read their approach in the stars.

James' mother arrived first, Antoinette Passantino Cullins, a small, nervous lady with a large, date-sized mole set against one cheek that peered out like a fortuneteller's eye. Entering the house, her movements were birdlike; they were spare and precise. Looking through doorways, peeking around the corners, Annie finally set her luggage down in the newly carpeted hallway and said, "Honey, where the doors at?"

She looked into the second and third bedrooms, sparsely furnished. She peered around the open bathroom door frame, where the harvest gold toilet sat in full view of the hall, beside a laundry hamper.

Now, Carlie loved this woman. She loved Annie as much as anyone could love her mother-in-law, once you got to know her as a human being and not as a force of criticism—and she also loved her own mother, her own parents, despite knowing them as human beings, which in turn encourages any child to be a force of criticism. But she wanted to continue to love them both. That's what was at stake here. To preserve and protect the love they had.

"Hey…where *are* the doors?" James said, genuinely confused.

Carlie planted her hands on her hips in full-blown amazement. "Oh, my gosh. They never put the doors on! This is just too much—you know, I'm gonna have a word with somebody."

Annie tightened her jaw, crimping her lips at the thought of defecating out in the open like wild animal.

"Mom," Carlie said, embracing her a second time. "We're so glad you're here. Let's get you a hotel room."

* * *

Mary Alice Robicheaux was due to arrive that evening and would call from the bus station on the northeast end of Copeland. When she disembarked, her face, no doubt, would be pinched and sallow from avoiding the black passengers that, to Carlie's mortification, her mother still referred to as colored. In fact, she wouldn't sleep the entire ride for fear of touching the armrests, for fear of public germs in the air, her nose protected by an old but clean cotton handkerchief. While Carlie dozed, she could see the matronly form of her mother, a thin spike of a woman, descending the bus step by step while trying to avoid the handrail. Much less vocal than Annie, and perhaps by virtue of raising six daughters, Mary Alice was prone to quiet approval or disapproval. A matriarchal telepathy that carried over vast distances, which Carlie unfailingly heard in the back of her mind with each little thing she did. *Wash your hands thoroughly under the nail; don't touch stray cats; avoid public water fountains.* Having just popped out a kid of her own, and now compounded with this anticipation, Carlie's body crashed. She napped for several hours. Elsewhere in the house Annie doted on James nearly as much as her grandbaby. With Bradey's bassinet centered on the kitchen table, she burrowed through the refrigerator; she cooed; she wiggled a wooden spoon at his uncoordinated eyes; she commandeered the stove with an apron cinched around her waist and prepped dinner, fulfilling the role of mother *in absentia* and passing little noshes and nibbles and tidbits to James while he sat in the den, television burbling and the newspaper in his lap. Later that evening, when the smell of ozone portended rain with still no call from Mary Alice, they threw old blankets in the yard and had a picnic supper on the grass. They drew out a lawn chair for Annie, whose joints were unaccustomed to eating so low to the ground; in the spirit of fresh air, even if still tender and sore, Carlie carted out armloads of soft pillows for her, James, and Bradey to sit at Annie's feet. They ate fried asparagus patties and macaroni salad.

All eyes were fixed on Bradey, propped on a pillow, as Carlie played with his hands. Antoinette leaned to her knees, picking away any stray ants that marched within a three foot radius of him. "Should he be out here?" she asked again, studying the dirt. "What if he gets chiggers?"

"He's not going to get chiggers, Ma. He's not even touching the ground."

"I don't like this air. It's clammy," she added. "No good. He could catch a death."

"He's not going to catch anything. Look, we've been cooped up in that house so long, let's just enjoy the outdoors. See what Carlie's been doing with the yard? See that—"

"Clematis."

"—clematis she just put in? Isn't it nice?"

"You almost caught a death when I brought you home."

"I know, I know." Then James said, "Didn't Aunt Zinny raise plants like that? With the flowers?"

Annie stiffened, looking as though someone broke wind in front of her, loudly. "I wouldn't know. We don't talk."

When Carlie gave him a questioning look, James explained, "This has been going on for about two years. They had a falling out, some argument on the phone."

"She hung up on me!"

"Two *years*?" Carlie said. "Have you tried calling…"

"Me? Why should I call? She should be the one to call. Anyway, good riddance. You should've heard the things she said. I've got no more to say about it." Having dropped that subject, Annie refocused her attentions on Bradey. Just seeing the wobbly newborn made her break out in a small-toothed grin. She wiggled one red lacquered nail and said, *skitch skitch skitch*, on his belly. "So what about the christening gown for little peanuts here? You got something in mind? I brought my crochet and patterns."

James had stretched out on his elbows, a plate of cold macaroni resting on his stomach. He looked up to Carlie, wrinkling his forehead. "Christening? What is he, the U.S.S. Poopdeck? Is he setting out to sea?" Carlie only vaguely grinned, still reeling from the thought of nursing a family grudge for two years.

"For when he's baptized, Butch," Antoinette corrected.

"Baptized." James popped his shoulder. He tugged at his son's tiny, stocking foot. "No, Ma. Bradey's not getting baptized."

Annie's lips went rigid.

Then from around the garage came voices. In a flash, Carlie expected to see the cotton-white head of Mary Alice Robicheaux appear around the walk; instead, there emerged a throng of younger women, all dark haired and laughing with shouts of *surprise!* Carlie gasped, then squealed, struggling up from the pillows. Four of her five sisters surrounded her in an avalanche of hugs. There was Francine, the eldest; Ruthie, the youngest; Nan, Carlie's childhood tormentor as a pudgy girl; and Thelma, one of the twins who refused to be identified as twins. Annie remained seated and James stayed on the ground, reticent in the overwhelming surge of in-laws. They all looked like younger, older, thinner, heavier, shorter versions of Carlie herself. The younger ones had husbands back home, or had had husbands and now had small children; the older ones were either stubbornly single or woefully single. Of the two toddlers present, one squalled from a bouncing hip while the other meekly pressed her face into her mother's legs. Robicheauxs swarmed over the small picnic. Carlie dragged out more lawn chairs, hustled for more blankets, more food, more drinks, whatever she could grab—aided by her sisters—from the cupboards and fridge. She, Carlie, was the sister who got away, who left home, met a man, and sailed away into adventure. Florida, the Great White North of Massachusetts, and now South Carolina! How exotic! The Eastern Seaboard, the Atlantic Ocean—Ooh-la-la. They had taken personal leave from jobs at the chemical finishing plant; they had left husbands lists of what to eat in the fridge, who to contact, what to do in their absence, all to visit the sister who had made it out in the big world beyond Iberville Parish.

"So where's Momma?"

Francine pulled a cigarette from her purse, but didn't light it. Some of the girls exchanged glances. "Momma couldn't come at the last minute. Daddy—well, Daddy took a fall."

"Took a fall?" Carlie said. "You make him sound like an old man."

"From a chair. He decided to fix a light bulb—"

"—which wasn't even broken," Nan added. "He's really been forgetting himself lately."

"And fractured his pelvis. Momma is looking after him. Holly stayed behind to help. We figured the four of us might be as good as one Mary Alice." Francine winked at her sister.

Within a few minutes the sisters had settled into chairs and on the grass, cooing with Bradey, chatting and telling stories. James patiently waited and at the first lull, spoke up with a curious smile, "So where's everybody staying?"

"Why, with y'all, of course…" Ruthie turned her innocent wide eyes upon him and the entire chorus of women rang with laughter.

Francine pulled a can of Schlitz from her lips to say, "Don't worry, James, we figured we get a room somewhere. We passed a couple motels on the way in."

"No, no," Carlie said, dismayed, "Y'all can certainly stay here—we don't have many beds, but we got a lot of space, and…"

Y'all? James thought. He cleared his throat. "And we don't have any doors on the rooms or bath. Remember?"

"No doors?" Thelma said, laughing. "Shoot, James, how long have you had to get this barn done? Ray could've built me the Taj Mahal by now."

Still smiling, James began his rebuttal, but Nan cackled over him.

"Since when do you need doors?" she asked. "It'd be like we're all at home again. You remember when Thelma went tearing out the house in nothing but a hair net?"

"Oh, please don't tell that story again…"

"How old *were* you?"

Much of the evening unraveled into conversation this way. After his first few words, James kept silent, as if he had been dowsed with a bucket of ice water. It was always this way with Carlie's family, he felt—bullied into silence by a clan of garrulous women. During the crab boils that happened in their low-lying yards each summer, James got lost amid the cracking claws and damp newspaper, the heavy back-and-forth talking and warm juices spurting across the table, which always seemed to spatter on his glasses. And then with the stories. They would pour stories—everything about Carlie—on top of his head. Carlie as an infant, Carlie as a teenager, sweet and adventurous Carlie, the entire catalog of Carlie as if they were educating him on the subject of his own wife. He wanted to tell them, *You don't know her like I know her*. That she was not the Carlie they kept feeding him, like medicine. The sheer animated bulk of Robicheauxs left him agitated and alienated—and now he began to feel like an outsider even in his own backyard. Taking a cue from her son, Antoinette fell into the same stony disposition, but watched whoever spoke with the intensity of a tennis match. Anecdotes bounded from the Robicheaux children to details of Bradey's future, until Francine pulled the tab of another beer and asked, "So what about the christening gown? You plan to make one or you want to use one of Momma's?"

At that, Annie, who had kept sullen and quiet, nearly leapt, "That's what I wanted to know! You should hear what they have to say."

All eyes landed on them: Carlie seated upright amid the pillows, Bradey stirring in her lap, James reclining at her knee. The circle of Michelangelo's holy family in picnic repose.

"What's to say?" James crunched into a pickle spear, chewing for a moment. "He's not getting baptized. It's something Carlie and I agreed on a long time ago when we decided to get married. Back when we were living in Florida."

Carlie cringed more than smiled. It felt as though she had just admitted to having sex before marriage.

"He doesn't need anyone shoving their mumbo jumbo down his throat." James playfully goaded Bradey in the belly, adding, "Right, little man?" Antoinette silenced herself—not that she had been speaking, but her noticeable lack of objection created an autumnal hush, a dry leaf-rattle in the air. Then an uneasy laughter shook from two of the sisters, hesitant but delightfully scandalized. *You're such a mess*, they said. *Too much!* James faced the women from his recumbent position on the ground, placing an arm behind his head. "This is the twentieth century, after all—at this point organized religion is all either superstition or mind control. Wouldn't you agree?"

At once Carlie saw the baited hook, but before she could jerk it back in, Nan bit.

"I don't really care what century it is," her sister said, bobbing an infant on her knee. "I think we all need to believe in something bigger than ourselves. Otherwise we get big egos."

"Big egos?" He offered a blank, Socratic expression. "Are you telling me that big egos are a worse consequence than centuries of manipulation, tyranny, and war? Think about it for moment, if you took—"

"James, let's not get into this..."

"What's to get into? We're all adults here. I think we can have a frank discussion of religion."

"Wait, does that mean you're not taking him to Mass?" Ruthie spoke softly, puzzled.

"Well," Carlie said, and even though Mary Alice was five hundred miles away, she felt the prickle of her mother's gaze, "that doesn't mean we're not ever taking him to Mass—I mean we plan to expose him to lots of things."

"Baloney!" Annie shouted, at last finding her voice, strained and swollen. "Butch, I don't believe it. I know you got faith."

"Mom, we're going to raise Bradey the best way—"

"How come, when you was eight years old, you would put dead birds in your trouser pockets?"

"Here we go."

"I was forever pulling dead sparrows out the wash. I'd yell at him, Butch! And he'd tell me, Ma, I thought I could bring them back to life! He thought he could work miracles, this one." Commanding attention at last, Annie clicked her teeth together in a nervous habit, a sound not unlike knitting needles. Then, her tone darkening, she held up one finger to prepare everyone for the next damning piece of evidence. "One years old," she said. "Couldn't talk, couldn't do nothing. Yet I knew." She tapped the side of her head, squinting shrewdly.

"Ma, come on. Don't get on with all these stories."

"I knew when quiet was too quiet. I'd left Butch in the crib, making sandwiches, bottom floor of that house we used to live in on East Garfield. But I knew something was wrong, between the bologna and mayo. Wanna know how I knew?" She pointed one crooked finger up to the graying clouds overhead. She tapped her nose, a gesture to the unspoken pact she held with the Big Man Upstairs, and then pointed that same fingernail toward James. "That's how. I run in and sees you lying there, turning blue in the face, and I says—I nearly died seeing you like that, my first and only boy—and I says, God, help me with this child, I can't do it alone! And I reach in with these two fingers, these two right here, and pull out a big glob of mucus like you never seen. At once, you breathe again. Presto. You always had such trouble with your sinuses."

"Mom, what on earth is that supposed to prove?"

"Prove? Prove? Listen to the way he talks to me. I guess it don't prove nothing to you, Mr. Smarty Pants. It didn't prove nothing to your Uncle Chick, neither, God rest his soul. Chick who thinks he's going to be a big man and says to me one day, Annie, I'm signing up with the war. Right then, I get this smell, one I don't like. Gardenias, so faint and sickly sweet they could've been right outside the window, but we never had none, and it was the middle of January to boot. Bad news, I know right away. So I tried to stop him and say, Chick, don't go! You're gonna die! He laughs at me. Eighteen years old, knows everything already. Nine months later, Chick's in France. I'm rinsing dishes one day and *whooof!* Gardenias. I drop the dish, the last of my mother's wedding pattern. Like someone hit me in the face with a funeral wreath. Two days after, we get a telegram: sure enough, Chick is dead. His entire squad walked right into kraut fire under bad marching orders; this was right before Cantigny. After that, don't matter where I am in the world, whenever someone I love passes on, I always smell gardenias. That's how I knew Butch was in trouble. I got a whiff of that terrible flower."

"I thought it was because you knew when quiet was too quiet." James muttered into his beer. And then, unable to stop himself—because this was *his* mother, the ambassador to his identity, his life, because mothers must carry the burden of being the commemorative body of their children—he added, "Listen to yourself, the story changes each time you tell it. You only say this stuff because you think it justifies what happens. But guess what: it doesn't. It only keeps you from thinking about it. And that's precisely what I don't want for Bradey."

Annie went silent, struck dumb, her ears red as if someone had smacked them. With her arms folded, she averted her face from the group, her lips pressed tightly together. No one spoke.

And then out of politeness, which was even worse for James to witness, Ruthie started a story about how she once dreamed that an angel fell to earth, and a month later, the A in St. Thomas High dropped from the entrance and shattered at her feet. And one by one they began relating tales of odd happenstances, dreams and visitations and déjà vu, all the moments of premonition that kept them protected from the future.

* * *

Perhaps most of all, the Robicheaux siblings reminded James of his own cousins, of being the only boy in a chorus of older girls, staring like a small wayward child into the foreboding wood of womanhood, all piney legs and dark undergrowth. Except that he knew from his adolescence that he *could* enter that female territory—could enter that conversation, that world of women. His cousins had schooled him well. All older by a few years, they coddled him, they adored him—*dance with us, Butch; play dress up with us, Butch*—to where he had developed an intimate knowledge of Eddie Fisher and sewing empire waistlines. How they would ask him to hold the measuring tape to their bodies as they made alterations; how they had no qualms milling around in slips and training bras in his company; how they begged to practice slow dances with him while they swooned about their crushes. How he would try on their incomplete gowns and undergarments after they had left; how he would then furtively fondle himself in the dark sewing closet. And remembering that, the ease and fluidity of being almost female, scared him. Because now, after all, he was a husband, he was a father, a doctorate, a homeowner, someone with a mortgage and a twenty-year plan. He didn't want to be reminded of that nine-year-old boy who now looked alarmingly fey, queer, the effeminate fait accompli of his cousins.

His mother and the sisters stayed at the Motor Inn across town, but during the day, they took over his house. They were in the kitchen, chatting loudly over the whir of a hand mixer. They were in his living room, covering every cushion of the sectional sofa. They draped themselves over the arms of furniture and leaned in the doorways, laughing and having a good old time. They filled his fridge with foreign and hostile foods to the point where he would bellow out, "Carlie, where the hell is the lunch you packed me?" His hands jammed inside, parting the aisles of Tupperware. "I can't find it anywhere!" From the living room, one would chide back anonymously, "Oh, relax, James. You ain't going to go hungry." Also in that first week, laundry began to appear: lingerie, slips, and bras strung up to dry in the bathroom. All these nether-things surrounded his head when he stood to pee, tickling his flushed forehead and cheek. Toddlers who didn't belong to him waddled up to stare while he ate alone, or endured jarring rides on their mothers' hobby horse knees while the women talked, or teethed on ice-cold unopened beer bottles. He would turn the volume up on the television and still get no respite. Annie sat beside him, taciturnly crocheting, finding solidarity in his displeasure, happy to be sharing his ire that he did not want to share, wanted to enjoy alone, because if shared he was still, again, his momma's boy in this world of strong energetic women.

James began to put in longer hours at the lab and office, but that provided little solace. Admittedly, I picture him as a Robert Crumb caricature, vexed by thoughts of these robust women while bent over his paperwork. Coke-bottle lenses flashing under a fallen swoop of dark hair, stoop-shouldered and stubbly, his forehead sprouting nervous drops of sweat. The irritations of his professional life might have been a nuisance, but they had not yet threatened his sense of self. The urine sample poster—which had proved a weather-vane of things to come—was only the first of many public ordinances tacked up all over the facilities. He found himself confronted by them in the hallways, on cork boards, behind acrylic display cases, staring at him from bathroom mirrors, and even riveted to metal posts along the footpaths between buildings. The messages, dauntless in their ubiquity, revealed hairline cracks in reality: *87% of All Accidents can be Prevented by Washing Your Hands. Yield Right of Way to Pedestrians without Vehicles. No Admittance Unless with Key.* The bureaucratic madness of these signs assured James that he was indeed the one stable point in an unstable world. Sure, there were no days when the custodians became kings or technicians rode into work on three hundred pound sausages, but the posters' inverse logic created a Rabelaisian carnival to the workplace. And those who were in charge, as James would come to know, certainly were the village fools.

At 3:00 p.m. one Friday, James found himself in the only spare chair in Phil Doyle's office. James had his legs crossed and waited patiently for Doyle to finish on the phone. The office was a step up from the bunker in which James worked, though by no means befitting the mover-and-shaker attitude that Doyle exuded. It was still windowless, had the same metal desk with rubber top, but it wasn't bolted to the wall. A slightly higher ceiling, more room for an extra chair or two, and few if any texts or manuals on the shelves. He didn't know what to expect from a mid-level manager's office. Usually Phil reserved the conference room even for such small, two-man meetings as this: plush chairs, wood paneling, bright slits of window around drawn blinds. Down the hall the secretarial pool clacked away on fifteen electric typewriters, humming and punching like a newsroom. Doyle reached from his desk and closed the door.

"All right, so what's up? Why are we here today?"

"I'm not sure." James shifted his posture, trying to be polite. "You called the meeting."

He drummed the desktop, a hollow metal sound which reverberated through its drawers. Phil snapped his fingers. "Right you are. I'm sorry I couldn't get us the meeting room...we could reschedule instead?"

"This is fine with me."

"We might as well be talking next to a water cooler, huh? Hardly enough room for our thoughts to breathe in here." He leaned in his chair to peek down the hall. "I had asked Leanne to bring us some coffee."

James glanced at his watch.

"Well, I suppose we can get started." He rapped the desk again and pulled up some mimeographs. "I'll be brief." He passed them to James. "Band-aid brief—one yank, ouch, but it's over: I'm getting a red flag that you're overspending on the glass project."

"How can that be possible? We're under budget nearly every month—"

"Mmm..." Doyle tapped the top page that James held. Thirty percent of their project funding had been reallocated to another research team. James flushed red.

"But our budget was solidified back in August."

Phil put his hands up in an apologetic defense. "It's a production-based system. Right now Derek Johnson's team is onto something hot within the same department. But don't worry, the budget will be reapportioned when you can show us some results. 'The money goes with them that shows,' James."

"I can't show you anything until we've had time—and resources—to properly work on the project."

"Hey, you guys are the geniuses. I have faith," Phil smiled distractedly, flipping through the dossier on his desk. "The other thing...There's a question from the higher-ups about this Toriyama character you've been contacting..."

"Toshiyama. He's not a character, he's a mathematician at Harvard. I co-authored two articles with him, one which was instrumental in getting me hired."

Doyle grimaced, confidentially, to alert him of dangerous waters ahead. "James. You know he needs to be a fully vetted sub-contractor before he can have any project involvement with the Site. We're talking about a possible major security infraction—I just want to cut it off at the pass."

"I do know that. I put in a sub-contractor request with you over a month ago. You told me not to worry about it."

Phil Doyle leaned back again to study James, thoughtfully chewing his lip. "You know. I bet that was before the revised budget."

After the meeting, James returned to his subterranean floor in a weak-kneed rage and hurried to the hall bathroom where, under the pale lighting, he puked his heart out. Steadying himself over the bowl, he still had Doyle's memos crushed in one hand. After heaving twice, his ragged breathing subsided. A silence.

From two stalls over, a voice echoed: "Meatloaf Tuesday. It'll get you every time." Then a toilet flushed and the sound of Whit's sneakers treaded to the sinks. A rush from the faucet, a few paper towels, then the sneakers again as he left. He and Whit were the only two who ever used this bathroom. After Whit had left, James unlatched the stall and approached the mirrors. He splashed cold water on his face, still shaking, still wracked in his guts. Little blood vessels had broken out on his cheeks and nose. Down in this concrete room, amazingly, none of the usual posters appeared. No *87% of All Accidents can be Prevented by Washing Your Hands.* He looked at the musty green suggestion box and waited, water dripping from his nose. Then he tore off a pair of slips from his pad, his wet hands blotting the paper. In silence James scrawled down a long, acidic message—filling up one slip, then another, and another—on the ineptitude and inefficiency of his workplace, which, the longer he wrote, somehow bled into his wife, his home life, the mass occupation undergoing his house. When he was finished, he studied eleven scraps of paper arrayed on the damp counter. Now that they were out, James didn't quite know what to do. They seemed dangerous, hot. He thought about wadding them up and carrying them on his person, but that wouldn't do. While digging into his pocket for a key or a mint, one might tumble out. The trashcan seemed no better; anything could spill out when it was emptied. So he folded them by halves into a tight packet and stuffed all his hostility into the box, unsigned. He felt a little better, a little calmer. He had formally filed his complaint; he was on the record, on the books, about where he stood. The universe now knew his official position. James studied the box, contented.

A moment later he tried (unsuccessfully) to tear it off the wall.

* * *

Back in the lab, James suited up. Eye shields, white smock. Clipboard binder. The fluorescent drone of overhead lighting ultrasonically scrubbed down every thought clinging to his synapses, wiping him clean, new, *tabula rasa*.

With nine inches of lead glass in front of him, Whit worked the slave manipulators at one hot cell. They were bombarding more elements with irradiated isotopes.

"How'd the little pow-wow with Doyle go?" Whit moved his lips precious little, concentrating on maneuvering the controls precisely. There were always these tiny conversations around hazardous materials.

"I don't want to discuss it." James checked the display without having to move his eyes. He jotted time and increment. The purifying power of numbers. "Thirty percent of our funding got slashed."

Whit carefully raised his cheeks into a half-mast grimace, but did not chuckle. Any small movement would disturb his handling. "Welcome to the Bureaucratic Graft. Everybody gets their fingers in the pie."

"It's such a lousy game." James lifted his glasses to his brow, trying to read a small printout. "I bust my ass to bring in this funding, and now we can't touch it? I'll have to come in on the weekends just to make up the difference."

Whit's eyes remained steady. "Let me cue you in on a little secret," he said, softer now. "These midlevel managers, they're free agents. They only get promoted when a team under their management does well. Do poor, and they'll grin in your face and put a call in to the glue factory. Because they have several ponies in the paddock to bet on. So don't let him fool you. He's not interested in our work, only in what our work can do for him."

James said nothing. The catalytic hum of cooling systems, of delicate machinery throughout the room. Whit said, "So how's that little baby boy of yours doing?"

Because one admission leads to another, or because he had already evacuated his body and his mind in the bathroom stall just ten minutes ago, James, who liked to keep his professional relationships professional, let his irritation slip: "I wouldn't know. I'm a stranger in my own damn house."

Aside from the casual babble, Whit himself had always been cagey around James, too. Not just because of the age difference, James thought, but the geographical difference. He had heard from Phil that the local hangers-on at the plant could be bitter, vicious even, largely because they were indolent and under-qualified. They were a legacy of charity cases, an unofficial settlement for the whole displacement-upset when the plant was built. Whit kept his eyes fixed through the yellow glass square, but was acutely interested in this tiny admission. "Oh?"

"Her family." James shook his head, making more notations. "Forget I said anything." And they let the subject drop.

* * *

Later, at the end of the day, James ran across Whit again in the parking lot. The older man hailed him from a distance, then nodded as James stowed his briefcase. The car James drove was a brand new station wagon, baby blue and chrome with wood paneling. Its door slammed shut like a bank vault. Whit stopped and let out a low whistle; James couldn't suppress a grin of pride. And that would have been all, a simple acknowledgment at the end of a long workday. Except Whit paused, reflected for a moment, then turned around.

"You know Shirley, South Carolina?" Before exiting the building, Whit had changed into short pants and a polo shirt; his dark glasses were impenetrable in the evening sun. "Those are my people. Whole town named after my family. You ever been?"

"No."

"Course not. Wanna know why? Cause there were only ever two hundred seventy-five people in the entire damn town. Wanna know why else?"

"Why?"

"Cause they built Parking Lot E over where it used to be." He sniffed. "My grandpa lived somewhere between spaces 38-47. So next time you park in E, you can say you been to Shirley, South Carolina."

James blinked, then broke a hesitant smile. He nodded toward Whit's El Camino, to the gun rack in the rear window. "Is that why they let you through the gate with that thing? Reparations?"

Whit snorted. "Hell, it's not illegal to drive around with an empty piece of wood." He drew out his jagged grin. "Now, if you're looking to get yourself fired, that's when you put something in it."

"Shirley, South Carolina, huh."

"Who says you can never go home?" Whit gave him a slap on the shoulder. "Dr. Cullins, this is the second time in my life that I can see you are in dire need of some liquid refreshment. Let me buy you that drink." He added, "A late congratulations for that son of yours."

Never before had James considered bar-hopping—as he thought of it—after work. It wasn't respectable for a family man. But faced with the stress and discomfort he now felt at home, trampled under by all those women, a rebellious streak took hold of him. "Okay," he said. "You're on."

James followed Whit's El Camino along the dusty outskirts of Copeland to a place called the Sugar Shack. It was a tiny cinderblock bar painted cotton candy pink, situated on an empty dirt lot littered with pull-tabs, tire tracks, and flattened beer cans. The few windows, James noticed, were barred like a county jail. Its pink walls would look laughable if not for the trash, and the metal bars, and the single, sad A/C unit dripping into a muddy cesspool that he had to leap over just to get to the door.

Whit Shirley, as a biologist, was an expert in local ecologies—*all* the local ecologies, he liked to say—which was how he became an unofficial emissary between SRS and the hunters who tried to poach on its government-protected land, who risked federal criminal charges for an eight-point buck, or worse, getting hosed by machine-gun-toting MPs who wheel up in jeeps at the sound of far-off gun reports, there to safeguard U.S. nuclear secrets more than the whitetail deer. Whit was a deft negotiator due to being a local himself but also, frankly, because poaching was part of his own personal ecology. When not playing the part of government employee he would, for a couple hundred bucks, take men out with him to hunt deer or turkey—regardless of season or size—on tracts of the 70,000 hectare reserve he knew to be unpatrolled for the day. Or at least where thought he knew, which was how he ran into James at St. Joseph's hospital on the day of Bradey's birth.

Inside the Sugar Shack, it was dank and dark as a gym locker, a male dormitory made up of one long bar, two rickety tables, and several tatty green stools. The face of the air conditioner rustled with colorful plastic streamers, blowing tepid air. A fine sweat seemed to cling on everything. They took their seats at the bar where Whit made brief introductions to the bartender and one or two other men. Non-committal head-nods and cold stares in James' direction. What they saw, of course, was a scrawny, pallid, pencil-pushing thirtysomething from Long Island, New York. The beaky nose, the nasal voice. Then Whit, diplomat that he was, added, *Jim here's recently in the family way*, and a lock turned. At hearing such news, these men whistled low through their teeth; they placed one hand to a sympathetic heart; they mumbled through beery grins, *Dead man walking*. They said, *Let us bow our heads and pray*. He might not have looked liked them, but he proved to be shackled to the same chain-gang of matrimony and fatherhood. A brother-in-arms, a cousin from some far-flung place. Like Idaho. James grimaced and nodded.

They listened to the politics of war on the radio. Protests at home, body counts abroad. It saturated the air, the silence and brooding. Outside those thick cement walls, thousands of miles overseas, Vietnam continued to grind toward its fatalistic never-ending conclusion. He smelled it in the sweat of the men around him, bent-shouldered around tin cans of beer, the masculinity and soured politics stinking from their pores like an infection. James found it reassuring, sharing this bond of angry male blood—even though he sat among them now in a short-sleeved oxford, the pocket stained purple from a leaky pen. James himself had marched down to the recruitment center early one morning in 1965 to enlist. He had puffed out his naked chest, hollow as a bird's, stood grandly on feet as flat as boneless steaks, barked out the unreadable letters of the eye chart, and immediately was 4F rejected. Then, he got the hell out. But the important factor here was not lost, especially in the realm of patriots—he *wanted* to go. In the Sugar Shack, other men would mumble largely the same: wife, family, or old football injuries had kept them from the duty that so many ridiculed or shirked. So they thought of themselves as the vanguard on the home front. This is how men are taught to build rapport, after all—by saluting the raised flag of a common complaint. Or more accurately, by rallying against a common enemy. For these particular men, that meant government, taxes, dried-up salaries, job losses, the shriveling death of local business, old family animosities, and outside interlopers. All those things that drained the virility, like succubi, of heterosexual male power. And while James technically fell into the last category, being an outsider, he pledged allegiance by grousing about that most common denominator of barroom complaint: women. Not only women, but five of them, and in-laws as well. All those invading forces—driving him out of his home. Well, he won the award for that. The men groaned; they slapped the bar, affirmed in their judgment of his character. There was a brief five seconds of hoopla and commiseration in which a sodden, loudmouthed twenty-year-old at the far end—married himself for the past three years—vowed to buy James five more beers, one for each of his miseries. Then most everyone turned his attention back to the bartender's radio, tucked amid the bottles of Johnny Walker, where it continued a report on the Pentagon Papers. Jeers and catcalls ensued.

"Well, Dr. Cullins," Whit said, tipping his can in tribute. "I would certainly hate to be in your shoes. A wife with her sisters is a dangerous combination. Nothing spells disaster faster than when women get with their own." Again Whit had that air of retired golf pro, like a vision of Bobby Jones, sagaciously tanned and wrinkled, dispensing advice. The cool and knowing demeanor, James thought, of a man who didn't need a long explanation to understand the whole story.

James scowled at the shelves of half-empty liquor bottles. "You've had experience with this then."

"Boy, I got my PhD in getting screwed. Take my last wife, you get her together with her sisters, any Saturday night, and it's all kinds of howling and laughing and carrying on. Man-hungry is what they got when sitting around together. Like they were still schoolgirls—or wolves, one of the two. And not hungry for any man they already had, that's for sure."

By now, a glaze of alcohol was taking hold in James' eyes. He said, "They all left their husbands behind—did you know that? Can you believe it?"

"What?"

"My wife's sisters."

"Yeah, I can believe it, that's what I'm saying. Anyway, at a certain age, these kind of women get boy-hungry. Like they weren't already feeling the change of life. But you see, I figured not Maureen, no sir. That girl's too good. She can joke and howl with the best of them, but would turn red as a beet if any man so much as walked by with his fly down in front of her."

"Taking off cross-country without your husband, without a second glance…that in itself is like an act of infidelity, don't you think? Really, it's like breaking the pact. It's like spitting on the sacred institution of marriage."

"I know, that's what I'm trying to tell you about. Anyway, Maureen ran off with some air conditioner repair-boy at least ten years younger, the one who was working on getting our place centralized. Recommended, I should add, by none other than Dear Sister Justine. Like she was passing him on from one of those swingers' forums out of certain disreputable publications, you know what I'm talking about?" Whit tapped the side of his glasses. "Anyway, I'd come around to her family's place to try and get things square, and those women wouldn't have nothing to do with me. Mother hens, clucked and sassed me right off the porch. Wouldn't let me even speak to her. And you know they had to have been talking Maureen into it that entire time, too. 'Go on and do it, girl. Life's too short.' Taking all this female empowerment business into recreational directions. Hell, she was the one begging to get married in the first place. Now I have to pay to keep those two shacked up in their little love nest out on Silver Bluff. Like a bait and switch—Me for the Money, Him for the Show. I can't even afford myself a can of corn niblets by the time my paycheck gets cut up each month."

"Christ," James said, his face glistening now. He sipped his beer, which had sweated down from chill to lukewarm. "And you said that was your last wife?"

Whit snorted and grinned. "God willing my last. You don't want to know about the other three."

At the far end of the bar, the senate hearings began to play, which caused the young rowdy to boo and chuck peanuts at the radio. The bartender, a vinegary old man, shouted at him and slapped a dishtowel against the counter.

Lowering his voice, James asked, "Do you think I should be worried?"

"Oh sure." Whit ordered another beer, took a mouthful, swished it around casually, and swallowed. "But if you want to diagnose your situation, you got to do it carefully. What do they drink?"

"I don't know. You can go to my liquor cabinet and count up the empty bottles."

"If your gin's gone, you got trouble. Only whores drink gin. Number two: you ever walk into the room and they all clam up?"

"Maybe. Why?"

"Mm-hm." Whit took another swig. "Ever say anything to your wife you wish you hadn't? You know, when you get too hotheaded?"

"What do you mean?"

"I mean that she can use against you, but hasn't realized yet. Small things. The kind of thing that's not a big deal until it gets a little encouragement from her sisters. Pumping her up with doubt and distrust. Once that happens, it won't matter if you get them out of your house or not, because the damage will already have been done. Now, don't get me wrong—I'm not a misogynist. I love women. I respect them. But they're evil. Women listen in their sleep, Jim. Did you know that? Nothing turns off. Do you talk in your sleep? If so, you're already screwed. Got all your dirt. They're the worst kind of opportunists, exploit all your weaknesses. Not even their fault, probably. They're probably just hardwired for it, after centuries of having to negotiate a man's world; figuring out where their power lies and where it don't, and negotiating all those back alleyways. A long history of angst is what we're talking about here, which is a dangerous thing. So then they getcha when you're most vulnerable. They wait for it, they believe in timing. They wait until your fortieth birthday. They wait until your car drops its transmission.

They wait until you lose a job to tell you they been cheating. The minute you're soaking your troubles in the bathtub, they admit they're leaving your sorry ass. Two words through a bathroom door. That's it. That's all she wrote. Leaving you naked, shivering and wet, worse off than the day you were born." Whit cackled to himself, pressing the can to his lips. "Oh, sweet Jesus, they do believe in some timing."

Another uproar near the radio and shower of debris, cans clinking to the floor. This time the bartender grabbed a baseball bat, his silvery comb-over flying up, and silently pointed his weapon at the young buck at the end of the bar like he was aiming for a homer.

Whit let out a short, foamy laugh, palming his lips dry. Then, puzzled by the menacing expression gathered on James' face, Whit slapped his shoulder and gave the perfunctory caveat, the ending to every story he had ever told in that bar: "But I wouldn't worry about it. You're still young."

* * *

After that, James began smothering his wife every chance he got. Groggily fondling her in the dark, sliding on top, tenting their bodies with the bed sheet. Caressing her awake at five in the morning for a brief coitus before he had to leave for work. Only then could he leave his wife with some confidence, through that old catalyst of control: sex. Between work and home, the Sugar Shack became a regular stop those few weeks that the Sisters Robicheaux occupied the house, one that James kept secret; but to be clear, this was about the need for control, not the story of my father becoming an alcoholic. Alcoholism itself wouldn't know what to do with James. Every trip he would have only two cans of near-beer, maybe three, and then he ordered nothing but 7-Ups with cherry. In the dank recesses of the Sugar Shack, in a bar full of roughnecks, my father ordered Shirley Temples by name—and everyone loved it. Regardless of what he told Annie, of what he thought he left behind as a child, James still carried the universe around in his pocket.

No, what James needed more than beer, more than musky male camaraderie, was a secret to restore the balance in his favor—a vantage point to observe others from—and regain a sense of himself. He sauntered home those evenings around seven or later, once the women had retired to the living room; he made his hellos; he scavenged the stove for a cold supper. After, he would stoop to kiss Antoinette on the cheek, then squish in close to Carlie on the sofa for a few minutes, surveying the faces and conversations with an animal gaze. Aware that he was in the game—as much at home now as at work—he gauged reactions, looked for telltale glances his way. He smiled unctuously, looking for the Judas at his table. Sometimes he would pop on the television set, just to piss on everyone's conversation. "Oh, James, crank that down, would you? You can't have everything your way." A remark by Nan that he silently ignored. They all knew he had been working overtime at the Site so few questions were ever raised, but each evening James lingered on the sofa long enough to drape an arm around Carlie, wanting her to smell the beer on him, wanting to flaunt the musk of his regained autonomy. Wanting her not to know the specifics, but to sniff out that he had a secret. To stumble with the realization that the world was not a direct line between his work and her sisters—to *recognize* it—which then makes one's autonomy complete. But all she did was give him room. Carlie smiled, chatted with her sisters, and patted him on the knee.

For her part, Carlie couldn't be concerned. She had a newborn baby who needed feeding every few hours, napping, changing; she had a house full of siblings; she had a mother-in-law around twenty-four hours a day who acted even more aggrieved than her husband. Annie had been staying at the house ever since Carlie screwed the doors in place, whereas the sisters still slept at the hotel. Regardless, while James was at work, Annie behaved like an ousted politico. No longer at the center of her child's universe, she tucked herself into a corner and knitted afghans all day, clicking her teeth. Yes, she came to the table at lunch, but chewed solemnly while the other women chatted. She would sit by the glass doors and gaze out, saying nothing. Waiting, it seemed, solely for James to return home. When he did, Annie wasn't any more verbose, just more at ease, content to sit near him like an old family dog. As a family of matriarchs, the Robicheaux women never quite gave up on trying to include James' mother in conversation; Annie gave, dry-single word answers to any direct question, then resumed clicking her teeth. A sound, Carlie thought, like water dripping down a deep stone well: echoing its resentful silence. She dwelled more and more on how Annie had shut out her own sister over a silly argument. And how it might happen to them.

Shortly before their departure, the Robicheaux sisters (sans Carlie) shared one last hurrah with a daytrip to Charleston. In the rare quiet of that afternoon, Carlie prepared to wake Bradey for his feeding when she saw her mother-in-law's tiny body creep into the nursery. She watched from the door as Annie leaned over the cradle. The older woman didn't dare touch the rails, but peered into it, as if the slightest disturbance could disrupt his peace. Then Carlie realized that she wasn't simply watching Bradey sleep—she was watching hawkishly, and listening, as if waiting for the exact instant when something would go wrong. Waiting perhaps for the slightest sputter or spit bubble to signal respiratory failure. After a long moment, Annie lifted her face to Carlie and grinned. Then she spoke perhaps her only words to Carlie in the past three weeks. "He breathes good. Hear that? What a pair of lungs."

Gently, Carlie moved beside her and inhaled to prepare herself for what must be done. "Annie—Mom. I got a proposition for you," she began. "I know you're mostly by yourself up there in New York, and well, we'd love for you to be closer to your grandchildren—that is, if you'd like to. I mean, if you're interested in moving to Copeland to be closer to your son and Bradey, then we'd love to have you. You could move in with us as long as you needed to, we could help you find a place and get you all set up. I know it might be a big change, but that way, you wouldn't have to feel so far away." While Carlie explained, the big smile on Annie's face slowly drooped and, for an instant, Carlie thought she might cry.

After a considerable pause Annie regained her voice and said, "Oh, honey, I couldn't do that."

"I'm serious, Mom. You could if you wanted."

But Annie only laughed, saying *Ahhh* as if Carlie were a prankster, and patted her hand.

"I want you to know," she said. "You're a part of our lives, and we want to keep it that way. You'll always have a place with us here."

Annie opened her mouth to speak, but then closed it. She tucked her fists under her arms, suddenly cold. "I think Butch might be home early today. Don't you? I bet he will." After giving Carlie's knuckles one last pat, she walked out of the room, absently rubbing her arms.

The next morning, Carlie saw her mother-in-law standing at the edge of the yard with her suitcase and hat, waiting on a taxi. She dropped the laundry basket and ran to get James.

He jumped up from his coffee and cinched together a bathrobe as Carlie explained the situation. "You did what?"

"She's up by the mailbox. All I did was invite her to move down yesterday—it's something you've talked about before, I didn't think it would be a problem."

"It's because I should have invited her. Why do you do these things without me?" James cracked the deadbolt on the front door and jogged outside. "Ma! What's going on? What's wrong?" He slowed as he neared her.

It wasn't gardenias that morning—or if it was, Annie didn't let on. She didn't answer for a moment, but simply stared down the road with her mouth clamped tight. "It's your Aunt Zinny," she said at last. "She's dead."

James sighed and felt the last of his patience run dry. "Mom," he said, propping himself against the mailbox. "If you want to go, then fine, all right? We're not going to stop you. We'll take you to the train station, whatever you want. But you don't need to go through this performance."

Antoinette kept her eyes locked to the road. Her voice was small and dry. "I know she's dead."

"Look, just drop that stuff, okay? Or should I call Aunt Zinny right now? Maybe I should call her and put the phone to your ear."

At that, she finally blew—all the steam from her three-week visit—and wailed, "What do you know? I called last night!"

James straightened, "Wait, you called Zinny? What made you…"

"Your Uncle Herb picked up. Says she'd been in the hospital for over a month—a month. And I didn't know *nothing*. They couldn't get a hold of me, didn't know where I was, not after…"

"What do you mean they couldn't get a hold of you?"

"They didn't want to, Smarty!" From around the bend of pines, a checkered cab crawled up the road. Annie kept staring as though she didn't see it. "For the funeral," she said. "All over. All done. It was last week, and I didn't even know."

The cab braked, squealing to a slow halt in front of them. After idling for a moment, the driver leaned over the passenger seat and pumped down the window. Gently, James placed his hand over Annie's thin knuckles and took the suitcase from her. He waved the driver on; he'd take his mother himself.

* * *

One by one, the sisters departed. They packed their clothes, hoisted their children and battered luggage, and kissed their goodbyes. They floated out of Carlie's life like dandelion seeds. Francine, Ruthie, Nan, Thelma—she named their names as they went.

After the last sister had left, the house was still and quiet. She and James took up no words. Bradey's month-old voice made their place all the more empty. Grunts and wailing, hiccups of air.

They stood at the double vanity before the mirror, preparing for bed. James squirted nasal drops while Carlie flossed meticulously.

"Finally, we can get back to normal," James said, his voice sounding like dead air in the middle of the night. He tilted his head back to massage the saline into each sinus. Carlie said nothing. He picked up a toothbrush, wet it, and streaked paste on its bristles. "This has all been way too much." He began brushing vigorously. "It's like they were purposely trying to sabotage everything."

Carlie unwound a new string of floss. "They? Meaning my sisters?"

"Yeah, your sisters." He spat. "My mom, too. Christ, all the theatrics. From the first day, everyone barging in and thinking they can take control of what we're trying to build here. I still can't believe you asked Mom to live with us—I mean, eventually, yeah absolutely, but *Jesus*. Imagine if she went ahead and said yes."

A subtle, tingling curiosity crawled over Carlie's skin, as if she were once again looking at the house blueprints to find something nebulously off. She held the floss in her fingers, numb where it wound around the tips. After a moment she asked, "What are we trying to build?" with the dawning awareness that they just might be working on separate projects.

James stilled his hand but kept the toothbrush dangling in one corner of his mouth. "A *family*," he said.

"James, they are family."

"But they are not *our* family." He removed the toothbrush, studying his wife in the mirror. "They're *your* sisters, it's my mother. It's time we got on with our lives and made a family of our own here." He returned to cleaning his teeth with the unspoken emphasis: *unbelievable.*

He was right. Carlie couldn't believe it.

3

The seeds of my father's paranoia, of his distrust, germinated over a long season. Longer than his acquaintance with Whit Shirley, longer than the Sisters' household occupation. Months. Years, even. And yet, Whit was right. It's true: the people we love will one day betray us. They will throw away our tokens of love; they will knock us down while running from the fire of their own bad hearts; they will stoop to selfish and ignoble deeds, and lie. Such things happen. But what do we get for being right about them? A lifetime of looking at our lovers—across the silent breakfast table, riding wordlessly in the car—always anticipating the knife.

After lunch, Freddie trails behind us, chewing his lip in a preoccupied sweat, when "The Girl from Ipanema" dances from his coat pocket for the twelfth time today. When he checks his phone, he yelps, laughing. It's not Henri this time. It's a callback. A Chad, or Thad, something I didn't quite catch. As soon as he picks up, Freddie's a different man: energetic, jovial, and casually warming up his pitch. He catches my eye and waves us on. When we don't move, he apologizes to Chad and mutes the phone. "Go on ahead. Go, change," he says. "This will take a little while, but once I'm done here, we can break out the champagne. I guaran-fucking-tee it."

My jeans are still gummy and darkly stained by soup, so I continue with Mom. I lay my hand on her shoulder as I guide the wheelchair along. For many years, Carlie saw her long suffering relationship with James as an exercise in virtue. I can hear her telling me: *It's just what people do, babe.* Sticking together, toughing it out, weathering the storm. But what's selfless about two people staying together for thirty years, waging a daily war of attrition, making each other miserable? What exactly is being honored there? What happens when the storm is, in fact, two irreconcilable personalities?

Back in the hotel, I peel out of my jeans and hang them over the sink. I keep the suite door open and one ear toward Mom while I change. When I return, I have a fat black photo album under my arm. It's something I pulled aside while packing the condo, something I haven't seen in decades. This album, one volume from a set of twenty, are from my mother's many years of cataloging her side of the family. I'm not sure how much of her collection my father kept and moved with them to Florida. But I only recall boxing about five albums. As for the antiques she preserved over the years—the family milking stools, the telephone tables, the mantel clocks—I saw none.

I wheel Mom beside the bed, by the window, where we can sit together. The pages are filled with black and white photographs of great aunts and uncles, of small barefoot children, of dour faces in bonnets and overalls, of ropey men on porch steps or behind plows. I can't identify any of them, except for my great-grandparents and one or two of my grandmother Mary Alice, when she was young. However, my mother has kept meticulous notes under each image. So we flip through them, the album on her lap. She takes great interest, tapping her finger to specific photos that raise a thought, squinting at them. Mumbling indistinct affirmations or questions to herself.

I check my watch, glance at the door. I try to get Mom to tell me stories about the people in the photos, but she mostly hangs in a quiet reverie, stuttering a single word or two. Child, is one. Great woman, is another. And a whole series of *yeses*. I'm not sure how many names take shape in her mind anymore. We come to the end and she opens the album again, from the start. She slowly wanders from page to page twice more, and still no sign of Freddie.

I sit beside her but can't pay attention to the album anymore. The day is getting late, the light longer across the wall. I want us to see the house. In his absence, I make a mental bet with Freddie: as long as Mom is still interested in the album, we won't leave him behind.

Nearly an hour and a half passes before Freddie returns. I hear him slip into our adjacent suite. He stifles a chest cough, sounding breathless. Another moment passes and he quietly appears in the doorway.

By now, I've stretched out on Mom's bed, my arms and legs crossed, waiting. He reeks of smoke. From the slick sheen on his face, it looks like he's eaten an entire pack of cigarettes, filters and all.

I don't budge from the bed. "Champagne?"

He scans the room, his eyes lingering on the mundane details. He shakes his head imperceptibly. "Small fish," he says. "He wasn't reliable. But I did get another name. Another lead."

He stands as if waiting to be invited in. I notice something in his hand, dangling at his side: a flat paper bag. An envelope, really.

"We need to get going," I say. "Can you help me get Mom into the cab?"

"Wait." He raises the envelope and takes two tentative strides toward the bed. "A present," he says, brightening a little, and hands it to me. I sit up. He briefly regards the photo album in Mom's lap, a nervous, distracted smile on his face. "You looked like you could use a pick-me-up."

The envelope is paper thin and unsealed. I blow it open and shake its contents free. A bumper sticker slides into my hand. It's of a confederate battle flag, except the crossbars are set against the exuberant colors of a gay pride rainbow. I set the envelope down beside me. "Where on earth did you get this?"

"Headshop," he says.

"Not even two hours in this town, and you manage to locate the one headshop."

He shrugs, but is clearly pleased with himself. "For all the Southern Gentility, this place has got some pretty disreputable establishments."

I simply nod and hesitate, then carefully slip it back into the bag.

"My Confederate Fag." He kisses me and grins. "Let's stick it to the back of the truck."

4

Here's the straight juice. Avery's not keen on me talking to you, so I'll be quick to the point. When we got together, it really wasn't under the most honorable intentions, I admit. One, I'll be honest here, I wasn't in the best financial straits at the time. I mean, if you think big, if you have plans, if you want to try to *do* something with your short time on earth, do something for the world, too, while you're at it, then that takes capital. Money runs off me like water. It's my element, is what I'm saying. Look, people get this wrong about me: I don't need it, not in a monomaniacal sort of way. I just live it in. It makes me move. Fuck, it makes the entire world move, it's how any of us get from Point A to Point B, and anyone who thinks that's distasteful is in la-la land. So yeah, there was something both cute and endearing and, yes, fiscally and erotically attractive about little Avery with his three separate savings accounts—the Vacation Fund, the Dream Home Fund, the Emergency Fund—his 401(k), his Roth IRA, his belief in economic *terra firma*. The man's always got money on his brain and in his pocket, don't let his day job fool you. And before your imagination runs away with you, I want to make it clear: I have never asked Avery for money. Not once. I mean, yes, of course, I did before we were really together. But after? Not a chance. I have my principles. That's not what we're about.

As for Two: honestly, I really dig short dudes. They're compact, they're neat, and most of all, they've always got something to prove. I love a man who's got something to prove. It means he's always thinking, he's moving, he's acting and reacting.

Related to Two, you probably don't want to hear about your son doing the nasty, so I'll skip that part.

So yeah, that's where we began, and I don't want to get sappy but—I don't know how to say this. Here: do you know what it's like to have someone make coffee for you in the morning? And I don't mean like the morning-after, silk kimono stuff, like Oh, Look, I Have Made Coffee For You, See What I Have Done for Us? But I mean, just make coffee. And it's always there. Granted, it's cold by the time I get up, but it's always there. He even wraps a little dish towel around the coffee press to try to keep it warm for me, even though it'll be hours before I see it. And he used to pack me lunch. Let me say that again: he used to pack me lunch. I don't know if you know this, but I don't exactly have regular working hours. He'd pack a little lunch for himself and tote it to work, thrifty Avery, to eat with the other drones, and he'd make me one too. An identical little lunch on the second shelf of the fridge.

I must sound like an asshole to you. Of course you don't know what that's like. You were the one always making the coffee or packing the lunch. But I want him to know that I appreciate it. I've always appreciated it, even if I never touched his silly little sandwiches. This is different for me. I guess I'm getting old, getting tired. Or comfortable. No, these aren't the right words. I've said a lot of shit in my life, a lot of it more eloquent than what I'm dishing to you right; some of it less. But what it comes down to is this: I love him. I love your son. Sure I've loved other guys—many at the same time—but for the first time in my life, I'm happy to just *be* with somebody. When I met you in Florida, when I saw how Avery acted around you, how you changed him, I realized for the first time that I had something to lose. I really had something that I could lose.

So here's the deal: you watch my back, and I'll rub your bunions or whatever it is that you need. Because the honest truth is, I am scared shitless. You scare the shit out of me. Your son is starting to scare the shit out of me. He stares right through me now, like he's ready to leave me on the side of the road. Like he already has left me behind. I know he thinks I'm a fuck-up, but we're all fucked up. Him, you, me. It's just part of the natural condition.

Shit. Here he comes. Look at him stare—who looks so cold-blooded carrying a bag of Hardee's, for chrissake? All right, the bottom line is, he adores you. And I feel like I'm hanging by a thread here. I feel like you're the only chance I've got left. So if you can show me a little love, I will...you know. I'll do what I can. Remember me. Because I need to keep my head down from here on out. You won't hear another peep out of me for the rest of this trip, I promise you that.

5

By the time I return to the cab, all is quiet. It feels like I've walked into the middle of a conversation. Freddie avoids eye contact, feigning interest in the line of cars that crawl up to the take-out window. He bites the cuticle on his thumb. I pass Mom a chocolate milkshake, which she takes with both hands. After our disastrous lunch, I decided to get her something quick to eat. It took me a solid ten minutes to decipher what she might like.

"Here." I hand Freddie a small bag. He peeks in and the smell of warm grease blooms inside the cab.

"Fries?"

"My blood sugar's crashing. I just want two or three. You take the rest."

Noisily, he digs in and brings a few french fries to his mouth. But after the first bite, he pauses in his chewing, staring at the potatoes as if seeing his own reflection. Freddie drops them back into the bag, morosely rubbing the salt crystals from his fingertips. "I don't need these," he says. He crumples the bag shut and sets it on the dash, out of arm's reach, in front of Mom.

"Suit yourself."

We take the bypass to the south side of town, heading toward the old house. In between the red lights, I punch the dial and we listen to some state politician chastise same-sex parents for a while. The radio static is reminiscent of that feverish night many years ago from my earlier life: the same airwaves, more or less, the same air. The same town. Fragments of experience now mirrored, reflected in reverse. *A child is not like getting a puppy*, the voice says, drifting through the speakers. *You can't just take it back to the pound when it's lost its fun.*

Home again. Too bad no one told Stacey and Yvette that they really needed a dachshund in their lives, not a son.

I reach in front of Mom and punch the radio off.

Freddie speaks up, his voice to the window, "Enlightened populace in this state."

"We can marry here," I say. "You can't say the same for Cleveland."

I hit a speed bump too fast and the truck shudders. We all bounce in our seats. Freddie slips into nibbling on his cuticle again. After another bend in the road, he perks up from a moment of quiet reverie. "Let's do it," he says. I can't see his face around Mom, can't see if he's smirking at his own reflection. I can't hear any irony in his tone, either, and the absence unsettles me. There is, however, a quickening sensation to his silence. A pins-and-needles of discovery.

"Do what?"

"Tonight," he says. "Today. Let's go to the courthouse here. Why not?" He then leans on the dashboard, around Mom, to gauge my expression. I keep my eyes on the road. "I mean, hell, this is our big trip, right? We're changing lives, getting into something new now. Let's mark the occasion, let's paint the town. And we've already got a witness right here." He shifts to include Mom, placing an awkward hand on her knee. Startled from her thoughts, she pulls the straw from her mouth and stares Freddie full in the face. She twists the straw between her fingers, watching him. "I bet your mom would love to see you get married, wouldn't she? Don't you think so?" As we near a stop sign, he looks to her, "What do you think, Carlie?"

"*Don't*," I say, pumping the brakes. We come to a jerking halt. Freddie slides forward, and I throw my arm out to keep Mom from meeting the dash. I lower my voice, collecting myself. "Don't play with her like that."

Slowly, Mom slips the straw back into her mouth, scrutinizing me, then Freddie, then back to me. She wipes a small dribble of milkshake from her chin. She says, "Maybe?"

I cut my eyes to Freddie. He says softly, "I wasn't playing with her."

I don't say anything. We leave the intersection. Freddie sneaks a glance at me from behind Mom's head, expectantly. "Four years ago," I say, "you would have been spouting the same nonsense as that idiot on the radio. You once called Emile a freeloader, if I remember correctly."

"That was about kids," he says. "Who wants kids? This is different."

"I can't take you seriously."

"I am being serious," he says. "I'm telling you: I'm being serious. I mean it."

When I don't respond, Freddie falls silent. He looks sick, pallid. I want to ask if he's all right—I want to ask what the hell has gotten into him—but before I can do either, he snatches the bag of fries from the dashboard and slouches against the door.

"Here we are," I say. "This is it. This is the turn."

We enter the old neighborhood. As we cruise between the hills and pines, I am so giddy that I feel close to vomiting. A peculiar mix of familiarity and change unnerves me, and I have the urge to recite the street names, to catalog the old neighbors' houses—the Stovers, the Gentrys, the Shellbanks—but I keep it to myself. Mom chews on the plastic straw. Something like consternation knots her forehead, or maybe brain-freeze, while watching the yards pass by. I talk to her, ask her what she remembers. When Carlie and James drove into this neighborhood for the first time, they saw only a few fenced lots with a dozen horse heads leaning over the rails, shaking off the flies. Decades later, all the lots are developed, of course. Houses and horse stables are neatly pressed together on an acre of land. Immaculate lawns, smooth blacktop, and American flags in the front yard. The horses are still here, stupified. Idling behind their fences like oversized lapdogs, wearing blankets and blinders.

"I don't think I ever heard my father say the word 'horse.' Isn't that odd?" I scrutinize the houses for familiar details, signs of change. Most, I think, have expanded paddocks now. "Not once in my entire life. We lived surrounded by them, and I can't remember a single time when he uttered the word 'horse.' Maybe it was an act of denial. Did Dad ever talk about the horses?"

She swallows thickly, chocolate gathering at her lips, and says, "Maybe? Maybe yes."

"I have absolutely no idea what he thought of horses. I know he hated dogs. He was a staunch opponent of me getting a dog. And I think the same probably went for children. I don't think he ever wanted them," I say. "Or, he wanted children. Wife and kids, the package deal, that sort of thing. He just never wanted having them around. Too distracting, I think. Too much maintenance."

Freddie quietly digs his hand into the bag, chewing. "Let's not go down this path again."

"No path. Just an idle remark."

Freddie shifts against the door, popping another fry into his mouth. We all lean into the next sharp turn, nearing our old street, and I can feel my heart spastically jumping. Then Freddie clears his throat and says, "Okay. If marriage is out, how about this. When we get back to Cleveland, let's go to the pound. Let's go to the baby pound and pick out a nice, chubby, towheaded two year old. Or maybe a Chinese baby. I hear they're still pretty available, with all that state-mandated baby ditching stuff. We'll name her Spot. You, your mother, Spot and me. We'll be one big happy."

I watch a foal galloping in its paddock as we pass by. "The turtle will be jealous," I say.

"We'll get one for her, too. And when they cease to be entertaining, we can build a race track. Pin numbers to their bibs. Can you imagine a corral full of two year olds? I bet they'd love to chase a mechanical bunny. They'd go nuts. We'd make a mint."

"Toddler races. Ever the entrepreneur."

He blows a kiss, then licks his fingers. "Just an idle remark."

It's been almost twenty years since I've seen these houses, these streets. The last time I was here, I was an eighteen year old leaping from my father's car and literally heading for the woods. An anxious nausea creeps into my throat and I can barely keep my hands steady on the wheel. I want to fall out of the truck and kiss the asphalt. I want to laugh at the people who live here and hug them at the same time, scorn them for all their suburban anxieties. For instance: look at the signs! All these signs! This is a subdivision with no road outlets, no through-traffic, but there are signs posted everywhere. Signs that assure this property is protected by an electrified invisible fence. Neighborhood watch signs. Signs that forbid dogs to poop. Several real estate signs aerate neighboring lawns with their black metal prongs. They seem to vie for attention. There are also equestrian caution signs. Big yellow diamonds with black horse silhouettes, as if this is somehow more visible than an eight-hundred-pound animal with a human attached.

They're a menace. The horses, I mean. I've grown up around them, have seen the neighbors trot them behind our house on sunny days, have attempted to be on friendly terms with them as a child. But their heads look like feet. They are large and unwieldy and easily spooked. "Spooked," of course, means they want to kill you for deigning to walk in their general vicinity. And if they don't wind up crushing your skull, then you have to put up with the people who own them. The *Equestrians*. Those who casually drop polo or dressage into conversations, who acquire and board their animals the way some people collect vintage cars. Or, they cultivate a different kind of class performance: wearing sun hats and dungarees (they *would* call them dungarees) smeared with dirt from a morning of hard labor. Getting back to nature by grooming a $35,000 beast. Yes, nothing says pride like a horse. Quivering its haughty haunches, lifting the tight silken tail, and letting loose with the first few steaming apples of the morning. To nobly shit where one stands. That should be our motto. I need a bumper sticker that says that.

Through a final stretch of neighboring homes, pines, and pampas grass, the house comes into view. From this distance, it looks like a small party is being thrown at the Cullins' old residence. Cars dot the driveway and disappointment plunges into my chest. This will be it then. I had harbored some fantasy of knocking on the door. Of speaking with the owners. Of taking my mother inside and re-connecting her—here, at last—to me. But now, we can only crawl by, then turn this lumbering albatross around in the cul-de-sac and pass the house for a final glance before returning to the hotel. Tourists to our own history, staring through the fishbowl of a stale-smelling truck cab, kept at arm's length.

"Sweet Jesus." I hammer the brakes. Everything poorly secured in the payload, every shoebox, picture frame, and table lamp, clatters to a metallic halt.

"What?" Freddie loses a few fries in his lap and bolts upright. "What's wrong?"

Of all the signs in the neighborhood, staked in our yard is a placard, decorated with an iconic horse head and palmetto tree, that reads: *For Sale*. Thirty years ago, when my parents first envisioned this barn of a house, they saw a new beginning, the frames and trusses on which to build their lives. Now, a fever chill shivers up my forearms. We have come full circle in the vision of foolish Cullins family endeavors, where past and future collide and blast into a thousand confusing possibilities.

"They're having an open house," I say, trying to grasp the magnitude of this thing while Mom pokes into the bottom of the cup, sucking the last sweet milk crystals of her shake. "They're having an open house—of our house."

For a long time we all sit in the cab, watching the house. We watch a scattering of people come and go, lingering on the porch steps. We watch a large man pull a flier from the box, hustle back to his idling subcompact, and then motor on. We watch as if the owners themselves might spontaneously come out to greet us.

The engine ticks, cooling. Freddie whispers, "You want to buy the place. I can smell it."

"No," I say. "It would never fit in the truck."

I expected a lot of things. That the house would be bulldozed to the ground. That it would have been gutted and reshaped. But I never expected it to look the same. Carlie sucks on her straw, slurping at the empty bottom. I rub her back, kneading the muscle between her shoulders in a comforting motion. As if gearing ourselves for an autopsy report. It takes a while for me to notice the changes. Our old driveway has been paved over, bordered with ornamental grasses. The dark wood façade has been replaced with wood-grained vinyl siding. The rickety balcony which Mr. Clarence once jury-rigged has now been completely removed and, in place of the door, an Art Deco stained glass window has been installed, sparkling with blues and amethysts. We watch a young couple leave the front door, studying a brochure between them.

Freddie rubs his eye. "Well?" he says. "This is what we're here for. Let's go make a scene."

"I have no intention of making a scene."

"Oh, please."

Distractedly, I open the door about an inch and then close it again. "Mom, do you want to go in? This is our house, Ma, remember? This is the old house. We're in Copeland," I say. Sandwiched between Freddie and me, she squints intently at the house.

Freddie whispers, "Do you want me to get the wheelchair?"

"I don't want to rush her."

She understands something there, I can tell. The house where she lived for thirty years as a wife and mother. She oversaw the whole development; she stained and painted and wallpapered; she cut carpet, and hammered nails, and nearly delivered her firstborn on the kitchen floor. I realize I'm sweating, my spine damp against the vinyl seat.

"What do you say, Mom? Shall we go in?" I crack the door again, just a little, enough to hear the rubber seal pop.

She stares at the house for a moment longer and says, "No." Simple and flat as that. Almost a whisper of air. "No, thank you." Her tone and enunciation, her nervous glances reveal that she is never sure who might be a stranger. Even those of us with some flicker of familiarity. She can't be sure. She can never trust fully.

Gently, I set her cup on the dash. I take her cold hands in mine and warm her knuckles, so that she will look at me. "I know we've been on the road a long time today. And we still have farther to go before we're through. But you can trust me, Mom. I am your son. I will not let anything bad happen to you. I promise. I am still your son."

She looks at my face, as if for the first time. Even stronger and more attentive than in the wee hours this morning, when I knelt beside her wheelchair in the nursing home. A clear, pained light cracks in her eyes. She says: "Bradey?"

She slips her hands from mine, limp now, and raises her fingertips to her face. She grazes her cheek, as if touching a bruise.

The vinyl wheezes as I shift against the seat. Slowly, I pull my door tight until it clicks shut. I start the engine. "Let's go," I say. "Let's get out of here."

6

The years fall away. How does this happen, so unnoticed? They slip by while we're distracted by a thousand daily errands. While we're in line at the grocery store, checking out the tabloid covers; while we pack lunch the night before work. Each morning we grease the gears and hear the whispery whir of the bike chain, they slip further away. For my parents, their years got lost between preschool and the purchase of new toddler clothes, between mortgage payments, and new cars and the maintenance of clunkers. They came off with the wedding ring to wash dishes and then got bumped, rattling down the drain. They were burned in the exhaust of the mid-morning commute to work. As Bradey grew, so did James' research: he invented seven new processes, licensed new patents, appeared in trade magazines, and was awarded a snazzy paperweight for outstanding achievement in the field of nuclear glass and microwave technologies. His team grew, too: half a dozen research assistants, lower level technicians, and interns, with Whit still on as a primary. The Rambler, amazingly, was still rambling: a living icon of their youth and union.

For Carlie, the years had furnished few acquaintances. There were James' colleagues and coworkers, and the wives, of course, the preschool mothers, the immediate neighbors. Faces traded and friends swapped like gift exchanges, like white elephant parties. The neighborhood swelled. Fifty new houses had been built, with as many new families. With them, she tried a fitful variety of volunteer organizations, which always petered out in deference to caring for Bradey.

By the time Bradey was two years old, they talked of a new baby. James begged off, ("It's just not a good time right now") spearheading two major new projects at the site. Carlie took Bradey to half-day preschool, where she discovered half the children were named Bradey, even some of the girls. The following year, they enrolled him in a private Episcopal school. ("I thought you didn't believe in that mumbo jumbo," Carlie reminded him, smirking. To which James replied, "Are you kidding me? Those people have deep pockets. If we want Bradey to get a good education, this is the way to go.") Within four short years, Bradey had developed into a child-shaped wrecking ball, a flash of shaggy black hair and dirty pink toes. He careened through the house whenever he heard the mailman brake at the top of the yard, whenever cardinals sang at the patio birdbath, whenever Carlie called him; they heard his bare feet beating down the hall in their sleep. Carlie and James could only watch, amazed. The boy had an infectious glee which couldn't be rubbed off, even when caught, even when his cheeks were scrubbed with a wet dishtowel to de-crust the seemingly permanent smears of ketchup and mustard. In short, the child had only one direction: forward. A tiny scar shone on his left cheek where he had a face-to-face collision with a neighborhood schnauzer at only two years old. At four, they installed a deadbolt on the balcony door to prevent him from blasting off into an early demise.

Currently, he buzzed past Carlie's legs, squealing *save me!* as James growled and gave chase. He, James, didn't catch his wife's cold expression as he ran around the table, so she called to him, low: "James." In her hands she held a stack of birthday invitations for Bradey's kindergarten class. Each was neatly addressed and decorated in cowboy stickers. All week they had been going at it, arguing about what to do for their child's fourth birthday party. Or, more specifically, Carlie had already planned a party and James vetoed it. Last night had been their biggest blow-out yet. "James!"

"What?" he said, a little breathless. He let Bradey tear into the living room without him. "We're just playing."

Carlie kneaded her right eye. It was already a lost cause—his birthday was the following day. But she didn't want her point to go unheard. Which was how their conversations went as of late. "We can't just keep him boxed up in this house. He needs children his own age to play with. Not a thirty-five year old."

James partially ignored this, watching after Bradey in the other room. "He has kids his own age. That's what school is for."

"You know what I'm talking about." She slapped the invites down on the table.

James groaned, rolling his neck. "I thought we settled this? Look, next year, a party. All right? A big party. With clowns and wagon rides and a million five year olds tearing the whole house apart. But for one more year, let's just have him to ourselves, okay?"

Daddy! from the other room.

"GrrROWR!" James said and stalked into the living room. After a moment, Carlie popped open the trash can, scooped up the invitations, and dumped them in.

In this way, the discussion dropped, just as other things had been dropped, too. Time alone together. A weekend picnic. A pool membership. Ideas for small vacations that came and went: driving into the mountains to see the autumn leaves. Camping in the coastal maritime forests. More significant plans got swallowed whole: the dream of scattering his father's ashes somewhere in the Finger Lakes. (This, he had always promised Annie. However, Grandpa Cullins remained on the bookshelf until I was seven before finally being interred twenty miles down the road.) For Carlie, she missed attending Ruthie's second wedding. (After another blow-out fight, involving some embarrassment with the neighbors, who were apparently within earshot, even with an acre and a half between them.) From there, compromise became a weapon of reciprocity. Carlie struck back and fought with James to get rid of his high school science and tennis trophies, that they didn't have the space for such junk. Just let them go. Then came the declining health of Carlie's father. (*You have five sisters and a mom looking after him. Carlie, honestly, what would you do there?*) Eventually James capitulated on that one, using his vacation days to travel with Carlie to Louisiana, only to find himself alone one afternoon with his Alzheimic father-in-law, desperately trying to convince the older man not to pee in the house plants. Battles won and lost. Dreams postponed.

More than the routines and mundanities, this, ultimately, was how time passed for James and Carlie, how it passes for us all: by simply letting go.

* * *

Inside the kitchen Carlie was frosting a birthday cake, attempting to recreate the round yellow face of H.R. Pufnstuf, a children's puppet she found mildly disturbing. She shifted hands with the pastry bag, squeezing tighter. Its purple-ringed eyes reminded her of broken blood vessels, black-eyes. The shining badges of domestic violence or alcohol abuse she saw on her neighborhood street growing up. Through the kitchen window, she heard James and Bradey playing with the wiffle ball set he received for his fourth birthday. She kept one eye on the side yard, hearing faintly, "Strike three! Oh no, you're out!" James groaned in the playful tone he used to dramatize Bradey's success or failure. "But wait! We can try this again—new batter! Hold tight of the bat. Now don't let it go this time." There was a pause while renegotiating the bat and stance. Then a slightly impatient fluster, the beats of his speech hardening. "No, Bradey, grip it. Grip it tight."

She had been noticing bruises lately. Large purple veined welts on Bradey's hips and legs when she put him to bed. The first time she saw one, she was almost impressed. "Wow, kiddo. You got to be more careful. What did you do, jump out of an airplane today?" The second time she noticed, it was less charming. Cautiously, she asked, "Bradey, honey, when did this happen?" Bradey just grinned sheepishly and squirmed into his PJs. The third and forth bruises to appear kept her silent. Early on, she had asked James more or less directly, "Do you know where that bruise came from?" Sitting in his red recliner, distracted by the television, he gave a non-committal, "Nah, what bruise?" She didn't ask again.

Carlie found herself staring at the phone, darkly daydreaming, purple icing streaked down one elbow. There were the numbers for poison control, for the fire department, for the ambulance, and for the police taped on the inside of the receiver.

James came inside, sliding the heavy glass door shut behind him. She peeked through the window to see Bradey sitting by himself in the yard, dejectedly plucking weeds.

"Carlie," James said. "I think there's something wrong with our son."

She kept bent over the pastry bag. "Just because he isn't athletically inclined doesn't mean there's something wrong with him."

"I'm serious," he said. "It's like he can't keep the bat in his hands. The thing is plastic. It weighs two ounces, tops." Then he added, "He slings his arms around like wet noodles. No control."

"James, leave him alone." She brushed her stray hair back—already a long thatch was going silver—then snatched up a handful of candles and the cake plate. "Come on. It's time for cake."

By the time Bradey clambered into the dining room, his dejection had been safely left in the yard. He sat at the head of the long dining room table like a tiny tyrant king, deliriously happy, bouncing on his knees. As they sang, Carlie brought out the tray. But her mouth got caught on *happy* as her eyes roved—glancing from the cake—and noticed the fresh plum-sized welt on Bradey's left arm. For a moment, she almost dropped the cake. For a moment, she almost hurled H.R. Pufnstuf at her husband, crying obscenities at the scene of her child's fourth birthday. Instead, she steadied the platter on the table, clearing her throat. She did it again, unable to clear it, as if a long hair had caught in her esophagus. Deftly, she—mother, wife—struck a matchhead with her thumbnail and lit all four big candles until they were glowing brightly.

"All right Sweetie, big breath now." Carlie knelt, unable to draw one herself. Bradey opened his mouth into a wide O and stuck out his chest, ready to blow the house down. "Come on, long long long, go go go!" James cheered. Carlie's eyes were watering now, unable to cough up or swallow down whatever stuck in her throat, seeing in the hypnotic flames a dizzy premonition in which she had to grab her son, now, this instant, and run.

Instead, Mother and Father stood over their son's chair, when their smiles—already strained—began to flicker. The tiny candle flames danced, then waved like undersea grass. Finally, they realigned, perfectly aglow.

Rasping, Bradey could not muster the breath to blow out a single candle.

7

A.L.L. Acute Lymphocytic Leukemia.

After three weeks of blood tests and biopsies, after a bone marrow aspiration which took two hours of commanding, bribing, and pleading before the four year old would submit, in frustrated tears, to dropping his pants and balling up on the cold medical examination table for a four inch, sixteen-gauge needle, James and Carlie sat before the doctor's desk with Bradey fidgeting—bruised, stuck, poked, and palpitated—in their laps. The office was small, made harder and more spartan by the late August light filing through the blinds behind the medical examiner. Dr. Morosi was a short, stubby man whose breath wafted antiseptic mouthwash with every utterance. He clasped both hands on top of the desk and paused to gather his thoughts, studying his own hairy wrists, a large gold Rolex jutting beneath his cuff. He had already spoken once with the parents while Bradey played in the children's center. He could still see the news of Bradey's diagnosis moving through their veins, slow as a glacier. Cold and smooth-gliding through their brains, freezing them with its enormity, thawing only over time. Which was usually the case with parents. He had shut the door to cancel the hall noise. Still there seeped a subconscious murmur of nurses' shoes, small electronic bleeps, pages over the intercom. Now it was time to explain everything to the child, and in doing so, address them as a family, bring them back into the world together.

Dr. Morosi withdrew a child's framed drawing from his wall as an instructional aid. He leaned over his desk to where Bradey could see, and tapped the glass with his pen. "There's a war going on inside your body, Bradley," he began.

"Bradey," Carlie and Bradey corrected.

Dr. Morosi cleared his throat. "Bradey." He began again, pointing with the nib of his pen to several crayoned circles and squiggles. Each shape had a cartoon face. "These are the good guys inside your bloodstream. They help fight off the foreign invaders that make you sick. Platelets, red blood cells, and most importantly, the white blood cells." He pointed to a large blob with a starred helmet, clicking the pen in and out as he spoke. "They're like the generals, they tell everybody else in your bloodstream what to do, keeping everything in order when you get sick. Except that you've got a lot of lazy generals inside you, and they're crowding out the good ones. And in turn, everybody else in your army gets confused. Your platelet count, for example, results in these bruises. A drop in red blood cells is responsible for the fatigue and weakness you've been experiencing. And so all we want to do is help you get rid of the lazy generals. Make room for some good ones so you can stay healthy." He handed the drawing to the boy and folded his knuckles.

Bradey studied the framed picture intensely. He knew from his parents' attention that this was big, this was all important. He nodded gravely. All his generals lay before him on the page, the cells with wide eyes and mouths, goofy and inept. Dangerous. They all looked like the smiling, disembodied head of H.R. Pufnstuf.

"You and I will be seeing a lot of each other," the doctor said. His smile was panoramic.

Dr. Morosi sent them off that day with the field manual for Bradey's life. A three inch, three-ring binder filled with an index of all the possible pharmaceutical cocktails used in combating his lazy generals. Carlie began memorizing it immediately, beginning with the A's, then poked around in later chapters. Each entry had a chemical description of what the med was supposed to do, then a whopping paragraph that began *Common Side Effects*. These varied, but included such possibilities as mouth sores, fatigue, diarrhea, hair loss, allergic reaction, vomiting, anemia, depression, epileptic seizure, hypoglycemia, sore throat, high blood pressure, kidney damage, bones loss, impaired fertility, brain tumor, and basal cell skin carcinoma. But after that, in fine print, every entry had the same tiny addendum. *Less Common: coma, death.*

"Why do they always put it in fine print?" Carlie had whispered as James piloted the car, Bradey asleep and silent as a newborn in the backseat.

"Because they think you'll overlook it," James said, grimly driving them home. "Because they think the size of the type font will somehow diminish the threat."

Carlie flipped through the pages, unable to read anymore, feeling flush. It felt as though in some bargain with God she had actively traded child abuse for cancer. "We're going to kill him," she said. "We're going to kill our own son trying to save him. We're going to cripple him for life. Look at this—anemia, kidney damage—we're going to give him more diseases fighting the disease. We can't do this."

Without waiting a beat, James only said, "There's nothing else we can do."

She put the binder at her feet, feeling carsick. Carlie craned around to get a good, reassuring look at her son, and was pricked with ice to find him not asleep. Instead, Bradey was strapped into the backseat, upright in his purple windbreaker, serenely staring out the window.

* * *

The human brain is a great organizer of overwhelming facts and developments. Call it compartmentalizing, call it feng shui—it adapts with remarkable speed, rearranging the furniture in its mental room to maximize new spaces. Carlie got to know her son's regimen with the precision of a registered nurse. The busy to and fro of clinics in Atlanta and Augusta; chemical names; dosages and counter-dosages; warning signs of bad reactions. James got to know the games of the health insurance industry (whose common side effects included gastric ulcers, migraine, mental fatigue, double billing, financial strain, and a growing sense of the injustice of privatized healthcare). They fought separate battles.

There was the cadence of prednisone and vincristine, methotrexate and leucovorin. Pronouncing these words gave Carlie mastery over them, mastery over her son's condition. Invoking their names, like those of the saints, guided her spiritually through this modern medical landscape. Carlie and Bradey also learned the nurses by name, learned who excelled at tapping veins, who worked what days of the week. Saline flushes, central ports, spit up pans, spinal taps, and bone marrows. The constant bee-sting of blood work. The premier child cancer research hospital in the Southeast happened to be only a three hour drive from Copeland by interstate. She put in a lot of road time, back and forth to Atlanta. The prognosis went from six months, to six years, to "Bradey's taking to the treatment very well. He should lead a full and long life."

The changes were enormous. Prednisone saw her once-finicky child turn into a muscular eater. At the dinner table Bradey would declare his love for cauliflower and heap them upon his plate. He would eat pudgy fistfuls of cold white rice for snacks, licking the individual grains from his fingers. At two in the morning, he would awake and cry for his momma, not because of bad dreams or for a glass of water, but to demand chicken-on-the-bone. When warned of mood swings by Dr. Morosi, Carlie envisioned a foul little temper, storming in and out of rooms or collapsing in the K-Mart aisles in a tantrum. Instead, this child, this same child who loved nothing better than to ignore whatever she said and dash, giggling, into fire ant mounds or mud holes or steaming piles of horse manure, had suddenly developed a serious passion for cleaning. She opened his bedroom door one Saturday morning to discover the room in clinical order, the small shoes lined neatly in the closet, the toys in their box, the desk straightened, the bed made and tucked as best he could—while Bradey himself sat cross-legged on the carpet, engrossed in organizing his coloring books by theme. Doggies, trucks, athletes. Next, he wanted to operate the vacuum cleaner. He spread his ambitions to the entire house, dividing and conquering by rooms, dusting and ordering anything up to three feet high, while Carlie observed from the doorway in wonder. Once, she allowed him, at his request, to use an ammonia floor cleaner in the kitchen under close supervision. She didn't know whether to be elated or panicked. She had careful questions for the doctor. When James came home in the evening, dropping his work clothes piece by piece en route to the recliner, Bradey would follow behind. Shoe, shoe, sock, sock, tie, coat. Bradey would gather each item from its place on the floor or furniture. Then, standing squarely in front of the television screen just as James eased into his chair, he would present the bouquet of castoffs, a full armload, and chastise his exhausted father without a single word. Carlie laughed out loud. Bradey, the Mean Clean Machine.

There's a picture from this era documenting Bradey's prednisone freak-out, glued into an early family album. At four years old, he holds the shaft of a broom and is tied in an oversized apron. He looks like a swollen but determined gnome, minus the beard, his eyes lost inside rosy, steroid-puffed cheeks. But away from the house, he was still a child and his curiosity went toward a child's interests. At Minnie's, he ran wonderfully amok, eliciting only the common fears: soiled and ruined clothes, thorn bushes, the danger of water snakes. Carlie took him there often. Enough so that she could breathe easy, and not think how the medication was irreparably altering his brain chemistry.

And then, there were the bills.

"Four thousand dollars," James would start in, seated at the head of the dining room table. Another unexpected side effect: Carlie and James socialized like never before, throwing dinner parties, inviting guests every week despite tightening their belt straps. Large brisket, whole hams, guinea fowl, whatever they could get their hands on in the low, fly-specked freezer bins of the Winn Dixie. With their guests enthralled, he would continue: "Four *thousand*. Insurance says they won't cover it. I say why not? She says because they don't cover prescription lenses. Lenses? I say, what the hell are you talking about? Your plan doesn't cover optometry, she says. Sweet little thing on the other end of the line. I try not to get mad, I know she just works the phones, shuffles the papers, it's not her fault. But I gag in disbelief. I shout. How could I not? *Optometry?!* It's listed as optometry—these idiots don't know the difference between *oncology* and eyeglasses!" he says. "They try to get you at every end." He lifts his water glass but puts it back down for one last rejoinder, smiling despite himself. "Who on earth gets four thousand dollar eyeglasses anyway? That's what I want to know." At that, everyone would laugh, and the air would lift. James would shake his head, lift his glass in homage to Map Price, and toast, "I wonder what the poor folk are doing." And the table would again ring in laughter, at the ironic relief, a blessed understanding of the narrow margins by which everything could be much, much worse. The Convivial Dr. Cullins. In company, he could joke. Alone at home, he kept meticulous records: an entire bookshelf lined with three-ring binders, each ordered and dated since Bradey's diagnosis. Alone at the kitchen table, his stomach would gurgle like a science fair volcano while pouring over the numbers, the hidden mistakes, the calculated ineptitude. Hours spent on the phone with the insurance company, while his supper broke down into amino acids, eased by pepsin tablets. At work, he used his lunch hour to set up meetings with the administration. He fought over the benefits package that was slowly, discretely being pulled away from him.

But in the anecdotal lulls, in the public clinking of stemware, a heavy specter would inevitably settle over the mirth. When the silence of eating threatened to undermine the casual atmosphere, freighted with alienation and pity and self-doubt, Carlie would add, as if an afterthought, "But, you know, contending with cancer is no more difficult than raising any other small child." Gently scripted, her voice tinted with down-home charm. "It's still just a matter of having to shoehorn your own life into your child's routine. Like T-ball and daycare."

"Just a stage of life." James would make eye contact with his wife, in front of all these witnesses, and deliver a broad smile of *C'est la vie.* As if the logical progression went: Marriage, House, Child, Cancer. The guests would return the smile, mouths bulging with asparagus tips, and approve the script. Grace in adversity.

Only then could James and Carlie relax.

Breathe into a brown paper bag. Sip your water slowly. Repeat after me: *everything is normal, everything is normal, everything is normal.*

8

When doling out his advice, Whit was right about one thing: Carlie believed in timing.

She waited for the best time to remind her husband of her evening plans—the best time being the last possible moment, when nothing could be done, and arguments would be the briefest. As the back door jingled shut, he peeled out of his clothes, necktie, coat, and she waited for him to shed the grievances of his workday. The puff of air, the sigh of home, his muted voice in the bedroom with the door open. James thumped into the den with Bradey, giggling, locked onto one of his legs like an iron boot. On the stove lay warmed dishes, Corningware, gently steaming.

James stopped before going to the television, peering and sniffing into the kitchen. "Amazing," he said. "Dinner's actually on time tonight." Bradey detached himself and rolled toward his Peter Rabbit doll on the carpet. Snatching it up, he scurried down the hall.

"It's not on time, it's early."

"I see," he said, popping on the television. His arms dangled heavily by his sides. "And why is it early?"

"Because I'm going out this evening. I've got a Garden Club meeting."

"Why didn't you tell me this before now?"

"I did. I'm telling you this again."

"So you're not eating."

"No, I'm not. They always have little things, coffee and hors d'oeuvres and whatnot. I've left chops, cheese potatoes, and green beans for you. It's all here."

"And Bradey's not eating. He's having coffee cake and oyster crackers for supper, too."

"Bradey's already eaten."

James studied the Barcalounger for a moment, undecided, then seated himself at the rolltop desk for some work. After shuffling through a disorganized stack of medical bills, he clicked on a small oscillating fan. He began scribbling, leafing through a smeary ledger. Carlie moved efficiently around the kitchen, putting things away.

After a time, he said, "How much do they charge per meeting? For hors d'oeuvres?"

"They don't charge per meeting. It's just annual dues."

"But you're paying people money to be your friend."

"I am not paying people to be my friend. I'm paying them to get me out of the house. I like gardening, so I like the Garden Club."

James searched for a pen that worked, scratching their dry ballpoints against the pad. "It just sounds unnecessary. That's all I'm saying. It seems to me that you get out of the house just fine every day." He spoke evenly, using his thoroughly reasonable tone. He had been adopting many new tones and speaking styles over the past few years that they raised Bradey.

Carlie snapped down a Tupperware lid, and held her tongue. Whisking to the back door, she grabbed a light jacket and her purse. She paused, looking for her keys. Quickly, she dug through her purse. "Have you seen my keys?"

"How should I know where your keys are?"

"Sweetie," she called down the hall, "have you seen Momma's keys?" An unintelligible reply. She saw the spare for the Rambler dangling by the door and snatched that instead. "All right, I should be back at 8:00." She waited for acknowledgment. "James?"

He sat hunkered over the rolltop desk. The television was on a low banter, cockeyed toward his empty lounge chair. The oscillating fan ruffled his hair and papers with each slow pass. "Don't forget to take Bradey," was all he said.

Carlie clicked the one spare key in her hand like an insect, watching her silent husband. "I'm not going to forget Bradey," she said, already striding down the hall to collect her child. She marched back through the room, her purse slung over one shoulder and her child on her hip. The door slammed shut.

"Bye," James said afterward, not looking up from his notes.

* * *

By the time Carlie arrived home, it was pitch dark. The meeting had gone long. Truthfully, she didn't like them very much and had debated quitting. She couldn't relate well to the other women, who seemed to want to gab about everything but horticulture. After the first perfunctory ten minutes, out came the coffee and crumbcake, and then it was all about family pets and children and husbands. Carlie had even brought books to the first meeting she attended, small reference materials, which proved to be a mistake.

The host that night, Evelyn, had raised her brows and said, "Oh, wow, we have ourselves a bona fide arborist here," which in turn raised a round of self-conscious laughter.

"Looks like we're outclassed, ladies."

"Where'd you get those?" asked another.

"Just at the library." Carlie blushed and discretely tucked them back into her handbag at the first opportunity.

Sometimes, she thought about wandering out into the woods and starting her own club. Set up a half-circle of Bradey's stuffed animals and conduct meetings, like she had with Francine when they were little girls. Sometimes, going crazy seemed like a nice idea.

Carlie reached over to pull Bradey, still sleeping, into her tired arms. He slumped over her like a sleeping cat, one hand clutching Peter Rabbit, whose ears were thoroughly chewed. It was past time for Petey to go into the wash, and maybe get a few extra stitches. An extra surgical procedure for the poor rabbit. Peter usually got stuck when Bradey got stuck, blood work or chemo. She gathered up the shoe and sock that her son had kicked off. That was how his universe was made fair. A buddy in needles.

Only now, out of the car, did Carlie notice that the back porch lights were off.

"Great," she said. "All right, babe, hold tight to Momma." She shuffled along the walkway in the dark, brushing past the ligustrum bushes and taking one step at a time up to the deck. Carlie stubbed her foot against a potted peace lily and fumbled for the door.

It was locked.

She shifted Bradey to the other shoulder, and dug around in her purse, unable to see. "James," she called. "I don't have my keys." She pawed through the purse one-handed, coming up only with the Rambler's spare. "James." She banged on the door with her palm. "James, are you up? Lord, child, you're getting heavy." She moved to the glass door and rapped sharply on that. It reverberated like a bird hitting a window pane. She hoisted Bradey up one more time, cupped her free hand, and tried to peer through. The recliner was empty, the television off. The stove light was left on in the kitchen as a night light.

"James, the door's locked!" she called out, rattling the handle.

A shadow moved past the glass inset in the door. "Finally," she muttered and stepped back. She waited. When nothing happened, Carlie approached the handle again and noticed the silhouette still squared behind the darkened glass. "James? What's wrong?"

Through the glass, he spoke. "What time is it now." Muffled, the question was flat and inflectionless.

"I don't know. Look, open the door."

"What time is it now, and what time did you tell me that you would be home." He spoke each word clear and succinctly to be heard through the door.

Her hand slipped from the knob.

"Over two hours, I've been waiting."

"James, it's not even 10:00…"

"So you're saying you intended to lie to me."

She couldn't reply.

"No, it's okay, you just lied, that's all. If you told me 8:00 and then break that, I don't know what else you'd call it."

"I didn't lie to you! Open the damn door!" She banged the glass, felt her voice razz through Bradey's thin chest against her. He stirred with an irritated *Momma…*

"Just admit it. Say that you lied. Come clean with it. Admit that you lied to me, your husband, and I will open this door." And then he shouted: "I have work in the morning! I have to pay doctor's bills, grocery bills, insurance! Do you understand this?" A pause. Then, without shouting: "You like staying out so late? Then stay. Goodnight, Carlie." At this last utterance, his voice was small, diminished, thrown over his shoulder as he shuffled through the bathroom back to bed.

She cupped a hand to her mouth and squeezed.

Carlie stood shuddering with Bradey in her arms, for how long, she didn't know. It felt as if she had rubbed her face after handling hot peppers: her cheeks and eyes blotchy and burning. Blurring up, she nearly tripped down the deck stairs back to the car door. The night was watery, a trembling cup on the brink of being dropped and shattering. Carlie guided herself unsteadily to the car. She laid Bradey in the backseat, quietly arranging a nest of thin blankets around his shoulders and legs for him to sleep. She pulled herself into the driver's seat and sat, huddled up. One moment passed, then two. Suddenly, the porch light snapped on.

James sauntered out onto the deck in his boxers and bathrobe, standing at the top of the steps. He left the backdoor open.

"All right," he called out. "Come on." Elbows jutting, hands braced on his hips. He stared at the car and waited.

Fixed on James, she slid her palm over the driver's side lock with a small click.

"Get inside. We'll discuss this in the morning. I need to get to bed."

After a long delay, he swung his arms open, wide, in an exasperated *entrée vous*. "I'm not going to stand here waiting all night."

At last, she popped the lock open. All her fight was gone. With the world still runny, Carlie gathered Bradey in her arms one last time and silently trudged up the porch steps. As she came near, James, for reasons unknown to himself—after waiting for his wife to drag her body from the car, after watching her lump their child into her arms and plod along the walkway like some shambling creature, purposefully slow, keeping him waiting and waiting, making him wait all night in the tepid air—he simply reached out and pushed her. It seemed like an involuntary reflex. As if he did it just to see what would happen, from an observational distance, as an experiment. She stumbled, clattered against the porch bench where empty plant pots spilled every which way, and hit the ground. Bradey started crying, wild eyed with shock in the tangle of his mother's body. James stood there—unable to apologize, he was so speechless—and didn't move to help her up. But Carlie didn't get up. Instead, she began hurling terracotta pots at him, one after another with her free hand while Bradey wailed. "Son of a bitch," he shouted, deflecting one, dodging another. "What are you doing? Stop it!" They missed, they smacked his shoulders, they shattered against the porch. One caught him in the ear, knocking him temporarily senseless; James staggered back, his glasses dangling. Carlie struggled up and hustled to the car.

He straightened his eyeglasses, which turned to quicksilver in the sudden flash of the headlights. James held up one hand to ward off the glare, a trickle of blood at his eyebrow.

"What the hell are you doing? Turn those off—right now!"

She cranked the engine.

"Carlie!" As soon as he began hopping down the steps, Carlie thrust the car into reverse and accelerated backward out of the winding drive. She clipped the mailbox, braking only a moment to ratchet her seatbelt over her shoulder. Then, slamming the Rambler into first gear, she was gone.

* * *

James made it to the street—barefoot and with his robe fluttering—in time to see the Rambler's red taillights weave through the trees. He stood only a second, huffing air, staring at the splintered wreckage of the mailbox. "I'm going to have to fix that, too," he shouted, seeing his breath bloom in the torpid moisture. "I have to fix every goddamn thing!" He ran inside to grab his keys to the station wagon. He banged back through the door and, this time, didn't lock it, didn't even slam it shut in his haste.

James peeled out of the drive, kicking up sand as the tires spun. Speeding around dark curves, he clicked on the headlights before nearly swerving off the road. That was better. He could see more; he could see clearly. What he did was an accident—what she did was on purpose. James adjusted his glasses. He hadn't caught sight of her yet. Just chased the streetlights, pooling through the darkness. The station wagon's metal bulk steadily gained speed, but to where, he didn't know. A red traffic signal lit up, bleary against the damp asphalt. He braked hard. No other cars came to the intersection as he idled steam. Getting him out of bed like this, making him chase her like some slatternly teenage daughter, it nauseated him. There was a word he'd never used before. *Slatternly.* A good one. He liked it. It implied all sorts of things. Loose clothes, loose flesh. The sound of it alone implied poor moral character. Buttons sloppily open. Hurried flight in the middle of night with smeared make-up, slips, brassieres, and whatever the hell else trailing in the getaway. He was glad they had a boy. He wouldn't have to worry about him in the same way. Where on earth could she go at this hour? The Garden Club women? Doubtful. He didn't even know the house, anyway. A motel? No, he was pretty sure she had no money on her.

And then it occurred to him: the only place Carlie could go.

Slapping on his blinker, James hooked a right turn and cut through the red. He headed toward Breezy Hill. When the windshield fogged up, he hastily wiped a porthole with the heel of his hand. Low lying mist hung over the road. James kept his chest pressed toward the wheel, as if pushing the car through the poor visibility. Before long, he was in the rural valley of Auscauga Lake Road.

The road dipped steeply and he remembered to brake this time, turning into the narrow wooded cut that was Minnie Price's drive.

He barked, triumphant. The front porch light was on. A beacon, a white flag, a red lamp, a neon sign. He knew it.

James parked in front of the house, wrestled with the gate, and marched up the porch. He banged on the front door and waited. Then he decided to bang while waiting. To bang until the door flew open or until he saw his wife fly out the back porch.

When Minnie drew the bolt, he stopped banging. Her face appeared in the sliver of doorway, pinched with caution. Then, seeing that it was James, her expression fell into exaggerated relief. Minnie had a blue robe drawn around her slack body. That's when James remembered he was still in his own bathrobe. "James!" she said. "Well, we're glad you're here."

"I bet." He braced his hands against the small of his back and decided to say nothing else.

"Wait right here one moment," she said. "I'll be right back." She disappeared, leaving the door partially open. It was dim inside, a few antique lamps glowing like votives. He tried to listen for Carlie's voice, for other movement.

"All right, James," she said, approaching the door. When it swung fully open, Minnie had a purse slung over her shoulder and an army service revolver wagging in his direction. "The back porch, dear."

His throat hitched. In a bizarre stroke, James recognized the weapon even without its holster…it was the same gun from the photograph in Map's bedroom. The one where Map stood pistol-packing and bare ass-naked to the wind, which he had found so unsettling. At this moment, James would have shouted if his nervous system hadn't seized up. He would have shoulder-tackled this old witch and wrestled the gun from her, but he couldn't and so didn't. Furthermore, he didn't have to. James looked down to find the weapon already in his hand. Map's pistol. His throat constricted tighter, gauzy and unpleasant. Perhaps he felt in his mind the confusion that followed, as if taking another man's penis in his hand. The queer, delightful exhilaration. Indeed, the horn handgrips felt like vitrified flesh against his palm. Thick, hard, and warming to his grip.

"This way, dear heart," Minnie said, cinching her robe tighter and flapping down the steps in her slippers.

Numb, James followed around the side of the house. The grass was dewy and tickled his feet. He weighed the gun in his hand. It was heavy, balanced-feeling. He wondered if he should point it at her and pull the trigger. He didn't know what he was supposed to do now.

Minnie led them to the screen door, which was propped open with a brick, and stopped him from entering. "You may want to shoot first and ask questions later," she said.

The back porch was lit up, too, and in that muddled light James saw a black shimmering coil. A water moccasin, five feet long, had curled up on her welcome mat.

"I don't know how he got in," she said. "But he's been there all day and, needless to say, I need him out. Mommy Cat nearly lost nine of her lives and most of her fur trying to get through the screen door."

Remembering at last how to speak, he croaked, "Whoa, Minnie, no. I can't." He turned toward her smiling face.

"Oh, it's easy. You just point that end at it and pull the trigger."

"No, I mean I've never fired a gun before."

"What fun!" She clapped one hand to her chest. "What an experience! You'll have to write in your diary about it when you get home."

"I really don't think this is a good idea."

"Oh, a lot better than me giving it another go. I've put two holes in my porch already. See? There and there. My eyesight isn't worth a hoot anymore."

"Minnie," he said. She held the door open expectantly.

The moccasin batted its tongue, roused into anxiety from the commotion. It stretched, began to unfurl itself.

"There he goes!"

James briefly thought of using a broom to flush it out, but he had also seen what had happened to some ecologists at the Site when handling snakes. How those reptiles could leap up. He'd seen Whit get bitten on more than one occasion during location tests; had seen those barbed fangs sink right into the meat between his thumb and forefinger; had seen Whit visit the toxicology lab, sweating like he had malaria, for treatment afterward. He didn't want to get snakebitten. Not tonight, or any night for that matter. A rash of sweat rose on James' forehead as he leveled the pistol with both hands. Here he was, out in the boonies, the Edenic scene revisited. (And as it turns out, the revanchists were right: it is Adam and Eve, not Adam and Steve. Except that Eve is a sixty-four year old lesbian, and Adam, poor Adam, is suffering from a homoerotic dilemma through the heavy signifier of a dead man's disembodied penis.) When he caught a glimpse of Carlie—ever so quickly—peeking through the glass, it became impossible to sort out his rage from all the psychosexual energy pent up in that handgun. He squeezed his eyes shut.

Pop.

An orgasmic jolt shivered through his forearms. It leaped from his elbows, kicked his wrists, an arc light of God.

The snake sprang like a loaded jack, three feet high, straight up. In its motion, a thin question mark of blood squirted into the air. It landed on the boards with a limp thump, shot dead-zero through the skull.

"Bravo!"

"I got it," James said, his ears concussed. He could hardly hear his own amazement.

"Good shooting, Tex." With two fingers, Minnie removed the pistol from his grip like a used handkerchief. "I'd offer you a snort of whiskey, but I'm afraid the saloon's closed. It's fairly late."

James only nodded, the cold nausea of relief in his stomach. "Minnie," he said as she ushered him toward the station wagon. "I came here…"

"Oh, I know why you're here," she said. "You got my S.O.S. My mental distress signals. Now if I can find Mommy Cat all will be right with the world."

"No," James said and turned, stopping Minnie. All this rushing, all this distraction, it was too clever. "Listen to me. I don't want Carlie coming out here again. You get me?"

Minnie hesitated, a quizzical smile—a viperous smile, he now saw— "I'm not sure I know what you're talking about, dear heart."

"You know what I mean," he said. "I'm not an idiot."

Then, quite suddenly, Minnie was just an old woman again, a deflated, crestfallen old woman. "Have I done something to offend you?"

He groped for evidence. The Rambler, he now noticed, wasn't under the carport or in the drive…but that didn't mean she hadn't been around. Blushing, backpedalling, James muttered, "If she does, I mean. If she shows up out here tonight. Make sure to send her back home." And he turned to the station wagon before waiting for a response.

"Oh, okay, dear heart," Minnie said. "I'll certainly do just that."

James slammed the car door, catching the tails of his soiled bathrobe, and started the engine. He never wanted to hold another pistol again.

* * *

When James arrived back at the house, the only light came from the living room. He navigated the hall in the dark, stopping in the foyer. Carlie faced him in the rocking chair. She had Bradey between them, gently slumped into the crook of her neck. James studied the gentle rhythm of her rocking.

"Where did you go," he asked.

Carlie watched him through narrow eyes, her head resting back. She had one arm hooked around Bradey's bottom for support, the other on his head. She looked exhausted and mean. Menacing. To James, it must have seemed a vengeful posture: the mother cradling a child in her arms, away from her husband, the visible bruise on her swollen elbow. "I drove around," she said, stroking Bradey's hair. He was asleep now, dead to the world. "You?"

"I drove around, too."

James stood there, muddy bathrobe open.

"In your underwear."

"It's a balmy night."

"Good thing a cop didn't pull you over."

"He might have been jealous."

"He might have made a move on you."

"He wouldn't even have bought me dinner," James said. "Goodnight. I'm going to bed."

Just as he started away, she said, "I didn't lock the door on you, if you noticed." She waited, rocking gently. "You remember that."

He lingered only for a moment, his back to her, shoulders hunched. Then, he spoke, struggling with the words, "You know, someday, you will lose me. You will lose me and be afraid, because only then will you finally realize what you have in me. Everything in me, you take for granted right now. But someday it'll be too late." With one final goodnight he shuffled off to bed.

"James," Carlie said to herself, stroking Bradey's hair. "You don't realize what you already lost."

9

Back at the hotel I stand in the shower, hot as I can take it, and vomit a little. A thin rill of stomach acid mostly, redolent of crab though I only had one bite. I raise my head to let the water beat into my mouth, then I swish and spit.

"She's sleeping," Freddie says, and I jump. I didn't hear the bathroom door open. After returning from the house, I had put Mom down for a nap. She embraced it, exhausted, but then spent the next thirty minutes going back and forth to the bathroom, doing nothing but being anxious, irritable.

"Good. Hand me those jeans, will you?" His silhouette passes behind the shower curtain and then my bisque-stained jeans, half-damp from earlier in the day, are thrown over the rod. I hold them under the water, drown them, and begin to scrub vigorously with a bar of soap. Freddie takes a long piss and for a while the only sounds in our tiny bathroom are his water hitting the toilet and the shower drumming against the tub, a hollow, plastic roaring that fills my ears. He lets the lid fall, but doesn't flush.

"Mind if I join you?"

"I want you to keep an eye on Mom while I'm in here." I snap the denim tight to rub between the fibers, then squeeze hard to wring the excess water out. I sling them over the towel rack in the shower.

"She's fast asleep, trust me. I sang 'Au clair de la lune' to her and she went out like a lamb," he says. I see him through the curtain shucking off his clothes, fumbling with one shoe. "I'm of the opinion that every lullaby should end with sexual gratification." He slips in behind me and winces from the spray, protecting himself. "Holy shit, you look boiled alive. Crank that down a bit." His own flesh is sallow and a touch bloated, streaking red where the water hits his legs. I look at Freddie and see myself turning to fat. Nothing but shit food and a hamster wheel for exercise since we've been on this trip. The hair on his chest almost seems to be thinning.

I turn to adjust the knobs and stay that way, bracing my arms against the tile to let the water crash over my shoulders and neck, to soak up every bit of heat. When Freddie speaks again, the steam and narrow space mute his voice. "You probably shouldn't take it too hard, what your Mom said back there. He was her first-born, and the illness, and all that jazz. That's got to be a lot to carry."

"Freddie," I say, spitting water. "Shut up."

"Here." He soaps my back, kneads his thumbs into my muscle. Freddie begins to hum. From the melody, I assume it's the lullaby that he mentioned, and after a few bars, he croons in an uneven, tuneless way, "Ouvrez votre porte / Pour le Dieu d'Amour." After a verse, he says, "I meant what I said, you know. On our way to the house. What if we got married?"

I rotate my head under the water pressure to drown out the world, then resurface. An acidic nausea returns to my throat. I can feel myself getting angry. "I don't understand where this is coming from."

"What do you mean?" he says. "I love you."

"And you loved me before. We've been together for four years now. Why are you suddenly keen on this idea?" Freddie's hands slacken as he formulates a response, but I interrupt him. "Forget it. Tell me about the cocktail lounge," I say.

He rubs his hands over me, squeezing my hips, then looping up to the tense knot in the small of my back. My body responds, excites at his touch despite my irritation. "No prospects yet," he says. "I don't know why it's taking me so long. But the wheels are turning. Fortune will yet find favor with the bold."

"The bold aren't so young anymore," I say. "What happens if you can't come up with the ten grand?" He generously re-lathers his hands with the bar, taking his time, shuck-shucking the bubbles together. "The entire enterprise goes under, doesn't it. How much do you stand to lose if that happens? How much have you and Henri sunk into this place?"

Freddie puts his hands right where my neck meets my shoulders. To stop now would admit pain, defeat. "Nothing will be lost," he says. Then, he eases me around by the shoulders and leans down to kiss me. He's nervous. It's meant to be a sincere gesture but his mouth twitches. His breath has a vinegary, metallic tang, and I think: this is desperation. This is desperation I'm tasting.

When we part, I ask, "What's that?" I cock my head so that water isn't drilling against my ear. "Did you hear something?"

Freddie squints at me.

"I think I heard Mom."

"Oh, for fuck's sake."

Then, a definite crash from beyond the door. It is the sharp, clumsy sound of porcelain breaking. I push past Freddie to slip out the shower and grab a towel, still hard. As soon as I hit the cold air of our adjoining suite, I hear her moaning, yelling, calling for help—and see that the door between our rooms is closed. Freddie must have closed it. When I grab the handle, it doesn't give. Mom cries out on the other side, a slurred choking sound. I throw my shoulder against the door once, twice, but it doesn't budge. Her wailing gets louder. By now, Freddie is dripping wet with a towel around his waist, struck dumb. "You closed the fucking door," I shout at him, then hammer my fist against it. "It locks, it locks from the other side!" I snatch a pair of shorts, yanking them as best I can up my wet thighs. In two strides, I'm in the hall, running barefoot for the stairwell.

* * *

She was, thankfully, unhurt in any serious way. Some swelling, a nasty bruise purpling her knee, but nothing was broken. By the time I returned with the desk clerk, we found her clinging to the edge of the tub, exhausted, nearly having cried herself out. My mother had dragged herself into the bathroom through miles of her own shit. The clerk was the same young woman from earlier this morning. When we first breached the room, she covered her nose and retreated a pace.

Apparently, while Freddie and I were showering together, Mom had awoken from her nap in a state of urgency. When she called for assistance, no one came. No one responded. Without help, she shat herself in a fit of explosive diarrhea, then had fallen out of bed, still struggling for the toilet. She then proceeded to crawl on the floor, leaving long mucilaginous streaks through the carpet. Feces had twisted through the sheets, had speckled the nightstand and baseboard throughout the room. It had saturated her skirt. From the volume of it, her guts must have been twisting up to this moment for days.

The clerk ducked into the hall, radioing for custodial services. I struggled with Mom alone. I stripped her down and hosed us both off there in the tub. For whatever reason, while working the washcloth over her body, I remember seeing, intensely, her teeth. That she still had strong, small teeth. Her old silvery fillings were still firmly in place. With her face close to mine, her breath had the faintly sour, milky smell of infants.

Afterward, we had quietly packed our belongings while the housekeeping staff roared away in the fouled room with an industrial strength wet-dry vac. They slapped mops against the wall, sprayed disinfectant foam everywhere, and plied the carpet again and again with the vacuum. We kept the suite door closed.

While I packed, Freddie sat on the edge of the mattress. He leaned far over, as if hyperventilating, elbows on his knees, tenting his hands over his mouth. I told him to load the truck. When I helped Mom to her wheelchair, freshly dressed and ruddy from the scrubbing, he looked at me from behind his hands. *Privacy*, he said. *It was to give her a little privacy. That's all.*

Only after the ordeal, after we have checked out of the hotel and the panic has subsided, does my outrage settle in. While securing Mom into the bench seat, the scene replays in my mind. I look up to see that Freddie still hasn't finished loading our luggage into the truck. I find him by the cargo bay, fumbling to fold her walker.

"Leave it," I tell him.

"I got this," he says. "I'm figuring it out. See?"

I take it from his hands and break it down in two, three snaps.

"Do you want me to get the door—?"

"Just get in the cab." Reluctantly, he disappears on the passenger side. I slam down the cargo door. It bounces once, and I hook the latch. When I lock it, I realize, suddenly, that he was hiding something. There, slapped haphazardly across the bottom, is the bumper sticker: that rainbow pride stars-and-bars. We had been riding around with it all day.

I punch the door as hard as I can. It reverberates, right from the center of the X.

* * *

In their own contest of loss, who knows which of my parents really won. When their own relationship, in one sense, had finally ended, they were of course fighting. It was an ongoing argument about nothing: just the constant underlying friction that began with James' retirement a year earlier—or his first attempt at retirement, I should say. It was the first time in over forty years that he was truly jobless. More important, it was the first time in forty years that he and my mother had to live alone in close quarters with each other, twenty-four hours a day. I had many late night phone calls from Carlie. Your father this, your father that. I'm going to wind up shooting him, so help me god, I'm glad we don't own a gun. Positions of power were changing. Without his job, he became aimless, useless—an infuriating reversal of Carlie's dilemma that began in 1971, when James first left her in Minerva's bedroom for the career that would occupy his life. (*See? See?* she wanted to say to him, to stick the words between his ribs like a paring knife. *So many years riding on his high-horse, and now I'm supposed to be understanding? I'm supposed to be sympathetic?*) James resented this new status yet was always underfoot, trying to keep himself relevant after years of controlling the income, wanting to apply his expertise to a household where he had none. A man who knew where no pots were kept. Who couldn't sew a button onto his shirt or wound up with pink socks in the wash. Who could only boil pasta and pour cereal. After forty years of marriage, he utterly depended on his wife's knowhow if he was to do anything for himself. The old patriarch drained of his potency. But Carlie's mixed vindication would be short-lived. By his second year of retirement, James had been offered the appointment with Florida State. He jumped at the chance, spending a hundred days out of the year in Tallahassee, living like a bachelor on frozen dinners, and then expecting his wife to resume her role as cook and housemaid when he returned to Copeland.

So, the last minutes in which my parents were truly themselves—or at least, together as the people I had known all my life—they had been quarreling. They are stuck in time, in this memory I've created, on an errand to the pharmacy: A silver-haired crank and a deflated old biddy. Sour, cantankerous, but endearing from afar. Carlie waits in the car after a spring downpour, the kind that leaves the afternoon panting for more air. The humidity redoubles and stirs up the thick, heady stink of asphalt. It makes James' body hair sticky. The fact that Carlie had driven, and not him, precipitated more bickering. Inside Eckerd Drug, he waits at the counter. His cheeks, usually waxen, are ruddy with impatience. The pharmacist has disappeared now for a solid ten minutes. James mumbles to himself, snorts under his breath at the delay, at the poor customer service. As he waits, a flat droning sound begins to expand from his inner ear like tinnitus. An unshakable annoyance that grows with each passing second, louder than it should be. When the pharmacist returns to the register, his wallet is already out, credit card ready to go, ready to pay too much for a bottle of heart pills, insurance covering squat compared to the premiums he pays. Grabbing the medication to leave, the sound has now become feverish, overwhelming. He worries that he might be having a heart attack. But here, James realizes that the sound is not in his head. Then the pharmacist looks to the door, puzzled. It is in fact a car horn. A sustained, unrelenting honk. Someone, perhaps, with her palm pressed firmly into the wheel. He hurries, red-faced. He passes through the automated doors into the heat of the day and the car horn blooms clearer than imaginable. The horn. The horn to his car. Now he has lost all compunction. This embarrassing public display leaves him at wit's end. "I'm coming, Jesus *Christ*!" he shouts. Still the horn does not subside. A few strangers on the sidewalk rubberneck, exchanging distasteful glances. His nose—why not—stuffs up at the scent of scalded flowers in the air, gardenias, a rarity for James' sinuses to detect even that much, but he is too aggravated to even notice. However, the anger he feels sits cold and leaden and useless in his gut, the moment he opens the passenger door. The simplest, mundane gesture: how many times has he opened this particular car door in his life? A thousand, ten thousand? But just this once, he pulls the handle to discover his wife—his partner and nemesis, vowed to love—with her face buried in the steering wheel. James drops the white paper bag and crawls over the bucket seats to her, unable to say her name. Maybe in the aftermath, while watching over her in the hospital bed, James saw what had been lost in their relationship. Yes, he had his accomplishments: degrees from Harvard and MIT, his grant funding and national advisory positions, his projects and patents. And yet Carlie was the person on whom he depended desperately—unwilling to admit it—like a mother. She who, in so many ways, had fed him, dressed him, sheltered him, attended to all the peripheral details of his life so he could get on with his career. All that suddenly became visible, because it was suddenly gone. Maybe this alone precipitated the slow decline toward James' suicide years later. Or maybe, James saw in the moment of my mother's collapse, in the loss of her selfhood, not what he had finally lost but what he had finally gained: that he at last could put Carlie in his pocket, like a broken sparrow, and carry her around, close to him—without all the messy human complications—forever.

One thing that he never knew, however: that she was already leaving him. This, after years of such an acrimonious marriage. True to James' worst fear, Carlie had been conferring with a lawyer. Each week that he left for Tallahassee, enjoying his appointment at FSU and microwaving frozen lasagna, she was seeking legal counsel. The relapse into his career was the last straw for her. When the stroke happened, she was less than a month away from serving him the papers. Truer still, those weeks he traveled, she'd rack up the phone bills with me. All those late night conversations Carlie and I shared were leading to this one climax that never happened, and I can still hear the litany of my own calculated resentment, my constant advice to her that, selfishly, was more for my own satisfaction than hers: divorce him, divorce him, divorce him—and set yourself free.

10

L-asparaginase: \el-as-PA-rə-jə, nās,-,nāz\
[Alternatively, Franco-formatted by Carlie Robicheaux Cullins: *L'asparaginase* \la SPEHR zjin ĀZ\]

Is classified as an enzyme, a cytotoxic chemotherapy drug purified from bacteria cells. It destroys the amino acid asparagine in the bloodstream, thereby necessitating all cells to manufacture their own asparagine for their proteins, which, incidentally, cancer cells cannot produce. L-asparaginase is administered either through I.M. (intra-muscular) or I.V. (intra-venous) injection. The drug cleaves amine from asparagine in order to destroy the food source of cancer cells, and releases ammonia—a chemical redolent of Bradey's cleaning spree—into the host's bloodstream.

* * *

At 2:00 a.m., the night before Carlie's thirty-sixth birthday, she awoke with a sudden pressure in her head. They had nothing planned for it, the birthday, maybe grill burgers on the porch, or try to take Bradey to the Variety for dinner. If the day passed uneventfully, she would be thankful. Carlie sat upright, her eyes pinched shut in the darkness. The radio dial of the alarm clock dimly glowed beside her husband's sleeping figure. It felt like a vacuum between her ears, ringing in the silence, and then there it was: a choked, impassioned *Momma!*

Carlie moaned and kicked off the covers, "Jesus Christ, child. Every night it's bad dreams. Coming, sweetie!" Bumping down the hallway, she came to Bradey's bedroom and popped on the light. She scrunched her face up and covered her eyes, trying to see, "What is it, babe. Did you have a nightmare?"

Bradey was sitting up against his mound of pillows. "Momma," he said, his face purple and veined, his head tilted against backboard gulping at air like a prisoner. "I can't breathe."

"James!" Carlie ripped his shirt buttons open and felt his small, warm chest; touched, eased, tested his throat. "James call the hospital!" There was a crash and a thud from the back of the house. She held Bradey's cheeks and angled his mouth toward the light. What she could see was red and swollen. Bradey continued to rasp in small, sharp inhalations. Hiccups that dragged in and never seemed to release air. "Goddamn it, I told them! Come on, sweetie." Carlie bundled him into her arms with a blanket.

In the kitchen, James stood shirtless with the phone to his ear. Without his glasses, his eyes were tiny, uncomprehending dots in his face. "Yes, no, I don't...wait, here she..." he said into the receiver.

Carlie snatched the phone from his hand, while one-arming Bradey. "He's having an allergic reaction," she pointed to James and said, "Tylenol." James grabbed the bottle from the cupboard and filled a juice glass with water. "Well, if I had to pick one, I'd say it'd have to be the goddamn L'asparaginase, he's had a reaction before, and I *told* Dr. Morosi—" She popped the dose into Bradey and offered the water. "Come on, baby, try and swallow. That's it, just try and swallow. Yes? All right, good. Yes, we'll be there straightaway."

She let the phone fall from her shoulder, clattering both cord and cradle to the kitchen floor.

"Where are you going?" James called, fumbling with the phone.

"Atlanta," she said, running out the door.

In the passenger seat, Bradey sat upright, Indian-style in the folds of his blanket, like a tiny precious Kannon. He sat groggy-faced, his eyes ancient toadlike slits, watching the night road. His cheeks were slick. His breathing had regulated, thin as it was.

After half an hour, Carlie's had not.

The interstate unfolded, black and endless beneath her accelerator foot. In her haste, Carlie forgot her purse but remembered to grab jackets for them both. Bradey was still in his PJs and blankets. Carlie only wore sweatpants and an old T-shirt with ice cream stains down the front. Forty miles, fifty. She traveled the same route I would hitchhike almost twenty years later. On the night I ran away, I felt like I watched them from the road. Stuck between the pull of two worlds, I stood by every mile marker that their headlights flashed by with my thumb stuck out. I saw them in every passing car. Maybe she caught a glimpse of me then, too—seeing a future she didn't yet understand. The nerves began to tingle in her fingertips; the wheel jittered at higher speeds. Bradey canted his head to watch her expression.

It began to rain, suddenly. A downpour hit the windshield like handfuls of rice. Carlie slapped on the wipers and, as soon as she did, found a pair of dull red taillights staring straight back at her. A truck, an enormous iron box, had somehow appeared, merged onto the highway, and trundled along no faster than twenty-five miles an hour. Carlie hammered the brakes with both feet. The Rambler squealed, sluicing an erratic line for five hundred yards or better, as Bradey was thrust into the seatbelt straps. All his downy black hair and blankets yawned forward, sucked toward the dash. Everything loose in the car came flying, magnetized: pencil stubs, spare coins, tissue boxes, and toys. In that instant, all sound ceased, and Carlie could hear the collision before it happened. Her arm thrust out to protect her child. She could see the hood crumple into the guard-catch bumper of the giant truck; she could see the steering wheel and dashboard console rush to meet their faces; she could see her child as he sprang through the seatbelt, rebounded head-first off the dashboard, and launched through the windshield.

She saw it was a chicken truck.

They didn't collide, but only kissed the red wash of taillights. The truck rumbled on, oblivious to the near impact. From its cargo of wire cages, white feathers fluttered through her highbeams like snow, pasting themselves to the Rambler's windshield as the wipers beat, matching the whump in Carlie's heart. A colony of fluffed and huddled chickens look down on them from above. Hundreds of them, murmuring little fusses, shedding white feathers from the truck like confetti, like a tickertape parade. The caustic smell of seared, wet rubber hung in the air.

And there, tied to the rear gate of the truck, was a blue banner flapping in the rain: *Happy Birthday! Parsee Farms turns 35!* Carlie began cackling, she couldn't help it. She whooped and got teary eyed. When recounting this story years later, she will say that this was exactly what she needed to keep sane. Beside her Bradey breathed deeply, if asthmatically, wide-eyed. The warm unearthly light pollution of Atlanta glowed in the far distance.

Carlie followed that truck all the way into the city.

* * *

When they admitted Bradey at the clinic, the nurses were alert and waiting. They were dressed in blue smocks with prints of teddy bears. It was four in the morning and these women had the eleventh hour humor of all third shift medical professionals.

"He's going to be okay," they said, wheeling her child away in a small chair.

Carlie had made it. The chicken car was parked outside, thoroughly plastered in white feathers. She left little puddles where she stood. One of the nurses briefly returned to hand her a short towel, rough but pleasantly dry, and even gave her a handful of coins for coffee. She had survived being a parent for one more night.

With the cafeteria closed, Carlie dried out in the lobby, picking over the vending machines. In her flip-flops, it seemed like she came directly from the pool. Breathing again, wet and grateful. She plunked the change for crackers and punched up the coffee dispenser, preparing for a long night in the waiting room. Twenty bench seats, vinyl, metal armrests dividing the cushions. Not a single one she could stretch out on, but she felt giddy, relaxed. As soon as Carlie retrieved the little steaming paper cup, the older nurse reappeared behind her.

"Oh, hi!" Carlie startled at her sudden reappearance. She had just turned away and here she was again.

"Mrs. Cullins..." The nurse looked wan, clutching a clipboard to her chest.

In the interim, it turned out—a scant ten minutes, no time at all, just enough to sort through the loose dimes and nickels and punch in the plastic buttons, E and 4, Caff. and Black—that they had misread the chart. Carlie crimped the cardboard welt of her coffee cup as she listened. She worked her bitten fingernails against it, scratching. Well, okay, we just got here, she sighed. We can deal with this. All part of the go-with-the-flow routine. Expected unexpectedness. How long will it take? What needs to be done? A flush? An injection? Monitoring, a reconfiguring and reconnoitering? Some counter-treatment, prep, cleanse, anti-anti-anaphylactic? What?

Carlie held the cup. The last thing she remembers from that night was that coffee cup, the tingling sensation in her fingertips where they held the thin, hot paper, going numb.

Bradey was dead.

III

The Half-Life of Love

1

If James was distrustful of the world and its machinations, if he harbored little faith in what he could not control, be it political systems, religion, or his wife, then Bradey's death corroborated a conspiracy that ran deeper than the vagaries of human behavior. Previous scares—such as Ronnie Shorr's suicide attempt, Minnie's unnerving eccentricities, the Robicheaux sisters' siege of his home—only hinted at the deeper issue. Yes, people were not to be trusted, but the problem lay with the universe itself. When Bradey died, so did James' principle faith in order, in objective goodwill. He remembered the hospital nursery, holding the eight pounds of baby boy in his arms, the rightness of it. Bradey, his son, was the next generational step in the Cullins evolution—the next stage of his DNA, his cells and, in some way, his experiences. And he had now outlived his own son. Nothing had, or could have, intercepted his child from the freak whim of a misread chart. The exact series of steps and missteps that led to his son's death were staggering. Logic failed. It failed to such a degree that, James felt, it wasn't even random: it was *intentional*. The universe, James discovered, was hardwired for perversity, not rational thinking. It was governed by a malicious caprice.

So if James ever began to believe in a God, it was one of a Lovecraftian design. Alien and malevolent. Anyone and everyone, he realized, might be a pawn in its game to destroy his heart—which is to say that, once I came into the picture, he wasn't sure about the whole offspring thing anymore. Children became the tiny agents of terminal disorder. They exposed your most monstrous failures through their own vulnerability. His own mother knew it, keeping crib-side vigils to prevent infants from spontaneously asphyxiating. James proved that he couldn't even do that much, the most fundamental of his responsibilities as a parent. Consequently, he was all paranoid energy around me as a child. Whenever I wanted to visit the playground on Mead Street on weekend afternoons, he viewed me with suspicion. Whenever I wanted to ride with him to the grocery store, he froze trancelike, foreseeing visions of disaster, as if each request I made was an elaborate ploy to off myself. The only year I played T-ball, James tried to talk me out of it, because Carlie demanded that he be the one to drive me to and from practice. All during the scrimmages, he'd shuffle behind the fence like he had to pee, chewing his lips, and then clutching the chain links at every pop-fly—visualizing the one errant ball, no doubt, that would arc through the dazzling sun and smash right into my brainpan. He'd drive home with cuts on his palms from holding the metal so tight.

It probably didn't help that, in my youth, I pretended to play with Bradey all over the house. It was more of a morbid affectation than anything. Who, as a grade schooler, isn't enamored with the idea of dark family secrets? Every child suspects, while poking around his parents' belongings, that he was adopted. Even stronger is the suspicion that he has a secret other. A dead twin. A ghost in the playroom, one who steals your lost toys. A mischievous angel who chucks that rotten persimmon at you from the top of the tree—pop on the head, and you turn in time to see the air displaced among the leaves. The concept shook me with its potential: I had a brother, and he was dead. Other kids at school had siblings who whined in the backseat, who tormented them with wet willies and Indian rub burns, who encumbered them through their neighborhoods, through their whole lives it seemed, with training wheels or threats or incessant tattling. My older brother was the sibling that every kid wished for. "Tragically cut down in the prime of his life," I'd tell my third grade buddies on the playground—a phrase I often heard applied by adults to adults, to older people who could drive, and who usually died in automobile accidents. Bradey had legacy, he had power, he had the augury of mysterious illness. L'Aspereginese. Methotrexate. Acute Lymphocytic Leukemia. I had purposely memorized these words for the playground and classroom. They cast the spell, lent me the power to mesmerize, to say, *My world is not your world.* After I enrolled in his same Episcopalian school, Bradey's presence shone, it radiated like the hushed aura of martyrdom when teachers and adults conversed around me. Other kids watched in awe, asked me questions, challenged his historical existence, fed me attention through their wonder or skepticism. It didn't matter that the Bradey I imagined—a streetwise older kid who showed me the ropes, standing roguishly by the lockers between classes, teaching me all the best tactics for dealing with bullies—would've been three years younger than me.

Sometimes, my eight-year-old affectation for Bradey went too far, and Carlie would be called in for parent meetings. On one particular occasion, I was held after school. The principal, the headmaster, had me stand by his desk while Carlie seated herself. I don't remember his name now, Father Something, but his pate was shaved and shiny as a bullet, with a thick welt of flesh where his neck met the collar. Some of the kids said he played football in college, but was barred from the NFL for unnecessary roughness.

Once Carlie was settled into his office, he fitted his fingers together and explained my crime. His eyes were not ungentle when he spoke. When Carlie was confused, he tried again, reluctant to repeat himself, or too burdened by the woeful gravity of the situation.

He said, "Your son ran around the playground, putting his tongue on the other children."

My mother blinked. "Come again?"

I kept my eyes on the carpet, where her ankles, in nylon stockings, were crossed. I whispered, "I was just playing."

"He told them that he had cancer. And that he could give them cancer by licking them."

Carlie's hand flew to her mouth. That was it then: the worst was confirmed. I was horrible, I was disgusting, I was about to be disowned. *Take this child! We can't do anything with him!*

Until she snorted. I looked up for the first time and saw my mother's cheeks quiver, the color of persimmons. She was suppressing a laugh.

The headmaster wrinkled one brow. "Mrs. Cullins, three children were in *tears* by the time the bell sounded for fourth period language arts."

"Sweetie, did you really chase those children around," she composed herself, "and try to lick them?"

"I wasn't really giving them cancer," I said. Then: "It was Marcus. He said it was in my blood. That it had to be."

When I saw my mother's face drop, the plunge of heartbreak in her eyes, I knew I was on the right track. Marcus Fletcher, of course, had said no such thing. That's what I had told *him*. Both adults looked concerned, softening; they looked open to invention now. "So I told him that wasn't true, but if it was, then he could get it, too. I told him if I spit on him, he could catch it." I held out my hands, painting that moment by the monkeybars, working up to what I thought was the best part. "He dared me. He kept daring me and daring me. He said I didn't have cancer, he said my brother never had cancer, and that he never even existed at all, so I knew I had to set him straight. I knew right then it was make-or-break time. But I couldn't work up any spit. So you know what I did? I licked him in the face."

When I broke from my reverie, I was slightly confused to find that they didn't share my sense of accomplishment. No? Too much? Okay. I lowered my head, finding that spot on the carpet. "But, you know, I didn't really give them cancer."

"Thank you, Father," she said, and enveloped my hand in hers. "We'll need to have a little talk." And she led me to the car. On the ride home, she tried to reprimand me, but wound up convulsing with laughter so hard that she cried. What I had done was mean, it was cruel to the other children. But she said this while wiping tears from her cheeks, giggling and snorting to herself. A little window opened up for me on the subject of Bradey then. The kind of attention I had come to expect and crave at school never translated well at home. Carlie and James were the experts on that subject and guarded their knowledge. But here, she was tickled. So I amped up my performance.

That evening, I saw an ad for a new laundry detergent, A.L.L., and subsequently began to torture the household with it. I crooned the jingle all through the living room and hallway, imitating Leon Redbone's warbling baritone—*A-L-L, stain-lifter that's ALL!*—knowing full well the acronym's marvelous coincidence with my brother's disease. Two minutes into my song, I was told to tone it down by James, but mostly I was ignored.

By the time we sat down to supper, Carlie still hadn't told James of my misadventure at school. In that period of their relationship, she rarely spoke to him about our days, especially when I got into trouble, or when she would sign me out of school to have lunch together. He kept his attention fixed to the television behind me, which broadcast Reagan addressing Gorbachev for the one hundredth time. James' plate made the rounds for second helpings.

"Bradey," I said, "Would you like some more asparagus?" I talked to him as if he was a dog, begging beside the table. I had, in fact, wanted a dog for much of that year.

James looked to Carlie, his mouth full of chopped steak. "What's going on?"

She shook her head, her eyes focused on her plate, chewing. "You've got plenty of asparagus left on your plate," she said. "Finish what you have first." James turned up the volume a hair with the remote.

"I think *Bradey* would like some more asparagus," I said, holding my hand out for the plate to be passed.

"All right that's enough of that," Carlie said. "Eat your carrots."

James glanced at me, then to Carlie. He looked upset, but unwilling to enter the conversation. I could almost feel the prickly heat on his cheek.

"Bradey does not like carrots," I informed them.

Carlie put her elbow on the table—a major infraction at dinner time—and bore into me with her eyes. "You stop this, right now," she said. "It's not cute." I didn't say anything, which she took for tacit agreement. Her tension eased a little as she returned to her fork. "Now eat your carrots."

"Bradey does not eat—"

And then she slapped my face. I knocked my milk glass all over the table, and James kicked back, raising his plate with both hands, to avoid the spillage. The shock was immediate, on all sides. Carlie and I looked at each other as if we had stumbled into an electrified fence. She leapt up first—to apologize, to console, to offer more asparagus—before I ran back to my room wailing.

She followed me, of course, which is all that I wanted, and after knocking lightly on the bedroom door and asking to be invited in, she huddled with me on the bed until I stopped crying. I remember hugging close enough to feel her own ragged breathing, seeing that her eyes were squeezed shut, and in that calming lull, I heard the car door slam outside. I listened against my mother's chest as James fired up the station wagon. Its shot suspension rattled and groaned as he slowly accelerated out of the drive, away from the cold supper we had left him with, all alone at the table.

In this way, I learned about grief from my parents: that there is no contending with it. No one moment, no one month or year, can allow us to adequately purge it and then move on. Grief is simply another child, precocious and alive. You nurture it, give so much of your life over to it, watch it grow. Then one day it comes of age and flies from the nest you have made. And your home is that much emptier for its leaving.

2

Carlie exorcised the house on a Monday. After the shriveled and miserly affair of Bradey's funeral (the turnaround was so brief that her sisters couldn't make it in time; few people showed, sending condolence cards and sympathy flowers by the bushel instead) she worked through the rooms with the efficient detachment of a hired housekeeper. Someone who hovered on the periphery of their inhabited lives, someone who, thankfully, didn't speak their language. Even with Bradey's cleaning mania, there was still much to do. Two full days, from six in the morning until midnight, Carlie separated his tiny clothes from the wash, folded them with the toddler garments he had outgrown and, with a rude rip of duct tape, boxed them for storage. She imagined crawling around the house on all fours, wailing, collecting every little whorl of black hair he left behind. She could rebuild him anew, stitch him back together from hair and old band-aids. But Carlie swallowed this impulse down; otherwise she'd have no appetite, no ability, to do what needed to be done. Instead, she scavenged the house for stray toys: Lincoln Logs lost between the couch cushions, felt eye masks and play capes she had sewn him wadded behind the dresser, Matchbox cars half-buried in the flower bed. She collected the small Golden Books scattered throughout the house; dried-out Crayola markers interspersed with check stubs on the rolltop desk; a milk-ringed plastic cup that had gotten kicked under the sofa; and the moldering crust of a cheese sandwich in his school bag. She found the birthday card, a rough cut red construction paper flower that Bradey had made her. Everything got boxed, labeled, and stowed in the crawl space beneath the stairs. Then, without packing a single bag of her own, without even snapping off her cleaning gloves or headband, Carlie got in the car, drove to Minnie's, and stayed for a month.

* * *

James took two days of personal leave, that was all. With his son buried and his wife disappeared, he wanted back into the desert. He wanted emotional dehydration. He wanted the asceticism of work.

On his first day back, without a lunch, he went to the cafeteria and fell in line with the anonymous hive of warm bodies, glad to be faceless, glad to be keeping his head down, when Phil Doyle called to him from across the bustle. He approached James at the end of a long table and stood, measuring him, in quiet pity. After a moment of consideration, he hoisted one checked knee over the bench and straddled it. "I know what you're going through," Doyle said. "And I sympathize." James nodded, staring into his cafeteria tray. A thick brown slab floated in gravy. Meatloaf Tuesday. "You know, the wife and I, we had our first and only miscarry," he said. Doyle had an apple in his hand, deep red, which he turned over and over, inspecting the skin for blemishes. "It was a crazy time. I didn't know what to do. The idea of a baby meant so much to Leslie. That's when we found out, you know, that she wouldn't be able to conceive. It was like the bottom dropped out of the future." While Doyle spoke, he flipped out a pen knife, the same one James had seen him use to clean his cuticles, and began to peel the apple. Neat, thin ribbons of skin curled to the table. Farther down the bench, a clutch of technicians had pushed their trays away and were chatting, smoking. "I cried, I admit it. But afterward, I kind of just ran dry. Meanwhile, there's this big to-do going on around me. A big fuss, you know, with Leslie, her family, our friends. It just never let up, this constant morbid business. This constant breaking down. I don't want you to get the wrong impression of me, but I was lying there in bed one night when it suddenly occurred to me: what's the big fucking deal? You know what I'm saying? But you've got to give them their space. You've got your own needs, and they go largely ignored for the hysterics of the woman. It's a big deal for them. They've got all these nesting instincts that suddenly go haywire—and what're you supposed to do?" Doyle sliced out a thin wedge of apple and popped it in his mouth, crunching. He scooted a fraction of an inch closer, lowered his voice. "But let me tell you something, it was the best thing that could have happened. Not having that kid. I mean it, I wouldn't have it any other way now. These weeks to come? They're going to be the best in your life. All those hormones go into overdrive. You know what I'm saying? You get the worst and best of it. Leslie and me found ourselves. I mean, we found ourselves all over the house, if you get my drift. I'm not just talking about the kitchen table and living room floor; I'm talking about the kitchen sink. I'm talking about the refrigerator. I'm talking about the patio furniture at four o'clock in the afternoon with just a thin screen of azaleas between us and that big beautiful world. She was hungry in ways she had never been." Doyle swallowed, appraising James as though deciding whether or not to let him in on a secret. "You know about Whit's first marriage, right?"

James toyed with the fork in his hand, but still hadn't touched the meatloaf. "No," he said.

Doyle hunkered in, confidential. "Well, after they had their first kid, she got strange with him. You know, that happens with us. With the men. Suddenly your house isn't your house anymore. Your life isn't your life. But with Whit, she'd lock doors. She'd leave the house with that kid for days on end. Staying with relatives, staying God knows where. Before, when she was all 'I want children,' she was glued to him. Once she had her baby, that was it. He was just a stranger now, buddy. He wasn't a husband anymore, he wasn't a man, just a donor. It's never the man's baby. She breastfed that kid until he was eight. Hormones and bonds. That's what I'm talking about. Right there." Phil Doyle gently laid his apple core on James' tray. "It's hard right now, I know. But you've got your wife. Think about that when you go home to her tonight. This is the time when she really needs you. You'll be close like you never believed. These will be the best weeks of your life." Doyle placed a hand on his shoulder. "I swear."

* * *

This last time, when Carlie took off for Minerva's, James didn't come racing out. He couldn't show his face over there again, not after his last interaction with Minnie. Instead, he called. The first day that the phone broke the silence, Minnie measured Carlie's vacant stare at the kitchen table, and picked up the phone. No response after her hello, just nervous breathing on the other end. The next time, Carlie took the phone. And James spoke. He began calling every day, just courtesy calls to check up on her, never being much of a conversationalist over the phone: *You doing okay? Okay, good. Take your time.* And: *I re-edged the walkway today. It was getting overgrown.* Also: *I repainted the hall. It was too dark. I couldn't see and kept bumping into the picture frames. Now it's bright yellow. It glows. It makes its own light.* But after a while, the phone began ringing in the middle of the night, its analog bell suddenly jarring Carlie awake like a heart attack, and she would pick up from her bedding on the couch. (She had refused Map's room, determined not to trade one morass of loss for another.) In those moments a hazy voice whispered out from the heavy receiver, thinly transmitted, as if tuned through a radio dial: *You can't just leave me. You belong home. You can't run off like your sisters.* And then it hung up.

Minnie gave her space, asked no questions, and expected nothing. She did all the talking. She told stories about a dear friend she had as a young woman, a pen pal who maintained correspondence even while imprisoned in the Japanese internment camps of World War II. (Minnie had an old pocket-sized photo tucked into a diary: "Isn't she the most gorgeous thing you've ever seen?") Similar anecdotes popped up. They worked Minnie's yard and went for rambling strolls through the woods after lunch, the cloud of Bradey lingering after. To distract herself, Carlie carried a tattered pocket guide for the native herbs and wildflowers, which she had found wedged in Minnie's bookcase. While Minnie flounced through the bracken to relieve her bladder, Carlie bent down with the dog-eared paperback, examining some wild weed. "Spiderwort," she'd utter, flipping to page eighty-seven. "Toadflax; devil's bit. Wild bleeding heart and gill-over-the-ground." They sounded like ingredients for the fairy potions or mud pies she and her sisters would make as small kids. With how often Minnie had to pee, she was reminded of her own pregnancy, wondering wildly, jealously, if the old woman herself wasn't pregnant. Annunciated in her late sixties. Anything seemed possible now. And maybe Carlie wasn't so far off. These walks were the only time she left the cottage on Auscauga Lake Road. She worked on re-laying stones for the walkway and cultivating azaleas. Without her own wardrobe, she wore Map's clothes, caked with dirt at the knees.

One wet, depressed afternoon in mid-September, both women rested on the back porch while a rainstorm rolled through the sky. Through the downpour they watched a thicket of mandevilla, which had grown high through the pine branches, slowly open in asters of deep red and yellow. Minnie had just returned to the porch from the bathroom again, easing into the wicker chair beside Carlie. She had arrived in time for the full bloom, like the final phase of a lunar eclipse, and whispered her usual benediction: *Suwannee*. Carlie said nothing, watching intently. "You know," Minnie said, "I've never done a thing but let it be. Every winter I think it's done for. But here we are."

Below, the creek stormed, overflowed, foaming white against the stone levee to Minnie's yard. The women were sitting quietly. In due time, the rain skimpered out, falling through the canopy in a sporadic murmur. The sky continued rumbling like dish racks sliding in and out of the washer, clanging together distantly. Then came a break in cloud cover, mopping the yard with sparse sunshine. The full musky anise of the mandevilla reached the porch.

"I could live out here," Carlie said.

"An excellent idea." Minnie sat utterly still. "You are most welcome to."

"Almost."

"Ah."

"I just think," Carlie thought for a moment, "the solitude. It could take root, inside you. Change who you are."

Without turning her gaze: "Do you think it's changed who I am, dear heart?"

"Minnie," Carlie said, in a rare moment of frankness. "I don't know who you are." She went on, "You have all these stories about other people. But here you are. And now, without Map. Don't you get afraid? Doesn't it overwhelm you, the loneliness?"

"Dear heart," Minnie said. "Map was good company. But I have always lived alone." Again without looking, she reached over and touched Carlie's hand, rubbing the knuckles. "Besides, there are better things to be overwhelmed by. Shall we go for a dip?"

Thinking it a joke, Carlie only smirked. But then Minnie stood and began stripping in front of her. Off went the blouse, slacks, brassiere. Then the wig. Standing bald-headed, and with only her owlish glasses on her face, Minnie walked surefooted down to the creek, crooning "Wild nights! Wild nights!" as she eased into its flooded waters. Eventually, left alone on the porch, Carlie thought, *Okay, screw it.* She followed. She held the work-shirt collar closed at the throat like a bathrobe, quickly shedding Map's old clothes on the bank. The washout had turned the creek bend into a deep and gentle pool, which ran richly warm, marbled with thin cold currents. Minnie rolled in and out of the water along the sandbar like a dolphin, while Carlie kept up to her chin. She watched

Minnie, uncomfortable with the ambiguity of her own need, her own hunger. After the initial invitation, Carlie found herself alarmed by the space of the moment, by the room for possibilities. "This is the best view in the entire county," Minnie said from her back, gazing through the twilit trees. The sparse seaweed of her remaining hair trailed out. "Go limp, relax. Look up." Carlie submerged herself, letting her own hair spread the surface like a drowning victim. Here they are, in one more revision of paradise: Lilith and Eve, the older and younger, peacefully unmoored in the primordial stew of the universe. When Eve rolled over to face the sky, all the space of that floating world reeled with vertigo. Tree forms spiraled above her, darkening like a ragged tapestry. Her hearing plugged with water. Her mouth sprayed a cloud of spume like whale. A cold joy crept into her stomach.

A week later, Carlie returned to the house. James, perennially seated at the rolltop desk, unshaven and unwashed, was bent over his paperwork. She stood in the doorway, with no baggage, dressed in the same clothes that she had left in. She waited silently for him to notice her. Once he did, she did not wait for him to speak. She knew what she wanted and laid it down with four simple words.

She wanted another child.

3

More than once in my life, I have been accused of being heteronormative. Or more accurately: homonormative. To paraphrase Freddie, this is a special species of sanitized queen who licks the boot heels of society while they're planted in her face, one who trades a mile of self-respect for an inch of respectability. Before we started dating, Freddie used to pin these names on me as a come-on, a prove-me-wrong flirt, though I was by no means his only offender. In my circle, Stacy and Yvette, who hadn't yet had Emile, were screening for donors. Joey worked, and still works, as a paralegal for Lambda Legal, spending eighty-plus hours a week up to his Adam's apple in briefings on family law and health care. As for me, I had been in a long-term relationship with an architect named Thom Shakar, a gorgeous, semi-closeted man who hid behind a self-deprecating humor and a habit for writing prompt thank-you notes. Whenever we all met for drinks, the table became a debating grounds for marriage and children—the struggle for those recognizable forms of family. But Freddie would have none of it. When he was at his least tolerant, contempt would raise a welt across his face and he'd shout and gesture. More often, he'd laugh behind the smoking gun of his cigarette and calmly squash the discussion, flicking ash into the square glass tray. *Fuck marriage rights. Seriously. That's not progress. The dream of wedding bells has corrupted the shit out of the best people I've known. No, see, it's like putting on blackface and doing the buck and wing—it's sick representationalism of mainstream control. I don't want to pretend that I'm a straight man in a straight relationship. Wearing a straight jacket, living the straight life. But you know what? Forget it. Better that you don't listen to me. Go ahead and make believe. That way, you can live your life untroubled, file for joint taxes, and one day you'll wake up and never have to remember being queer again. It was all just a bad fucking dream because you chose the straight and narrow.* Though addressing the table, Freddie's diatribes were always aimed indirectly at me. With Thom seated between us, he would bait me with his sardonic glances, flashing like a fish hook in the depths of the Little Jefferson Bar, while Yvette tried to keep Stacy from jabbing a broken beer bottle into his face. *Oh, America, When will you be worth your million trannies and terrorist drag queens?* He'd croon, spitting cracked ice cubes back into his glass.

I wonder now: Where did this Freddie go? When did he get so domesticated, like the rest of us?

Most of our friends discounted him for the usual reasons: fear of closeness, fear of commitment. But there's a greater fear out there. However dubious his motives were, Freddie had a point. Polyamory works its way into all our lives and, uncomfortable with the possibilities, many of us do our best to ignore it. It blurs the steadfast boundaries of our identities—gay or straight. I think of the people we depend on and who have, in turn, depended on us. Those with whom we've talked until six in the morning, solving the world's problems. Those who leave a bag full of their garden tomatoes at our doorstep, or a novel in the mailbox with a note. Those who pay us a thousand small kindnesses—ringing our doorbell with coffees, doughnut holes, paper berets for Bastille Day—without a second thought. Those who show us how to laugh at ourselves, who have faith in our ridiculous ideas, who knock on our door in the middle of the night on the verge of a breakdown, to whom we freely offer a couch, an ear, and a bottle of red wine. Those who call out our despicable behaviors and challenge us to be better than we are. Friends, neighbors, landlords, teachers—all who have come so close to our lives that we remember the smell of their breath, with whom we feel in the quiet lulls of conversation a radiant, ringing peace. How can we not fall in love with all of these people, just a little?

Minerva understood both well, the competing urges between normativity and the far-reaching territory of love. From piecing together the letters and stories, anyone can see that Minerva herself was a lesbian outwardly living the prescribed American life. Inside-out of the box. A lot remains ambiguous this far from events, but the old earmarks are clear. In those weeks living alone together, did she and Carlie make love? In some fashion, I'm sure. I'm equally sure she loved Map, and others still. Even more than Freddie, I believe, Minnie had embraced a sexual democracy: a willingness to absorb and be absorbed by the people around her. It's irresistible. Once we open our emotional borders to others, a little Walt Whitman flutters patriotically, deep in our chest. But I want to know more about that flamboyant couple, hiding out in a boondocks Xanadu, throwing their grand New Year fêtes in celebration of what they were. (Years ago, James and Carlie had been in the heart of the gayest annual outpost in South Carolina. Did they know it?) Who were Map and Minerva? Did they share some form of love, or was it a contractual convenience? Were they a brother and sister of sorts, pretending to be a straight couple in the sticks so they could live their lives away from the scrutiny of others? Straight-jacketed, as Freddie would have it. Such marriage pacts were common during that era. WWII made so much space in our national geography—not just for Rosie the Riveter, but for Rosie and Rita to rivet together, for G.I. Joe to discover the joys of deploying with John. It begot a single-sexed homefront. It created a burgeoning haven for homosexuals in the mobilized port of San Francisco. So what happened to those spaces after the war ended?

Sure, we got San Francisco, demobilized. But all across this great country, Maps came back from the war and buddied-up with Minnies, and together as pioneers they hid out, staying alive, in the great mainstream frontier. This is the truer Edenic scene reprised—all those Adams and Eves, living out one identity while enacting another, determined like hell not to get thrown out of the Garden.

If it seems like I'm forcing the issue, suggesting comparisons between my life and those lives of my parents, of Minnie and Map, making connections where they don't exist—well, then, sneer if you like. But don't condescend to pity or forgiveness. I don't need either. I'm only practicing an ancient form of navigation. Look up in the evening sky, right now. See those stars beginning to form in the twilight? Point out for me Ursa Major. Look for Orion's belt. Tell me, do they look anything like a bear, an archer? Of course not. We draw the lines, we make connections between the points of light. All contrived, maybe. But we can still use them to guide our way. When I close my eyes to sleep, in my field of vision I see their constellations—James and Carlie, Freddie, Yvette and Stacy, Minnie and Map—trying to figure out where I am and where to go. And I know that James and Carlie, when they laid their heads on the pillow, have done the same, even though the stars they saw were different. As does Freddie in what fevered sleep he gets. As do Yvette and Stacy, with little Emile tossing in the next room. As does Minnie in the grave.

Homo and hetero, normative and non—and everyone between the binaries. All any of us can ask for in this world is safe passage.

* * *

We relocated to a motel on the outskirts of town. The penumbra of evening falls around us, blue-blacking the pine trees as we settle in. A steady rhythm of big rigs and pickup trucks swoosh by on US-78 like the pull of the surf, their headlights cutting an oily glare across the large window that fronts our room. Freddie paces just beyond the window, watching the traffic and openly smoking a cigarette down to its filter. Even in the twilight, dried sweat stains darkened the back and underarms of his shirt. He stubs the butt out on a stucco pillar and flicks it into the parking lot, toward the moving truck.

After a meal from the Mexican place up the road, Mom is in bed with the starchy comforter drawn to her chin. The photo album still lies on the mattress beside her. I had undressed her for the second time today and helped her into a clean nightgown. Her thighs, I noticed, were mottled with bruises. A deep yellow swelling had puffed her knee from where she fell off the bed. Some of the spots were simply the burst capillaries of old age, but others—thumb-sized welts and faded purple blotches—from a history I don't know. I ran my fingertips over them and she flinched, more tickled, I think, than tender.

I keep the reading lamp on, angled down. My journal is open and smeared with the ink of a cheap pen. The old atlas is spread under my arm for the next morning's route, one last stop before leaving this place forever. The old secondary road names came back to me as soon as I mapped it out. Vaucluse. Tiger's Ferry. Auscauga Lake Road.

Freddie slips in, bringing with him a plume of acrid tar and tepid night air. The heavy, pneumatic weight of the door wheezes shut behind him. For the moment, I keep writing in my journal, blotting my hand on a paper napkin from dinner. Freddie settles into the single overstuffed chair, tucked into the far, dark corner. When he tries to speak, he has to clear the gauze from his throat. He tries again, not loud but clear: "What'd you do with the bumper sticker?"

"What do you think I did with it?" I don't say this to challenge him.

"I know you peeled it off," he says. "But I want to know if you saved it or threw it away."

I cap the pen, take the last of the napkins to rub the smear from my fingertips. They stick and pill to shreds, making a mess. "It was a two dollar bumper sticker, Freddie."

"Five dollars," he corrects. "But that wasn't the point."

"It would have to come off anyway. It's a rental truck."

"That's not the point," he says, slouched into the chair, staring at nothing.

I throw the napkin bits into the wastebasket. There's something I have been thinking of doing this entire trip, and now it seems right. Now seems as good a time as any. I stand and retrieve my checkbook from our suitcases, then return to the desk. I uncap the leaky pen one more time. I can feel Freddie stir, cautious and curious, as I carefully make out the check.

He sits straight in the chair, defensive, as I walk it over. He delicately receives it from my hand with a small, nervous snort and glances up to me, confused. It's made out to him, of course. For ten thousand dollars.

"Are you serious?" His voice is almost inaudible.

"Fix it up," I tell him. I return to the desk chair slowly. My body feels as though I have been cycling for days and days and days.

"Wait," he says suddenly. He stands, the check trembling in his hand like a ticket. "What is this really for? What does this mean?"

It takes me too long to face him. When I do, his complexion is sickly and washed out, undercast by the single lamp in the room. "I want you to succeed, Freddie. I want you to be happy," I say. The finality of that word rings in the silence between us. It hardly needs adding, but I might as well finish the job: "Neither of us has been happy for quite some time."

I catch sight, at that moment, of the glistening bead of sweat clinging to his cheek. He looks at the check pinched between his fingers. Pay to the order of Frederick Luq Smithfield. Ten thousand dollars and no cents. His face quivers, then flushes, as he swears and proceeds to tear and fold and tear the check, glassy-eyed, into tiny pieces. When they won't shred any further, he throws them at my head. The pieces bloom as soon as they contact air and scatter like confetti over my knees. In two strides Freddie grabs the door, bangs it hard because of the security latch, then flings it wide open, and is gone.

Mom stirs with a choke and snort, rises with difficulty to her elbow to find no one in the room but me. No Freddie. No James. No Bradey. No one else but me. The highway traffic runs more clearly. I sit with the shreds in my lap, watching the band of pines and starry night get smaller, narrower, as the pneumatic pump slowly, slowly draws the door to a close.

4

The tenderness of those first few nights together were edged with talk of babies, small caresses, whispers in the periphery of a post-coital sleep. Carlie kept to the pill at James' insistence, just for a little while longer. She planned for the child they would have, curled against his back, asking for his input on names while James feigned sleep. During the day, he effaced the question. He didn't say no, but rather, not now. He said, I'm tired, I'm not thinking straight right now. He said, It's too early, too soon. Once the nocturnal tenderness began to wear off and their conjugal relations dawned into terse daylight, Carlie grew impatient. Words were of no use. So she began to throw red socks into the wash with his white shirts and underwear. She left the newspaper out in the rain; when it didn't rain, threw it into the shower and plopped the soggy heap on the doorstep. The rabbit ears went missing. She burned his bacon in the morning.

"I need time," he said again, sitting in his bathrobe and watching, mesmerized, from behind a ruined sports section as black smoke billowed up from the stove.

"When? How long?" She braced her hips.

"These things can't be measured."

"You're a scientist. Guesstimate."

He returned to the paper. "I can't let go as easily as you."

Clang went the spatula into the sink. Carlie marched from the room. "I'm not letting go." James carefully ran water into the skillet, steam and grease spitting from its charred bottom.

Later, outside, the conversation continued. Carlie confronted James as he scrubbed a golden film of pine pollen from the station wagon. Baby blue and faux-wood paneling, gleaming chrome luggage rack. The family car he had pushed for, with a frame heavy as pig-iron. "We need to move forward," she said, standing at his back. "If we are to stay sane, we need to move forward."

"Moob forward," James echoed, his sinuses swollen and runny with allergens. "I amb moobing forward. Habbing anudder child is not moobing forward. Ids looking to the patht—ids replacing one child with anudder. Ids trying to undo the patht."

"The what?"

"The pastht. You're trying to replace the pastht."

Her slippers snapped and gritted back down the walkway. Carlie spent the afternoon tearing the house apart, digging through closets, wrenching out the steamer trunks, splitting open cardboard boxes. At last she came to his desk, late that evening, and hissed, "I am not trying to replace my child." Slapping a yellowed sheet of legal paper over the electric bill, she pointed: *big.fam.kids*. "One thing in my column. It's the only goddamned thing there."

James, who had his handkerchief out, blew one nostril, then the other. "I'm the one who had to do everything," he said, staring blankly into the dim corona of the banker's lamp, staring at nothing at all, certainly not the marriage plan he had drawn up over ten years ago. "I planned the funeral, bought his casket, and paid the mortician. I have already paid. There's nothing more you can ask from me." Solemnly, he tilted his head back and squirted decongestant into his sinuses, his eyes watering with each pump.

It's hard to explain why, at such an impasse, my parents stayed together. To loosely paraphrase Heidegger, we can only understand things when they cease to function—what blows our minds are those things that endure. That Freddie's chain-smoking grandfather lived through the invasion of Normandy (and the venereal consequences of a dozen French prostitutes) to reach the ripe age of one hundred and two. That the Sentinelese of the Andaman Islands have successfully repelled face-to-face contact with the western world for centuries, armed with nothing but bows and javelins. Or that, despite losing their child, despite watching the bond of familial love unravel in their hands, despite becoming petty antagonists in the everyday drama of their lives, James and Carlie Cullins stayed married. Here, we can only hypothesize. We could make a cosmic fate of it, throw in an indelicate metaphor, say that they were bound like positively and negatively charged ions in an atom, diametrically opposed in the deepest essence of their being but held in motion by a common force. The truth, I believe, is less pretty. Smaller, meaner. They had an opportunity for a clean break, to leave it all behind. Why not divorce? To quote another philosopher, this time an old high school teacher: *Times change, people don't.* What does this mean, exactly? Most essentially, that our motivations are always the same. There are the physical drives: comfort, pleasure, satiety. But perhaps the reason why we partner up as human beings, why we have concocted elaborate ceremonies, devised an official system of legal, state, and federal recognition toward an enduring union, with all sorts of oaths and vows and pledges and exclusions, *until death to do us part*, perhaps all this can be traced back to the one true psychological motivation that sprang from the first primordial moments when we scraped our knuckles against the earth: fear. And what is the source of all fear, at its heart, whether it's fear of dying or fear of the dark? Nothing less than the absolute terror of being alone.

So the truth is, Carlie left James inside at his desk with that miserable slip of paper. Big. Fam. Kids. She stood at the deck railings and overlooked the yellow forsythia in the yard as the last minutes of evening waned. With the sun paling, clouds had amassed from the horizon and released a hot spitting shower that lasted for perhaps two minutes, hardly enough to dampen her shoulders or cast a rain shadow on the patio tiles, leaving everything more sticky and miserable than before it had begun. She watched until night spread and the vegetation took on its own luminescence, mulling over the one reason she never gave for why she wanted another child: "I don't want to be alone." An utterance to which James, confusion in his eyes, might reasonably respond, "What are you talking about? You're not alone. I'm here, too." And in that moment they would at last see each other perfectly. They would understand with irrevocable clarity the differences that stood between them, and go their separate ways. Because the revelation, unspoken, would be clear: "You are not enough."

But out on the porch, such existential phenomenology meant squat to Carlie. She didn't want to understand what ceased to function in their relationship. Rather, she decided to get behind what was broken and just *push*. So after years of James' style of lovemaking—the furtive crawling at night between the sheets, as if sex was a word that needed to be whispered—she announced one fresh Sunday morning to God, the world, and her reflection above the bureau, "I'm not taking birth control anymore." An earring flashed in the mirror as she fastened its backing to her lobe. She then sorted through her jewelry box for a matching bracelet.

James sat on the bed behind her, tugging on an athletic sock. He had planned to mow the lawn that day and liked to protect his ankles from the itchy grass clippings. He stopped and rubbed his feet against the carpet. One sock on, one sock off. "You what?"

"I've stopped taking birth control. I thought you might like to know."

"When?"

"Today," she said, fitting the other earring together. "It's a decision I've made."

"A decision you made," he repeated, computing the idea. "What's wrong with the pills? We can afford the pills. Easily. The pills are not a problem."

"The pills are a problem." Carlie turned from the bureau, looking directly toward him for the first time in a week, and smiled a simple, radiant smile. "They're against my religion."

Stunned, James could only sit on the bed and watch as Carlie plucked up her purse. "Where are you going?" he asked as she passed from the bedroom.

"To church," she called from the laundry room. The back door closed with a jingle.

So began Carlie's life of deceit, and her long conspiracy to get me into the world.

5

Nothing sanctions spite like a popular cosmology. So that first Sunday, she actually did go to church. She had been doing just fine as a lapsed, if still respectful Catholic, but now Carlie wanted to fill herself with the life she had before James. Like loading a gun or funneling gasoline into a glass bottle. St. Mary's of the Hill was the only option, being the only Catholic church in the entire county. Proudly ornate, its bells could be heard ringing over the treetops of downtown Copeland well into the quiet afternoon. Carlie took a seat in the rear pew, ran her fingers over the varnished wood, and fell into comfortable observance. All the familiar smells of ritual and practice returned: the clean pews, the perfumed women, and later, the tickling aroma of incense from the altar. Carlie closed her eyes and let the pipe organ blow its music against her sweaty pores, like a blast of cool air conditioning. She would soak herself in mass like a rag in turpentine, would return home reeking of the stuff. She wanted to drag its heady funk into the house, wanted to make him dizzy, intoxicated, nauseated. He would then smell that she was dangerous, highly combustible. That, if he was reckless, she could burn the entire house down. Carlie inhaled the melodic drone of the homily; she searched the arched windows for the head of St. John the Baptist, for the brutal Deposition of Christ. She professed her faith down to the last definite article. She sang, just for the fun of it, in Latin. Had there been no one else in her row, she would have knelt without the kneeler pads just for old time's sake. To feel the cold hard floor beneath her patella, the pinched nerves tingling, the bone and skin. She looked forward to offering a sign of peace to everyone within reaching distance; she would hurdle over pews to hug small children, cross the aisle to affirm the elderly with a touch. When it came time to transubstantiate, she fell in line to receive the body and blood.

And it almost worked. But waiting in line for communion, slowly processing with everyone else, she couldn't go back. The words of consecration caught up with her. The refrain to "Bread of Heaven, on Thee We Feed" buzzed in her ear. And the idea of communion began to rub against her—not as Carlie Robicheaux or the wife of James Cullins, but as this new Carlie Cullins—like an itch, like a wool suit hugging her body. As communion was presented, it seemed wrong, it seemed needling, pestering, this *take my body*, this *take my blood*—isn't that what they were always doing? These people? This incessant, insatiable take-take-taking? *Jesus Christ*, how exhausting! Why couldn't they leave Him alone for once? What if, instead of demanding, instead of taking, grasping, gulping, swilling, they gave back a little for once? Opened their own artery over the cup. See how that felt. Spill a little of their own blood. Or, here's a novel idea, bring their own goddamn loaf of bread!

"Why don't you do something for your own self instead of sucking me dry!"

The little priest, with his long, pocked cheeks, blushed. The congregation was so deep in the habit of ritual that it seemed to register Carlie's outburst as if it were a siren that had passed outside. They looked up, they looked around. Only the organist, to his credit, dropped a note, a brief breath in the pipes that caused the choir to stumble, unaware of what they had tripped over. Carlie popped her mouth open and quickly squatted so the priest, stunned, could place the host on her tongue. Parishioners whispered under the music, scanning the nave. With hands still knitted prayerfully together, Carlie marched by her pew, head bowed, straight past the baptismal font and out the vestibule doors.

Safely outside, she stayed at the top of the high, terrazzo steps to clear her mind. After a moment Carlie scraped the dense wafer from her palate and, since spitting it over the rail seemed too sacrilegious, let it drop into her open purse. She breathed. Instead of scurrying to the car, Carlie took her time: she tasted the air, observed the way magnolia leaves scattered the sunlight, the muffled din of organ music and hosannas inside, the traffic signals mutely regulating the empty intersections. She saw the plantings across the street, those by the church walkway. Native azaleas, golden forsythia again. The silvery green foliage, the litter of fuzzy magnolia cones crushed in the street. The absence. She felt she was on Minnie's screened porch staring into empty space. She was waiting for an epiphany.

After the service, when the heavy doors pushed open to daylight, Carlie was still waiting. She stood aside and watched the people pour over the church steps. Below, they pooled in large circles and chatted, stoppering the flow of foot traffic for those few who searched for their cars. All the social connections paused to jig on their lines, flashing smiles and hellos. And she, again, an anonymous fish. The priest, in his vestments, noticed her while shaking hands with the exiting congregants. When he at last approached her, Carlie said, transfixed, "Father, do you know what that is?"

He adjusted his glasses and glanced over his shoulder, "I'm afraid I…"

"*H. ventricosa aureomarginata.* That's a classic hosta. Lord, how pathetic it looks. I bet it's never bloomed." This last thought was apparently too much. With it, Carlie excused herself and negotiated between the crowds, leaving the little clergyman baffled again. She re-emerged at the flower bed where she knelt, in her skirt and heels, in the dirt. What the priest hadn't seen was a little plant among the mulch, looking like a withered, yellowing head of spinach. A moment later Carlie called out, "I got it!" holding the plant up by its fibrous roots system for him to see and catching the attention of those nearby. "It's in sad shape but the roots are still healthy! I think it'll be all right!" The priest didn't know what he was witnessing, exactly, but this woman was apparently taking the plant.

He held up a palm and began, "Those are donated..."

"Thank you!" she waved, tooting the Rambler's horn, as she pulled from the parking lot. Carlie drove around town for hours with the hosta in the passenger seat, watching the trees drop their first leaves, breathing the damp fragrance of September into her lungs—a smell not unlike the moss that grew creekside at Minnie's—until James, all alone and chewing his nails, had to make his own lunch.

* * *

Over time, the Rambler began to disintegrate, resembling a crumpled toy more than an automobile. Its navy blue paint job had discolored around the hood; dings had pocked the wheel wells; the passenger windows had clouded; and now, loose topsoil filled the seat crevices. For weeks, Carlie drove the Rambler all around town with a shovel in the trunk. It rattled beside a basket in which she had thrown gardening gloves, a spade, band-aids, and the like. Sometimes people honked as they passed by, seeing her in a roadside ditch spearing the ground with her shovel, or on her knees gently shaking the rhizomes of some plant from the sand. Carlie would wipe her underarms with a handkerchief and wave. Mostly the cars whooshed by. By the end of another afternoon, the Rambler chugged along the new bypass home, its backseat populated by cardboard boxes, each bursting with scrappy foliage and shaking dirt everywhere, scrawny limbs wagging to the beat of the wind. From all the points of public access, the ditches, the uneven shoulders, the lots for lease, she dug up the town and put it in her yard.

Carlie's plant gathering was not indiscriminate, but neither could she explain her system. It was intuitive. Different days required different rules, and they were always shifting. Some days were for plants on the edge of disaster, those that had trailed too far out into the sun for too long and were nearly killed to a crusty brown. Other days, saplings. She kept meticulous lists, crinkled and soiled legal pads at the potters bench, detailing the plants she gathered—their names, their condition, the date, and location from which they were retrieved. Though she had begun with that one hosta (which was beginning to recover now, if not thrive, its leaves a glaucous green and variegated with frosty white streaks), she tended toward the wild and brambling. The native. The unnoticed. Carolina sweetspire. Jessamine. Tea olive. Mimosa. Nandina. Ligustrum. She checked off their names in pencil; Minnie had given her the old pocket guide. She accrued just shy of sixty plants; most failed, some took root, and before long she began propagating, too; her bench was stationed with scores of clippings, a supply of black plastic pots and torn bags of mulch. Any given weekday, Carlie studied the yard and its transplants like a chessboard. An omniscient, unseen force played at the other end. She looked for light, for shade, for soil conditions, while sweat trickled down her neck.

It got so that she was rarely in the house, only in the evenings and on Saturdays, when James was sure to be home. When not in the thickets around town, she was in the yard, toiling to get plants rooted before winter fell. After a while, the Sunday morning tension between her and James had thickened into a stifling unrest, and the conversation reset.

"Where're you going?"

"I told you before."

"You don't look like you're dressed for church."

"I didn't know you were such an expert."

"You're seeing someone, aren't you?"

"That's right, James—how'd you guess?"

The real fight, always reserved for when she was at the threshold of the door, popped off like cheap firecrackers, unexpectedly quick and furious.

"Step out that door," he dared. "Step out and see what happens!"

"Lock it and see how much glass this house has left in it after I'm done!"

After the door had slammed shut, after the air had settled, James would drop back into his nappy red Barcalounger, zone out in front of the television, and so practice his own form of centeredness in the universe. Null. The Aleph. The portal where all light and sound waves intersect. At work he had tried to regain the old camaraderie with Whit, but the man was never around. Or when he was, he acted strange. Ever since one disastrous personnel meeting with Phil Doyle, Whit dodged about the grounds, ducking and hiding. The last time James bumped into him was in a stairwell. *They're trying to disappear me*, a voice said, seemingly from inside James' skull. He turned to see Whit skulking in the shadows, like the Deep Throat of paunchy sport fishermen, smoking a nub with one hand and eating a baloney sandwich with the other. *Why are you eating lunch in the stairwell?* Whit took a puff and a bite. *He's been messing with my file, James. I been working here since before the paint was dry, and now Doyle tells me my credentials aren't in order. Documentation, that's how he's getting me. And that's how they'll come for you too.* When a door opened two flights above, Whit snuffed his butt and slipped out without another word. The most stable places in James' life now seemed to be the cloistered bathroom at work and the television at home. Years later his monastic devotion to the latter would evolve into something more visceral, a form of habitual self-medication. Basking in the glow of infomercials and political talk shows like the light therapy sessions for seasonal depression, waiting out the winter months of his mental life. Being nowhere and everywhere from his recliner.

When Carlie returned to the house a few hours later, she hung her purse without a glance in his direction. James said nothing, moved nothing, his gaze steady on the shifting electronic transmission of the television screen. He waited only a beat for her to fully enter the house, and then hit her with his one deadpan question: "Do we get to have lunch today?" He had snacked and waited. And waited. Carlie tightened her silence and, with fresh dirt still under her nails, marched through his field of vision to the kitchen. A brief interference with the Aleph. James didn't shift, keeping his attention on a daytime detective show. He said, "How's the Rambler?" He had considered sabotaging it, ruining the starter. Then he wondered if Carlie would sabotage the station wagon, hire somebody to cut the brake lines.

"Cranky," she said. "Mule-headed." Then more honestly: "The clutch is acting up again."

"You should try taking better care of it."

"Don't ask about the car and then act like it's me."

"Makes no difference to me if you drive it into the ground. But when it goes, that's it. Two cars is too much upkeep."

Carlie plunked the mayo jar on the counter. "So how do you expect me to get the groceries if I don't have a car?"

"Simple," James said. "I'll do the shopping when I get home from work. I have to do everything else as it is."

* * *

Another hot, sticky autumn in the sandhills, cooling by night. The roadside leaves bronzed, a less than spectacular show below the fall-line, the foliage turning to a dull, baked red at their brightest. More than therapy, the plant gathering provided a sense of purpose. A personal satisfaction that helped Carlie escape a house that, for her, still festered with the wounds of personal loss. Away from the house, her mind could begin to scab over. Also, in isolation, the mind begins to fantasize. As a younger man, I often daydreamed in a bookstore where I worked, when the aisles were empty and full of silent dust jackets, that a dashing, bright stranger would wander in, spark up a conversation in which we finished the other's sentences, and arrest all the dull days in my life. Or I'd be walking through the park on some autumn evening where that same stranger—or a variation—would be jogging by with his dog. *Hey, didn't you... Weren't you the one...?* Of course, that simply doesn't happen. People go gray and bitter waiting for kismet. You have to go about your life and appreciate those daydreams for what they are—an entertaining substitute for romance.

Carlie I can't imagine had such fantasies. When I was a child, after any spat she would promise herself, "If your daddy and me ever get divorced, that's it. I will never be married again." But maybe as a younger woman, she did. Maybe while toiling with her fingers in the dirt, she began to fantasize. When sweating through thickets of greenbrier and slapping at mosquitoes, she conjured a man from the pure distracted ether of her mind. A sweeter balm rubbed into the periphery of her thoughts. Or perhaps the man was created solely from James' fear.

That Monday, Carlie was breaking back stalks of pokeweed on the corner of Edgewood and Richland Avenues, getting deeper into the dense bracken after a wild rose she had glimpsed, when she came across a stone overgrown with foliage. It looked like a foundation slab, roughly three feet square, a remnant from some old house, no doubt. But as Carlie uncovered its face, she saw an inscription. The chiseled letters were brackish and weepy with grime, hardly legible after years of weathering. She traced them with the tip of her hand spade:

Venus Durchgang 1882
Deutsche Station II
5h 26m 52s 6 W 33° 33' 51" N

She thought she kept misreading it. While trying to make sense of the words, Carlie heard a crashing and crunching through the woods and suddenly was possessed by a wild thought: that it was James. He was coming for her, tearing after her through the woods in his suit and paisley tie. That, much like that night he pursued her in his bathrobe, he had just been sitting in his office with a bee under his bonnet, stewing, until the world was out of proportion, out of his grasp, and now he would set her straight, he would make her understand exactly what she was doing to him, he would show her the wreckage and pain that she alone had caused. As soon as he caught up with her Carlie whirled around, brandishing the spade like a knife, and shouted, *What?*

A man and child stood together, frozen hand-in-hand. The boy rubbed his nose. Fair-haired and wearing glasses, he looked to be a few years older than Bradey. "Are you going to kill us?"

His father broke into a grin. "We can come back later."

It took Carlie a moment to gather her words, stuck on the picture they made: the father taking his son's hand, rambling through the woods to discover this mosquito-bitten, wild-haired crazy woman. "Wait, I'm sorry," Carlie said, breathless as though she had run a mile. She still had her work gloves on. She pulled them off, her hands shaking. "I am so sorry. You and your son scared me. I was just…gardening."

"Gardening?" A crease ran across the man's forehead, warming his expression.

"He's not my *dad*," the boy said, breathing through his mouth. "Why does everybody think you're my dad?"

"It's because we're both so darn good-looking." The man apologized and introduced himself as Lee. If not exactly good-looking, something about him did seem exotic. The gray hair, maybe, because he only looked forty, forty-one. Or because his hair was shaved so short, and his sideburns so trim, that the silver in them glinted like fine grains of sand. He offered a hand to shake. "I'm sorry, Miss…?"

"Missus," she said. "Cullins." Then, to soften her tone. "Carlie. My name's Carlie."

The man nodded. "Ryan's a loaner model. My nephew." And he squeezed the boy's neck to harass him.

The man, Lee, sheepishly pointed at the stone behind her. "We just came out to see the marker," he said. "Ryan here's an aspiring astronomer. Just got himself a brand spanking new telescope for his birthday." The boy was already leaning up on the stone to study it. He wore athletic socks to his knees and had his name lasso-stitched across the back of his tee. She could see it now, that he was an uncle. Protective, but in a brotherly way. A relaxed authority figure.

"I'm sorry—the what now? You know this thing?"

"It has to do with the planet Venus," the boy said, wiping his nose again.

"Here," Lee said. He invited Carlie closer to the stone marker and read the inscription aloud in weak German, then translated, "The Transit of Venus, 1882. German Station Two. And that's the longitude and latitude." To Carlie he said, "That's how they used to measure the distance between us and the sun. Every once in a while, Venus would eclipse the sun—"

"No, it wasn't an eclipse, it was just a black dot," Ryan said. He had begun walking tightrope circles around the adults, heel to toe. "You have to tell it right. Venus is the size of three earth moons, it's just farther away."

"Okay, Smart Guy," he said. His smile was conscientious and boylike despite the premature gray. "Apparently, I don't know enough. Anyway, they rigged up this measuring equipment at strategic points all over the world to track its movement. And that's how a bunch of German scientists wound up in our little hometown, of all places, back before any of us were ever born."

Lee looked to find Ryan, who kept walking his circles. "Don't you want to see this?"

"I've already seen it."

"So when does the next eclipse," Carlie cleared her throat, "dot-thing, whatever, happen?"

"Not until, oh…2012 or so." Lee squeezed his nephew's shoulder, wrangling him by his side. "We just came from checking out that over there." He pointed through the pine trunks to a heavily oxidized iron trellis that Carlie wouldn't even have noticed, overgrown with kudzu as it was. "It housed the observatory equipment."

In a quiet voice, she asked, "It just looks like a gate. What happened to the rest of it?"

"Well, the heliometer. It got broken up and scattered around town. People didn't know what it was so they used the different parts as garden arbors, compost bins, jungle gyms, and the like." Lee cocked an eyebrow, and though he made no eye contact, it somehow felt like an intimate act of complicity. The sharing of a quietly amazing secret. "Can you imagine that? All this stuff, all this old German equipment. It's all just sitting around town in people's backyards."

A smile grew on Carlie's face. Later, she would look it up at the library and see all the exotic places the Germans chose to observe the transit: South Africa, New South Wales, Brazil. And then, among that roster, Copeland, South Carolina. The little town she called home was on the map.

Lee Corbett, as his nephew would attest, was not himself an astronomer. He was a piano tuner. And he also turned out to be younger than appearances. Thirty-eight. Only thirty-eight, and so familiar.

Ryan began tugging on his forearm, abashed and ready to continue on. "All right, Knucklehead, hang on." Lee turned as he was being led away, laughing at the boy's force. "Well, Carlie. Mrs. Cullins. I'm sure we'll meet again when the moons align."

She waved and hollered to Ryan that it was nice meeting him.

Venus would not come again for another thirty-five years, but Carlie could see a black mote in her vision where those two, nearly the image of father and son, had passed before her eyes.

* * *

Doors were shut all over the house, both real and imaginary, as their lives became divided territories. The rooms, undusted, low-lit, became a place of cold storage, suspending the raw data of their lives. Habits formed now that would persist well into my adolescence. Carlie rattled oven pans and crocks around in the kitchen; played her vinyl while studying arborist guides on the living room sofa; and relocated her collection of hand lotions to the front bathroom. She had moved into the third bedroom, my future bedroom, the room that was supposed to accommodate their abundance of children. James turned the den into a hamster cage, collecting piles of old newspapers around his Barcalounger. He kept his work organized in a mnemonic system on the dining room table, no longer in use, and gargled shirtless in the master bath while rehearsing project presentations to his colognes and deodorants.

During this time, Carlie found herself thinking about that man, Lee Corbett, at odd hours. While brushing her teeth and staring into the mirror. Cutting off the garden spigot to a cool trickle, forgetting what she had meant to do. Or on her weekly visits to Minnie's, over tea and store-bought snack cakes, her ears would be buzzing with Minnie's chatter but her mind would vacate.

"Why, I think you should ride him for all he's worth," Minnie suggested. "Ride him until he blows or begs for mercy, one or the other."

Carlie's eyebrows sprang up and Minnie came back into sharp focus, teacup and saucer poised delicately beneath her chin. "I'm sorry?"

"Your car, the Rambler. I know that's what I would do." She sipped her tea with a small, prim smile and added, "What do you think I meant?" Minnie excused herself, set the cup down, and jockeyed off to the bathroom. Even in Carlie's dreamy preoccupation, she noticed Minnie's frequent interruptions, the quick exit to a nearby bathroom. Extracting her from the safety zone of her home proved more and more difficult. The toilet flushed. "He's trying to use it as an excuse to lock me up. Like the Matchstick Girl," Carlie said as Minnie returned. "But I have some money squirreled away from my Aunt Ruby. Why don't you go out car browsing with me on Wednesday? I need a go-to ready for when the Rambler does die."

"Oh, I would love to, dear heart. But I would only push you to buy the most expensive roadster on the lot. Compunction is lost on old age. Besides, James would hang me as a co-conspirator."

"No," Carlie said, tasting her tea again, "I think James is afraid of you."

"Why, Suwannee," Minnie chuckled. "Isn't that a thought?"

She hadn't told Minnie about Lee Corbett. There was no need to, she had only met the man once, by accident, but she did tell her about the limestone marker and the Transit of Venus, to which Minnie responded, "Such a scholar!" and asked to hear more. She thought of more, much more, on the long car rides to and from Minnie's cottage, positively vibrating during those high hours of emotional daydreaming every week while the Rambler fell apart around her.

6

The same morning that Whit Shirley lost his job, James was up at 4:00 a.m.—pacing and rehearsing project specifications in front of the bathroom mirror, practicing his responses while washing his underarms and gargling in the shower—for the most important business lunch of his career. It wasn't a prospect that he relished. Whit's paranoia had been justified: James received official word that they were pulling Whit from the project, reassigning him to other sectors as a second tier assistant, ostensibly to fill vacancies made by the worsening economy. The demotion was incremental, yanked for half an hour here, an hour there. "Custodial duties," Whit had said grimly. "They got me all but wheeling around a mop bucket." Eventually, Phil Doyle came into the cold-lab one morning with a lower level manager while both James and Whit were reviewing data from the latest ceramic samples. When they entered, Phil had been engrossed in a cuticle, biting his teeth together to sever the offending hangnail, and casually disengaged himself to lean on a work counter. It was the lower level manager, a small man with damp curlicues of hair, who spoke. "Whit Shirley?" He looked to the two men, then at Phil, who nodded in Whit's direction. "Your schedule with the physical plant has been extended, so clock in promptly at 1:00."

From then on, Whit never saw more than five hours a week in the lab. Occasionally, James spotted him across the grounds during odd hours, wearing a shower cap and rubber gloves, and wheeling what looked like a sanitation cart from the physical plant. Only once did Whit catch him by surprise outside the lab, dressed in that godawful getup, unable to swallow down the indignity in his voice. Whereas he would have once gritted his teeth and said, "I'd like to slam that sonofabitch's pretty little fingers in a car door," Whit now said, "James, they got me on a pay reduction. You gotta help." James nodded vacantly, "Sure, sure. I'll see what I can do. I'll see what I can do," and hurried off. He told himself he would, too, when the time was right. For now, he avoided Whit at all costs, nearly sprinting when he had to cross between buildings, and holing up in his office for the scant hours Whit was in the lab. Phil Doyle had been punishing him it seemed, first by extracting Whit, and then by pulling so much funding from the main project that it teetered on the edge of collapse. But now two investors from France were interested in subcontracting the research for a related invention, and for the time being Phil Doyle's unaccountable spleen had turned to manic enthusiasm. All week he hooted, "My go-to guy!" and "Tuesday, 12:30 sharp!" whenever he saw James in the halls, like a basketball coach pumping and pointing to his star player.

James crawled through the tangle of commuter traffic early that morning—a flat gray day, a wet muck of pine straw and leaves already plastered to the roads—only to be barred from Lot B3 by an armed security blockade, outfitted in their military fatigues, helmets, and bracing AK-47s at the sling. A small congestion of cars and pedestrian onlookers were barred from the third aisle, where James had an assigned space. As one MP dispersed the crowd to the sidewalks, James saw another who carried at arm's length, tagged as evidence, a bolt-action rifle and a 12 gauge shotgun. He gawked, thinking, *What kind of idiot…* Then the security detail loosened to reveal a mule-brown El Camino as the center of attention, its doors broken opened like wings, while two other MPs continued to search the interior, tearing gashes through the upholstery. And that was when James saw them hoist Whit's handcuffed body from the pavement; a jagged grin on his sixty-one year old face, blood at the temple. His characteristic dark glasses were broken, scratched and bent at the ear, and as he was dragged up, he looked clearly in James' direction.

In that moment, James thought: the guns. The guns aren't loaded. Strangely, that was the first thing that came to his mind, the thing he knew in a heartbeat from the bruised grin cocked on Whit's face. Whit had gotten himself intentionally fired. He must have. Just to prove what he could do. To prove his dignity and swagger and to shame the authorities and dodge a long-term jail sentence in the same breath. Right then, James felt the heat flush his face and came very close to screaming through window, *We were a team!*, spittle flecking the glass, shrill enough to be escorted into custody himself and prematurely end his career. Instead, when the cars behind him began to honk, he broke eye contact and motored on.

All that morning he skirted the sensational buzz from the other personnel, the lab techs and secretaries, until Phil Doyle cornered him down one hall, bracing his shoulders like a brother-in-arms who had barely escaped death, to whisper, "They were hollow-points, you know. I hear they found an additional sixty rounds in the glove compartment. I'm glad they dropped the fucker before he got inside." Phil pressed a hand to his own forehead, visibly angered and ill. He noticed the hollow stare in James' eyes. "Hey, hey, focus. We need you to bring it today, Jim, don't let this distract you. It's time to focus on the future here. Are you with me?" Phil clapped James' shoulders to buoy him, not realizing that James wanted to twist his head off like a bottle cap. James nodded vaguely. Phil smiled. "All right. Today's the big day. Twelve-thirty: the French are coming! The French are coming! You bring the brain; I'll bring the game." He then slapped James on the shoulder once more, the encouragement of a real trooper, and strolled down the hall.

* * *

By 12:30 James was still in a mental fugue. He found himself at the Highlands, a Continental restaurant in downtown Copeland, seated between Phil Doyle and, perplexingly, Bob Pendergast—PenderGasbag, as Phil called him. Here, the two men carried on like best friends. During a break in the conversation, Phil casually leaned in to whisper, "Don't worry about Bob. There'll be enough to go around." James felt feverish. Immediately, he understood. Bob—mustachioed like Phil but with shiny, ruddy jowls—had gotten wind of this meeting. He had smelled money, carrion on the side of the road. Both men, James saw, circled the table like jackals as they chatted, vultures to opportunity, who were not above indulging on the government dime, apparently. Phil ordered filet mignon; Bob, beef tartar and a little champagne. Between bites of small delicate meat, between laughing at their own ice-breakers, they turned their hundred-watt smiles onto the guests, keeping them transfixed, it seemed, to the table. They talked of the oil embargoes; they boasted of stellar days ahead for the nuclear industry. Compared to their overseas counterparts, they looked and behaved like used car salesmen. Tweedle-Dee and Tweedle-Dum, Whit had named them. The monikers stuck in James' head.

Across the table sat two French representatives, Messrs. Bessette and Durand, from a private European nuclear corporation. They were soft-spoken men, slow to raise a fork or water goblet to their lips, dressed in impeccably pressed dark suits. One was bespectacled and thin; the other, immaculately balding. Crisp white linens dressed the table between them with a set of chilled water glasses. They politely asked for water without gas, no ice. They drank beers with lunch, imported bottles poured into small glasses. Waiters maneuvered by their elbows. Occasionally the men conferred among themselves. James had taken French language in both high school and college but couldn't follow what they said. Outside the café windows, Whiskey Road split into two one-way streets, bisected by a wide, shady median of crepe myrtles. James sat in a sick daze, staring out the window. In the center of the table was a silver vase, sweating with wilted daisies.

Their company, Messr. Bessette said, had seen Dr. Cullins' recently published article—the petroleum and micro-crystalline sealant—and was very excited about this potential technology. "We're all very excited," Phil chimed in. "Our technology is a frontrunner in the industry." Making clear, of course, that Dr. Cullins' technology was not his own. It was the property of SRS and the U.S. government. Neither owner nor spokesman, James was the inventor at this lunch, the token scientist. He knew what was expected of him. To sit as still as a trophy prize and a pocket calculator and to only respond, when both managers looked to him glowingly, to the technical questions. While James outlined the details, all four men smoked around the table, tapping their cigarettes into little glass ashtrays. Soon a gauzy wreath of smoke pervaded the air; James took to sniffing and clearing his throat sporadically, his sinuses clotting. Phil leaned back, looking more than ever like the local meteorologist: wide lapels, checked suit, neatly combed mustache.

Durand asked in a delicate, nasal voice, "So at this point, could you please explain to us possible applications. What is it you see this sealant most suitable for?"

"At this point? It'd be reckless of me to speculate. We're aiming small-scale first, commercial appliances, things of that nature. Though it probably couldn't fix a crack in a microwave yet," James said.

"But we foresee the applications to be myriad," Phil corrected.

"Industrial?" Bob prompted.

"Most definitely," he said. "Reactors, primarily. A reactor nowadays costs well over a hundred million bucks, USD, to build. Think of the expense it could save if you could stop leakage on older models. And nuclear isn't the only industry that deals with radiation. We're thinking medical, too."

James shot him a cold stare. "This is not exactly something you can slap on."

Bessette asked, "How close to complete development?"

"I'm not sure," James responded slowly. "My production team has been slashed. So it's probably still years away."

"Oh, that's a conservative estimate," Bob jumped in this time. "Isn't it, Phil? You're closer to the project than me."

"You betcha. That's why we have our top people, like Dr. Cullins here, assigned to it."

The French reps turned to each other looking concerned, looking for the information they were apparently promised, looking as though they had just crossed the Atlantic Ocean for tap water and a conversation on American sports. By the time the waiter arrived to trade out the ashtrays, Phil had managed to take James aside in the men's room. "I can't believe this," James said the moment they entered. "I really can't believe this."

Phil had locked the door. "What are you doing out there?" He kept his hands in his pockets, his cheeks dimpled in a neutral smile. James stopped short of the sink, disconcerted to see the bathroom was one private stall, a small space between the two men.

"I'm trying to answer their questions."

"No, you're not. You're sabotaging the best opportunity you've had since arriving in this little shithole. And you're making the rest of us look like shmucks." Phil ambled over to the mirror, the threat in his voice aimed at his own reflection. To squeeze aside, James had to straddle the toilet.

"I don't know what you've been telling these people," James said, collecting himself. "I don't know what you've been shoveling to mislead them, but it stinks. I created the framework for this sealant. I clocked over two thousand hours of my own time to work on the compound. No one knows it better than me."

"Boy, you eggheads really earn those PhDs, don't you?" Phil took his time, meticulously rinsing his fingers under the faucet.

"Excuse me?"

He plucked one, two linen hand towels and dabbed his fingers dry. "You think I'm telling them what they want to hear. See—I know how your mind works, James. You're easier to read than an odometer. All of you number-crunchers are. But no. I'm telling them what they *need* to hear. And only what they need to hear. Because it is my job, my responsibility, to provide you with this opportunity. An opportunity to do something meaningful. It's like leading a horse to water. But you're not going to drink. You're not going to drink, because you are a righteous prick, James. You are simplistic and stubborn. You think you've got the honor of the gods on your side because you think you work in an objective field. But the gods aren't objective. They're bureaucrats, and you're a peon who thinks his shit smells like daisies. So here you have this opportunity: these guys are willing to pay big money for first crack at something that doesn't exist yet. We know that. Hell, *they* know that. That's just how industry works. So those two icy-assed frogs sit out there *wanting* to believe in you and your work, wanting to *fund* its development. And what are you going to do with it? You're going to walk in here, and stick to your pencil-pushing numbers, and you're going to let, how much?, two thousand hours of your hard labor go to shit. Because—over goddamn canapés—you're going to ruin your budget, you're going to ruin *my* budget, and with it you're going to ruin something you believe in."

With no room to stand, James sat on the toilet lid, his knees scrunched together. Razor bumps flared red on his neck and cheeks from where he had shaved that morning.

"Now let me be clear." Phil held an index finger, numeral one, in front of James' face like an eye exam. "This sealant stuff? It's not your idea. It's my idea. Because it's my project to delegate. And if you're telling me that you can't rise to the challenge we're setting out there," he pointed beyond the bathroom door, "then I will take my project and find someone who can."

Doyle let that thought linger, then slowly drew himself upright. Beside the sink was a decorative basket with chocolate mints. He snapped up two and, flipping one to James, unbolted the door.

Back at the table Bob craned around, a little flush-faced with champagne, and beamed, "We were just kicking around some ideas for this little wonder-putty. Say, James, how many rads you figure it can withstand?" All four men faced James for an answer. He had hardly touched his food; the linen napkin lay crumpled in his lap. "As outlined in my article," James said, clearing his throat, "at the present moment, we don't hypothesize more than 10,000 rads, with a temperature resistance between 40 – 600 degrees Fahrenheit." He looked to Phil, then to Bessette and Durand. "However…it's not inconceivable that, possibly, it may at some point withstand twice that amount." The representatives nodded eagerly and whispered over their cigarettes.

After lunch adjourned, everyone stood on the sidewalk in the pleasant sunshine, giving damp handshakes. Before parting for separate cars, Phil turned to James for one last word. Except James wasn't paying attention. Instead, his glassy countenance, typically immune to all peripheral stimuli, was mesmerized by a terrible mirage down the boulevard. Phil squinted and said, "Hey…isn't that your wife?"

The group of men shuffled for a better view, a murmur of interest. "What's she doing there, James?"

Where the streetside tapered into undeveloped lots, weedy and overgrown, a tall woman squatted over a spray of sedge and crabgrass like a milkmaid among the pastures. Cutoff jeans, wobbly tits, and a big floppy sun hat, ripping up big chunks of something. Aiming that visible derrière, bent over, at the downtown traffic. James felt a sharp stabbing pain between his ribs. He had no answer, no response, and had to force the words from his tongue, murmuring, then blurting with feigned laughter: "No, no, that's not my wife. I don't know who that is!" He turned to block the men's view, fumbling to adjust his briefcase clasps.

"Well, whatever she's doing," Bob said, peering around James. "I'd sure pay good money for her to keep doing it!" Laughing hoarsely, he slapped Durand on the shoulder and led the two men down the sidewalk.

Phil kept his face toward the warming sun, waving as the party dispersed to their cars. "I think you need a break, James. Some time to recoup," he said. "I want all your documentation on the sealant given to

George Gifford by Monday." Briskly slapping one shoulder, he added. "See you back at home base."

It took all of his strength, once alone, to dislodge his feet from the concrete. But once his feet were free, there was no stopping him. Within seconds he was in the station wagon, its engine quaking like an iron tank as it ate up the asphalt and lurched onto the curb three feet from his wife, who, while he blared the horn, spun around like a startled alley cat, matted with sweat and dirt. James pumped down the passenger window, shouting, "What the hell is wrong with you! You should be committed! You should be in a straightjacket and committed!" And then he began to throw whatever he could grab from the wagon's console—loose coins, dried felt pens, wadded receipts, a half-eaten package of Smarties—at the speechless target of his wife, raining a salvo of trash in her general vicinity, until the light turned green. Then he executed a U-turn with shuddering force and accelerated out of town.

Carlie knelt in the soil, amid the litter and weeds. A moment later—five minutes, maybe ten—another car cruised up to the same curb, a pistachio green Chevy Vega, gently idling. It was Lee Corbett. Lolling one elbow out the window, he grinned and asked, "So you ready to grab some lunch?"

"Yes," Carlie replied firmly, her eyes bitter and honed on her husband's exhaust, vanishing down Whiskey Road. "Let's."

* * *

Moments before James' business lunch had dissolved into a fiasco, Carlie had been hunkered in the thigh-high sawgrass of an abandoned lot, digging up what she believed to be crocus bulbs, when a low voice said from behind, "Vandal." A man, owner of the voice, waited from the sidewalk, a small paper bag cradled in one arm. He was dressed as though ready to climb telephone poles. He gave a little wave. "Lee Corbett. We met the other day?"

Carlie forced a smile through the sweat on her face. "I remember."

"I saw you from the hardware store."

Kneeling among the bulbs, Carlie nodded and speared her hand trowel into the clay to give it a rest. "So where's your surrogate son?"

"At school at the moment."

"Oh." The memory of schedules and yearly school cycles flickered over her face. "Yeah, I should've known that."

Perhaps noting her vague unease, he added, "But back with my sister, in the grander scheme of things. I have to renew him every few weeks or so." He nodded at the cardboard box filled with loose soil and shoots. "I see your still gardening. So is this some kind of parole work or a vigilante thing?"

Carlie straightened and peeled off her gloves, a rivulet of sweat trickling down her collarbone. She grinned absently, adjusting her bra, "A little of both, maybe."

"Yeah, I figured you had a lawless streak in you." Lee Corbett weighed the bag in his palm. "Look, I need to grab something to eat before my stomach digests itself. Would you want to join me?"

Carlie gave a mirthless laugh, seeing his bluntness, and rubbed her runny nose with the arch of one wrist. "Thank you, Mr. Corbett, but I think I'll pass. I'm not exactly dressed for dining out."

"It's Lee," he said. "And don't worry, I happen to know a great place that doesn't even care what you smell like."

"Oh, you're a flatterer. You must get that from your nephew." She slapped her neck, where a horsefly buzzed. "But I really don't think so."

"All right," he said. "It's no big deal."

And as they lingered one second too long, Carlie ventured to say, because the thought occurred to her, and because he had already erased the dirt line between polite strangers, "You know, I had uncles like you. Always full of shit," she said, grinning. "So tell me something. Are there really pieces of that observatory all over this town?"

His smile opened wide and toothy. "Absolutely." And with that opening, he added, "Look, I gotta run and grab my car before it gets towed. While I'm gone, think about following me for an egg sandwich or something. I could use a little conversation."

"Uh-huh," she said. Ridiculous, was what she thought after he left, further thinking she had better pack up her tools and go while the getting was good. He seemed like a lonely man, if a little too brazen. A little like a brother she never had. Mischievous, but mostly harmless. While unearthing another bulb, she thought of the gray dolor of his eyes, the sad heaviness of his mouth even when smiling. She imagined what James would say about having lunch with another man. He'd be outraged, of course. Livid. Blood vessels breaking along his nostrils. *Gallivanting*, he'd call it, as he did any time she left the house alone. The thought amused her. Such paranoia, you couldn't take seriously. And then, bent over to grab her spade, mid-thought, Carlie found herself mentally pushed through a plate-glass window. Because there was the station wagon, blaring in her face, and James sputtering behind the glass in a rabid fury, chucking trash at her, here to break the illusion of a neurosis that, from a distance, could be cynically amusing. And then, just as quickly, the station wagon disappeared. He really was stalking her. Carlie was no longer amused, but stunned. Stunned long enough for Lee Corbett to return, as everything else returned to her as well—the dusty air, a jay calling in the mimosa tree, the particulate cloud of exhaust, the blood pressure warming her veins. And Carlie said, "Okay, buster. All right. I'll take you up on that offer."

They ate fried egg sandwiches and coffee at the Mile Track Kitchen. Tucked between the polo fields and the mile track, the Kitchen operated out the back of a two-story farmhouse. A hideaway that served the horse people—not those who owned them, but those who worked them. Those who mucked the stalls or hammered the hardware for their hooves, those who ejaculated stallions for their semen, or mid-wifed the broodmares, reaching up to the elbow in horse placenta. Carlie took her coffee black and allowed herself to drown in it; allowed herself to float around in the cup like a steam bath. People came and went through the screen door, leaving behind sandwich crusts or greasy egg plates, and a ragged newspaper that circulated from table to table. The house sat under the shade of live oaks, cool with the screen doors open and comfortably ramshackled. She gazed out the window to empty fields.

Carlie spoke into the lip of her cup, completely sedate. "I've lived in this town for over five years, longer really, and had no idea this place existed. Seems like you know a secret about everything here."

"That's only because everything here has got one," Lee said, dusting the crumbs from his fingers. "So tell me yours. You're a botanist for the nuclear site, aren't you? You're testing how radioactive the local flora's getting."

"No, I'm not a botanist," she said, almost adding, "I'm just a homemaker," but stopped somewhere between the "just" and the "home." She had never been ashamed of it before. She even had taken three years of college as a home economics major before dropping out. Now she felt a disconnection, an insufficiency in such labels that lead her to keep her mouth shut. That he would assume she had an advanced degree, that she herself was a scientist, well. That tickled something in the roof of her mouth, filled her head with a subtle effervescence not unlike a gin and tonic. Carlie simply shook her head, suppressing a hiccup.

"All right. Let me guess again: you run a nursery. Or wait, landscaping. Guerrilla tactics."

She couldn't restrain the hiccups and laughter this time, self-consciously splaying her fingers over her mouth to hide the volume.

"What's so funny?"

"You're serious?" Carlie said, rubbing her chest. "No. I do not own my own nursery. Nor landscaping business. Amazing as that may seem."

"But you plan to?"

"Are you kidding me?" She nearly snorted. "I can't do that."

"Why? Why can't you?"

Carlie squared her elbows on the table, slightly frustrated that she had to answer. "Because it takes money, for one. And planning. A whole lot of planning. You just can't up and do that kind of stuff."

Lee shrugged, diligently wiping his palms clean. There seemed to be a patina of mechanical grease under his nails. Whenever he turned to stare out the window, the gray bristles in his hair winked like flecks of mica. "So plan," he said. "What's stopping you from doing that much? Save your pennies. Start a fundraiser."

Carlie could only close her eyes and produce one of those guileless, toothy grins that were her last defense against any small, impossibly simple truth. His words pinged against her like pebbles on a windowpane. "Listen, Buster, I don't ever recall saying I even wanted to start a nursery."

"So you're an enthusiast, is what you're saying."

"Sure, I'm an enthusiast. An enthusiast who's quite content to sit here and enjoy her coffee without having to race out and start up a business, thank you very much."

Lee acquiesced, clearly tempted to tease one last time. Instead, he let her change the subject. Carlie talked about James, about Massachusetts, about growing up with her large family in Louisiana. Suddenly, she found herself mentioning Bradey, surprised to hear her own voice speaking with an ease as though his death had happened years ago. When the subject had passed Carlie felt a dizzy relief, akin to tight-roping a gorge and realizing the vertiginous drop only after she had made it across. Lee asked her questions about her sisters. Which of her siblings was the greatest nuisance in childhood, who had changed the most, how often they saw each other. He asked her about the kind of plants she found, what she propagated. He prompted her into a twenty minute explanation between *phalaenopsis* and other *dendrobia*. "You don't want to hear about that, it'd bore you to tears." "No, I know what you're talking about. Those little flowers, they look like this," he used his hands to explain. "But I didn't know they could live on air." Carlie felt as though she hadn't talked this much in years. She had always chatted with Minnie, but now things came spilling out of her freshly, with a purpose it seemed. A two-way torrent that wasn't just conversational, but eager, swallowed up whole in big thirsty gulps and then replenished. She discovered that Lee had been raised solely by women. As the baby of the family, he had been coddled between two sisters, his mother, and a gaggle of aunts. His father had died in a tractor accident two weeks before he was born, so Lee was heralded by his sisters as the golden child of their daddy. So when his sister, Therese, lost her husband due to "Pregnancy, a mortgaged future, and other responsibilities," Lee had stepped in for Ryan. A big brother, if not father figure.

Their lunch, eaten in the first thirty minutes, lasted three hours. Over that time, the screen door popped with the coming and going of horse handlers and late afternoon retirees. The scrambled copy of the day's newspaper migrated from table to table; autumn breezed through the open windows, fluttering its pages like fallen leaves.

"You know," he said, "there's something that I think you'd want to see. I got this job tomorrow, at the Pink House."

"Pink House?" By now, Carlie was absently twirling the handle of her empty coffee cup. "What, and where, on earth is that?"

"On Easy Street," he said. "Where else could it be? It's this mansion. A place left over from the old money days. You should stop by tomorrow afternoon sometime. There's something you'd especially get a kick out of."

Carlie hesitated. "I can't imagine the people who live there would appreciate that much."

"The people who own it now don't live here. They're from the great white North, off-season—snow bunny money. It'd just be you and me."

When he had said this, the temperature in Carlie's face rose, and she felt lightheaded. She focused her attention on the watery grounds in the bottom of her cup. "I really don't think I can do that."

Easily, and with such honesty that she felt abashed, Lee said, "All right, I understand. But I'll probably be there until five working on their piano, if you decide to drop by for minute." He stood from the table and began working his wallet out.

Carlie refused to let him pay, and their easiness dissolved into being strangers again. On their way out, Carlie paused on the back porch to look across the training fields. The late autumn afternoon hit her hard, the lambent sunshine curling to smoke where the horses galloped. Here, she felt detached, an observer to her own life. Lee stood in the dirt lot, not knowing if he should wait. "This is all I wanted when I was little," she explained, then descended the steps. "I wanted nothing more than to work on a horse farm. Get up before the world was light and rake the stalls. Groom the horses, counting strokes. Watch the fields get misty as the sun peeked up. Then sit down to a big family breakfast just as the day really got started."

"So what did you do instead?"

Carlie laughed, "What do you mean? I was in the fifth grade! I was fussing with my sisters over the bathroom and daydreaming in geography class." Again, Lee shrugged like he knew no better, as if he had fallen through the cracks of adulthood and never had to grow up in the world. Too long in parting, they unlocked their separate cars in awkward silence, until Carlie waved goodbye and said, "You make everything sound so stupidly easy," before slipping away.

* * *

When she returned to the house later that afternoon, James was already home. She had almost pushed the day's earlier encounter from her mind. Almost. Carlie lingered at the back door for moment, hanging up her purse. He was stretched out in his Barcalounger, hadn't even changed from work, awash in the television with its sound knob dialed down to mute. He might have been watching abstract shapes on the screen, the way its pale light broadcast then changed every few seconds against his glasses. Carlie hesitated, then walked directly through his field of vision to the kitchen. At the sink, she said, "You're home early." Running cold water over the nicks and dried scratches on her hands. The water, knuckle-achingly cold, spattered into the metal basin. "I was thinking about making stuffed peppers tonight." She cut the tap and toweled her hands.

Lying prostrate in the chair, unchanged in his crumpled suit, James looked as though he'd been run over by a car. "What the hell were you doing today." He asked this in a pure monotone, focused on the soundless images.

She placed an empty skillet on the stove, reconsidered her response, and continued to set out more pots and pans. "Clippings, James. I go out and gather clippings, if you haven't noticed." Carlie glanced through the kitchen window, beyond which the effulgence of the backyard garden lay. Dusk was coming early. The frogs began to chirr. "Actually, today, I was transplanting."

"Transplanting," he said with his eyes closed, tasting the sound of the word. He lay with his chin on his chest, using minimal effort to speak. "Just doing some transplanting out in the middle of town. Tell me something. Can I ask you something and you answer me honestly?"

Carlie stopped and folded her arms tightly.

"Why do you insist on drawing so much attention to yourself? This is what I don't get. What happened to you in your childhood that you feel the need, the sick compulsion, to parade through the middle of downtown like that..."

"Like what? With these?" Carlie slapped out a pair of chunky garden gloves from her back pocket, misshapen from a month of briars and pulling weeds. "Where do you think they sell these, the lingerie department?"

"I can't think of another reason. You must simply want people to see you. Can anyone tell me of another reason that a married woman, in the peak of day, would traffic herself in the busiest intersection of town?" He didn't move an inch. He spoke languidly, slowly, as though reasoning with a child.

"Maybe I want to start my own nursery. Did you ever think of that? Maybe I need a little purpose in my life. Maybe a little more than just waiting around all day to fix you dinner."

"Of course, it's my fault. It's all my fault. Let me tell you something. You looked ridiculous out there. All the people who have seen you today will think you are an indigent, a destitute woman scrabbling shamelessly around town."

With that, she reflexively became aware of herself, as if James had held up a cracked mirror. For the first time since early this morning, she could see the tendrils of sweat-dried hair hanging limply from her face, the faint residual salt ringing her collarbone, the pouchy eyes, the baggy top that slouched from her shoulders and breasts and hips, the stickiness of her joints. She became aware of the cold sore, tender inside her cheek; the fat callus rubbing her little toe. Good God. Carlie turned scarlet from her cheeks to her chest. This is what she was today, sitting at that restaurant, eating, oblivious to her own seedy odor. And she could smell it now, too: a whiff coming from her body, a bitterness, like tannins in a musky bottle of wine.

He asked, "What else do you do when I'm not around?"

Fighting back every impulse in her body to begin hurling things, to bring the skillet down over his supine head, she said, "I don't know, James. Why don't you tell me? You apparently feel the need to spy on me. That's what you were doing today, wasn't it?" She filled a pot to boil, water rushing from the tap. "What's the matter, too cheap to hire a P.I.? Or maybe I should call your office ten times a day with hourly reports. That would save you both time and money."

"You know, that might not be a bad idea."

Carlie cut her eyes at him, bloodveined with murderous intent. Bang went the pot on the stove.

James lay there, impassive. "That way, I can at least know when my career is about to go down the toilet. You really must want to get me fired. That's what I think it is. Why else would you put yourself on display like that? It's not like I don't work for the government," he held up an open palm, one scale of the balance, and then the other, "it's not like they don't keep meticulous dossiers on us at work, looking for any liabilities, for any little abnormalities."

"Oh, at last! Yeah, yes, exactly! Exactly! I think that would be fantastic! In fact, I lie awake nights plotting what to do to you next."

"And now you're screaming. You should seek help."

"You're the one who tried to run me over with the car!"

"I did not try to run you over."

Carlie threw the rice she had been measuring into the sink. The grains exploded all over the counter, and she stormed past him.

"And where are you going now? More transplants? Won't you need your gloves, or is that pretext over?"

"Out to dinner." She snatched her purse. "Take care of yourself, if you can manage it."

"I hope you enjoy yourself. Because when the Rambler dies, that's it. No more."

Carlie laughed, open and viciously. "What—you think you're clipping my wings? You think I'm some sixteen-year-old daughter?"

"No. There's an energy crisis going on. I know you can't pay attention to such things, but I need to be a responsible citizen and conserve—"

Here she stalked back into the room and jerked the television's plug from the socket. "There. Start with that."

In his calm, with his eyes on the dead screen, he said, "If I find out that you've been cheating on me, mark my words: I will make sure you never get a dime."

One tick of the clock, and she was gone. As soon as the door slammed shut for the evening, reverberating in the air, James threw his hands up. "Enjoy yourself!" He shouted now in earnest, "You only ruined my career! Treat yourself, you deserve it, after all your hard work today!" He kicked a TV tray at the foot of the recliner, sending newspapers, bills, and timesheets flying into the air. "Celebrate!" And then he sprang to his feet and attacked the silage of papers on the rolltop desk with both hands. Punting the waste basket and chairs, knocking his framed Certificates of Achievement off the walls where they hit the ground and shattered, stomping on the flurry of papers. Bawling to the heights of the empty house, his voice, engorged with blood, twisted into such a guttural outrage that the words he barked were almost incomprehensible: "Go out whenever you goddamn well please, spend my money, spend my sweat and my goddamn money, while I break my fucking hump!"

With this, the banker's lamp had been smashed—by him, he supposed—leaving a large, rough gouge in the desk top. A few sheets wafted down around James, his face purpled and distorted, but he began to calm, to breathe, suppressing a near heart attack, while the chain to the ceiling fan sprang back and forth, back and forth over his head, and the lights glowed a sodium yellow on the empty porch outside.

* * *

Late the following morning, Carlie took note of the carnage and, silently, went about cleaning it up. She swept glass with great satisfaction, still in her bathrobe; she snorted at the explosion of papers and sorted them, straightened the desk; she pried the jagged splinters from the deep gouge in its right pedestal. (What the hell had he hit it with?) With every silent, uncomplaining chore to repair their domestic order, she won a little victory—by his own game, no less. To verbally recognize what James had done would be pointless. To gasp, to mutter to herself out loud, to swear this and that and make oaths or dire promises to him, *in absentia*, would only give the moment its lingering power. If he wanted to break every stick of furniture in the house, let him. It made everything so easy. They could pile the shards three stories high and light an enormous bonfire in the night. Watch it all illuminate the sky. With her hair tied back in a kerchief, she sanded the gouge as best she could, then applied a layer of varnish and sealant, blowing on the gloss to see it glisten evenly. Carlie showered and dressed. From the doorway, she surveyed her handiwork, the newly cleaned den, redolent with fresh bruises and scars. So stupidly easy.

And then she left.

Carlie had no intention of staying long. And she certainly had no intention of sleeping with Lee Corbett. She intended to meet with him, have a brief glimpse at another life, and then apologize and say she couldn't do this. Couldn't see him, couldn't know him, couldn't befriend him. That she would, in fact, be leaving town. And soon. She had done it before with their child no less, off the cuff, late at night. That was when she had something to protect. Now, she could do it in broad daylight, for herself. She saw her future release itself, shimmering like the gasoline mirage that wafted up while she refilled the Rambler, the chimerical haze rising where the tank met and the pump spent its fuel. She would see how far this old dilapidated car could take her. Carlie carried with her an envelope with little over fifteen hundred dollars, the inheritance from Aunt Ruby she planned to buy another car with. He could keep his money, if that's what it all came down to. She could make her own way. She had been resourceful enough before they were married. That was part of the terrifying allure, too: the emptiness and the unknown. Head out on her own. Maybe stay with her sisters for a while. Maybe not. Break off ever seeing Lee again, leave her husband, and then move someplace out west. Arizona. Somewhere arid, where the landscape was painted in broad blazing strokes. Sunsets you could sizzle bacon on. Lots of cacti. Succulents. After the fight last night, this Louisiana native began fantasizing about the desert. Searing sun and dry heat. Mirages that maybe held a vision of her future. She could feel the butterfly in her breastbone tremble.

When Carlie pulled up the long gravel drive to the courtyard of the Pink House, she almost turned around, seeing the four-car garage with all its doors shuttered, until she noticed Lee's single Chevy Vega parked under the shade of the portico. It looked to her, of all things, like a pea-green Batmobile. When she had said as much in the parking lot of the Kitchen, Lee feigned woundedness, "What, you don't like it? Ryan loves it."

Stepping from the car, Carlie heard music. Faraway, it seemed at first to come from the sky, the clouds passing languorously overhead; but the sound came from indoors, a strained melody drifting out of the latticed windows, which were heavy with wisteria gone to seed.

The Pink House wasn't so high as sprawling. Palatial. It had the architectural design of a Spanish cloister, the pink stucco walls draped in jasmine, occasionally dipping to reveal a rondelle garden or punctuated by a small gated archway. The exposed wooden beams of the portico were trellised with climbing wildflower, something as country as sweet potato vine maybe, winking with tiny white blossoms. Bougainvillea clung to the pilasters, shedding piles of brown papery bracts to the drive.

She had dressed as if for church. Not fusty nor flashy, but simply: a crisp pair of dark slacks. A light blouse draped at the shoulder with a thin shawl she had crocheted. A shiny black clutch purse in her hand. Her going-away clothes. Carlie paused before the front door. She stood listening at the top of the steps to the faint piano refrain; it broke, then played again. A different octave. A new little phrase tested. Something like a fragmented memory, trying to remember a tune.

And then Carlie did something she had never done before and probably never did since: without knocking, she put her hand on the brass latch and let herself in.

Her shoes tapped along the polished floors, paused, and timidly advanced. Alabaster surfaces. Marble interiors. Brass flower vases, empty. Mirrors, busts, an unsuitably Victorian sofa in the foyer. At once, the music was louder, clearer. It filled up the halls, it breathed through the walls and ceiling as if the entire house were one huge lung. She followed to where she thought the sound emanated, and her footfalls followed her.

In a glass enclosed rotunda, the music stopped.

"Carlie?" His voice all but echoed.

The windows, a nearly continuous circle, overlooked a shallow green pool nearly as still as the silence in the room.

Lee sat at a concert grand piano that dominated the room. It was a Steinway, with an intricately scrolled music stand and a rosewood veneer that flamed red where the sun hit it. Warm chestnut brown. The lid had been propped elegantly open, two oily chamois rags hanging over its lip. The soundboard and strings shone like gold.

And this was the fact of Lee Corbett: with the sleeves of a gray utility shirt rolled to the elbow, he sat at the piano bench where, seconds ago, a fragment of an etude rolled out from his indelicate fingers. Now he twisted on the leather bench, tempted to rise but he remained seated. Carlie stood four or five arm lengths away from him. "Let me finish up here real quick…"

"Don't rush," Carlie said and smiled a little sadly. "I already saw the surprise."

"Oh yeah?" He planted one hand on his knee.

"The gardens," she said.

"Nah," he smirked, gauging her from the corner of his eye. "That's not the surprise." Without another word, he casually rose from the bench and picked up a tuning lever and a roll of felt masking, the end of his sentence dangling like a baited hook.

Carlie didn't bite. Instead, she said, "So this is your job? You get paid to break into people's houses and play with their stuff?"

"That's the long and short of it." He leaned under the piano's hood like an auto-mechanic. "Got to keep them in tune, keep them in shape while the house is vacant. You don't want your $40,000 dollar masterpiece sounding like a cat in heat." Working unseen, he muted two of the three strings that form a note. "I'm supposed to fix that before the party descends for the winter."

Carlie didn't move, just quietly observed the room from the same spot where she entered. "And I suppose this was your boyhood dream. Something you wanted to do and so you just did it."

He laughed at himself. "Maybe."

Then he began talking out the process. Using the same gentle tone Carlie heard while he spoke to his nephew, that he used when broaching any new subject and sought to humble himself with humor. Carlie saw this world of pianos, these elegant, mammoth instruments that simply collected dust in big empty houses most of the year; and how they must cramp up during that idle time, rejoicing as Lee stole in like a thief, like a cat burglar with his bag of odd tools, to coax from them sonatas and waltzes that drifted out to no one. As he spoke, Lee reached back and forth, distractedly: his knuckles deep in the strings, or working the tuning pins, or at the keys testing an octave. "When tuning a piano, you don't start at the beginning. You start in the middle and work out. Middle C. You have to listen, you have to hear. Listen for the temperament of the instrument and get that octave in tune. You hear that wobble? We're going to narrow that gap. Each instrument is different. No standard measure." While adjusting a pin, he strained his neck to see Carlie. "The inaccurate sciences," he said.

Easing back onto the bench, Lee pantomimed cracking his knuckles and ran a scale up the keyboard. Pausing to hear the dying fall, he nodded. He played a few intervals, a few chords, and the harmony rang true throughout the room. To Carlie's ear, the music had sounded fine before she even walked through the door, but now, the resonance was clear, the purity of each sound penetrated the rotunda like sunlight through a prism.

Lee withdrew a sheaf of sheet music from his canvas duffel, a worn green army bag. "This," he announced, "is what I wanted to show you."

Having arranged the sheets, he began to play. The tune was lively, abrasively upbeat. Splashy major chords that bounced like a ticker tape parade through city streets. Or like bombs falling gaily around your ears. "Guess what it is." His hands jumped up and down the keys, play-acting at the instrument as he easily controlled it.

"I have no idea."

"'The Transit of Venus.' A Sousa march of all things," he laughed. "Scored in honor of the occasion. I found it in their library. Now I don't believe in signs, but you have to admit, that's a pretty amazing coincidence." He ran out one last crescendo and let the notes hang, then die, in the air. "And all just God-awfully wrong. Personally, I'd go for something a little more of a nocturne." He worked the *sostenuto*. "That communicates a more graceful movement. Tinkling, silvery, melodic. But definitely in a minor key."

Carlie nodded.

"All right." Lee slapped his knees, finished. "You got me. I really just wanted to show you the gardens." He hopped off the bench. "Shall we go take a look?"

The house and gardens, in their stillness, felt like a museum after hours. The vast spaces were made private by garden enclosures, each revealing hidden accents: concrete fountains, plinths with large urns sprouting ornamental grasses, shrubbery pleached to form natural fences. The autumn sky cranked its mood-lighting down to a cool afterglow, a romantic tint if it weren't for the disturbing cry of peahens roosting from the defunct caretaker's house nearby. Lee and Carlie talked sporadically; they strolled and pointed. Japanese maples popped out like firecrackers, their dainty leaflets burning orange and red in a town where evergreens simply browned and the few deciduous leaves shrugged their shoulders, gave up, and fell without a final blush. Walking the gravel paths, they came to a tiled patio shaded by a pergola. Underneath was a chaise lounge, wide as a clam shell and printed in *toile de Jouy* palm fronds. They seated themselves. An antique tea cart stood by their side.

She had come to tell him she was leaving town. But something else was happening. She was kissing. Or being kissed. Or both. Surprised by her own fumbling lips that didn't work so well. She nearly coughed, sputtered, but held her breath instead. She hadn't kissed another man in perhaps fifteen years; the foreignness of it electrified her. New possibilities swam up into her head, too quick, like oxygen bubbles that nearly made her queasy—sure, she could leave with Lee. She had the Rambler and fifteen hundred dollars in her purse. She could see his tightened forearms easily draped over the steering wheel, rolling along the state highways of America. He could tune pianos out in the Great West. She could start a nursery amid all the painted rock; hearty succulents, aloe, cacti for sale. They could live in a small adobe house. They could change their names. She would go by Robicheaux again. They could have children.

Over the rooftop, a peacock cried twice, like a baby shrieking awake in middle of the night. Beneath the deadened tingling of her lips, something hard dissolved in the center of Carlie's chest like a clod thrown into a cold river. The old German philosopher scored his point as Carlie understood at last what something was, by seeing what it wasn't. She went limp and quietly began to cry.

Lee stopped, pulled away from her face. He wiped a tear with his thumb.

"What's wrong?"

Carlie, drying up with honesty, said, "I just want my family back."

* * *

February saw the first snow in five years, weak little flakes falling through the sky. A light dusting to begin with, then lacy icicles that grew heavy enough to bend pine saplings, powdered sugar that lay undisturbed on the roofs of cars and over the frozen grass. A gentler memory of their winters in Massachusetts. What Carlie was thinking: that Bradey had missed his first snow. Sitting bundled in the rocker, an unread book in her lap, she stared out the darkening windows. If Carlie had expected some form of cosmic homecoming by leaving Lee Corbett behind, if she looked for some indication of having made the right choice, any sign of assurance at all, then she would have been sorely disappointed, perhaps even suicidal. Instead, she had settled for catatonia. James kept to his habits and she made new ones of her own. The guest bedroom became suffocating, so Carlie moved into the living room like a hermit, sleeping on the couch under the windows. For months, she spent her waking hours in the rocking chair, doing little else than flipping through family albums, books, magazines, huddled within the flocculent mood-music of her Herb Alpert or Harry Belafonte records. Occasionally she mustered the energy to cook, or at least gaze into a pot of boiling water. Some evenings she pulled out executive stationery notebooks with a vague purpose in mind, but they sat open, blank for hours on the arm of the chair, before being set aside.

Boots stomped on the side porch, one-one, two-two, and then the sliding glass door rumbled open behind its thick curtain. She hadn't known he was outside. James was from this weather, and the winters they braved in Massachusetts were record-breaking, but already his nose was raw and wet as he tracked a weak slush indoors and unbound his scarf. He threw an armload of logs into the fireplace, so far unused, and deposited himself on the hearth. He breathed.

"I thought you could use this," he said. "This room gets cold."

She turned her face to him, which looked perpetually raw itself these past months, rosy under the strands of black hair, and distracted. He had performed this gesture without being asked. James stayed in the room. He leaned forward on his knees and fidgeted with his new facial hair, scratching at the beard on his cheeks that he let go unshaved. He had been losing his scrawniness, gaining a weary weight, a fleshiness to his shoulders and belly.

After this prolonged silence, he said, "I overheard some of the guys at work this week." He said, "They were talking about this thing called the Rhythm Method. I was thinking maybe we could give it a try."

By now, they had not had sex for six months. Twenty-four sexless weeks. One hundred and sixty-eight sanitized nights spent listening to the susurrant call of cotton whispering against skin, while their bodies lay like stones in opposite ends of the house. Whether James was reaching out, attempting to negotiate life on her terms, whether he was actively broaching some form of compromise, or whether the agony of day-to-day celibacy—trapped in the cage between home and work, with only two square feet to prowl in—had finally driven him to concede one facet of his stubborn determination, didn't matter. It was an opening, however partial. The rocking chair creaked as Carlie leaned back to get a better look at her husband.

"And it's a Catholic thing, right? So you wouldn't have any problem with it, would you?"

"No," she said. "Not at all."

"And it works, right?"

An enigmatic grin flickered on her face—just briefly showing itself before withdrawing—as a timid creature peers up from its tiny dark hole in the ground. "Oh yes," she replied. "It works."

Three weeks later, Carlie was pregnant.

* * *

I learned about Lee Corbett in my early twenties, in college for the first time after a delayed start. (A recurring theme for me.) There is a phase of life when many parents look at their sons and daughters as potential confidants, living on their own for the first time, resembling adults. But this was something more. Three years had passed since I sprang from my father's station wagon, and in that time Carlie made frequent bids to reach out to me, to bridge the gap between my life and theirs. Each gesture, each anecdote she shared was laced with the indirect question: *Who are you exactly? Tell me a story. Give me a hint*. But what could I tell her? What could I say when I was so distracted with sex? My mind swam with all the hotheads and flirts and doe-eyed fawns lingering in my bed sheets. This one with the aureoles pebbled like coarse beach sand; the stocky one with his muscled hips, smooth as pears; the one with perfectly dimpled buttocks I still could draw from memory. Like any young man my age, desire was the axis on which my life rotated. Three years in Atlanta had eventually led me north to Illinois, hopping on and off new boys, boarding love and then letting it go like a Greyhound bus. And again, like most any young man my age, I kept that life hidden. I kept it my own. So when my mother met my face, she saw the grit of foreign cities, the indelible touch of strangers—and was left fumbling for a way to reach me herself.

She had flown up to see me in Chicago, and we had a tourist lunch along the Navy Pier. This wouldn't be the last time that I saw Carlie before her stroke, but it would be the time I remember most. For whatever reason (or a combination of them, most likely: James' retirement, her growing resentment, and my encouraging her to leave him), she started in on this story of my conception. I didn't get so many finely etched details, of course. But they were there, in the lines on her face as she ate; in the way she thoughtfully kabobbed walnut to apple to raisin on her fork; in the slow chewing, the lingering swallow, the deliberate pause before lifting her glass to sip from its plastic straw. Casually told. Early at the mention of another man's name, I expected the story to end with a startling revelation of my paternity, so much so that the wind on the Navy Pier sent glassy shivers up my neck, and I almost blurted it out for her, because she was taking so long to reveal the truth to me. It seemed so clear. I thought of my father's rabid jealousy in my childhood, his mistrust with me. I thought a profound piece of a cosmic puzzle had just fallen into place. But no. By the end, Carlie had finished without any mention of the melodrama running through my head, and I saw only my mother with another forkful of Waldorf salad: a fifty-seven year-old woman, wrapped in a summer scarf, who had been carrying the heavy secret of a minor infidelity around with her all these years.

Lee Corbett, a decade after she had known him, got trapped in a carburetor fire. This was the last contact she had with him, if you could call it that: page twelve of the local newspaper. She briefly toyed with the idea of visiting the hospital, but daily life swept in and ushered her away, as it usually does, from such romanticized gestures. By then, she had her family back again—in some form, anyway. Carlie never learned if Lee died there in the hospital as befits the tragic requirements (no follow up article, naturally, though she did search), or if he lived to become a bloated drunkard and went out west himself, tinkling on the ivories with fingers that recalled the salty puff of her cheeks that afternoon, and sleeping under the starry skies of Arizona.

So I didn't push the obvious question. I had begun to know who I was: the progeny of five different people. James Cullins and Carlie Robicheaux, the Sapphic Minerva Price, an illegible Map, and at last, the lingering note of Lee Corbett. There, with tourists loitering by our elbow and snapping photographs from the pier, she offered the following advice: "Whoever you find, sugar, make sure it's someone you can do things with. Share the same interests. Someone who can get up and do. Don't make the same mistakes I did. Don't let a year of love lead you by the nose into a lifetime of frustration. Fighting all the time. Shouting. It's for the birds." She studied an apple slice on the end of her fork. "Or hell. I don't know. Make the same mistakes." She laughed. "What do I know? Without them, I wouldn't be right here. Talking with you."

7

I saw Minnie's house for the first and last time when I was eight years old. My mother had pulled me from school early that day. She did this sometimes. Showed up on random weekdays without warning and pulled me out, usually to have lunch, occasionally just to run errands with her, and one time to take me to the zoo an hour away in Columbia. I remember that the school administrators, without exchanging words in front of me, disapproved of these unnecessary absences. On this occasion, however, Carlie was called to the school. The school was officially Episcopalian, with chapel twice a week before class, but held a sort of laissez faire attitude about God and sin. However, Marcus Fletcher and I had been found behind the gym with our shorts around our ankles, during recess, pricking the tips of our penises with dried sandspurs to see how long we could stand the sensation. We had invented a game of space pirates and this, of course, was the logical initiation into the crew. After the science teacher found and separated us, I waited for nearly half an hour—this time, by special request, in the assistant principal's office—for my mother to show up.

Mr. Hamilton was a narrow man with no chin and a large mustache. His office was cramped and quiet and only lit by the red afternoon sunlight through the blinds. It felt like everyone else had gone home, that the entire school was vacant, though I knew they were just in class in the next building over. He sat behind his desk and stared at me, two fingers stroking his mustache, as I waited, legs dangling, hands in my lap, engulfed in the office chair.

When my mother showed up, she was not her usual self. In the half-light of the office door, her hair was disheveled, her face was taut and distressed, and an absentmindedness seemed to halt her movements. She glanced around the tiny office as if coming out of a trance, then saw me, and snapped fully to attention, smoothing her forehead. Her large silhouette seemed to fill the entire room. And she stood, not sat, patiently as Mr. Hamilton greeted her and explained the situation.

After he had finished, a humming silence filled the room. The sunlight struck my mother at such an angle that I couldn't read the expression on her face. She said, "I'm sorry. Why did you call me in?" There was the tiniest ant of annoyance in her voice, and I felt relieved.

Mr. Hamilton leaned back in his chair and stroked his mustache again, considering how to frame his words. "I believe that little Avery might benefit from a psychological evaluation."

Five, six seconds of silence pressed against those words. And then popped: Carlie laughed. She guffawed, good-naturedly, like someone, an uncle most likely, had been stringing her along for a joke. "Mr. Hamilton," she said. "I'm surprised at you. Haven't you raised boys of your own? Don't you know little boys are prone to all sorts of bizarre behavior?"

"Mrs. Cullins, this hasn't been the first incident."

"And I don't suppose it'll be the last, either. This is what detention's for, isn't it? Or does every child who has to sit out at recess have to be... *subjected* to a psychiatric examination?"

"It's not a psychiatric evaluation, Mrs. Cullins, it's psychological. It's just a simple battery of tests."

"I don't care what it is. I think that degree on the wall has gone to your head."

The assistant principal's eyelids fluttered. His thumb and forefinger paused briefly, bracketing his mouth as he gathered his words. "Your son has been exhibiting abnormal behaviors. Signs of sexual deviancy. It's my feeling that the earlier one can identify—"

All the good humor in my mother's voice hardened. "My son is just fine the way he is. You're the one who should be ashamed. He's just a child yet, just eight years old. Who knows where he'll go in life. You're a grown man and here you are putting ideas in his head."

And with that, she grabbed me by the wrist, and signed me out of school.

In the car, she fell quiet, melancholy again, strained by occasional attempts to be chipper. We stopped at a drive-thru, and she bought me french fries, and as I licked the salt from my fingers, we drove out of town. She didn't say why or where we were going, but from the silence in the car, and the unwarranted appearance of fastfood, I knew not to ask. We drove for what seemed like ages. I watched the road above the dashboard change from town intersections to highway, then into a narrow country road that dipped and swerved through the poorer, half-deserted towns that dotted the outskirts of Copeland. We passed an old-fashioned gas station, a fishcamp, a creepy-looking daycare. Eventually, the forest surrounding us grew taller and enshrouded the car as the road we traveled descended steeply into the valley. I had remembered this part of the road. On the few occasions we took it, if my mother drove fast enough, I could feel my stomach lift from the sudden drop. A kind of roller coaster, a tickling giddiness in all my guts. This time, however, she slowed at the bottom of the valley road, and I heard the turn signal click on.

From my vantage, half-buried in the passenger seat, it seemed to me that we drove straight into the trees, but I heard gravel popping under the tires. My mother pulled the handbrake and left the car idling. "I'll be right back," she said, hopping out. I watched her crunch around front of the car and saw the top of a wide chainlink gate. I clutched the takeout bag tighter, cold with grease, and sat on my knees for a better view. I saw the blue eaves of a house to the left of my mother. She worked to free the gate clasp and pushed the hinges wide open. The metal groaned like it hadn't been budged in years. Back in the car, she popped the brake and drove us another twenty feet until the tires caught hard, smooth concrete, and we stopped under a carport.

The blue house was small and cabin-like, perched atop a tiny knoll. This low in the valley, mist hung around the trees. I could hear water in the distance. I hugged the takeout bag to my chest, feeling the air, chilly against my arms. My mother closed the passenger door for me. She moved slowly, lingering under the carport. "Remember those stories I would tell you about Minnie and Map? This is their house. Was their house," she corrected.

I said nothing. My mother looked around with a furrowed expression like she was sizing up rain on the air. She breathed deeply, her eyes closed.

I asked, "Why are we here?"

"They're selling it, babe."

"Who?"

"I don't know. The bank. Whoever has rights to it now."

"Who has rights?"

"I don't know who," she said again. "I never claimed to have all the answers, babe."

"But not us?"

"No, not us. Not legal ones, at any rate." Hugging her elbows, she followed a little path of stepping stones to a screened back porch; slowly, I trailed behind. The screens sagged and were torn from disuse, or too much use, mildewy and gray. The door was off one hinge, and when she carefully opened it, my mother looked in and sighed. She braced it open for me as I mounted the steps after her. The entire porch was carpeted in bristly green plastic, like a welcome mat, and was littered with beer bottles, cigarette butts, and old cast-off clothes. There was a broken piece of furniture or two, a chair, I think. Large mud dauber nests were piped along the walls and window casings. "Teenagers," my mother said. "That's all. No one's here." The view from the porch was a good one. It swooped down the hill to a rolling creek, which rushed and murmured loudly from a recent rain, and led to darker, older woods. Fairy tale woods, from what I could see. I turned to find that my mother was not sharing the view with me. She had one hand cupped to the colorful glass window pane on the back door, trying to see in. She tried the handle. It hardly even rattled. Even I could see that the jambs surrounding the door were so warped and swollen from the damp that, if it had been unlocked, it still would've been impossible crack open. That's when I saw my mother sliding a broken broom handle from the debris on the porch.

"Stand back, sugar," she said and, averting her face, bapped once, twice, and a final, hard third time against the glass inset in the door. At the third strike, it cracked with a flat musical chime. She knocked in the remaining glass with the handle, reached through, and within a moment, with all her weight, broke open the door.

The house breathed as she stood inside the darkened dinette. The air it expelled was colder, more ancient than anything in the valley woods. All the furniture was still there. A dinner table was set against the wall, under an oil lamp, and in the den I could see a couch, a coat rack. Cups were still in the glassed-in cupboard, though a shelf had fallen and it looked as though raccoons had pushed through the debris. My mother stood with her back to me, taking it all in. She then turned and offered her hand. "It's all right, sweetie, you can come in. Or you can stay out there if you like. I won't be but a few minutes."

I held out my hand and carefully stepped over the glass on the carpet. The deep pile was soggy under our sneakers as we approached the den. It was the most open room and held the most light, filtered as it was through a large window opaque with years of grime. The wood paneling buckled from the walls because of the moisture. Big black stains spotted the ceiling, fringed with gray-green mold. A marble-topped coffee table sat in the middle of the room, still laid out with ivory figurines, dusty and clotted with cobwebbing. Something had torn open one of the sofa cushions, dragging the stuffing out. Dead beetles, meal worms, or flies speckled every surface.

Then I saw the most amazing thing: inert, near the front door, was an organ. I gingerly slipped my hand from my mother's grip and approached the console.

"Map and Minnie used to sit side-by-side on that and play it every New Year's," she said.

I pumped a single, silent key.

"It needs electricity to play."

The thick layer of dust, gritty beneath my fingertip, hardly came up. I streaked my finger through it, more purposefully. It yielded and sprang again. I set the french fry bag on the bench to free both hands. The pressure of the keys was wonderful. To feel the resistance at first, then the yield, the give. *K-thunk. K-thunk.* How oiled they felt, how smooth and weighted.

After a moment, my mother disappeared into the hall. I heard her poking around the bedrooms—I didn't want to follow her into those narrow rooms, but stayed in the open space with the organ. I couldn't imagine the music it made, but I could imagine mastering it. All these keys and switches and sliders and pedals must have done something wonderful. It looked like the control center that piloted the house, that could pilot a starship. I grew more confident and firm, pumping and hammering the keys, flicking the hard plastic switches. I left tiny round prints on every part I touched. Motes of dust bloomed up even in the weak light. I dialed in the coordinates. We were taking off now, rising from the soddened earth above the treetops. Slowly, I rotated the hulk of a house in midair, pointing it towards school. And then we were off, lightspeed. We were going back; we were going back to save Marcus Fletcher. One didn't leave his crew behind.

I'm not sure how long I sat and pretended to play. But there came a moment when I heard something, beyond my own imagination, and stopped abruptly to listen. There is a sound that human absence makes: a ringing in the ears, a slight creaking. The sound of emptiness crowding in.

I called out to my mom and waited for her response. I called again.

I knew then from the silence in the house that she was gone. That my mother had left me. I listened to the house, intently. I stared at the black stains that streaked the walls, at the ubiquitous dust. I didn't have the word for it then, but I knew in that moment what a sarcophagus was. I understood that there were ornate places where we locked away all the dead things of this world. To trap them. To keep them from getting out. And I knew that I was alone inside of one.

An hour ago, my mother had been my only defender. But I suddenly realized why she brought me here. It wasn't to show me anything. It was to abandon me. This was the perfect place to get rid of a little boy who was deviant, who was abnormal.

I ran hard. I ran for the back door with the sarcophagus closing its lid around me. When I hit the porch, she wasn't there either. My mother was far, far away from me. I saw her all the way down the hill, sitting at the creek with her back to me. I called out to her. She didn't turn. Once again I bolted, this time off the porch through the weeds, down that steep hill, nearly losing my feet, feeling the sandspurs stick into my athletic socks and rake against my knees, with my heart caught in my throat so that I couldn't call her name, that I felt like I would never reach her. But of course I did. And when I came up beside her, breathless, wanting to wail, wanting to cry and flail my fists against her chest for leaving me like that, I caught myself. I stopped and swallowed hard.

It was not often that I saw my mother cry. My mother hammered nails; she smashed her toes while hauling bricks; she cursed under her breath. But here, tears had gathered in her eyes. She sat on the stone wall that dropped off to the stream with a parcel of envelopes gripped in one hand. She had opened two or three and held those letters in the other hand, no longer reading them. Her eyes glistened, maybe a drop or two had slipped down, unnoticed, but the rest held. She held them there, pulled them back into herself, in a sheer act of strength.

I asked her why she was crying. Children can't leave grief alone. They have to poke at it. More than anything, I asked her so that she would have to look at me, see me. This wasn't something I was used to.

"People are gone," she said. Her voice was thin and bitter, and she just continued to stare at the water. "There are people who are gone forever, babe." She opened her hand and let those three letters scatter below the wall. They hit the water's surface, gentle as leaves, and were whisked downstream, pirouetting against branches and rocks that disturbed the current.

Finally, she looked at me and smiled weakly. "But I have you." Hooking one arm around me, she pulled me close to her body. She buried her face against the top of my head and held me so tightly that it was uncomfortable, but I knew not to push away. She said, "I'll always have you."

8

The pregnancy, as you know, was interminable. By her second trimester, Carlie was already measuring large for her dates, but thought nothing of it. For the moment, she lugged around, more or less, the same uncomfortable and effulgent burden of any expectant mother. By the time warning bells did start to ring, she would have no interest in paying attention.

Summer again, the basking month of July, and Carlie struggled from the driver's seat of a now terminally ill Rambler. The car, lingering in its last days, had one side mirror strapped on with twine while the other had fallen off completely; paint shed from its joints when Carlie slammed the door. Despite James' dire promise, mechanics had saved it twice from the brink of extinction. By now, Carlie had the middle-aged silver streak in her dark hair that would define the prime years of her life. Crow's feet (crane's, she would later call them) recessed from her eyes. There was a difference in her carriage, too. A self-assuredness that hardened her face, a dogged determination in every movement of her girth. Carlie did not linger to inhale the breadth and beauty of the woods around her, but tramped directly to Minnie's back porch. No more airy wonder. On iron rails her course was set, her mind and body both Ahab and the Whale. She was looking for her Lamaze partner.

She pressed up to the screen door, her belly busting under a sunflower tunic and her hair pulled through a matching headkerchief, both already losing their relevance in popular fashion. Carlie squinted through the screen.

"Ready?" She spoke to the wicker chair where Minnie had fallen into a catnap. The older woman snapped to attention, righted her wig, and snatched up a satchel overloaded with an umbrella and other emergency supplies: reading material, first aid, cotton pads, a light jacket.

"Aye, aye." Minnie struggled to her feet and took the porch steps a little nervously. "O Captain, my Captain," she said, to tease herself, bracing for the unsteady seas to come. That Carlie had lured Minnie from her hermitage was no small miracle. She hadn't left the cottage for over a year, ever since incontinence took hold of her life—phoning in her groceries, only dashing out for the briefest and most necessary trips. Her sense of security had been reduced to four small musty rooms in the wood, like a recluse, where her bladder could do its worst without much more consequence than cleaning herself up. Of course, she never told Carlie this much, but it was evident. This is where we all end up, Carlie thought, and so on these Lamaze trips into Copeland she made frequent excuses to stop—gas, gum for her popped eardrums, the need to use a payphone—so Minnie could discretely exit to a public bathroom if need be, and maybe preserve a little self-respect.

When Carlie had told James of the pregnancy, she braced for cataclysm. From the moment she knew herself to be pregnant, images from the impending showdown began to play in her subconscious. Accusations. Grandiose fights. *You lied to me! It was your idea!* Ultimatums. Implied demands for an abortion, though she doubted James would outright say it. Those mornings before she had told him, in the ritual half-hour that she drank her coffee on the porch, Carlie's imagination bloomed into terrible pictures. Wild scenarios that amazed and tantalized her more than frightened her. Daydreams where James lost all control and beat her, knocked her to the ground and kicked her stomach to make her miscarry. Where he grabbed her by the neck with both hands, red faced and wild. Where he set the house on fire and ran into the night, naked for some reason, with a can of gasoline.

More disturbing than anything she had anticipated or dreamed, however, was his lack of response. Carlie had waited until she was almost showing to tell him. They had enjoyed two months of each other. Not unstrained, but still tactile, speaking with that wordless, human connection of skin touching skin. They had been watching the evening sun descend, James snorting antihistamines. A few gurgling squirts into each nostril, which he pinched, and then he would try to breathe. It sounded as though he was forcing raw egg whites down his sinuses. Carlie had wanted them to sit on the patio and, acquiescing for the first time in ages, James needed to fortify himself against the early spring. He had made them Harvey Wallbangers, which he placed on a small table before flopping into his patio chair. Carlie refused her drink. Then she confessed to him. He was silent for a long time, stalled in the act of sucking Galliano from his mustache, and she studied his every non-movement for a response. It was as though, by a fatalistic inertia, he was trying to separate all the particles of his being and drift away on the evening breeze.

"You've beaten me," was all James said, after ample consideration. He set his drink down. Weeks of allergen attacks had destroyed his sinuses: his eyes were red watery welts behind their glasses, his cheeks pimpled and rashy, his nose a polleny starburst that forced him to breathe through his mouth, so that when he finally spoke it sounded as if he were speaking through a snorkel. "You win, Carlie," he said, clogged up like a pipe, unable or indifferent to raising his head from the back of the chair. "But don't expect anything from me."

Carlie drew her legs up into the chair. "Don't say things like that."

But he didn't say anything again. Dusk fell and the moisture in the air turned clammy, weaving a fog through the trees. When he said nothing further, Carlie retired indoors, leaving the mosquito coils smoking thinly around him.

From that point on, James never breathed a word about her pregnancy. They immediately lost that physical intimacy that had carefully nudged to life over the winter—no touching, no more bodily recognition as they squeezed past each other in the kitchen or bath. But neither did he stop talking to Carlie all together. He simply ceased to acknowledge that she was pregnant. The words themselves—child, baby, term, due date, any of it—were casually lost from his vocabulary. It was as though she carried a huge cosmological void in the center of her body: a swirling black hole where her belly should be, which James refused to stare into. Whenever she spoke of prenatal kicks and shifts in the womb, or of wallpaper for the new baby room, James changed the subject as if she had not been talking. Whenever she mentioned an upcoming appointment with Dr. Schoenhauer, James never said a word or even uttered a grunt to indicate that he had heard. At the mention of fees and hospital issues, he only nodded his head in a distracted manner, his attention hooked on more intricate issues: inaccuracies in the electric bill, balancing the checkbook, a fork twined with spaghetti, the nightly news report. When neighbors rang the door with prepared casseroles and chilled roasts in hand, James would give an amiable smile and decline the offering, leaving the neighbors puzzled on the front doorstep. Occasionally, he accepted the dishes if pressed, and Carlie would stumble across a Jell-O salad sweating by itself on the hall stand, or a coagulated bowl of creamed chipped beef in the coat closet, absently deposited by James as if he were Alzheimic, or as if household elves had left bizarre offerings in the dead of night. These hidden foodstuffs often languished around the house for days, patiently awaiting discovery.

The extent of this denial—more than that, the ease with which James fabricated normalcy—startled her. So much so, that at a company picnic Phil's secretary, Leanne Gibbons, accosted Carlie with an audible gasp. The woman held her polished nails at her breast, tempted to reach out and test Carlie's belly to see if it was a prank. "James never mentioned…How long have you two been expecting?" This was the same woman who, seven years earlier, held a warm cup of James' urine. Her forehead looked either worried or threatened by this new huge gap of information.

Carlie faltered, offering a weak-chinned smile. "Six months." James' motives were unclear: whether this was a form of psychological revenge or self-defense, she didn't know. But the cancellation was complete, at work and at home. The sheer simplicity of his belief made it happen like an act of absolute faith. A virgin conception in reverse. A Denunciation with the angels—We take it all back! God declares—an immaculate abortion. She had carefully watched James behind the steering wheel as they drove home from that picnic, puckering his lips and whistling down tempo and off-key to Sheb Wooley's "Purple People Eater" on the radio.

* * *

And so, months into this disturbing neutrality, Carlie breached the agreement. Sloshing in the tub, James had been soaking his sore muscles after using the push-mower earlier that morning. Unplanned, Carlie tapped the bathroom door with her nails, alerting the captive audience inside, and said she wanted to do Lamaze. Her mind worked furiously. Now it would come, now would be their explosion, the verbal immolation that would take their entire house up in flames, but she couldn't *not* do it. She could already imagine the bathwater burbling, agitating to a volcanic head. James loathed group activities; he saw community courses as soft-headed New Age pyramid schemes. She could predict the response: *What? Don't you already know how to breathe?* Quickly, Carlie fired off her reasons through the keyhole, "I don't want to take drugs again, James, I don't want drugs. I want to be fully here this time. I want to know my child when she comes into this world. I can't do this without you." She was surprised how thick with emotion her voice sounded; once the words got out, her throat felt bruised. She was surprised that she had said *my*, that she had said *she*. She was determined to make him affirm the existence of this child.

Nothing. Tentatively, Carlie put her ear to the door. Water gently slopped. His breathing sounded labored, a deep, faraway hollowness from his throat. Faint drips from the fixture. She could practically hear the water beading on the mirror and cabinets inside the steamy interior, like a sauna. Then came a low, sea-dwelling groan from a primordial place, somewhere far beyond the bathroom. In it, a single word: *No.* The utterance was drawn out like a yowling, mewling Grendel, licking his wounds, rubbing the word into his face with weary, shriveled claws. "*No. no. no. no no no nononono.*"

The sound had been clear: for James, Lamaze classes were the final calculated tactic in nothing less than the destruction of his soul. Carlie retreated from the door and didn't bring it up again.

* * *

"Dads, it is a new era," the instructor announced from her position on the floor. She was a moon-faced elementary school teacher named Dana Joy-Hammonds who, on Wednesday nights, also doubled as the Pottery I instructor at the Community Center. "You, too, are instrumental in this miraculous process."

Carlie and Minnie sat, nearly capsizing—one in old age, the other in pregnancy—from the oversized ashram-like pillows that the Center provided. Minnie held Carlie tightly by the wrist, as if she might roll off her pillow and, like a turtle, unable to right herself. The instructor played ambient relaxation music: something between ocean waves and orcas, a deep amniotic sort of sound, beneath which Carlie could hear the squeak of sneakers from the basketball courts next door. The scoreboard sounded, then a referee whistled. The instructor maintained a pleasant, soothing tone of voice through the dull babble outside.

Minnie pulled a small legal pad and pen from her satchel, and began taking notes.

Ten other couples formed a half-moon around the center cushion that Dana Joy-Hammonds occupied, each woman reclining into her husband as instructed. Many of the couples were younger. Many first-time pregnancies. One couple couldn't have been more than nineteen years old. The boy was pimply and had a dirty upper lip; his eyes flickered around as if looking for the truancy officer. The girl, intensely focused, scrawled detailed notes in a heart-shaped journal. Carlie watched them from the corner of her eye. "All right, husbands—dads. Today, we're going to work on helping mom achieve deep relaxation, with comfort measures and massage. Relaxed muscles will help both mom and baby during delivery." Each time husband was uttered, Carlie's jaw twitched. Around the room, men sat Indian-style behind their wives. Men with beards or boyish cheeks or hairy chests, wide lapels and open collars, each with sweat on his forehead. Men feverishly grinning or flashing skeptical smirks. Now asked to perform the task of touching their wives, delicately in public, these men examined their own hands as if they were suddenly unfathomable instruments. For what? How do I? They flattened their palms, placed them on shoulders, like communion, like first contact. Oh.

Carlie dutifully leaned into Minnie's embrace, inching backward on her forearms. Minnie's fingers found her neck, cool and clammy, as if examining for swollen lymph nodes. The instructor, Dana, singled them out with a limp wave and said in a stage whisper, "You can just skip this step." She went back to directing massage techniques.

Carlie propped herself up on her elbows and glared. Minnie whispered below her ear, "I'm sorry, dear heart..."

Drifting through the room, the instructor intoned cadences of love and assurance.

"The baby remembers his birth," she said.

"The baby can feel the love binding his family," she said.

"When mom and dad are at ease," she said, "baby is at ease, too."

The tendons in Carlie's neck drew into tight knots. What were she and Minnie expected to do, sit and stare? Shouldn't they participate in these exercises of well-being, too? Were they not permitted to find that plateau of loving acceptance to bring her child into the world, as the other couples were? "Excuse me," Carlie raised her hand. "What are we supposed to do?" Was it because her partner was elderly? Or because they were two women? Because she had no husband at her side, were they just not worth this woman's time? Minnie's cold fingers tried again, unable to relax the steel cables in Carlie's shoulders. After all this work, she thought, after all the grief to be here, after duking it out with James, the shame and heartbreak, and then having to wait for a slot to open up, after cajoling Minnie—no small feat—away from her cottage, to be told just *skip it*?

"I'm sorry. Just return to the modified lotus position for now." Carlie put her arm down and straightened up as she was told; she closed her eyes and tried to clear her mind. Maybe there was no need to rush. Maybe being so eager to let go of her baby girl, to give this child up to the world, was a mistake. Perhaps conditions needed to be right before she did so.

The scoreboard bleated across the hall, followed by an uproarious cheer.

And then the nineteen-year-old girl clutched her pillow and let out a desperate, animal howl. All the first-timers snapped awake, eyes wide from the bowel-quaking scream, which seemed to imply that the child inside was all teeth and horns. For some, there was an inaudible, but vaguely perceptible, sensation of ears popping. Then they saw it: the wet stain spreading through her denim jeans.

Immediately, the small room exploded into confusion: some of the dads—by now, nerve-addled, tensely awaiting their own call to duty—sprang into action. Each vied to take charge. Each leapt up to coach, no matter who the pregnant woman was; they were prepared, they were determined, they were fulfilling their prescribed male role as protector and provider and leader. Shouts of Push, Relax, No, hold it until the ambulance arrives. Other shouts raised: she needed to get her pants off, right here, right now, goddammit! All these commands elbowed out any attempt by the instructor to rein the havoc in. A few sensible souls had deferred their authority and ran into the halls to call for help.

Minnie clapped and exclaimed, "How thrilling! Why, we all could drop them right here and now!" Except Carlie didn't hear a thing. She sat in her own universe, completely zenlike, envisioning her child. With her eyes still closed, at peace amid all the pandemonium, perhaps she began to discover the arcane deep-breathing techniques that could preserve the process indefinitely, that would maintain a beautiful mother-child stasis rather than breach it by ushering in a birth.

They continued the classes. For weeks, Carlie and Minnie showed up while the original couples began to disappear, two by two. Week after week, month after month, amazingly they returned long past when Carlie should have been due, until Dana Joy-Hammonds' nervous brown eyes signaled to Carlie that maybe she no longer needed the class, that maybe it would best for all if she took her unborn baby and withdrew, to drop off the radar of worldly maternity and meditate on her disturbingly newfound, prenatal enlightenment.

* * *

She gave James time, the only resource she had. Time to adjust to and accept the birth of their second child. More and more time. And so she held onto me, growing bigger and bigger. Week forty-one, week forty-two, week forty-three. After a while, it seemed preferable to carry me around forever, rather than birth a child into such a contentious home. Besides, the womb was permeable. She could talk to me and did so constantly; she could interpret my replies in the ticklish vibrato of my shifting. In those amniotic murmurings my mind, my understanding of the world, blossomed in the womb. But after such a moratorium, after being confined so long to her swollen and distended figure, we both slid into a process of attrition. Carlie became gaunt, fatless, despite her belly. Inside, primed for the world, the child began to atrophy. After waiting so long for change, it was Carlie's body, and not her will, that finally gave up.

For hours, Carlie lay listening to a choral assembly of crickets outside her bedroom window. It was the first of October. She hadn't slept, but she had been dreaming. Here, we were one. Me in my medium, Carlie in hers, both slowly separating. The only light beyond her window was a drifting, crepuscular dawn. Dirty, discontented rumblings in the sky; tumescent clouds warped the air, sounding much like jumbo jets violating the night. The wind grew, stirring gray disturbances through the trees and photinia bushes; still the crickets hung on in the pre-dawn hours. They sang, they prayed, they called for manna in the promise of rain. Their natural rhythms seeped into her skull, so that Carlie envisioned herself rising from bed, stepping barefoot out into the windy woods, wearing only her nightgown. In this dream, she searched for a place of water. Something ritualistic, clear, isolated. She returned to a creek she knew. Disembarking from the cold stone, she drew down to the embankment.

Through a foggy chill Carlie eased into the stream, the water lapping at her ankles, the cold meniscus climbing against the gooseflesh of her skin, alerting her blood, speeding her heart until sitting, sinking, she tilted her head into the water and it reached her heavy breasts, soaking into the nightgown. Here again in Minnie's element, the creek filled her ears, muted them to the world. She was surprised at the buoyancy of her own body. Floating downstream like a contented Ophelia, Carlie watched the forest canopy pass overhead, a tunnel of tree limbs and bracken. She passed beneath fallen trunks, ancient gray things carpeted in moss; she saw thin stalks of birch and sweetgum angling toward the light; a stinkbug marching along the guide-wire of a jasmine creeper; a nuthatch bedding down in damp lichen. Carlie placed her hands on either side of her stomach, a taut tumulus, feeling the child-rhythm pulse there. *It's time, it's time, it's time.* The nightgown rippled and folded in translucent waves. Clots of wet leaves and other debris gathered to her as she passed, clung to the raft of her body. Boatbugs spun around, crowning her hair. Serenely, Carlie felt the whole world release from her in a warm effluvium, before her body finally broke apart like jelly, dissolving in a hundred eddies in the water.

Her spine had sunk into the soft mattress. Inert and supine as in the imaginary stream.

She continued to wait, refusing to stir.

James' body lay in a gray heap beside her, turning every hour or so in bed, adjusting to a troubled sleep. He wheezed through his sinuses. Eventually, the clock radio went off on his nightstand. It was the sound of red sirens in Carlie's mind, of dire warnings. Of emergency lights flashing in a submarine, as all hands scrambled to their stations, going down for the final time. Under the abrasive buzz, the homely voice of a meteorologist forecast the day's weather. James snorted awake. Rain, the forecaster said. Thundershowers ahead. James fumbled with the off switch, then sat on the bed to regain his senses.

He didn't see that she was awake—had been awake all night—and so she watched him. Even in flannel bottoms and a T-shirt, he looked naked in the mornings. His eyes bare and disheveled. His footing unsure. A mole stumbling through tunnels to the bathroom.

Carlie said nothing that morning. While James showered, she waddled into the kitchen and had breakfast prepared by the time he toweled off. Grabbing his coat and briefcase to leave, James muttered a routine goodbye. Carlie clenched her teeth in what seemed a constipated smile, and waved him on his way.

The cramps had begun at about two in the morning, dull and menstrual; they picked up in sharpness an hour earlier. By her own estimation, Carlie had been in labor for nearly four hours.

Once James had left the driveway, Carlie bolted for her clothes, her dusty overnight bag, and the dilapidated Rambler in sixty seconds flat. Fifteen minutes later she was banging at Minnie's back door. She rapped incessantly and was near panic before Minnie finally answered with a slurred hello, unsteady on her feet, and naked except for a yellowed bedsheet dragged around her aged body like a Dionysian gown.

Carlie grimaced, panting, "You. Have. To. Drive. Me." And then in one gust: "Tothehospital."

Minnie rallied, tried to focus her attention. She looked past Carlie's shoulder as if James might be waiting in the car, sensing this final breach of territory.

"No James." Carlie shook her head, straining to keep herself together. "Work."

They tore off in the Gremlin as they were, racing through the hills of Graniteville toward the burgeoning metropolis of Augusta, Georgia, with Minnie bleary-eyed at the wheel, unable to properly savor her own joy. Carlie braced herself in the passenger seat and repeated her name whenever they began to drift—Minnie, Minnie, Minnie—like an invocation of love, despite huffing like a warthog and biting into the back of her own hand.

* * *

At some point we are all called out, ready to give birth to something we cannot control or comprehend. For James, this meant the long gestation of his own powerlessness at work. Phil Doyle was done with him. Over their years together, Doyle had benefited from several managerial re-organizations and remembered his enemies well. James was not Whit Shirley. He had been too high profile to demote without just cause, but Phil found other means to effectively cut the strings of James' career. Projects were re-appropriated. He was mysteriously dropped from crucial schedules. His hours got shuffled, his lab access restricted. In the wake of new hires, he had been reassigned permissions to a derelict lab all the way across the Site, rather than the few in his own building. A once-upon-a-time wunderkind, James had been blackballed to a professional Siberia: given "cold" projects and no resources, then censured for being unproductive. Occasionally, Phil deigned to acknowledge him, but only as an act of torment. While chatting up the newer physicists, Phil might catch James passing in his hawkish sights and interrupt himself, momentarily, to dog him: "Jim, didn't I ask for a Form 30? No? Well, drop one off with Lindsey before you leave today." Or, "Have I seen your timesheet for the microcrystalline project?" Only to pause reflectively, a finger pressed to his mustache: "Oh wait. You're not on that anymore, are you?"

James avoided leaving his office. After so many years, his spartan bunker resembled more of a forbidden library, the reclusive cell of a crank who preferred to be left alone, head-deep in his piles of books and paper, to shuffle through the neverending reams of conspiracy data. The four concrete walls bristled with push-pins tacking notices and project outlines; due dates and deadlines, with four different calendars to keep them all straight; forms in triplicate, color coded in white, canary yellow, and pink; carbon copies of requisitions and lab inventories; contact numbers and names; article clippings, graphs, and graphic models printed in dot matrix. The metal-bracketed shelves held a burden of three-ring binders, documenting every hour spent in the lab, each labeled in masking tape; cardboard filing boxes were heaped five high, beginning to mildew in the rear corner; a metal table littered with papers, broken pens, discarded fasteners, and an abused word processor. He had been right, after all. Bigger forces had been trying to crush him. The sole decorative element in his office was a print by M.C. Escher—pedestrian perhaps, but maybe what he saw in it reminded him of his work environment. The exchangeable conduits, pipes, and stairs running to different, impossible exit signs. And if he could only master the art of breaking physics, he could escape.

Ultimately, James had become something of an eccentric at the plant, a shut-in. This beetle-backed, bearded figure who scuttled across the Site grounds with sheaves of paper pinned under one arm, nervously conducting his work. He lunched at his desk, kept the windowless door closed at all times, just him and his vindicated paranoia, alone in this tiny room. In the center of it all, James hunkered over his work like a schoolboy, leaning from the edge of a swivel chair whose seat cushion was busted and patched with electrical tape. He kept a miniature wall-mounted fan aimed at his head. Its monotonous whir filled the dead air with a Vedic Om.

Amid this clutter, the telephone rang. Not the analog shrill of a ringer, but the newer, digital bleating. The mellow sound of hospital intercoms. James reached through his work and paused with his hand over the receiver, foreseeing what lay on the other end. After five rings, he picked it up. Lindsey—the new girl—on the phone. Phil wanted to see him in his office.

When James had entered Phil's office, he hardly let the door close behind him. This office was more spacious than his earlier one, with big brilliant windows behind the desk. Potted fronds sat in either corner. James stood at the door, without being offered a seat. The room was lit only by the slanting sun, as though they were meeting before official hours, off-the-books. Phil sat, legs crossed, hands folded cordially in his lap. He smiled at James, glum. There, on the center of Phil's new mahogany desk, was a green wooden box, a decrepit thing, which had been pried apart with a pair of scissors. Its contents had been upended in a neat pile on the ledger: tiny papers, all of which were written in James' scrawling hand.

There they were: all of his rages, insecurities, vulnerabilities. The private thoughts and monologues of James A. Cullins, kept fastidiously suppressed for over a decade, everything he had hidden and protected from this world suddenly made public. Every fear and shame and outrage that he had swallowed down, concealed in his carefully monitored behavior as he walked through the halls, smiled at coworkers, delivered lectures and project presentations. Wife. Sex. Work.

Phil inhaled deeply and released it, as though he faced a tough decision ahead. "James…" he said, finally. "This. This is deeply, deeply troubling." Phil's features were obscured, backlit from the windows. "I can see only two solutions here. One of which is quiet and dignified. The other," he exhaled again, the sound of a pained confession. "The other involves a lot of loud noises, a lot of painful, messy, loud noises which call into question the mental stability of one our top research scientists. A huge, embarrassing imbroglio."

James didn't move. The sunlight caught in his glasses like two cubes of ice. After a moment, all he said, softly, was, "Those were personal."

"Well, they were," Phil replied. "Now weren't they?"

James let himself out. Down the floors of the industrial stairwell, back in his basement office, James stood at the desk and watched the thousand sheaves of his life's work stir in the disturbance of a tiny fan. They hung from the walls, all these papers, arranged and coruscated like feathers about to take flight. A numb buzzing set through his body, a vertigo. The phone rang again. James picked it up without even realizing. Lindsey's still sweet cadence mentioned something he couldn't understand, and then a new voice crackled on the line. Unbelievably, it was Minnie Price:

"James?" She spoke, her voice a hesitant warble from some faraway place. "I thought you might like to know that your wife is about to give birth. We're at St. Joseph's hospital."

And with that, blood rushed back through his head, a high ringing in the inner ear. His numbness thawed. James didn't clear his office, but unearthed a single file box, already stowed under his desk and neatly bound with packing tape. Hastily, he shoved a few remaining classified documents down his pants, should he be stopped by security personnel. The world became sound, the clanging of a stairwell exit, then a passage of light, as James dashed out the corridor into the blinding sun.

Four stories up, Phil Doyle idly flipped through the hundred slips of paper on his desk. One was damning enough, but he had developed a taste, an enjoyment for reading them. Something salacious, like snooping through a personal diary. He was amazed at every page, at the outstanding stupidity of such an emotional paper trail, like a child shouting at the unfairness of his parents, until at last he reached the bottom of the pile, the very last scrap to be pushed into the box, which simply read:

Screw you, Phil. I quit.

* * *

Fetal macrosomia. Excessive prenatal development. A condition that affects roughly 10 % of babies. We return to the beginning.

When Carlie was first wheeled into the delivery room, her estranged obstetrician, Dr. Schoenhauer, nearly flipped. "Great God…" His mouth went dry, his scowl revealing a row of nicotine stained teeth, as the nurses flew around and Carlie huffed her Lamaze techniques. Dr. Schoenhauer reflexively fumbled through his breast pocket, just below the stethoscope, for a cigarette. Several weeks ago this patient, *Mrs. Cullins, Charlotte R.*, had dropped off the face of the earth, and the good doctor had assumed she either relocated, miscarried, possibly aborted, or simply found another OBGYN without bothering to contact him. Terribly irresponsible of any expectant mother, but not unheard of in his profession. And, admittedly, something of a relief. Now here she was. Dropped at his door with the most ridiculously distended fundal height ever recorded in the history of his practice. Dr. Schoenhauer began sterilizing his hands, an unlit cigarette trembling between his lips. A nurse removed and trashed it without him even noticing.

By the time Carlie was in the stirrups, open-kneed to the world, James had burst into the delivery room with an escort of nurses—his scrubs were hastily mis-fastened like a sloppy straightjacket, a sterile mask snapped around his ears—all without a second thought. As soon as he entered, the room became a vacuum: sucked of all sound and oxygen. The nurses stopped. The swinging doors flapped to a standstill behind James; a rivulet of sweat crawled unnoticed down the length of Carlie's jaw. Everyone waited for them to speak.

"I..." he said.

"You..." she said.

At last upon this primordial scene, braving his own pride to meet his wife on her most basic and blood-swollen terms, crossing into that ultima of womanhood, James—Dr. James A. Cullins, internationally renowned ex-nuclear physicist, later to become a well-paid independent consultant to the industry—immediately passed out on his feet. All noise resumed.

The shockwave of seeing him—of seeing her husband sprawled on the floor with the nurses rushing to help him—sent Carlie into convulsions of laughter so hard that they triggered the contraction from which neither of us, howling, would return. She couldn't breathe, her face was so strained with the effort. After forty-four weeks, she could keep me no longer. It was too late for a caesarian—I was already crowning—and Carlie, I believe, in her delirium and determination to be present, would not allow one anyway. Fortunately, she was a large woman. Large and wide enough in her bones to keep her alive. The delivery split her pelvis open: her hips dislocated with a thundercrack, heralded by a peeling scream, as she pushed the damply haired head of a staggering 17 lbs 6 oz boy from her womb.

All through that gestation, the many years of my parents' life had grown like biological masses, cysts of memory that colonized my brain tissue. Spark. Flash. A new memory. Celestial thunderstorms, electrical disturbances in the neural cortex like the surface of Jupiter. But here, as the soft red womb-light passed into the bright artificial fluorescence of the delivery room, I was at last chemically separated from my parents. In those last seconds, I lost all connection with them. I can't say I know what James felt or thought the day I was born, though I suspect that children are a little like lovers: that the first one is an experience which can never be quite replicated, one which renders all others a little bittersweet, a little nostalgic. But I do know what Carlie felt, as the last of her emotional enzymes squirted from her nervous system to mine. She believed that this one action would right their lives: this birth, and here, James' determination to be present for it. Already, a chasm had been bridged between them. The replacement baby was already working its magic of reconciliation. For the moment, it was enough. It would take decades to discover the inadequacy of such grand gestures to fully heal the past, and this moment would forever remain simply and only what it was: a bridge, a suspension between them, their feet never quite together on solid ground.

As for Minerva Price, she has no grand exit scene in my parents' lives. From the moment I entered, she began her departure, slow and unnoticed, the way so many people leave us. The fact is Minnie would drift into the isolation of her cottage, dying alone eighteen months later from complications with uremia. The gradual poisoning in her blood led to heart failure, and she passed away face down in the kitchen early one January morning. Her body wouldn't be discovered for nearly a month. All those letters she wrote to my mother would go unanswered. As we know, only one was ever sent. Crammed into a nightstand, they remained hidden long after Minnie was safely in the ground, where she shared that wooded plot with Map. *Dear Pony Paradise*. They were her own universal suggestion box, so similar to my father's secret writings. A world full of sublimated desire. In this way, perhaps she understood James better than my own mother. The sleight of hand of each letter, distracting and confessing in the same breath, asking for forgiveness and asking for love.

9

And that's the end of the story.

Mom and I wake at dawn in our motel room and are ready to go by the time the sun is cutting its wicked rays clean through the pine tops. She's chirping a little as we pack, humming to herself. I'd probably be in good spirits, too, if I had just spent the previous day expressing my bowels all over quaint decor of an overpriced hotel. She doesn't hum the lullaby that Freddie sang, but I'm reminded of it.

He never came back last night. There was no tearful and impassioned beating on the door at three in the morning. I make one last pass over the motel room with Mom's bag slung over my shoulder, making sure we leave nothing behind, and then pick up the phone. I dial his number. Straight to voicemail again. I leave another message and let the door wheeze shut after me.

When I check out in the office, I ask for an envelope. The attendant, a grizzled old woman with orange curls, looks me over without a word, then heaves herself off the stool with leaden feet. She returns with an envelope stamped with the logo of a local credit union. I shimmy in a bundle of neatly prepared documents, lick it, and write Freddie's name on the front. Folded inside are a personal letter, the confirmation for a flight number, detailed information on shuttle service to the airport, and another check.

I slide the envelope across the desk to her. "If a man comes by today asking about Room 108, please give him this," I say. I look to the truck, where sunlight winks off the metal and glass. I can just distinguish Mom's dark outline sitting behind the windshield, hunched and patient. "And if he never comes to claim it, tear it up. Throw it away."

Fresh morning traffic along US-78 cuts through the air, while the parking lot burns off dew. Already the sun is relentless, making new promises. I mount the cab, slam the door, and, after double-checking Mom's buckle, crank up the engine. As we motor through the lot, I look over the great long expanse of pine trees from the motel to Copeland, where gas station signs strain their necks up and shout their prices. Gashes in the distant tree-line indicate where the town begins, the craters of residential communities and shopping centers. On our way out, we pass the motel dumpsters, which are ringed by a wooden privacy fence, painted blue. The fence itself is half-hidden behind a row of stunted evergreens, planted too close together to grow. And that's exactly where I see feet. Bare ankles jutting into loafers. No socks.

It's Freddie, slumped against the dumpster fence in the bushes.

"Hang on, Ma. Hang on just one second." I set the brake and climb down with the motor idling. Standing over him, I call his name, twice. He doesn't even twitch. He's curled up like a bum, one arm tucked under his cheek, as if he suffered through a cold night. His hair is a mess. A light stain streaks the lapel of his coat, spattering to his shirt. Dried mud crusts the cuff of his slacks. I kick his shoe. Freddie stirs but doesn't open his eyes. I kneel down, "Get up. Freddie. Freddie?" When I pinch his knee and give it a good shake, Freddie's eyes bolt open.

He startles with a gasp, disoriented. Then his eyes settle on mine.

"You didn't leave me," he says.

"No, I didn't leave you."

"You didn't leave me here."

"No, I didn't. Now come on. Get your ass in the truck. Get up." I extend a hand and, with a grunt, heave him up. He's stiff, creaky.

"I walked to this bar last night," he says, standing unsteadily. He wobbles and leans against my shoulders; I lead him by the elbow. "I don't know. I don't know how far away it was. But it was full of these rednecks."

"I'm sure it was," I say.

"I got," he stifles a belch, or the urge to vomit. "I got a bit verbose," he says. "They looked at me like a…I thought they were going to kill me. I was terrified. I thought I was going to be lynched."

I aim us toward the truck. "I'm sure that half of them were figuring out how to take you home."

He halts. Even in his woozy state, he's substantial enough to make us both stop like we've run into a wall.

He looks down at me. "Really?" he says.

"How could they not?"

He closes his eyes and leans in to kiss me, but I stop his mouth with a hand. His breath smells like vomit. Instead, I hug him. I hug onto his chest and feel the familiar contours, the declivities and warm fleshiness of his arms, the spreading girth of his stomach. I squeeze and after a moment let go.

Words break from his chest as we shuffle forward, instead of sobs. "I had to walk along the highway shoulder, tripping over all kinds of broken bottles and dead animals. And human hair. I never knew there was so much human hair on the side of the road. On the way back, I thought about thumbing a ride, hooking up with some long-haul trucker, some burly bear, and I don't even like hairy men. Here-suite." He tries the word again: *Hirsute*. "But I thought, whatever. I've never been to Arizona, you know?"

"None of us have been to Arizona," I say. "Now come on. Get in the fucking truck. And please, try not to puke on my mother."

"I will not," he says, his throat hitching. He is full of misty-eyed resolve as we march toward the cab, and he mounts the first step tentatively. "I will not puke on your mother. I promise you, Avery. I promise." A new thought strikes him, and he falters one more time, hanging on the cab door. He squints at me, grimacing, full of sorrow and confusion. A sheen of liquor-sweat is already dotting his brow from the exertion. "I'm sorry I asked you to marry me."

"We can talk about that later," I say, easing him into the seat. "Come on." I help him with his belt.

He holds his hand against the door, softly, to prevent me from shutting it just yet. After considerable time, after regaining control of his voice, he asks, "Are we going home now?"

"Almost," I tell him, "but not yet. We're going on a ghost tour."

* * *

Decades later, there's still nothing much between Copeland and Graniteville. The landscape boasts a prefab Baptist church with Spanish outreach on its marquee, a bait shop or two, a few dilapidated white houses with weather-ruined card tables by the roadside, offering a perennial yard sale for passersby. Deeper into the valley, we pass a housing development, chopped out of the woods, that stalled in construction. Its service road is rutted with at least a year's worth of erosion, leading into nothing but scarred clay lots.

Mom watches it all with an air of familiarity, while beside her Freddie slips further down his seat with every bump, rigid as a convalescent. He looks as though his brain is in a vice, one that tightens with every fissure and pothole we tag in the highway. He talks with his eyes closed. I know the feeling: as if sunlight is making the veins in his eyelids burst. "I killed my battery talking to Henri last night," he says. "In that bar. It was called the Dew Drop Inn. I swear to god it was called the Dew Drop Inn." Something dry, like a laugh, passes from his lips. "It was painted pink. I only saw that when I got to the door. It was painted bubblegum pink and made of cinderblocks. It smelled like an old baloney sandwich inside."

"How is Henri?"

"Lonely," Freddie says. "Terrified." The wind whistles through the cab, cooling off what must be a terrible hangover. Freddie opens his eyes and slowly rotates his neck to squint out the window. "He's a sixty-eight year-old man on antidepressants. A sixty-eight year-old man who's real name is Henry. It always has been. Henry Selznick."

We follow the long, rollercoaster dip of Auscauga Lake Road, and I almost miss our turn. We pull into a weedy gravel turnabout, hardly visible from the road—the same spot along Auscauga Lake that my parents pulled into over thirty years ago. It's mostly a clearing now, raked through with a high sun and noontime heat. Scrub pines stand about chest-high across the property, along with some mangy sedge and tangles of greenbrier that are busy with pollinators. In the middle of it all a small knoll rises, still scarred where Minerva Price's house once stood. Like the housing complex we passed, whatever was supposed to be developed here never came to fruition, but it failed longer ago. Finances bottomed out or a company went under. Or someone got divorced, or died.

We help Mom out of the cab and into her wheelchair, where she catches her breath and studies the environment. Her knee has swollen to the size of a grapefruit, the color of an unripe plum. Despite the sun, a sweet loamy smell of water is on the air. "This is Minnie's place," I tell her.

Plant me in the yard. Before I ran away, this was my mother's frequent invocation, whenever she reflected on her own mortality. Usually with reams of genealogy charts under her elbows. The longer the list of the dead became, the more she said it.

Mom braces both gnarled hands against the wheelchair's tires, and tries to make them go forward. I take the handles, and the three of us walk toward the only place to go: the jagged slope where Minnie's house stood. With the ground so uneven, Freddie helps lead the wheelchair, pulling from one armrest until we clear the top of the hill. From this vantage, we can see can see the rust-brown waters of the creek. Beyond it, the old-growth woods have been clear-cut for half a mile, the earth bulldozed and planted with yellow pine saplings in an endless, orderly grid. In twenty-five years they'll reach maturity, be harvested for the sawmill, and the process will start over again.

Freddie shields his eyes. "What are we looking for?"

"Nothing in particular," I admit, then nod far to our left where the old-growth forest remains, thick with behemoth loblolly and silvery ropes of crossvine. "There's a tombstone somewhere out in those woods with my name on it. Or at least there used to be."

What compels us toward sites of the dead, when it's impossible enough to commune with the living? It's like visiting an old battlefield, something you have to let your imagination dance across, because nothing that remains will really evoke the old ghosts that you believe to be there. I see the ruins of the stone wall where Carlie and I sat when I was eight. A tumbledown deer path cleaves through it now and leads straight into the rippling banks of the water. The same length of water where Minnie skinny-dipped on warm summer nights, the same creek where I watched Carlie let go a little bit of herself, one page at a time. *Agape, Hoss Creek*. Mom squeezes the vinyl armrest, keeping her left hand curled close to her chest, near her throat. The toe of her orthopedic shoe grazes the dirt, skims the ground as if to test it, as if to remind herself of it. Minerva Price could be trudging naked up this hill toward us. Mom's eyes are narrowed and glassy, flecked white in the sun. Who knows what her memory is capable of conjuring. In another three years, the doctors told me, she will be completely wheelchair-bound.

With a muffled groan, Freddie squats down to his heels and lets his arms dangle off his knees, picking through the small stones embedded beneath his loafers. Idly, he rips up small weeds. Only when he begins to lay them out, one by one, on Mom's open armrest do I notice that they are in fact flowers. That he's picking tiny, pale blue wildflowers. Mom moves her good hand toward them and carefully pinches one to examine it. Then, she lets it drop and brushes the others off with her fingertips. As they sprinkle down over his knee, Freddie finds himself laughing. They're for you, he tells her, and begins setting them up again. And again, she lightly flicks them clear of the armrest.

Suddenly, I say, "I wish I had brought my father's ashes. It was a terrible idea, leaving him in Florida."

"Well, you were honoring his wishes, right? Not that he cared much about what you wanted."

"He cared."

"Yeah, I hear you." Freddie remains squatting, ripping at the tiny flowers. "The dead are blameless. He cared so much that when your mom had her stroke, he told you to stay out of Dodge. Said that—"

"I was glad, Freddie."

He stands with some difficulty, stiff-jointed and wincing. "What do you mean?"

"I mean I was glad he gave me the excuse. He called me back, more than once, but I hung up on him every time. I gave them both up for dead."

I can feel the numbness take over. If I could hop on my bike and pedal and grunt uphill for fifty solid miles, I would. I would find a forty-five degree incline and burn my calves and twist my quads up until they snapped. Until all the muscles and tendons in my legs finally sprang from the excessive build-up of lactic acid, and I would start rolling downhill, backwards, blind and gaining tremendous speed. Out-of-control, but free.

Freddie places a hand on Mom's chair to steady himself, seized by a passing head-pang. As soon as he touches the handle bar, it's as if I have permission to let go. I begin marching down to the bank. "Stay with her," I say.

"Avery?" His hand recoils a little, like he has been zapped.

"Stay with her," I call out. "Don't leave her alone." Already, I'm halfway down the hill. Grasshoppers and potato bugs spring from the grasses as my legs scissor through them, knee high. I aim for the crumbled wall, the deer path leading through muck straight into the water, where some of the stone remains. I can hear the creek bubbling in earnest now, a stronger rush than I imagined, especially in this wide, deep-amber bend of it. A few puddles stagnate around the rubble, cut off from the source, slick with iridescent colors, oily residues. I see boot prints in the mud and lean on the rocks long enough to strip off my own shoes and socks. High up above me I see Freddie and Mom, half obscured by weeds and the light. He calls out to me again. But I know he won't come down. He will stay by her side because he still wants to prove his love to me. He still wants to prove that he is worth loving.

The cold meniscus of Little Horse Creek slices through my ankles as I wade out, sloshing through the coppery water. It deepens quickly, from ankles to shins to knees. Mud sucks over my feet, stirring great motes of sediment with every step.

I can see now that Freddie and I will persist. We will continue to stay together, despite the corrosive arguments to come, despite the heavy debt I owe to my mother, despite the fact that what I hold in my heart for him now is more like remorse than anything else. Because it is hard to get rid of someone you have loved. It is harder to get rid of someone that you have loved than it is to get rid of yourself.

James knew that all too well. His suicide is no mystery to me. He had Parkinsons, yes. He was retired, yes. One could wax grandiloquently and say he was bereft of the purpose that drove him to be the man he was. But as he proved, you don't need a box of bullets to end your own life. What he couldn't do, finally, was get rid of his wife. What he couldn't do, despite both our best efforts, was get rid of me.

I reach the pool where Minerva must have prostrated herself under starry skies. Where Carlie floated, overripe with me in her last moments with Minnie. Already, my jeans are soaked up to the crotch. I close my eyes and feel the blood hammer through my legs against the freezing current. My toes, locked in mud, have gone numb.

I thought that when I hit the water, I would plunge in. I would let the cold current cut through me, cleanse me, that the force of its resistance would scoop me along and baptize me in its memory. But now that I'm out here, my mind has already jumped ahead fifteen minutes into the future, where I would be shivering behind the wheel of the truck, fully soaked on the vinyl bench seat. I would be the same person, only wetter.

So I turn my face to the sun instead. The water rushes around me, sounding like a head full of voices talking all at once. It grows louder, more immersive and indistinct, until I begin to feel weightless, until I could dissolve into the meaningless roar, into the confluence of noise that sounds so human, so ecstatic, so close to true language. Until, at last, I realize that I'm hearing my own name.

When I open my eyes, I see Freddie waving high atop the hillside. He cups one hand to his mouth and calls something I can't understand. He's laughing and windmilling one arm. And then Mom starts in, too, this seventy-three year old woman locked in a wheelchair; she raises one hand and gently waves at me, at the stranger in the creek. The breeze catches them, tall Freddie and Mom in her wheelchair, two shadow-burnt silhouettes high above me, waving manically, captured in some lunatic joy. Just the two of them, together. I raise my hand lightly in response.

Oh, my father. With all of your good intentions, where are you now? Tell me, please, who is it that can save us from being ourselves?

Acknowledgments

I am deeply indebted to my multiple families, each of whom in their own way have helped to shepherd this novel through its many visions and revisions: to Art Taylor, Tara Laskowski, and Kyle Semmel for their rigorous insights, friendship, and faith in our labor; to Paul Chesser, William Wright, and Martin Sheehan for being a continuous source of creative inspiration and wonder; to my most dear and immediate of families, George, Donna, Forrest, and Bell, for decades of unwavering love and support, despite my reluctance to talk shop; and most of all, to my best editor, Katie Rawson, for her patience, draft after draft, and her indefatigable belief in my need to tell stories.

About the Author

Brandon Wicks studied creative writing at George Mason University, where he received his M.F.A. He serves as an associate editor for *SmokeLong Quarterly* and teaches at the Community College of Philadelphia. This is his first novel.

www.bpwicks.com

Also from Santa Fe Writers Project

Dissonance ***by Lisa Lenard-Cook***

When Anna Kramer, a Los Alamos piano teacher, inherits the journals and scores of composer Hana Weissova, she is mystified by this bequest from a woman she does not know. Hana's music, however, soon begins to uncover forgotten emotions, while her journals, which begin in 1945 after she is released from a concentration camp, slowly reveal decades-old secrets that Anna and her family have kept buried.

"...this beautifully written novel defies its apparent fate: It weaves through the history of the bomb and the Holocaust without feeling depressing. To my mind, it is everything a novel should be."

—*Catherine Ryan Hyde,* Huffington Post

By Way of Water ***by Charlotte Gullick***

Struggling to feed their children in an unforgiving California forest when there are no logging jobs to be found, Jake and Dale Colby make personal vows that only make matters worse. Jake will not accept help from the government or his neighbors, and Dale won't allow him to hunt, believing her faith will sustain them. But one other member of the family makes a promise to herself. Seven-year-old Justy believes that she alone can hold the family together, even when her father's violence resurfaces.

"By Way of Water *is a work of exquisite beauty."*

— *Jayne Anne Phillips*

About Santa Fe Writers Project

SFWP is an independent press founded in 1998 that embraces a mission of artistic preservation, recognizing exciting new authors, and bringing out of print work back to the shelves.

Find us on Facebook, Twitter @sfwp, and at www.sfwp.com